CROSSROADS

For

Diana "Nana" Brush

Thank you for always believing
in me.

Dedicated to

Curtis & Erica Brown

Some love stories inspire.

This book is a work of historical fiction.

Cover art by Audrey Maher

ISBN 9781540343086

2022 — First Edition

Acknowledgments

I am blessed with a wonderful support system that is instrumental in my writing process. First, my husband, Travis and our three wonderful daughters, who have always been supportive and encouraging, even when writing, took long hours and sleepless nights.

My mother and father, who instilled a deep love of the written word in me as a child. I would have never realized the dream of writing a book without their support.

I also like to thank those people that influenced my work, Erica Brown, Chandra Grohman, Jackie Kruger, and Diana Brush. This would not have been possible without you acting as sounding boards, inspiring characters, book covers, storylines, and for being a large part of the process in countless ways.

A special thank you to Patt Hilmer, Dana Thomas, and Renae Sibbett for acting as story consultants, editors, and cheerleaders. Without whom, this book wouldn't have been possible.

Prologue

June 1879

Although it was a clear day with only the slightest of breezes, Glenna felt as though a gale was raging at her, beating at her back and filling her ears with its sound, blocking out Captain Tanner's words and leaving her with nothing except her own thoughts.

The image of her father's lifeless body swinging in time with the pitch of the ship was the only image that Glenna saw when her eyes closed, the feel of empty dread the only thing she felt when her eyes opened. The dread turned into ash and slipped into oblivion in the hours after her father's body had been pulled back from the rail that he had jumped from, and the rope removed from his neck.

"Sir Louis Perry, may you find peace in the hereafter denied you in this life."

Glenna felt the air being knocked out of her, catching in her chest. It felt as though she would never breathe again. She could recall Father Lucas's sermon on those who ended their own lives and what awaited them in the afterlife. Did she believe in the eternal separation of her father and mother because he had taken his own life? Did she believe he would find peace or torment? Had he damned his eternal soul?

Finding it impossible to watch as his body splashed into the sea and slipped beneath the waves, Glenna instead cast her eyes to the heavens and prayed for strength. The strength that her father had lacked. Prayed for the fortitude to forge on.

Pent-up air spilled from between her lips in a shuttering gasp and with it the emotion she had held in for so long. Now she felt — nothing.

One

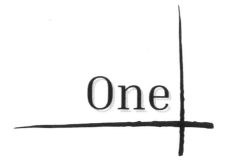

August 1884

Glenna swallowed hard, pushing past the lump in her throat as the wagon rolled to a stop.

"This is it. The homestead on Crossroads Spread." She glanced from Theodore, who was smiling brightly, back to the two-story ranch house with a large front porch. The main house was picturesque, with its whitewashed walls, large windows, and wide porch steps that were edged with bright wildflowers.

Off to the left and set back some stood a much smaller one-story bunkhouse. A large barn complete the idyllic picture: stables, henhouse, and a blossoming vegetable garden. The house and outbuildings stood as a stark contrast against the wild backdrop of the Northern Wyoming skyline.

"This is the Sterling residence?" Glenna could hear the disbelief in her voice. Could all the weeks of trial and seemingly endless days of travel have led her here?

Theodore laughed, "Not what you were expectin'?"

"No—not at all. Mr. Sterling gave a very brief description of a small family ranch I never dreamed of — this."

"The boys' grandfather started this place, built the homestead, and started to grow the herd from next ta' nothin'. By the time his sons and daughters were born, the Sterlings had already made a name for themselves as cattlemen. Clint's father, Clint Senior, built the big house and bunkhouse. He spared no expense to make it a very functional and comfortable home for his wife and the boys."

"It's — perfect," Glenna said in awe.

"Where'd you say you traveled in from again?"

"New York City."

Theodore gave her a worried look. "Ya didn't travel all this way alone?"

"I had companions during my travel. It was all arranged ahead of time."

"I'm mighty glad to hear that, when I saw you all alone in town, lookin' lost — well, if you were my kin' I wouldn't want you travelin' friendless."

"Thank you for the concern," Glenna smiled warmly at him, "Also for delivering me here, it is greatly appreciated."

"It was nothin', Ma'am. I couldn't see a woman in distress and not be of help. The Crossroads Ranch isn't much out of my way home. The Mrs. and I own a small piece close by and work some milk cows. It's nothin' to ranchin', but we scrape out a-livin'."

"I would love to make your wife's acquaintance," Glenna said sincerely.

"She would be mighty glad to meet you, miss Glenna. It will be nice to have more women folk 'round these parts." Theodore left his seat, came around to offer Glenna his hand, and helped her down. She clutched at the small carpetbag holding what meager valuables she still owned as she turned to face her future.

"Well, Ma'am, this is where I take my leave. I better be off or Hattie will have my hide."

"Thank you. I am sure I'll be fine from here," she assured him and waved as Theodore clambered back into the wagon seat and tipped his hat to her.

Holt cursed under his breath and cringed inwardly as the sound of knocking at the door interrupted the peace of Daisy's nap, arousing the sleeping child. Grinding his teeth, Holt picked up the wailing toddler and stormed down the stairs.

"What on earth?" He snapped as he angrily pulled open the front door. A surprised-looking woman stood on the other side.

"Oh! I apologize." The woman stammered, her dark brown eyes wide. "I should have been more careful not to rouse the child."

"Can I help ya?" Holt asked, his annoyance mounting as Daisy screeched in protest at being awakened.

"Yes, I'm looking for Mr. Sterling?" She looked at Holt hopefully and he noted her British accent.

Daisy's cries grew louder and Holt attempted to soothe her with a few quick bounces.

"Mr. Sterling?" Holt repeated and studied her for several seconds as Daisy sobbed and wriggled in his arms until she was facing the stranger. Daisy's cries didn't subside as her hands went out to the woman, begging to be held.

"May I?" the woman asked and inclined her head toward the child, who was now practically jumping out of Holt's arms.

"I'm not much in the habit of handin' children over to strangers," he muttered over the shrillness of Daisy's wailing.

The woman started to respond, although it was impossible to hear over the sobbing toddler. Holt relented and passed the little girl into the waiting arms of the woman who had interrupted her fitful nap.

With Daisy cradled in the woman's arms, Holt stepped out onto the porch. The woman had discarded her carpetbag and, humming

softly, moved to sit in the old rocker. The humming became a soft
lullaby, her voice carrying the tune beautifully as she rocked the little
girl. Before Holt knew it, the crying subsided to shutters and muted
moans. Holt watched in astonishment at the tender exchange as
Daisy curled into the embrace and her eyelids drooped.

The song ended and Holt wondered if he had ever heard
anything more peaceful in his life than the soft trilling of her voice.
Daisy's heavy eyes had fallen closed, her breathing even in sleep.
The stranger lifted her face, meeting Holt's gaze with an air of
elegance mixed with determination.

He had been so preoccupied with Daisy's cries when he first took
in the stranger. It was almost as if he hadn't really seen her at all.
The ill fitting nondescript dress cut from a thick gray cloth and
adorned only with plain buttons did nothing to detract from her
natural beauty.

Holt wasn't able to deny himself a minute to appreciate such a
woman. The slender curve of her neck, full rose-colored lips, and a
soft tint of pink lit her cheeks from the summer's heat. He had never
seen such deep brown, soulful eyes with the richness of color as the
ones that looked at him so earnestly as she was, cradling Daisy so
tenderly in her arms.

"I'm sorry I woke your daughter."

"She's my niece," Holt said simply.

"You must be Holt." She smiled with what looked like a touch of
disappointment he didn't quite understand. "Your brother mentioned
you several times." Her eyes turned down to the sleeping bundle in
her arms. "Hello, little Daisy." She whispered. "She is smaller than I
expected for a child of thirteen months. I suppose the loss of her
mother at such an early age made it hard for her to put on the needed
weight of a nursing infant."

"I'm sorry, you seem to know us, but I have no earthly idea who you might be."

"I thought — perhaps your brother would have — yet, if he didn't inform anyone — I suppose that explains the absence of a welcoming party when my coach arrived." She seemed to be talking to herself in disjointed sentences that Holt couldn't make heads or tails of.

When a few heartbeats had passed and Holt didn't respond to her statement, she pressed on, "My name is Glenna Eleanor Perry. I am your brother, Clint's fiancée."

Holt gaped at her in utter disbelief. "Clint's what?"

Glenna watched as Holt Sterling ran a hand through the mass of sand-colored hair and groaned loudly, repeating his brother's name in frustrated tones. It was hard to admit to herself that when he had first opened the door she had felt a rush of relief, believing him to be Clint, her intended and instantly liking the look of him.

Standing four to five inches above her, Holt was the very picture of an American cowman, dressed just as she would have expected in dust-covered boots, breaches, and a work-worn shirt that may at one time been the color of new grass yet had faded overtime. He looked at home and out of place all at once, standing on the front porch of such a fine house. Holt was undeniably handsome as well, with a strong jaw, wide shoulders, hair although mussed from his frustrated actions, kept laying in the most active ways about his forehead and ears framing his face so that it drew her eyes to the strong and defined features.

Inwardly she chided herself for hoping him to be Clint and felt a rush of guilt at the pang of disappointment that had followed his being the child's uncle instead of her father. She had not come all this way because Clint would be a handsome man. Or live in a finer home than he had described. She did not travel across countless miles of the countryside to be swept away by girlish notions. Glenna didn't give herself the time to wonder if his brother would share any likeness with Holt. It did not matter after all, only that he was true to his word and a good Christian man.

Holt cursed under his breath and looked at her as if he was just now realizing she was still seated in the swing. She felt the intensity of his blue eyes as he scrutinized her closely.

"I'm sorry, miss. But you can't possibly be Clint's fiancée."

She bristled a little at the comment and wondered if he thought her unfitting for his elder brother.

"Pardon me, would it be permissible for Daisy to be placed in her crib? After, you and I can go find your brother and clear up any concerns that you have."

Wetting his lips with the tip of his tongue, he nodded and reached for Daisy. Glenna passed the sleeping child to him without waking her and Holt slipped inside. It was a few seconds before she heard the sound of his footfalls returning.

She stood when Holt reappeared. "Mr. Sterling."

"Holt," he insisted. Striding to the porch railing and grasped it with both hands. "No one calls me Mr. Sterling."

"Very well, Holt. I can see the news I shared with you came as a surprise."

"You can say that again. Clint never once made mention of a fiancée."

"Mr. Sterling — Holt. Your brother wrote to several Eastern papers advertising for a wife. His advert stated that he had been widowed not long ago and needed a suitable caretaker for his two small children. A boy of five and a small girl not yet one year."

"You answered his advertisement." It wasn't a question.

"I did. Clint — expressed a desire for the permanent placement of a caretaker for his children. A stepmother — we corresponded for three months before the subject of marriage was even discussed. Once I accepted, arrangements for my arrival took place." Glenna relayed the information in a business-like tone.

"He paid your way?"

"Yes," she confirmed. "From New York City."

Glenna went to her carpetbag, and reaching inside, produced a small stack of letters. "It was not all one sided, Mr. Sterling. I was able to cover my accommodations during stops and meals. These are the letters I received from your brother. They confirm every word of my story…"

Holt scoffed, cutting her off. "What kind of woman accepts the marriage proposal of a man she has never met?"

Feeling as though she had just been slapped, Glenna turned so that Holt could not see the rush of angry color that touched her cheeks.

"It is easy to judge another when you have no idea of their circumstances," she said softly and stuffed the letters hastily back.

"I shouldn't have said that. I didn't mean to insult you." Glenna wasn't able to face the man or his intense gaze as she regained her composure.

"I know what you must think of me, my character, for answering such an advert, however I had my reasons, as did your brother, for placing it. If I was of questionable moral character or so very untrustworthy, I do not believe you would have so freely accepted my help with Daisy just now and the child would surely have never come to me so willingly."

"I haven't seen Daisy take to anyone such as that since the death of her mama," Holt relented, and Glenna bravely met his eyes in defiance, daring him to judge her harshly once more.
Glenna noted that Holt looked suddenly worn as if he had aged years in seconds. His sky-blue eyes dulled into a storm color gray that held no hint of kindness.

"I'm sorry, Miss Perry, for your trouble in comin' such a long way for nothin'. I'll arrange for your return to New York as soon as possible."

Glenna's brow furrowed, "Return?"

Holt let go of the railing and turned, towering over her. He looked down at her and said in a low, harsh voice, "There's nothin' here for you. Clint's dead."

Holt watched Glenna as a hand flew to her middle and she seemed to fight for breath.

"Dead?"

"Yes, these two weeks," Holt said in a sedate voice.

"Two weeks — what — how did it happen?" Her voice was soft and pained. Holt cursed his brother for finding such a fine woman, a beauty, who it seemed cared for him just to drag her across the country to learn of his passing.

"It doesn't matter how. He's gone and there isn't anything that can change that fact." Holt indicated he was not about to elaborate, and they both fell into silence.

Glenna blinked rapidly a few times as if fighting back tears, sagged on the porch railing just as Holt had done. Her hands gripped it so tightly they turned white.

"I — I sent him a telegraph — just over a month ago with last-minute details of my arrival." She whispered, with a faraway look in her eyes, "I can't make any sense of this."

"There is no sense to be had," Holt said solemnly.

Coming to herself, she blinked and seemed to not just look at Holt but see him. "I am very sorry for your loss." She breathed the words, and the sadness he heard there took Holt aback.

"Thank you kindly." Needing to put some distance between himself and Glenna. From the sorrow he saw in her face, Holt left the porch and started toward the barn. Letting the warm sunlight remove the coldness of grief.

"Mr. Sterling?" She called after him.

"I'd better hitch the wagon and get you into town before dusk to get you a room."

"Please," she had rushed after him, "to be quite honest, the trip from New York was daunting enough. I can not imagine coming all this way just to turn around."
Holt shook off the complaint and continued to stride toward the barn.

"You'll have to take the coach to the nearest train station," He said more to himself than to Glenna, adding, "By train, the trip will be an easy one and you'll get back long before winter sets in," Holt argued and again cursed Clint for leaving more of a mess of things that he would have to clean up.

"Mr. Sterling!" This time, her voice sounded higher and more desperate than it had before. The panic held in her tone made Holt hesitate and turn to face her; the hat had flown from her hair and hung at her back by its ribbons, exposing her face fully to his view.

Her delicate features showed lines of worry and stress. "I — I can't return — I have nothing to return to. All my plans for the future — all my hopes lay here, in this place."

"I'm sorry Miss Glenna. There ain't nothin' here for nobody… not anymore." Holt stopped himself, his eyes on the house rather than looking at her. "My brother was a good man, an honest man. He would have been better than his word to you. I am truly sorry you had to travel all this way for nothin'. I'll get you a room for the night in Buffalo and arrange your travel." He mentally calculated what it would take to find a coach in Buffalo to take her to the nearest rail lines in Merino, then cursed under his breath, spitting.

"Please Mr. Sterling, I have a proposition. If you insist on sending me away, allow me to at least earn my passage by working for you for a season. I can cook, keep the house, and tend to the children. It also gives you time to put other plans in place for the children after I'm gone. I will expect nothing from you but what I earn."

Holt frowned at her, then looked down at his boots, thinking over the proposition for some time.

"It's a hard life here at the foot of the Big Horn mountains runnin' cattle. Days start well before sunup and last till after sundown. There is always work that needs to be done and not a great deal of leisure time. Winters are hard and cold, with long months of nearly endless solitude."

"After five winters in New York City, I think I could stand some solitude," she mused. "I would be a help to you, as I would have been to your brother."

Holt furrowed his brows. "Keepin' a woman who is not a relative on the place would be highly inappropriate. I could not expose you, the children, or myself to any kind of scandal."

12

Glenna pulled herself up to her full height and glowered at him. "I was not seeking a proposal. I would never hold you to those offers or promises made by your bother. It was simply a mutually beneficial proposal. I can see how it was also a mistake."

"Wait." Holt protested.

"I can provide you with a small sum for your trouble to see me back to Buffalo, and I will find my way after that and allow you to be unburdened further by my sudden and unwelcome appearance." She pivoted sharply and walked with purpose away from him and back to the porch.

Holt wasn't able to suppress a grin at her retreating figure. He had liked the look of her immediately, but beyond that, he found himself admiring her as well. She was well-bred from a wealthy family; he was sure. Strong and used to having her way. That was clear in how she carried herself.

He knew his brother well enough to know he would have sought a mother for the children. That part of the story rang true to him. It made a kind of strange sense that Clint would make a woman like Glenna an offer. She was not like Clint's late wife Grace, and the differences would have been a comfort to a man still mourning his lost love.

Grace had been petite, short, with hair the color of golden corn, and timid. She was a wonderful wife and mother, though a childhood illness had taken a real toll on her, and Daisy's birth had not been easy. She was not long for this world after that.

Holt watched the tall, dark, and very handsome form of Glenna from across the distance that now separated them. Could he allow her to stay all winter? The children needed looking after, and he wouldn't have the time to give and run the cattle. She had been right, assuming he would need time to find a replacement situation for the children as well.

A replacement situation — the idea of sending Daisy or Finn away made a deep ache well inside him. The children would most likely be separated and farmed out to distant relatives or even strangers. How could he entertain the idea of not having his kin raised on the family ranch?

"Damn you, Clint. Damn you for puttin' either of us in this position. Damn you for dyin'." Holt felt a rush of frustration that mingled with grief.

Glenna gritted her teeth. A horrible habit that had developed over the last few years. There was embarrassingly little left in her coin purse. Nothing to offer Holt Sterling to entice him to take her into Buffalo, and if she gave him the coins, she would be left with nothing. Perhaps she could find work in town?

"Come inside. I'll put on some tea and we can work out the details." Holt was at her side.

"The details?"

"For your stayin'. We must come to some agreement and discuss livin' arrangements." He moved and opened the house door, holding it for her.

Glenna felt a rush of relief that surprised her and angered her all at the same time. Oh, how her life had changed. Head held high, Glenna gathered up her carpetbag and stepped over the threshold.

The inside of the house was just as delightfully surprising as the outside had been. The entry was large; high ceilings and clean, fresh-looking walls greeted her. To her right, a staircase wound its way to the second story.

To her left, a large welcoming room with windows draped in white curtains that stood open to allow light to flood each corner.

This room held a fine-looking fireplace, a small, well taken care of piano, lovely looking sofa, a small table with two chairs situated to admire the view, and towering shelves holding all manner of things. She didn't have time to capture every detail, as Holt had moved to lead her down the hall in front of them.

The hall held finely framed photos. She wished she could examine them fully, as she recognized a younger version of the man leading her in one of them just before they turned to the right and entered a large kitchen. She liked the look of it instantly. It had been set up for the ease and comfort of the cook. With two windows and one door now open to the summer sun, the room was bright and full of light.

A large cook stove stood near the door. Near it a cabinet with counter space for preparing food. Above this, a collection of pots and pans hung from pegs in the wall. A deep sink and other necessities to run a functional kitchen stood in convenient places around the area, a large table seated in the center taking up the rest of the spacious room. She could imagine a family seated around it, with the smell of food wafting in the air. The image was beautiful in her mind's eye.

Glenna watched Holt move to light a small fire and fill a pot with water, setting it to boil. She studied the room. The man, taking in both, wondered about the proposal she had made. Could she see herself becoming his employee? At least she had some knowledge of Clint from their correspondence, however, she knew little of Holt Sterling other than what Clint had felt necessary to share with her. Was she capable of committing to live in this place, so far away from anything or anyone?

Glenna found it a straightforward answer. Just as she had known, it was the right thing to do when she had stopped him from hitching up the wagon. Being a governess to two small children, taking care of this house and its garden, doing the cooking, cleaning, and washing laundry seemed like a dream come true to Glenna. She would stay.

Holt pulled two sets of cups from the cupboard, a small thing of sugar, and cream, placing each on the large table. Coming to her senses, Glenna pulled at the strings of her bonnet, leaving it to lay it on top of her bag that she had set aside, and walked to the pot of boiling water.

"Please allow me," she said and took the tin of tea leaves from Holt. He didn't try to stop her, instead, left her to steep the tea while he rummaged for some biscuits. Soon the tea was ready and Glenna strained the leaves out of the amber water. She poured the steaming liquid into the teapot provided and placed it on the table. Holt pulled out a chair for her, and Glenna gave him a small smile of thanks and took it.

"We don't have much call for tea. This is more of a coffee-house, but my mother insisted that we keep tea for guests."

"I am grateful for it," she said truthfully, as he poured the tea into both cups.

"How do you take it?" He asked, putting sugar into his cup.

"English." She smiled and lifted the cup to her lips without adding anything to it. The tea was strong and felt like home. Glenna instantly relaxed.

Holt added cream into his cup as well and gave a chuckle, the sound of which she instantly liked. "I guess I take mine like I take my coffee, strong and sweet." Glenna smiled when he tasted it and proceed to put another sugar cube into his cup.

She let her eyes drop to the remains of her tea and wondered about the man across from her. When she made no effort to further the conversation, he cleared his throat.

"I have no desire to send Finn and Daisy away. However, I can not see after their care or schoolin' myself and make a run at ranchin'

16

without Clint. I also can not live on the same spread with an unmarried woman who is not a relative. This isn't a grand English house, Miss Perry; there's no place for governesses." Glenna clasped her teacup as she waited for him to continue, silently hating that again her future rested on another's decision. She had thought momentarily when she had answered Clint's advert that she was taking back control of her life. How deeply wrong had she been?

"The way I see it — we better get hitched. There isn't anythin' else for it." Glenna listened to Holt sigh deeply as the declaration left his lips.

"Hitched?" She breathed, placing the cup back on the tabletop.

"Married," he corrected.

"I understand the vernacular." It was Glenna's turn to sigh. "I was not expecting the sudden turn of events."

"The marriage would be in name only. The house would be your domain. You mentioned you cook. I would expect that not only for the children but for myself and the cowhands in my employ, that's atop any household duties. Does this arrangement sound agreeable to you?"

Glenna looked closely at Holt, who was patiently waiting for her to speak.

"I understood the offer when it came from the children's father. He — Clint — made it very clear that he loved his wife, would always love his wife and his devotion to her would be lifelong. I made peace long ago with the idea of marrying for advantage rather than romantic notions, so the arrangement was acceptable to me.

"If you are insistent that my being a governess would not be possible and could tarnish both our reputations, I must understand *why* you would make such a drastic alteration to your own life as marriage?" Glenna paused, watching his face for any telltale sign he was going to take back his proposal. When his gaze didn't waver, she dropped her eyes, finding it impossible to continue the connection.

Finding her strength, Glenna rushed on, "Could you truly shackle yourself to a stranger, remove the possibility of a romantic attachment from your life just to keep your family intact? Because, Mr. Sterling, that is what you would be vowing at the altar. I could not bind myself to a man that would flounder — married in name only or not. Having a mistress will not now or in the future be acceptable. If there is another you would prefer to make this offer of marriage to, or you have other reservations, please inform me now."

Glenna dared to look up and noted that Holt was grinning over at her. "Was that humorous?"

"Not at all. I am impressed. You know your worth. It's admirable." He continued to smile as he went on, "There is no one else. And I have my reasons for makin' you the offer. Not all of them can be placed into words I'm 'feard. I *can* promise you not to act the part of a scoundrel."

Holt held out his right hand. Years before her residence in New York, this gesture would have horrified her with its vulgarity. Now the American practice of shaking hands to seal verbal agreements had become commonplace working among them, and she placed her hand within the warmth of his grip.

Images of what this new future would hold rushed forward to the forefront of her mind. It had been impossible not to spend her time imagining the start of her new life. The daydreams during the long days on the train had filled her mind with a myriad of possibilities, not one of them likely.

Of course, she had envisioned Clint taking one look at her and, in an instant, forming a connection that could someday grow into love, a childish fantasy that was replaced with other scenarios. She

18

had also pictured him being indifferent to her and living as strangers.

Even misplaced malice or hatred directed toward her for his predicament, perhaps. Once imagined him as a brute or violent man, yet she had pushed the idea away after revisiting his kind, well-thought-out and articulate letters. She felt confident she knew what kind of life she could have shared with Clint. Uncomplicated, and yes, sometimes lonely.

Holt, on the other hand, was an enigma. His desire to hold his family together was certainly admirable after he had already lost so much. Past the mention of him in Clint's letter, Glenna knew nothing about the man and he had not even known of her existence before today. Yet, here they were, strangers and newly engaged. A strange, cold, business arrangement of an engagement, to be sure.

Glenna swallowed. Holt was presenting her with security, stability, a home, a purpose outside herself, his respect, possibly friendship, and nothing more. It was altogether a different arrangement than she had expected to find herself in and yet so much the same. "I accept."

The handshake sealing the arrangement Holt drew back, "I'd better get my things moved out to the bunkhouse."

"Mr. Sterling, if we are to proceed with this — marriage, I could not in good conscience remove you from your own home to be banished to the bunkhouse."

"I'll stay out in the bunkhouse until after we are properly married. I'll stay in my room after that. I have no illusions about what kind of arrangement there will be between us."

Glenna dropped her eyes back to the teacup.

He stood. "Seein' how you'll be stayin', I better show you to a room and move my things to the bunkhouse until after the weddin'. Then I suppose it's off to chat with the Pastor."

She hurried to follow him and moved to gather her things, However Holt had already picked up her bag and hat.

"This is an awful small carpetbag," Holt observed.

"It holds everything I own in the world," she answered honestly.

Holt didn't press the matter further and inclined his head to indicate that Glenna should follow him.

At the top of the stairs, Holt seemed to hesitate for a minute before he nodded to himself as if an inner dialog had just taken place. He stopped at the first door to the right. "Finn, my nephew, and Daisy share this room." Holt pointed to the far door off to the right, just past where they now stood, as his words trailed off. He seemed lost in memories, and Glenna rushed to change the subject.

"Will I be meeting Finn this morning?"

Holt rubbed the back of his neck briefly before answering, "I hate to admit it, but it's been a bit harder than I had expected to look after both Finn and Daisy while carryin' on with the ranch work. While I worked out what was goin' to happen next, he's been stayin' on a nearby farm. Daisy does better at home." He paused. "I'll send for him."

His explanation drifted off. She understood that he suddenly found himself in an overwhelming situation and to have any help at all would have been welcome.

Feeling the need to give a subject change, Glenna looked down the hall and made mental notes on the rooms, "And the two off to the left?"

"My room is just there," Holt answered, indicating the door just opposite of them. "The last door goes to the attic. I'd appreciate it if — you would stay in these rooms only."

"Yes, of course." She nodded.

Holt pushed open the door, sat her carpetbag down in the doorway, and, stepping aside, allowed Glenna to enter first. The room was large and looked as if it hadn't been lived in for many years.

Glenna walked farther inside and in the dim light noted the furnishings, although outdated; were very attractive and looked as if they had been well taken care of.

"This — this was their room, wasn't it? Clint and Grace's." Glenna asked softly as the realization hit her. Holt only gave her a quick nod.

"My parents before them."

"I can't stay in this room," she protested. "It wouldn't be right."

"A room with no one livin' in it isn't of any use to no one. Clint — he moved in with the little ones after the loss of their mother — no ones been in here for months. I do apologize for the state of it. It will need a good scrubbin'." He said, sounding slightly uncomfortable as he yanked open a set of drapes, flooding the room with light and dust.

"I am not afraid of work," she assured him.

Holt looked at her for several heartbeats, their eyes locked, and Glenna tried not to become uncomfortable under his gaze.

"Well, then — I best leave you to it." Holt said finally and turned to go.

"Thank you," Glenna called after him. The words stopped his retreat, and Holt turned to look back at her from the door.

"Miss Perry, I am sorry for bein' so short with you when we first met. Clint left a whole mess of troubles when he passed and you your arrival took me just as much off guard as you learnin' that my brother is gone. I didn't mean to be insensitive."

"Please, do not let it bother you another moment. I cannot imagine what a shock my arrival gave you."

Holt nodded and made to leave. Just over the threshold, he wavered and turned to face her. "I am sorry about Clint, for your sake. It's selfish to only think of what his passing meant to me. I suppose you have also lost something in all of this. I'm a sad second prize."

Glenna wanted to disagree with him, but as her throat had welled up with unbidden emotion, was unable to answer and was grateful that Holt didn't wait for her to make a response. Glancing around the room, she made a shortlist of things that would need to be cleaned before she would be able to rest. There was no time to mourn the dead. No time to mourn Clint or the death of her hopes for the future and possible happiness.

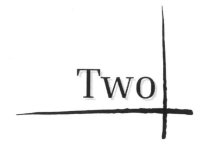

Two

Holt pulled the door closed behind him as he left the room and crept to the children's room. The curtains had been drawn, casting the room into premature dusk to allow Daisy to sleep. Walking as softly as possible, Holt relied on what little light still filtered into the space to guide his search.

The room was simple with little furnishings, making his task easy. A small box lay on the floor under the bed, pushed back far enough it wouldn't be a temptation for Finn or Daisy. This must be it, he was sure. Slipping out of the room as silently as he had entered, Holt shut the door behind him and, wasting no time once in the bright hallway, lifted the lid and wasn't disappointed with his find.

A stack of letters scribed in a delicate hand from Miss Glenna E. Perry to Mr. Clint Sterling lay at the very top. Holt flipped through some of the envelopes before noting that the box also contained other correspondence addressed to his brother. One from a solicitor and another from an inquiry agent's office based in New York. He noted many letters that still lay at the bottom of the box but couldn't spend the time looking through them now.

"Oh, big brother—what have you gone and gotten me into?" Holt cursed and placed all save one of the letters back in the box, the single correspondence tucked away in his shirt pocket, and retreated to his room. Once there, he hurriedly gathered the things that would need to be moved to the bunkhouse. Placing the box of letters in the back of his closet. There would be time to read them later; for now, he needed to sort a few things out for himself, like how he had just gotten himself engaged.

Holt slapped his hat atop his head, then walked quietly back down the hall and passed the closed door he knew Glenna was still behind. Once he was out to the bunkhouse and set up on the extra bed, he decided it was best to keep himself occupied and set to work saddling up his horse. There would be no putting off talking to the pastor.

Leading Ranger out of the barn he caught sight of Glenna, Daisy up from her nap held happily on Glenna's hip, babbling away. Holt stopped just short of showing his whereabouts and watched from his vantage point as Glenna crossed the space between the house and garden, Daisy in one arm, a basket hanging off the other.

The long sleeves of the nondescript, gray dress now rolled up to accommodate for the warm weather. She had found one of Grace's aprons, its crisp whiteness a stark contrast to the dullness of her skirt. Daisy, her cherub, cheeks rosy, clinging to Glenna, fistfuls of her dress clutched into tiny fists.

"Shall we see what's in the garden?" he heard Glenna question. Daisy answered in her own way, and Holt found himself caught up in the conversation.

"Perhaps there will be onions." he could hear Glenna speaking to Daisy.

"You can help me fix up some supper. Oh my! Is that an apple tree?" Glenna exclaimed as their path took them past the three tall apple trees that separated the garden from the smokehouse. She and Daisy made their way to the nearest tree, there spending time picking a few choice apples and placing them in the pockets of her apron, all the while involving Daisy in her every choice.

Turning his mind back to the task at hand, he finished leading Ranger out of the barn and into Glenna's line of sight. He tipped his hat in her direction as her eyes landed on him from the direction of the garden.

"I won't be gone long," he called to her. Then, before he could overthink his choice of leaving Daisy with Glenna, he swung onto his horse and spurred the animal into a run. The freedom of the ride helped to clear his head, and a new kind of reckless determination set in. This was his family's land, their legacy, and now it was his. It was his duty to keep it for Finn and Daisy — his duty.

It wasn't as if he didn't know other ranchers or trappers who had sent word back East for a wife, a few of them set up with wives by family. Wyoming was still sparsely populated and single women were few and far between. Holt had never considered the possibility for himself or his brother.

Their parents had been a love match. Because of their example, Clint had waited for and courted his wife Grace. Perhaps that is how Holt saw himself if he ever gave it much thought at all. Yet this — this sham of a marriage — a contract made of necessity. It all seemed too impersonal, and he wondered what his parents would think of it.

Shaking off the idea, he realized just how much time he had been focusing on the topic when Buffalo came into view. The ranch was set back and could be cut off for months by the winter snows, but in good weather was an easy distance from town.

Riding up to the church house, Holt dismounted and tied Ranger off just as the pastor came around the side of the building as if he had been waiting for Holt's arrival.

"Good morning," the other man smiled warmly.

"Mornin'." Holt tipped his hat, then took it off altogether. "Pastor Joseph, can I have a word?"

"Of course. What is on your mind?"

"I'm — gettin' married. Or rather, I need to. And soon."

Pastor Joseph raised one eyebrow. "Come inside Holt. I have a feeling there is a story behind that statement."

He led the way, and Holt knew from experience the Pastor wouldn't be made to rush into anything. He would make Holt sit and talk to him until he was satisfied. It would be no use to argue with him and followed him into the chapel. Taking a seat near the front, Pastor Joseph waited for Holt to sit and relate the whole story before he ventured to speak.

"And this is what you want, Holt?"

Holt let his hat dangle uselessly from his fingertips while he mulled over the question. "I can see the benefit of it."

"Yes — marriage has many benefits. I can see what drew your brother to make the decision to remarry. I could even understand your desire to follow suit, but what of this young woman? What benefits would she have in the arrangement?"

Holt sat baffled. Glenna said she had nothing to return to. There had been no other information. He had extended the option of marriage out of his need, not once considering pressing her about hers. Perhaps her letters could answer the question of why Glenna wished to stay, even to shackle herself to him, rather than return.

"I suppose those answers are held in Clint's letters," he finally answered.

"Letters that she presented to you?"

"She offered me the ones he sent as proof of her identity. I found the correspondence she sent to him later."

Holt waited while the pastor seemed to mull over something, then clasped Holt on the shoulder, "Rachel and I will be there for supper tonight. After that I will give you my answer. To prepare, let's get started on the marriage license and clear some time for the ceremony — for when?"

26

"Tomorrow," Holt answered.

———————————

"Well, it's just you and I for now, little Daisy. Shall we set to work?" Glenna asked the sweet little girl who had woken from her afternoon nap with a grin. Daisy patted Glenna on the cheek with one chubby hand.

"Will you play here for a little while?" she asked and placed Daisy in the high chair. She gave the child a dry biscuit from their tea to nibble on, then set to work cleaning up the remnants from the table. Holt had left well before lunch, and she had only prepared oatmeal sweetened with molasses for Daisy and herself. After the simple meal, Glenna stripped the bed in her new room, hauled and boiled water to wash with, then set Daisy down for another short nap while she washed the bedding.

The afternoon hours had been eaten up by the project. Now the sheets hung out in the warm summer air, drying fast with a slight breeze snapping their edges into a strange sort of dance. Daisy had awoken from her afternoon nap even more pleasantly than her short morning respite, and Glenna had the feeling that the little child was usually very good-natured. Now it was time to focus on the supper meal.

"Now, what to cook? We have carrots, onions, and potatoes from our excursion to the garden this morning." She glanced around, settled on what she was sure must be recipes held together in a well-used book.

Glenna looked over the recipes and frowned. Although many of the recipes looked as if they had been written with care in a very nice hand, they were old, frayed at the edges, ink smeared in several places from use, and many indefinable smudges of various foods.

Finding one that looked as though she could read it all and had simple ingredients, Glenna set to work. Having the chance to spend the afternoon familiarizing herself with the kitchen, its ingredients, or lack of, soon the smell of homemade biscuits and stew filled the air.

Daisy had stayed content after the biscuit by entertaining herself with an old cup and wooden spoon while Glenna hummed a tune she had learned as a child at the knee of her nurse. The house had been well taken care of, nevertheless it needed some basic cleaning and she made mental notes on things that would need to be done in the next few days.

There would be a great deal more washing that would need to be tended to, and the basket with items that needed to be sewn was large enough to keep her evenings occupied for some time. Just before the biscuits needed to come out of the oven, she heard the sound of a horse approaching and glanced out the window that faced the barn to confirm it was indeed Holt.

He went right to the barn; Glenna was sure to see after his mount before coming inside the house. She rushed to finish, and right on time, Holt entered for supper without Glenna needing to call for him. He washed up and placed a kiss on Daisy's fine golden hair. "It smells wonderful."

"I hope it tastes as well as it smells," Glenna answered, then felt brave enough to venture farther, "How was your trip into town?"

"Productive," he said simply.

She didn't press, although she wished he would elaborate. "Supper will be ready shortly, Mr. Sterling."

"Holt," he insisted.

"Yes, Holt. I just wanted to ask, how many will be joining us tonight? I haven't seen another soul all day."

"The boys are out on a drive. I don't expect to see hide-nor-hair of them until — Friday, maybe Saturday. Finn will be home tomorrow."

"It will just be the three of us tonight?"

"Not exactly," he said slowly. "We are expectin' some guests."

Glenna looked at him, the question plain on her face.

Rather than answering her, he said, "I'd better go wash up," and slid up to the sink, primed the pump, and set to scrubbing his hands with a sliver of lye soap.

Glenna bit her tongue. She supposed she would learn of the supper guests' identities shortly.

He finished and moved to dry his hands just as a knock sounded. Holt excused himself to answer the door, and Glenna made an attempt to smooth back the wild mass of curls that had come loose during the day's work to frame her face, pulled off the apron, and dusted off the front of her dress before the footsteps approached. Gathering up Daisy, she held the child to her like a shield.

"Glenna, let me introduce Pastor Thomas Joseph and his wife Rachel. This is Glenna Perry — my fiancé." His tongue seemed to stumble over the last word, and Glenna felt her smile falter.

"It is a great honor to be the first to welcome you, Miss Perry," Rachel said warmly and rushed forward to take Glenna's hand.

Rachel was younger than her husband, by a good deal, if Glenna had to guess. The woman was bright and lovely. She had those wonderful little wrinkles around her eyes that indicated her propensity to smile often. A cap of auburn hair and slender build complemented her charming smile.

"I am very glad to meet you both," Glenna returned the greeting.

"We never come to visit friends empty-handed." The pastor smiled and stepped forward, holding out a jar of preserves for her to take. "Strawberry rhubarb," he said proudly.

"Thank you. It looks delicious."

Daisy wriggled in her arms and pointed at the preserves.

"It seems Daisy is trying to tell us it's time to tuck in," Rachel laughed.

Placing the preserves on the counter, she attempted to balance Daisy on one hip while reaching for bowls. "Oh yes, everything is ready. I apologize for not having the table properly set; I didn't know to expect guests."

Holt stepped forward and reached for his niece. "The short notice is my fault."

"No explanation necessary," she said softly and placed the bowls on the table, adding spoons and cups.

Holt deposited Daisy in the highchair before pulling out a chair for Glenna. She felt a wash of confusion at the behavior. It had been so long since a man had shown her true civility that the gesture had seemed out of place.

Once everyone was seated, Glenna watched Holt as he placed his hand near her, palm up. He must have seen the confusion that followed.

"Do the English not say grace at supper?" Rachel asked in an amused tone.

Suddenly, Glenna seemed to remember the company in the house and looked across the table at the pair.

"Of course we say grace," she answered, feeling foolish, and slid her hand into Holt's. She tried not to acknowledge the surge of warmth that shot through her at the same time, making her skin tingle from the contact.

His long, lean fingers closed around her small hand. Glenna was keenly aware of the rough texture of his fingers speaking of hard work, the strength that marked his trade, and yet, how gently he cradled her hand.

The circle of hands continued until everyone, save Daisy, was connected, and Holt offered a prayer of thanks for the bounty before them, thanks for the hands that had prepared the meal, and ended the prayer asking for a blessing on those away from home working the cattle.

It was a simple prayer, and it touched her heart in ways that no other prayer had before. Realizing she had allowed her hand to rest in his a moment longer than necessary, Glenna pulled her arm away and felt a blush rising to her face. She had never held the hand of any man besides that of her father before, and now, in the space of hours, she had found her hand held within Holt's twice. She had forgotten herself with the contact.

<hr>

Holt couldn't help but notice the lingering of her hand in his as the prayer ended, the feel of her hand in his. The conversation never waned thanks to the efforts of Glenna, who seemed to find both the Josephs' very interesting.

"So, Miss Perry, you have indeed learned a great deal about us. Why don't you tell us something about yourself?" Pastor Joseph pressed.

"What would you like to know?" she countered while prodding Daisy to eat another bite.

"Well, it's clear from your accent you are a transplant from Great Britain. How long have you been in the states?"

"Five years. I was seventeen when I first set foot on American soil."

"That would make you twenty-two now. We are the same age," Rachel commented with delight.

"And you stayed in New York City these past five years?" came the next question.

"Yes."

"Did you like the City? I have always wanted to see a place so full of people they outnumber the cattle," Rachel giggled at the idea.

"I did not mind the city. As a youth, I spent time in London. New York is a very different type of city. The hurried movements of those that live life fast-paced seem somewhat universal."

"Oh, London! What a different life you must have had," Rachel wondered aloud.

"Do you still have family in England?" Pastor Joseph pressed.

"No." Holt watched as she shook her head slowly, her eyes darting downward. It was a motion that most people never caught because it was usually followed by a smile to hide the pain of loss. Glenna did just as he expected and smiled, cooing to Daisy and prodding her to take more food. Glenna had lost someone, someone she loved; he was sure of it.

"Is your family back East?" the questions continued.

"No," Holt could see Glenna's shoulders sagged a little under the scrutiny of so many eyes on her, "I have no family left." Again, the air of pain caused only by loss. She was an orphan, perhaps even before her journey across the sea. Is that why she had nothing to return to? There was no one waiting for her?

"I am sorry to hear that," Pastor Joseph said with genuine emotion.

32

Glenna gave him a polite nod, then turned her attention back to Daisy.

"Well, I am happy to have you here, Miss Perry. It will be refreshing to add a new face to the quilting circle and, of course, the Harvest Festival is right around the corner."

"Don't overwhelm her," Pastor Joseph chided his wife with a chuckle. "I am sure she will want to get settled in here before adding to her plate."

"We will see you at services on Sunday?"

"We will be there," Holt assured them when Glenna didn't answer. It was impossible not to notice the change in her demeanor. He would ask her about it later.

With Daisy on her hip, Glenna accepted the fast hug from Rachel as they parted. She watched from the porch as Pastor Joseph helped her into the wagon and took his seat at her side, waving back at them before taking the reins.

Holt stood a respectable distance from her, still as quiet as he had been during the meal, and his gaze still locked on her. The minute the wagon pulled away from the house, Glenna rounded on him.

"Did I pass inspection?" He seemed taken back a bit by her tone.

"That wasn't —"

"If you did not trust your brother's judgment as to my qualifications to run this household, to care for the children residing within, you should never have made such a rash proposal yourself. I gave you a perfectly reasonable alternative to marriage."

"Don't trust my brother?" Holt spat. "You are about to cross a line."

"I believed you to be an honorable man when we met. However, parading me around and having me inspected like — like cattle was mortifying. You didn't even have the decency to give me warning enough to set a proper table or still my nerves. How low you must think of me." Glenna trailed off as Holt took a step toward her.

"I don't think lowly of you. I don't know you from Adam. Before today, I had no idea you even existed. Clint never gave any indication he had sent away for — for a bride. I have only today to judge you by, and there you have me at a disadvantage."

"You're right. I at least knew Clint had a brother," she conceded. "I am sorry for becoming so easily upset."

"To be rightly honest, you are a conundrum to me." He tilted his head to one side a little, his eyes searching. "You are well educated, well-spoken; it's clear you are used to society far finer than anythin' you'll find in the wilds of cattle country. I can't seem to understand what on God's green earth would entice you to choose — this." He waved his hand around to encompass everything in their field of vision.

"What makes you believe I had very many choices to start with? Or that this wasn't more ideal?" she countered while patting Daisy softly on the back as the toddler was clearly up past her normal bedtime and was becoming fussy with lack of sleep.
Holt seemed to think about what she said for a few minutes before attempting a response.

"I apologize for makin' unfounded assumptions, but I am not the only one who has done so."

Glenna slowly nodded, "You are right. I, too, apologize for making assumptions."

34

Holt's stance relaxed a bit. "Pastor Joseph invited himself to supper and gave me no fair warnin', either. I had no intention of paradin' you about or havin' others to inspect you. I believe they're comin' to supper was only done with the best of intentions. These are good, honest, and hardworkin' people out here, Miss Glenna — for the most part."

Glenna didn't press about what he could mean adding in that last bit as Daisy's head started to loll on her shoulder. Holt stepped a bit closer and dropped his voice as if someone were listening to a very private conversation.

"You hold in your arms one of two things that mean anythin' to me in this whole world." His eyes were on Daisy as he talked, "My Ma' always said you could tell a lot about a person by how kids and animals reacted to them. I haven't seen Daisy take to anyone the way she took to you. I chose to trust you with her today, and I'm makin' the choice to trust you tonight with her care, because Daisy seems taken with you.

"That is why I want to get hitched. Because Finn and Daisy need a Ma' of their own. They need the lovin' and time only a Ma' can give. I asked you to marry me because it's proper. It will keep my family together. I trust my brother, Miss Glenna. I loved him too, but he was also keepin' things from me. And I believe one of those things may have got him killed."

Glenna felt shocked at his statement. Her mind working overtime, wondering what secrets Clint could have been keeping that would put his life in jeopardy, and what proof Holt had to make him suspicious.

"After all, I knew nothin' about you. It's reasonable to assume that Clint was keepin' more from me. It would explain how odd he had been actin'." Holt reasoned.

Glenna bit her lip to stop herself from responding. He had linked Clint's withholding of information on the state of his personal relationships to his behavior prior to his death. She wondered anew how Clint had passed, but knew it was not the time to venture into that discussion.

———————

After the evening chores were done and long into the sleepless hours, Holt lay awake in the bunkhouse. There was something about this mystery woman that he found intriguing, something he inherently trusted about her as well.

Rolling onto his side, Holt tried to quiet his mind and allow sleep to take over. After a time, he sighed and gave up the attempt. Lighting a lantern, he searched the pocket of his shirt now hanging on the back of a chair and fished out the single letter he had kept from the box now hidden in his room.

Sitting back down on the cot, he unfolded the letter, telling himself it wasn't an invasion of privacy as she had offered up her letters for his inspection. A small newspaper clipping fell out and onto his lap. Holt laid the letter aside and unfolded the clipping.

> *Wife needed: Young widower seeks a*
> *kindhearted, Christian woman to help*
> *rear two small children on a Wyoming*
> *cattle ranch. -C.L. Sterling*

It also listed contact information was also listed in the short advert. Holt wondered what in that simple advert could have enticed Glenna to write to his brother. Taking up the letter, he noted it contained several pages.

Dear Mr. C.L. Sterling,

This letter is in response to your advert placed in Street and Smith's New York Weekly. My name is Glenna Eleanor Perry. I am one and twenty, of English birth, however, I have resided in New York for the past four-and-a-half years.

I was educated in one of the finest finishing schools in Britain. I am a fair cook and talented with a needle and thread. Although I have never been on a cattle ranch before, I have no fear of hard work. I have a great fondness for the outdoors, gardens, small animals, and adore children.

I have enclosed character references for your consideration of my qualifications.

Sincerely,

G. E. Perry

He glanced over the reference letters she had sent, one from the owner of a boarding house that had employed Glenna as a seamstress and cook, another from a member of the clergy that gave glowing accounts of Glenna as an upstanding member of the congregation. The last was simply a short message from a woman who had employed Glenna to tend to her children for a time. By all accounts, Glenna was trustworthy, thoughtful, and a woman with high moral standards.

Holt cursed himself for not bringing more of the letters with him now that he was fully awake and wondering even more about the woman now sleeping in his home. He had heard of men advertising for housekeepers that later turned into wives, even knew a few that had sent word back East to relatives for a wife to be found for them and sent out on the frontier. It wasn't at all unheard of or out of place, given the small number of available women on the frontier.

He could understand why, yet was unable to stop it from bothering him that his brother had a whole part of his life, a rather large part Holt knew nothing about. He had advertised for a wife and caretaker of his children, had at least one response Holt knew of, written to her for some time, even proposed and arranged travel for her, and Holt was none the wiser.

Clint had acted off for days before leaving the day he died. Holt hadn't pressed Clint for information. The tension was high all over the state among the cattlemen. Conflicts over grazing rights, cattle drives over open range, and violence between cowboys, ranchers, and rustlers were escalating, making everyone tense.

Was Clint's strange behavior due to the demands of life on the ranch? Or did it have to do with Glenna? How had he shared meals at the same table, slept under the same roof, worked the same land without ever really knowing what was going on with his brother?

Holt felt a headache creeping in among the questions that piled one atop the other. Perhaps the other letters would hold some answers. He looked out the window at the dark house. Not wanting to risk waking Glenna or Daisy, there was no way to find out until he could retrieve more of the letters.

Three

The sun had long lit the sky before its rays crept over the mountain peaks and warmed the roof of the house. She watched the progression as she dressed, donning the only other dress she brought on the journey, only slightly better fitted than her everyday dress; it was a light purple that complimented the darkness of her hair and eyes.

Glenna hurried to wash her face and piled her curls into some semblance of order atop her head. There was no use in admiring her reflection. There were no jewels to drape from her neck and ears. No kid gloves for her hands. No fan, parasol, lace collar, or any adornments tucked neatly into her hair. There was no need for the self aggrandizement she had once felt necessary. Fastening her mother's broach to the base of her neck, she finally felt ready to face what this day held.

Wasting no further time, Glenna plucked up her bonnet and rushed to retrieve Daisy from her slumber. It was well past time she should have had the food cooking. She was busy stoking the fire when Holt appeared at the back door.

"Mornin', did little Daisy let you get any shut-eye?" Holt asked while placing a kiss on the toddler's brow as he passed the high chair. Daisy gave him a beaming smile.

Glenna took in his appearance and wondered if the man had slept a wink himself.

"Daisy did very well," she answered, not willing to explore the fact she had not slept well despite being exhausted or that it had nothing to do with the delightful child.

"That's encoragin'. She's had some pretty fitful nights as of late. Wakin' up inconsolable."

It was most likely that Daisy was reacting to the feeling of stress in the home. However, Glenna felt it was better to keep that thought to herself.

"You look very nice," Holt mused, taking in her appearance in a long glance. Glenna nervously touched the broach at her neck, then smoothed the lilac-colored skirt with trembling hands.

"I — I thought my best would be appropriate for the occasion," she said, her voice betraying the nerves that fluttered in her stomach at the sight of him. Holt, even disheveled, was very handsome to be sure. Glenna glanced at Holt from the corner of her eye. He looked startled for a split second.

"That's right. I'd better get myself cleaned up." Holt looked lost for a minute before slipping out of the room. Glenna busied herself with Daisy as the sound of his footfalls overhead kept Holt in the forefront of her mind.

The sound of a carriage approaching brought Glenna back to herself and gathering Daisy into her arms, she went to the front, curious as to who it could be.

Glenna smiled to herself as she recognized the battered hat of Mr. Theodore Coleman, even from a distance. As he drew closer, Glenna could see he had brought someone with him.

"Hello!" The woman seated next to Theodore waved enthusiastically as the wagon rolled to a stop in almost the same spot it had just the day previous.

Almost the instant the wheels had come to a halt, a black and white blur leaped from the wagon and rushed up the porch steps.

"Oh, my!" Glenna felt a momentary rush of panic as the dog bounded toward her. The apprehension was met with a wet tongue and wagging tail. He was a fine-looking black and white dog with one blue eye and one brown eye. She liked him instantly.

"Oh, hello! Hello!" Theodore was already down from the wagon seat and came around to give a hand down to the cheerful-looking woman who was beaming at them from her seat.

"It's good to see you again, Miss Glenna." He tipped his hat to her, then reached into the wagon box and produced a young boy.

"And you, Mr. Coleman."

In an instant, Glenna and Daisy found themselves wrapped in the arms of the older woman. "I told Theo we had to head over as soon as possible so I could meet you."

"Hattie, let the poor girl breathe," Theo laughed.

Hattie was a few inches shorter than Glenna, with hair the color of corn silk and striking blue eyes. Glenna knew as soon as she looked into them that this woman was a relative of Holt's. Her smile was warm, genuine, and held a kindness Glenna hadn't seen in years.

Next to her husband, they made a handsome couple. He was tall and lean, with black hair that had peppered with age. His brown eyes and tall frame played a pleasant-looking contrast to his wife's short and round stature. Glenna liked the look of them.

"Well, I might have guessed." Holt had appeared from behind Glenna, hastily tucking in a fresh shirt, his hair combed, and face freshly shaved. She thought he looked even more handsome than she had first thought him, if that were possible. He stepped around where her feet seemed to be rooted and placed a kiss on Hattie's cheek.

"Glenna, this beauty is my Aunt Hattie." Holt had his arm around Hattie's shoulders. Glenna could see the family traits they shared, "Hattie, this is Miss Glenna Perry."

"That failure of a guard dog is Blu, or Blu Dog, as everyone calls him. He's a pest, but the best darn cow dog you'll ever meet." Holt gave Blu a pat.

"Theo told me he dropped this poor thing off here yesterday, and I scolded him something awful." Hattie swatted at her husband, who had stepped up to join them, the little boy now walking at his side. "He really should have brought her over to our spread for the time being. I made him hitch up the wagon right away this morning. We are happy to have you come stay with us, Miss Perry, until arrangements can be made."

"No need." Holt shook his head and, lifting his eyes, met Glenna's gaze. "She'll be staying here at Crossroads, with Finn, Daisy, and I, as my wife."

Holt felt, rather than heard, the collective gasp of surprise from his aunt and uncle. Ignoring it, he stooped and smiled at Finn.

"How would you like that, Finn? To stay here with me and Miss Glenna." The eyes of his elder brother looked up at him from the face of his nephew.

Finn looked from Holt up at Glenna, who was still holding Daisy, then to Blu, who was sitting next to Glenna's feet, looking up at her as well, tongue lolling.

"Blu Dog likes her," Finn observed and Holt nodded, "Daisy likes her?"

"She does," Holt nodded.

"You like her too?" Finn asked innocently.

"Yes." Holt didn't hesitate to answer the question.

"I guess it would be okay," Finn relented. He looked from Holt to Blu and back up to Glenna. "You're pretty." It was a statement.

She smiled at him. "Thank you. It's very nice to meet you, Finn."

Finn stepped up and lifted his hand to shake hers. Holt could tell that the exchange humored Glenna as her mouth twitched upward. She took his hand and shook it.

"I am glad to meet you," Finn said in his most grown-up voice.

"We are all glad to meet you," Hattie added with a warm smile.

"I am very pleased to meet all of you."

"Well, why are we all standing around out here? Have you lost your manners, Holt?" His aunt scolded.

"No, Aunt Hattie," Holt chuckled and stood, "Why don't you come in and rest while I hitch up the wagon. Glenna, Daisy, and I were just about to head for town."

Hattie patted Holt on the cheek as she brushed past him. "Come on in with me, Glenna; let's leave the boys to it." Hattie linked her arm with Glenna and pulled her and Daisy inside the house, Blu right at their heels. Finn looked momentarily lost, then decided to follow them, leaving Holt alone with Theo.

Theo swiped off his hat, ran a hand over his brow with a handkerchief, before clapping Holt on the shoulder.

"Please, start from the beginnin'."

Holt sighed and took the porch stairs two at a time. Theo caught up with him halfway to the barn.

"I'm gatherin' you didn't know who she was when you drove her out to the homestead yesterday — was it just yesterday?" Holt sighed. "So much has already happened. It feels like weeks ago."

"She didn't give much information, and I didn't ask too many questions," Theo shrugged.

"Clint — Clint advertised for a wife, a stepmother for the kids. These last ten months without Grace must have worn on him. The two of them exchanged several letters, it seems, then he arranged her travel from back East."

"You — you are takin' his place?"

Holt stopped abruptly as they reached the barn and turned sharply to look at his uncle. "You and Aunt Hattie have been a godsend in helpin' me out with the kids, but you can't take them both on permanently. I need someone to be their caretaker unless I farm them out to other families —" He shook his head. "I can't run the place and look after them properly. It's the best solution."

Theo looked thoughtful. "Marriages have started on far worse terms, I suppose. What do you know about Miss Glenna, her qualities?"

"English born. She's been living in New York and sent Clint several reference letters. I am playin' catch up learnin' anything about her." Holt stopped talking, and after a second of pensive silence, added. "Daisy was taken with her the moment they met."

"And you? What do you think of her?" Theo raised one eyebrow.

"She's talented in the kitchen," Holt answered lamely.

"Oh boy," Theo chuckled.

"She's fine to look at." Holt could feel the heat creeping up his neck at the admission.

"A pretty wife that can keep you fed. Men have married knowing far less about their wives, I suppose."

Holt pulled the barn doors open and stomped inside.

44

"Will you be sleeping in our room?" Finn asked, seating himself at the kitchen table, his hand resting at the top of Blu's head lazily scratching the dog's ears.

"No," Glenna answered, unsure if Finn would be bothered by knowing she was staying in his parents room.

"When are you getting hitched?" Finn asked.

"We are getting married this morning." The words felt strange leaving her lips. Married. She was going to be a married woman in a few hours. She had thought herself prepared to yolk herself to Clint, a man she had felt she knew a little about, but fate, it seemed, had very different plans for Glenna. Could she truly commit to this life? Hard work and solitude? She thought of what she had left behind and looked from Finn petting Blu to Daisy and Hattie in turn. Yes, she could make the best of this.

After all, what use was it to question the choices that had led her to this point? She was here, had traveled great distances and lived through less than ideal circumstance to come to this place. Holt was not the groom she had expected. However, there was nothing to go back to. She was resolved to this new twist of fate.

"Theo and I will come into town with you and act as witnesses," Hattie said in a matter-of-fact tone. "Now, tell me how you found yourself here?"

Glenna obliged and retold her story with as little embellishments as possible. Hattie only asked a few clarifying questions, finally nodding, satisfied.

Glenna gave the woman a small smile, "Tell me how you are related to Holt? I didn't know he had any living relatives other than the children."

Hattie lowered herself into a chair and reached for Daisy. Glenna deposed the little girl into her great-aunt's arms and set to work making a pot of tea.

"Hester, the boy's mother, was my younger sister, twelve years my junior. Our family came from Illinois. We lost my two younger brothers on the wagon trail. A few years after we settled here, Hester was born. Clint senior's family had already established their ranch here when my family showed up. Hester and Clint senior grew up together, and it was clear from the time they were young the two of them would end up hitched."

"Was it that way with you and Mr. Coleman?" Glenna wondered.

"Theo? Oh heavens no," Hattie laughed, "Theo came by way of Nebraska. By that time, I was nearly twenty-five and considered an old maid. He didn't seem to mind my strong opinions or sharp tongue, and we married only a few weeks into the courtship. Not long after, he bought up some land close by and we settled in."

"He did mention to me that he lived close and raised some milk cows."

"He used to run cattle, then sold most of them to Clint a few years back after he was thrown from his horse. The hip injury plays up a bit now and then. I don't mind downsizing the operation one bit. It's a comfort for me to have Theo home more these days."

Glenna set the pot of tea at the table and added a few biscuits for Finn and Daisy on the tray, and took a seat.

"Do you have children nearby as well?"

"Theo and I were never blessed with any younglings. Clint and Holt are the closest things to it, and these little ones are the joy of our lives." Hattie placed a kiss on Daisy's head and handed her over to Glenna who cradled her before placing her in the high chair, placing a crumbled biscuit in front of her. Hattie had given Finn his share and the two women sipped at the tea.

"I don't mean to pry," Glenna started, and Hattie lifted one hand to quiet her.

"You are wondering why Theo and I didn't take the children." It was not a question. Glenna nodded.

Hattie looked warmly at both Finn and Daisy. Her gaze fell on Glenna. "We did offer. Holt refused. You see, years back, there was an illness that swept through town. I was mighty sick for a long time, doc said it damaged my heart. Just as soon as I felt well enough from that, I fell under another bout of sickness.

"It took a good deal longer to recover, and my old ticker has never been the same. I enjoy the littles from time to time for short stays, even those tucker me out beyond reason. Holt was scared, I suppose, that by leaving the younglings with us he'd put Theo in the same place he is, raising them alone."

Hattie explained the damaging effects of her past illnesses with a mature and even tone. The woman was matter-of-fact, not looking for sympathy in the hand she had been given. It made sense to Glenna now, knowing that Holt would refuse to put her life in danger just to ease his load.

"I was glad when Theo came to my rescue yesterday and even more pleased to know you both. I did not expect an extended family. It is a happy turn of events. I hope to learn as much as I can from you about life out here and how to best adapt." Glenna changed the subject with a smile.

"You seem to be doing a fine job on your own."

"I am still in a state." Glenna shook her head.

"Well, of course you are!" Hattie sat her cup down, "After such a long trek, you come to find no welcome reception, the need to make your own way to the ranch, only to learn your intended husband is dead. There has been no shortage of surprises and challenges for you."

"I am not the only one that has been caught up in this whirlwind." Glenna let her thoughts fill with Holt. "He is giving up a lot."

Hattie waved her hand to dismiss this line of thinking. "Holt has a good head on his shoulders. He must have thought it the best for all involved. It is a difficult place you both find yourselves in, but the boy isn't being forced into anything."

"He is pledging himself to a stranger for the sake of those he loves. Is it truly possible he isn't pining for — someone else? A lost love, perhaps? This one rash choice could leave him miserable."

"You must have put some thought into accepting Clint's proposal. You don't have any affection attached elsewhere?" Hattie pressed, not addressing Glenna's questions.

"No, I have never allowed myself to become close enough to anyone to form attachments," Glenna said with real honesty.

Hattie looked at her, thoughtful.

"The wagon is all hitched." The announcement from the back door stopped Hattie from questioning her further.

"I'll change Daisy before we all head out." Hattie volunteered and went to gather up Daisy.

Glenna automatically started to clean away the tea items from the table.

48

"Finn, why don't you go get a fresh shirt while I grab somethin' from upstairs," Holt said and waved to Finn to follow him.

Once he was out of earshot, Theo cleared his throat, "How are you holdin' up, Miss?"

Glenna smiled over at him, "As well as can be expected under such circumstances."

"I am sorry for bein' fool enough not to tell you about Clint."

"There was no way you could have known to correct the mistake. I don't believe I ever used his Christian name upon our meeting."

"I must confess I was thinkin' of Holt when you mentioned Mr. Sterling. But after thinkin' it over last night, I realized my mistake. Hattie was upset somethin' awful at me for leavin' you and insisted we head over as soon as I could hitch up."

"There is no need to worry. Holt was a true gentleman," she reassured him.

Theo nodded, ringing his hat a little in his hands. Glenna tilted her head a little to one side, "Was there somethin' you wanted to ask me, Mr. Coleman?"

"Theo, please. No one calls me Mr. anythin'."

"May I call you Theodore? I quite like the name."

"You sure can," he smiled broadly. "I don't mean to pry. Well, I suppose I do mean to pry, if only a little. I can see why this arrangement — this marriage would be beneficial to Holt and the children, yet I can't seem to understand your part in this."

"You see all the advantages on his side, only you mean?" Glenna asked her question in return, then rushed on, not allowing Theo time to speak, "Can it be so strange to you that I would be so eager to marry? I have no family, no fortune, no prospects, nothing to my name save what you saw me with yesterday. This seems like a happy turn of events for me indeed. By the end of the day, I will have a place to call home. One that is warm and lovely.

"I will also be entrusted with the care and education of two beautiful children. Surrounded each day by their laughter and vigor. To have the pleasure of watching them grow. Sharing his name will provide me many advantages — many more than I am sure Holt would be able to lay claim to.

"By the venture of marriage alone, I will have a degree of protection that is not available to single women. There is a sense of belonging and security in a marriage that nothing else can fulfill. On a more personal turn, I hope that Holt and I can share mutual respect and, in time, perhaps cultivate a friendship."

Theo listened openly to her, his expression revealing first his skepticism that turned into acceptance.

"So you see, Theodore, all of these things are something to be praised, proud of, and grateful for. It has been a very long time since I have had anything positive to look forward to or call my own. This is a very selfish act on my part, very selfish indeed, I'm afraid."

"I'm ready!" Finn bounded into the kitchen in a new shirt and freshly combed hair. "Holt said you'd read to me. Will you?"

"Of course, and teach you to read on your own," she replied, and Finn's eyes widened. "Would you like that?"

"Very much." Finn grinned.

"And will you teach me how things ought to run here?" Glenna asked. "I have never lived on a ranch and I'm worried I'm ill-equipped to make it a go alone."

"I can help you." Finn nodded eagerly as Blu tore into the space leading the way for Hattie and Daisy.

"Well, it looks like we are all ready to load up the wagons. Come on, Theo, us and the little ones can get a leg up while Holt finishes up here."

Hattie beckoned to Finn to follow her out.

Theo took a step toward her retreating form, stalled, and turned back to Glenna. "I meant no offense with my questions."

"This is your family and you care about them. It is only right that you are concerned."

"I ain't just concerned for them." He nodded in the direction everyone had disappeared to. "Your well-bein' should be considered in all this as well."

Glenna felt a flood of gratitude toward him.

"Thank you, Theodore. You have no idea how much that means to me."

Theo blushed high on his weathered cheeks.

Hattie called out for him to join her from the front of the house.

"I better get a move on." Theo started to move, stopping halfway across the kitchen. "Hattie and I will take the younglings with us so you and Holt can — um — have a little time together."

Before Glenna could protest and rebuff the offer, Theo had slapped his hat back onto his head and was gone.

Feeling a lot less secure in her choices than she was pretending to be, Glenna slumped a little, her shoulders falling with weariness. She had been honest with Theo about her reasons for marriage and knew it was to her advantage to go through with the ceremony.

However, the emotional fatigue she was feeling was as real as the physical. It had been a very long and trying to trek out west and coupled with all that had happened since her arrival, only added to her exhaustion.

She could hear Holt as he shut one of the doors on the second floor and started to descend the stairs. Glenna was glad for the few moments this gave her to compose herself and prepare to face him. Gathering up her shawl and hat, she went to meet him by the front door.

"It seems we've missed the mass exodus," he commented, looking out the door to see the Coleman's wagon had already pulled away from the house.

"I'm sorry. Theo and Hattie insisted on taking the children with them."

"No need to be sorry. Once Aunt Hattie has an idea, there is no dissuadin' her from it. Besides, the ride into town will give us the chance to chat."

⸻

Holt shut up the house, called Blu to his wagon, and gave Glenna his hand to help her into the seat. Once she was settled, he gathered the reins and hopped into the driver's seat next to her.

"I hope meetin' Theo and Hattie weren't too overwhelmin' for you. I hadn't expected them to show up this mornin' or insist on joinin' us in town," Holt said after the team of horses started to move down the lane.

"They are both marvelous," Glenna praised.

"I'm glad you think so." Holt looked at her from the corner of his eye. "Hattie, give you a lesson on the family connection?"

"She did."

"And how did you find Finn?"

He noticed her smile at this question.

"He is charming. I think we will be fast friends."

Blu placed both front paws on the back of their seat and stuck his head in between them, licking at her face. Glenna laughed. Holt smiled. Her laugh was infectious.

"Yes, and you Blu Dog. I like you very much as well." She scratched behind his ears.

"Traitor," Holt accused as Blu leaned closer to Glenna and into the scratch. "He's very taken with you."

"What breed is he?"

"Australian Shepherd and somethin' else — don't know what that somethin' else is, but he is one hell of a cow dog."

Blu licked at her fingers when she slowed her scratching, then, seeming satisfied with himself, settled down in the bed of the wagon to doze off.

There was a moment of quiet that passed before Holt pressed forward.

"There are a few things I figure we should know about each other. Now is as good a time as ever to learn them."

"Alright, what would you like to know?" she answered a little stiffly.

"At supper, you said you lived in New York for five years?" he wondered.

"Yes."

"Did you like city life?

"I managed to survive it," she said soberly. "Do you like ranch life?"

"I do. It wasn't always that way, but the older I get, the more I realize it's in my blood, this place — it's a part of me."

"It is very beautiful." She agreed.

Holt paused in his questions long enough to appreciate the surrounding space. Glenna was right; it was beautiful. God's land, he thought.

"I never thought to ask if you would mind attendin' Sunday service with us."

"I — would not mind attending with you and the children."

"Pastor Joseph is a very charismatic preacher. I think you'll enjoy his sermons," Holt remarked.

"I think Rachel is a woman I could grow very fond of as well," Glenna conceded.

Holt thought about her answer. "You didn't say if you were a religious person. Is that a subject you'd rather not speak about?"

Glenna shifted slightly in the seat next to him. "I was once a very devout follower. I still hold to many of the teachings of my childhood, however — I am not sure I still believe in an all-knowing and benevolent God. Or more aptly, I am not sure that if one does exist that he cares at all for me. I have seen no evidence of his hand in my life, rather an astonishing lack of it. I am sorry if you find that disappointing."

Holt stole another glance at her. The softness of her face had turned to hard, sharp edges.

"I'm not disappointed; I understand. I have had my struggles with belief." He said, then added with a tad more softness, "I am sorry for whatever happened to you that would make you believe God doesn't care for you."

"I will, regardless of my personal struggles with belief, teach to the children with diligence whatever gospel you wish. Faith is a very lovely thing to have and no one should be deprived of the chance to develop it."

"Faith is also a very fragile thing." Holt lamented feeling the truth of the statement deeply. Glenna didn't respond, so Holt dared to change the subject.

"What brought you to America?"

"A very large ship," Glenna chortled.

Holt wasn't able to stop himself from looking right at her this time. She didn't meet his gaze, however, he could see the humor playing on her attractive features.

"I'm sorry. I know what you meant by the inquiry. I felt the need to bring some levity into the conversation. Everything has been so somber —"

The laugh he had been holding behind the rush of surprise burst forth and leaped out of him.

"You are right," he nodded, "We have been a very gloomy pair, haven't we? That's a fine way to start wedded life."

Again, Glenna shifted a little in her seat. Holt noted that this time it was to get a better look at the few structures that had just come into view as the wagon crested a hill.

"Is that Buffalo already?" she queried.

"That's it." Holt slowed the wagon a bit and pointed into the distance. "Livery, blacksmiths, hotel, post office, cafe, bar, general store, and church." He indicated each in turn. "There are also homes and a few other places I am sure I'm forgettin'. It's a handsome little town, though."

"The drive from the railway depot to Crossroads seemed so much longer than today's journey," Glenna admitted softly.

Holt pulled the horses to a full stop. "Mind holding the reins?" Not waiting for her to answer, he handed them to her and jumped from the wagon. "Stay, Blu Dog." He commanded as he strode off the road and into the brush.

"What on earth are you doing?" Glenna called after him.

Holt didn't bother to answer her and set about his mission. Once he located what he was looking for, he pulled his pocket knife. Gathering up his prize, he started back to the wagon. Glenna's brow was furrowed.

"I thought some wildflowers would look well with the color of your dress." He stepped back up into the wagon and, sitting down, took the reins as he handed her the bundle of flowers. Glenna's eyes were wide in pleasant surprise.

She pushed the bouquet to her nose and inhaled deeply. "They are lovely. Thank you."

"I think we are ready. You have your bouquet. I have a ring. The preacher has the license." Holt went over the list out loud as he coaxed the horses to start pulling the wagon down the hill and into the outskirts of Buffalo.

"Ring? You have a ring?" Glenna questioned.

Holt patted his breast pocket. "Fetched it from the attic this morning. It was my mother's. Hope it fits."

"I would be honored to wear something from your mother," Glenna whispered. The feeling in her voice caught Holt off guard, and he looked over at her. Unshed tears glistened in her eyes. Feeling dumbfounded, he didn't know what to say that could be of comfort to her. The idea she might cry unsettled him.

"I — uh — it's just — well, I thought maybe you'd like to have it."

"I apologize," she rushed on, "You see, I have only this broach that once belonged to my mother. I was unable to bring any of her

56

things with me. All her letters, even my small locket with her portrait in it, were left behind. Those things seem trivial, I know, and I have learned that attachments to physical objects are unimportant in the grand scheme. However, to someone who has next to nothing linking them to their kin — the gesture is deeply appreciated."

She smiled over at him, and Holt felt his chest tighten. Unable to articulate his feelings, he just nodded as his thoughts wandered back to Crossroads. The hall was heavy with portraits and photos of his own family. Everything in the place held meaning and memories of those he loved. Sometimes they were painful reminders of what he had lost and other times, those memories kept him sane.

She had only arrived with the shawl on her shoulders, the hat she now wore, and the small carpetbag that was far too light to hold much. Glenna had told him it was all she had; he hadn't thought about it much at the time because of everything else that was going on. This made him wonder even more about Glenna and her past. How was it that such a fine woman could have ended up with so little? Holt's curiosity mixed with empathy. Nothing good could have transpired in Glenna's life to have led her to his door.

Four

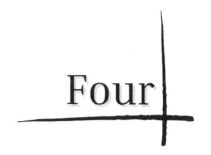

"Will you love, comfort, honor, and keep her, in sickness and in health, and, forsaking all others, keep only unto her for as long as you both shall live?"

"I will." Holt's voice sounded strong and sure as he recited his vows.

Glenna took strength from how sure he seemed and by the smiles of those gathered around them, Hattie and Rachel at her back, Daisy cradled in Hattie's embrace, Theo and Finn standing near Holt. The rest of the small chapel stood empty.

Pastor Joseph turned his attention to her. "Glenna Eleanor Perry, will you have this man to be your wedded husband, to live together after God's ordinance in the holy estate of Matrimony? Will you promise to love, comfort, honor, and serve him in sickness and in health, and forsaking all others, keep only unto him for as long as you both shall live?"

Her eyes had fallen as the vows were addressed to her, and the sight of her hands resting in Holt's had a calming effect on her and offered a sense of reassurance. She stilled herself and looked into the eyes of the man that would from now on be her husband.

"I will."

"I call upon those assembled to act as witnesses to Holt and Glenna committing themselves to each other in the sacred rights of marriage. Will you do all in your power to uphold them in the vows they have made this day?" Pastor Joseph waited to continue until both Theo and Hattie had given their answers. Glenna was not able to unlock her gaze from Holt's.

Under instruction from Pastor Joseph, Holt slipped his mother's ring onto Glenna's finger.

"In First John Chapter Three, we read 'Let us, love, not in word or speech, but in truth and action.' I hope that you will work together as partners to create a truly wonderful and blessed life as Mr. and Mrs. Holt Sterling. Amen. You may now kiss your bride."

Glenna let out a squeak of surprise when, without hesitation, Holt reached for her, one arm sliding around her waist, pulling her close as his other hand rested on her cheek. His lips pressed hers. The contact sent a wave of dizziness pulsating over her while the world swayed underfoot as it never had before. With a yell of laughter and whooping from the collective onlookers, he pulled away.

"Congratulations!" Rachel had stepped up, twirled Glenna on the spot, and gathered her into a quick embrace. Just as fast, Glenna found herself being hugged by Hattie, Daisy pressed between them.

"Welcome to the family, dear."

Glenna received a fast kiss on the cheek from Theo and a handshake from Finn before Pastor Joseph offered his congratulations, and in a whirlwind of activity that included signatures on their marriage license. Glenna found herself standing outside. Looking down; she realized she still had the bouquet tucked in her arms, and Blu was now dancing around their feet, happy to be allowed to join them.

"Uncle Holt," Finn ventured when the adult conversation had died down. "Will you get a photograph like the one Ma and Pa did? One to put in the hallway."

It felt as though her heart was stuck in her throat at Finn's question. She was a married woman, a Sterling, yet she knew in her bones she was not part of the family and did not have a place there.

Holt must have felt the same. "In time, perhaps. We did not give enough notice to sit for a photo today. How would you like to stop at Carson's and pick out a sweet to celebrate?"

"A taffy!" Finn squealed.

"A taffy sounds perfect," Holt agreed.

Glenna felt the fog lift and her practicality return. Nothing that had transpired changed who or what she was or what was expected of her. A caretaker, homemaker, a cook.

"Rachel, would you mind taking these for me? I am afraid they will not last the trip back without being put in some water." Glenna turned to the woman and handed her the wildflowers. Rachel took the flowers wide-eyed, smiled as she plucked the finest bloom, and stepped closer to Glenna.

"This one is too beautiful to keep." She tucked it onto the side of Glenna's hair, "There, perfect."

Holt watched Glenna closely as she walked through the shelves of Carson's General with Finn pointing out all his favorite sweets to her. Daisy had curled herself up close to her and fallen asleep on Glenna's shoulder. He had to admit to himself that the picture of them together felt right in a way he hadn't expected.

"Uncle Holt, can we get the taffy now?" Finn had turned to him and was pulling at his sleeve, begging.

"Sure," he laughed, catching her eye, "Would you like anythin'?" She looked momentarily surprised.

"Well — I was wondering — I haven't had time to look over any supplies you might have for schooling at the house. Would you know if there is a slate? Early readers perhaps?"

Holt wasn't sure and looked down at Finn to confirm, who simply shrugged.

"Please get anythin' you think would be useful."

She nodded, then paused before moving off. The hesitation was a stark contrast to the self-assured woman Glenna had presented herself as.

"Well, Master Finn Sterling. How are you today?" Finn had moved away from his side and was peering over the counter at Mr. Carson.

"Good morning, Mr. Carson. We came for taffy," Finn announced. Mr. Carson, once a man with a head of flaming red hair that had long since turned a steel gray, still sported a boyish grin, and he beamed down at Finn.

"A fine choice. I have some maple-flavored today. Unless you'd rather a licorice whip or a peppermint stick."

"We'll take the lot, Mr. Carson. and add in a bit of honey sesame brittle to boot." Holt watched Finn's eyes grow wide with his announcement.

"That's a lot of sweets. Is there a special occasion? A birthday perhaps?" Mr. Carson asked, bagging up the order.

"Yes, and no." Finn quickly answered for him, then rushed on, "No birthday. Uncle Holt got married!"

Mr. Carson stopped short and glanced at the two of them from over his shoulder. "Married?"

Finn nodded excitedly. "To celebrate, Uncle Holt said we could get some taffy."

Holt didn't feel the need to further the explanation Finn had given and just smiled as Carson gave him a questioning look.

"Well — a wedding. That is a reason to celebrate if I've ever heard of one." He went back to plucking the sweets out of their jars and placing them into the paper bag.

"A wedding? Who had a wedding?" Holt didn't have to look to know that it was the voice of Mrs. Carson that was ringing throughout the store. The woman, although well-intentioned, could hear news miles away and wasn't shy about sharing it or her thoughts with anyone that would stand still long enough to hear it.

"Holt's gone and gotten himself hitched," Mr. Carson addressed his wife as she appeared behind the counter from the door that attached their living quarters to the general store.

"No." The single word rang out clearly. Mrs. Carson caught herself and rushed on. "We had no idea."

"Want to meet her?" Finn asked.

"Oh — I'd love to," Mrs. Carson nodded.

"I'll get her." Finn dashed off.

"What a happy bit of surprising news," Mrs. Carson commented, then under her breath but loud enough for Holt to hear, she added, "Edith will be very sorry to learn of it."

Holt gave no indication he had heard. Rather, he turned and greeted Finn, Glenna, and Daisy. Reaching out, he lightened her load by placing the items she had chosen on the counter, then lifting Daisy out of her arms, who was now awake and eager to look at her surroundings.

"Glenna, I'd like you to meet the Carsons, Simon, and Phyllis." Glenna looked from Holt to the couple behind the counter and smiled. "Mr. and Mrs. Carson, this is my — wife."

To their credit, both greeted her warmly and welcomed her to town. Glenna complimented them on the store and its diverse stock. This seemed to endear her to them and for several minutes, they asked Glenna a multitude of questions, all of which she answered very politely.

"Is there anything I can help you find?" Mrs. Carson asked her kindly.

"Oh, you have such a wonderful selection. I believe I was able to find everything I was looking for. Thank you."

"Would you mind wrappin' this up, and we will be back to pick it up after a fast lunch at the cafe?" Holt asked, to which Finn cheered his agreement.

"Of course," Mr. Carson nodded as Holt held the door for Glenna and Finn. Daisy waved happily over his shoulder as they exited.

"This is a special day, Glenna. We never eat at the cafe! They have three kinds of pies you can choose from." Holt could hear Finn rattling away to her as he skipped, leading the way.

"You will have to tell me your very favorite kind, so I know which one to try," she responded.

Holt watched with amusement as Finn stopped his skipping and, reaching over, took Glenna's hand in his. The unexpected and tender action had clearly startled Glenna, however she cradled his hand in hers as they continued toward the cafe. Holt stayed a few strides behind, lost in his thoughts.

He was grateful the Carsons had been so kind, even in their bewilderment over his sudden marriage. Holt had known for some time they had designs on his marrying their younger daughter, a fine-looking woman in her own right. Edith had just never caught his fancy.

Holt supposed he had spent so much time away from home and delved right into ranch work when he was home that there was never time for proper courting, even if she had. If he was honest with himself, it was more than those things that had stopped him from forming lasting attachments to anyone female.

He had never been the type of man to seek attention from a lady where there was no interest on his part. Of course, he was aware that a few women over the years had sought after a deeper or more meaningful relationship from him. Holt, however, had always pictured himself a lifelong bachelor, believing that the kind of love he wanted, the once in a lifetime kind, the kind he had witnessed with his parents, his aunt, and uncle, or that of Clint and Grace, was something out of his reach.

Now, here he was — married. Married to a woman who, he had to admit, stirred something deep inside of him each time she looked his way, yet a stranger and a marriage of convenience, nothing more.

Passing the brush through her hair, Glenna took in her appearance in the mirror and dim light. Glenna was not sure what she had expected from marriage. Of course, while she hadn't ever really entertained the idea that Clint would rush to start a family with her; she also hadn't thought she would not be sharing a room with her husband at all, or that he would sleep separate from her, and as far as another building all together hadn't been in her mind. It was all so strange. Engaged to one brother, married to the other.

The last three days had been long extensions of her first afternoon, filled with meals, laundry, and time spent with the children. Holt would make small appearances from time to time, and always seemed too busy to be bothered. His willingness to be forever occupied with something or other sent a very clear message to Glenna about Holt's intention to keep their relationship as platonic as possible.

She had resolved herself to a loveless marriage long ago, even before reading Clint's advert, yet a marriage without even the smallest chance of friendship or common cordiality left her feeling depressed.

Determined to focus on the positive in her situation, Glenna put the brush down and finished dressing for bed. The room was comfortable enough, large and empty as it was. She did not have enough to give the space personal touches, so unpacking the two dresses, one nightgown, stockings, underclothes, one worn pair of boots, a hat, and shawl would have to do.

She had left her most prized possessions to unpack last; her mother's broach and her journals had found a home on the lovely desk. She had yet to find time to spend writing about the changes in her plans, although Glenna had made sure to press the flower Rachel had tucked into her hair. Besides the ring that rested on her finger, it was the only memento of her wedding day.

Holt watched from the bunkhouse as the candlelight that was shown in the window of Glenna's room extinguished, plunging the house into darkness.

He had made a trip into the house to remove the rest of her letters to Clint and was devouring them well into the late-night hours the past few nights. Tonight would be no different. He had learned through the letters that Clint had shared details about Grace's passing from complications after giving birth, how small and sickly Daisy had been, clinging to life for months after she lost her mother, how

Clint felt the little girl needed a full-time mother to help her thrive. Glenna had written to him about using goat's milk rather than cow's milk for the infant. It helped. She stopped spitting up as much and put on weight.

It seemed as though Clint had mentioned having a brother to her in more than one letter and that Holt was living away from the homestead. Holt didn't know how much of his past Clint had shared with Glenna, and not knowing made him feel anxious.

The later letters discussed mostly expectations on Finn's education and travel arrangements. Glenna would be looking at weeks of travel altogether, including stops. Clint had paid for and arranged everything, including a chaperone and travel companions.

Holt wasn't at all surprised at how well organized Clint had been with his meticulous planning. Clint had never been one to leave things to chance. He had never been reckless.

"So how did you go and get yourself killed, big brother?" Holt wondered aloud.

He sat down on the edge of the bed and opened the last of Glenna's letters. Turning the lamp up a little, he held the letter close to the light to read her dainty scrawl.

July 2, 1884

Dear Mr. Sterling,

I was pleased to read your last letter. It was wonderful to learn that Daisy is now eating more solid foods. I am sure it will help in her development. She will be walking and chatting up a storm before you know it. I received the tickets you sent and I am preparing for the journey west. The trip will take a total of about four and a half weeks, perhaps longer,

with ill weather. I will arrive in late August as
planned. I am looking forward to meeting you and the
children.

I appreciate the offer of your escort, however; I
feel certain that my trip will go as planned; there is
no reason for you to come all this way. You will lose
close to nine weeks of work to do so. That is, time
away from your children and your home would be
better served to stay there and see after the ranch. Do
not make yourself uneasy. I am sure the arrangements
that have been put in place will be more than
adequate.

As to your last question, I have no objection to
living under the same roof as your brother. Family
connections are well worth having and preserving if
possible. From your descriptions of him, Holt seems
like a fair-minded, as well as a generous man. You
have also mentioned his keen knowledge of cattle in
past correspondence and his strong work ethic. Such
assets must be a boon to you and a great help with the
ranch work.

I will send word of my progress by telegraph, as
promised.
Sincerely,
G.E. Perry

Holt reread the last paragraph. His inquiry about her feelings over sharing the homestead with his younger brother brought back flashes of memory. Glenna had been kind and charitable in her assessment of a man she had never met. Is that what had prompted Clint to draw up the papers that would put Holt on as co-owner to the ranch? Bits of conversation about the change rushed to the forefront of his memory.

"…I don't want you to stay on like a cowhand, Holt. I want you to be here, as my partner. Crossroads is as much yours as it is mine, brother… we are family and that's worth preserving…"

Holt glanced out the window and to the sleeping house bathed in moonlight. Clint had used her very words when telling him about his plans to put Holt's name on the ranch deed. Glenna had changed the course of his life, long before he had known of her existence. How could he ever express to her what that meant to him?

From what she had written to Clint, he knew her to be a thoughtful woman. Glenna had revealed little of herself beyond the attributes she must have felt would help ease Clint's mind in his choice of stepmother. She was capable; he had already assessed that much on his own in the very first day of their acquaintance, yet there was something about her, something she held back that tugged at his consciousness.

Why was it she never talked about her own family's past? Folding her letter back up and replacing it into the stack he had already read, Holt blew out the lamp and laid back on the cot. Sleep would not come easily, as his mind was racing.

———————

Friday morning dawned clear and bright. With the cleansing rays of golden light came a new sense of purpose in Glenna's mind. She gladly plucked Daisy out of her crib and changed her, trying to be quiet so as not to wake Finn.

She had a charge, and her life held direction for the first time in years. Daisy curled her small hand around one of Glenna's fingers and curled into her arms. Glenna felt suddenly as if the part of herself that had long been missing had been found. No longer working only for her survival, Glenna reveled in the knowledge she could act as caretaker, teacher, confidant, and friend to the children.

Holt must have risen quite early, for there was a warm fire already ablaze in the kitchen as she entered. He was no place to be seen, and she assumed he was seeing to the morning chores. Setting Daisy in the highchair with a rattle, Glenna set to work on breakfast. Soon the room smelled wonderfully of bacon, fried potatoes, and fresh coffee.

"Morning Auntie Glenna," Finn yawned from the doorway.

"Good morning Finn." Glenna beamed at the boy. Hearing the new title of "Auntie" from Finn gave her a thrill.

The boy yawned, rubbed the sleep from his eyes. "I better go collect the eggs from the hens." He pulled on his boots and hat, and slipped out the back door.

Glenna was spreading butter on thick slices of bread when Finn reentered with a have laden basket, Holt at his heels. Both removed their hats and stomped the morning dew from their booted feet.

She swallowed a rush of nerves at the sight of Holt. "Breakfast is almost ready if you would like to wash up."

Both took turns at the washbasin. Glenna set the last of the food at the table and everyone took a seat. Holt put his hands out, palm up, one for Finn to take, the other for Glenna. He said a blessing over the meal.

"What are your plans for the day?" Holt asked her casually as he spooned potatoes onto Finn's plate.

"I thought I might give the bedroom a thorough cleaning. That is unless you have something else you would like me to attend to?"

"No, I think you should make the room as comfortable as possible for your use. Finn can come to help me, so only Daisy will be underfoot."

Glenna placed some small bits of food in front of Daisy, "I think she and I will get along just fine today."

"The boys should be back today, or if things took longer than expected, tomorrow. I'll try to give you enough warnin' to prepare; they eat twice as much as any of us could."

"How many hands do you have working for you?" she asked, moving to retrieve the pot of coffee from the stove and offering to pour him a cup with a small gesture.

"Thank you, yes," he nodded and took the cup gratefully, "three. Gunner Clark worked with me as a hand in North Dakota. He's young, but a hard worker and trustworthy. Decker Hayes worked for Clint for about three years by the time I came back home. He is a bear of a man. Don't let his size intimidate you; he is as gentle as they come and loyal to a fault.

"Bowen Williams has been with us the longest. He first worked for my father when I was a youth. He stayed on to work for Clint and now myself. Bowen's the best cattleman I've ever seen. With all that's happened over the years, this place would have been long lost without him."

Glenna liked how well Holt spoke of those that worked for and with him. She noted that he mentioned only their most admirable qualities as he saw them and not their faults. It spoke to the kind of man Holt was as well.

"I look forward to being acquainted with them."

Holt thanked Glenna for the breakfast, and with Finn on his heels, set to leave, hesitating at the threshold, "I'll be moving my things back into the house. That is, if you are alright with it."

"Oh — yes, of course, it is, after all, *your* house," Glenna stammered, heat flooding her face.

"I'll — ah — be stayin' in my old room." Holt tossed the comment at her from over his shoulder before pushing at the door and disappearing with Finn.

Glenna surveyed the spot he had stood for many moments after his departure as she scrutinized the exchange. Undoubtedly, she knew that Holt would not want to stay indefinitely in the bunkhouse, and had expected him to reclaim his home once the hands returned. She had not, however, allowed herself to think further than those terms.

She was thankful he had not proposed that they share a room. After all, she had agreed to a marriage in all its complexities, save that of romantic attachment when the proposal had first been made… by Clint. She had not even thought to discuss the topic with Holt. Certainly, they had covered many topics over the past few days, naturally avoided anything remotely uncomfortable regarding their living situation.

What could he have meant by adding the last two words to his declaration? Was he preparing her for a time when her room would no longer be a solitary space… did Holt intend to pursue the possibility of having a family of his own someday? Of their own? And if that was his meaning, how did Glenna feel about the fact? He had kept his distance, sprinkles of polite conversation, nothing to indicate an interest of any kind. Had Holt changed his mind about their marriage? About her?

Reeling from her thoughts and feeling a bit flushed, Glenna busied herself with cleaning up after the meal. There was no use pondering or mooning over Holt's possible meanings unless she intended to confront him about it. For all she knew, it could very well have been a slip of the tongue.

Daisy crawled at her feet as Glenna took the curtains from the windows, removed the bed linens, and prepared them to all be washed. It took longer than she had expected to wash, sweep, dust, and scrub the room to her satisfaction and left her little time to prepare a hearty lunch. Neither Finn nor Holt seemed to mind the smaller spread and dug into the food with zest. After little in the way of conversation, the two departed.

Glenna hauled in water to boil for the washing before she returned to her room, proceeding to tuck neatly away in the drawers and closet the few personal items she had brought with her. Somehow, this one act made the transformation feel complete. Gathering up Daisy and the bucket of dirty water, she glanced over the space as they exited and smiled with satisfaction.

"When you are older, Daisy, I hope you appreciate the feeling of accomplishment a good day's work provides." Glenna cooed as she took the stairs to the kitchen.

Holt was just entering and dropped the bucket used for scraps to feed the pigs back into place.

"May I help?" he asked and reached for the bucket of water and quickly disposed of the murky water.

"Thank you."

Bouncing Daisy on her hip, she looked down at the little girl. "Do you want to show Uncle Holt what we practiced while cleaning this morning?" Daisy prattled something in response.

"Holt," Glenna said his name slowly.

Daisy reached over for Holt and babbled. The word came out in a jumble, yet recognizable. Holt's face split into a grin.

"Now hey, there little one! Did you just say my name?" Taking her from Glenna's grasp, Glenna watched as he tossed her above his head, making Daisy giggle in delight. Glenna wasn't able to resist a smile herself as Daisy laughed and tried out the sound of his name once more.

Holt tossed her again, then smiling broadly, cradled her and caught Glenna's gaze from over the top of Daisy's fine hair. Daisy curled up close to his chest, one hand reaching over to rest on his shoulder in a kind of hug. Glenna felt heat touch her cheeks under his penetrating gaze.

"I better see to the washing and get Daisy down for a nap," Glenna mumbled. Holt passed Daisy back to her and nodded.

"Finn and I will be gone for a spell; we're ridin' out to check on the crops in the long field."

Glenna only nodded, unsure she was quite following everything he had just said. Of course, she had no idea what crops a cattleman would be growing or what a long field could be. He stood, unmoving, not taking his eyes off her. Reaching into his vest pocket, Holt produced a small wax paper-wrapped rectangle.

"Aunt Hattie informed me that it's customary to give gifts after a weddin'. I know there is nothin' traditional about how this all started, but I figured it wasn't a bad custom, and I picked up a little somethin' for you." He held out the wrapped item toward her.

Glenna blinked a few times. "I — I am sorry I can't reciprocate the gesture." Her mind raced to the only item she had brought with her that was now of no use. The fine bone cufflinks with the letter C carved into them. At the time, it seemed an appropriate gift. Now she knew it had been an impractical and frivolous purchase. She also could never gift them to Holt — or anyone else, for that matter. Their purchase had been for another. A man she now honored by caring for his orphaned children, though, would never meet.

"I'm not expectin' — just open it," He grunted, bringing her back to herself.

Glenna pulled at the string, holding the paper closed while balancing Daisy in her arms. The wrappings fell away, and she wasn't able to stop the smile that touched her lips.

The small lavender soap was the very essence of thoughtfulness.

"I wasn't sure if you even like lavender. I can always return it and get somethin' else."

"Please don't," she protested. "I adore lavender." Drawing the soap nearer, she breathed in the scent more fully. "Thank you, Holt."

His stance relaxed a little as he returned her smile. Then he turned suddenly and pushed through the door, hat in hand.

She wondered if this was how their married life would pass? Friendly conversation punctuated with moments of awkwardness. She supposed it was a very fine way to pass the time; a minor discomfort in forced conversations was far better than a man who was boorish and brash or one that was mean-spirited and rude.

Holt had often proven himself to be considerate and kind. Glenna wrapped the soap back in the wax paper and tucked it away in her apron pocket.

Soon she had the large washtubs, washboard, stool, sliver of soap, and a basketful of linens, including the children's things and all the mending she had finished, all set outside the kitchen door to take advantage of the warm afternoon sun.

Daisy was content to bounce on her hip as Glenna took buckets of heated water from the stovetop out to the washtubs. When she was satisfied with the levels in each and the temperature, Glenna set Daisy down and allowed the toddler to play while she set to work.

One item at a time was submerged into the soapy water, scrubbed on the washboard, rinsed, rung out and placed on the line to dry. By the time she was done, Daisy was covered in a layer of dust and more than ready for her daily nap.

"Come here, sweet one." Glenna bent, scooped up the little girl, removed her simple clothes, and discarded them into the same water, scrubbed with one hand, then tossed into the rinse water before Daisy was dipped into the wash water with a squeal.

At first, Daisy protested by attempting to stand and reaching her arms out for Glenna to remove her from the now tepid water.

"Shhhh, it's alright. You are in just as much need of a good scrubbing as that poor dress of yours," Glenna cooed and set to work washing Daisy from head to toe as fast as the squirming little girl would allow, using a cup, dipped out some of the much cleaner water from the rinse tub for good measure, drenched Daisy in it to remove the remains suds before wrapping her in the clean towel she had brought out for just this purpose.

"There now, isn't that better?" Glenna smiled at her while she rubbed her dry.

"No!" Daisy said with a frown.

The word was so crisp and clear that it took Glenna back. She laughed and rubbed Daisy's hair with the towel.

"Let's find you something to wear." Daisy didn't seem to hold being forcibly washed against Glenna for very long, and just as her footsteps reached the stairs, Daisy's head was resting on Glenna's shoulder.

Washed, dried, in clean clothes, and tired, Daisy fell asleep the instant Glenna placed her into the crib.

Glenna sighed as she shut the door behind her. She was sure there was nothing so exhausting to a person as taking care of a toddler not yet walking. She was also sure there was little in life that was as rewarding. So much time had seemed to have rushed by rather than just two days since Daisy had reached out for her in a fit of exhausted tears and, in doing so, wrapped her little fingers around Glenna's heartstrings. She already adored the child.

At the bottom of the stairs, her footsteps halted in the hallway, and she took a few moments to take in the photos placed there. A faded photograph of a handsome couple with two small boys caught her eye, and she studied the image in great detail.

She knew it had to be an early image of Holt, Clint, and their parents. She moved to the next photograph, a very beautiful bride sitting in a decorative chair with her new husband standing behind her, hand placed lightly on her shoulder, the couple younger versions of Holt's parents.

Glenna allowed herself some time to enjoy peering through the images and catching a glimpse into the lives of the Sterling family, seeing the brothers grow into manhood. She already knew Holt's face and found herself fascinated with that of his brother, a man she felt she knew nevertheless would never meet.

Clint stood within an inch of his brother's height. His hair was darker than she had imagined, face a little fuller, with slightly narrower shoulders. Pausing to glimpse at Clint's wife in their wedding photo. The slender, fair-haired woman in the photo would never know her daughter. Her small son left with only a few vivid memories.

"I will not let them forget you," she vowed aloud. Surprised at herself and the strong feeling of sentimentality that was overpowering her, she resolved to keep the children's parents' memories alive for them in any way possible.

———————

Holt stilled himself for the introductions. Later would come the explanation he knew the three men would demand of him. There had been no sign of them until mid-afternoon on Saturday. Now the three riders were close enough to dismount and start leading their horses to the barn. Glenna and the children were inside preparing for that evening's meal.

"Holt!" Decker waved him over.

"How was the countin'?"

"We had some trouble locating a few strays, but Bowen spotted them and got them back to the herd just this mornin'."

"Good. Let's head into the barn and get these horses watered and fed."

"How are things here? Finn still with Theo and Hattie?" Decker asked as he removed the saddle from his horse.

"No, he's inside." Holt attempted to sound much more casual than he felt as he continued, "There's been a change of plans, Boys."

All three men looked over at him.

"How so Boss?" Gunner asked.

"Well — I got myself married for one."

Decker let out a low whistle. Gunner gaped open-mouthed at him.

"Who'd you trick into doin' that?" Bowen snorted.

"You'll all meet her shortly. I wanted to tell you 'bout her before we head inside."

"Well, good on ya, boss!" Gunner grinned. "One of those pretty town girls is my bet."

"No, there ain't a soul that knew his ugly mug that would marry him. I bet he is bluffin'," Decker laughed good-natured.

"If you're hitched then — you'll be keepin' the ranch runnin' — or sellin' and settin' up somewhere else?" Bowen wondered.

"That's the other thing I wanted to tell ya. I'm not sellin' Crossroads. The idea did cross my mind after Clint passed, thinkin' it would be too hard to stay on the place, but I can't see leavin'. I didn't figure on the littles stayin' — without a Ma', it would be too hard to run the cattle and raise them, even with the help of you sordid lot." He waved at the three others in an all-encompassing motion.

"Glenna, that's her name, is a good fit for both Finn and Daisy. I don't think you'll have any complaints about her cookin' neither."

"I'm glad to not have to be lookin' for another job," Decker laughed.

"You're too lazy for anyone else to put up with ya," Bowen spat at Decker, nudging the younger man in his ribs as he moved past him toward Holt. "Congratulations, Holt. It looks like things are workin' out after all."

Holt took Bowen's hand, and the two men shook. "Thanks, old friend."

"Well, I don't know 'bout the rest of ya, but I'm feelin' a might hungry, and we have a lady of the house to greet. Let's wash up boys, want to make a good first impression." Bowen took the lead and waved at Gunner and Decker to follow him to the bunkhouse.

Holt sighed; it had gone better than he thought it would.

***

When Holt had told her Decker was a large man, he had not fully described the breadth of the man. He was a giant, well over six feet tall, with shoulders that made it impossible to step through a doorway without turning to one side. Although physically imposing, the man instantly put anyone around him at ease with his charm. Both Daisy and Finn squealed in delight as he played with them while Glenna finished the last preparations for the evening meal.

78

Gunner, just now out of his teens, was eager to experience life and full of big dreams. He asked Glenna more than a dozen questions about life in the city, even offering to set the table for her while she pulled the cornbread out of the oven, so he could continue to talk to her about life outside Wyoming.

The older man, Bowen, seemed very content to sit back and put his feet up while he watched under half-hooded eyes at the chaos in the kitchen. The space had gone from large and accommodating to crowded in a flash when the four men had stormed in, Holt apologizing to her for their intrusion.

Of course, Glenna had welcomed the distraction and was glad to have the introductions past her. The three men looked very at home. Each had an easy and open banter with Holt. She wondered just how much he had told them about her... or Clint. What would any of them think of the arrangement?

Finn let out a howl of laughter as Decker, crawling on all fours around the table, growling like a bear, grabbed at his foot. Finn slipped away and slid under the table, away from the big man's grasp. Decker didn't let this deter him and he made to follow Finn, seizing the boy by the ankle, dragged him out from under the table, and tossed him, one-handed, into the air.

Finn squealed upon being caught; Decker roared with laughter. Daisy crawled up to the duo, babbling. Decker gathered her up, rubbing his bearded chin on her cheek, making Daisy giggle with glee.

"Decker is a favorite." Holt had leaned closer to her as if this was a great secret he was exposing.

"I can see that." Glenna smiled; it was impossible not to love the sound of children's laughter.

Decker stood, still holding both children, and grinned at her. "My Pa said it was good for littles to laugh and play as much as possible.

I guess seein' as I'm just a big kid myself, it always made sense to join in with 'em." He shrugged and deposited Finn into a chair, then ruffled up his hair with a large hand. Daisy let out one last laugh as Decker gave her cheek a playful pinch as he placed her in the high chair.

"I believe your father was correct, Decker. Play is a very important part of a child's development," she agreed, ladling stew into bowls.

Gunner was right there, taking each filled bowl from her hands and placing it on the table. A plate of fresh cornbread and fresh butter followed. Each took a seat at the table. Holt led them in a prayer of thanks. Glenna turned her attention to Daisy and the soft stewed vegetables and bits of meat she had dished up for her. Blowing lightly over the food, checking the temperature and placing the food in front of her.

"These are mighty good vittles, Miss." Gunner said with a mouth full of stew.

"Keep your trap shut until it's empty; no woman needs to see her hard work half-chewed, Boy," Bowen snapped with a disapproving shake of his head, his weathered face turned into a scowl.

"Sorry, Ma'am." Gunner looked sheepishly at her.

"I appreciate the compliment." She inclined her head to Gunner with a small nod.

"My apologies, I didn't mean to be so short. Gunner is right, this is a mighty good stew." Bowen interjected.

Glenna turned her attention to him. He must have been a good fifteen or more years older than Holt; however, she couldn't guess at his age. His face and hands weathered from years of working out on the range. He wasn't a bad-looking man, gruff and a little impatient with the others. She supposed it came with age and experience.

80

"Thank you, Bowen."

"I like everythin' she makes," Finn piped up.

"I do enjoy cooking. However, if this wash of compliments continues, I am afraid I will never live up to your expectations hereafter." Glenna felt odd being the center of attention in the room and refocused herself on making sure Daisy was eating.

"I doubt that, Ma'am. This house has been without the touch of a woman, save Hattie from time to time, for too long. We have survived off soggy oatmeal and dried bits of beef and called it supper. You'll hear nothin' exceptin' gratitude from us," Decker boomed.

"Especially grateful because Gunner won' be feedin' us any of that slop he calls grub no more," Bowen added, chuckling at the expression Gunner shot him.

"You weren't complainin' when that slop was fillin' your empty belly, old man." Both men laughed.

"None of us are much for cookin'. No know-how. You bein' here is a blessin', Ma'am." Decker agreed and took an impressively large bite out of his cornbread.

The good-natured banter continued as the men cleaned their plates, proceeding to eat seconds. Glenna watched carefully and learned a lot about the dynamic between all of them. There was mutual respect; that was clear. She liked how at ease and friendly each of them were, especially with the children. Holt, too, seemed to be more comfortable now that the cowhands were back; he laughed and joked right along with them.

"Will you play checkers with me, Bowen? I've been practicin' with Uncle Theo," Finn asked once his bowl was empty.

"I'd like a game, little man, but you'll have to roll me down the hall. I'm afraid I ate too much!" Bowen patted his middle to drive the point home.

Finn jumped up and pulled at Bowen's hand. Bowen overacted as though it was very hard to move and groaned down the hall while Finn laughed at his antics.

"I'll — uh — get started on the evenin' chores," Decker announced to anyone that was listening, tossed on his hat, and slipped out.

Holt also stood, his meal finished. "Daisy girl, it's time to get washed up." Taking up a washcloth, he moved to pluck her out of her high chair as Glenna began cleaning off the table.

"May I lend a hand?" Gunner asked.

"Thank you," she smiled and nodded.

Glenna took the water she had been heating during the meal and poured half into each washbasin set up for the dishes, while Gunner scraped any leftover bits into the slop bucket. Daisy babbled Holt's name while he swiped her face with a wet washcloth.

Her little hands pushed back at his larger one, turning her head away from him.

"Sorry, little one." He finished, despite her protest.

Glenna took the handful of dishes from Gunner and submerged them.

"Have you met Theo and Hattie yet, Glenna?" Gunner asked as he removed the items still left on the table.

"Yes," she answered, glancing at him from over her shoulder, "they are both wonderful."

"Were they — I mean — did they know about you and Holt, or are us boys the only ones to be blindsided by the news?"

"Gunner —" Holt said in a clipped, warning tone.

82

"Sorry, Boss."

"It's alright. We knew there must be questions," Glenna said softly.

"No one knew she was comin'," Holt hurried to explain. "Clint — he wanted to ensure the care of the children."

"You and Clint?" Gunner shook his head in disbelief. Then his eyes grew two sizes. "Ya didn't know about him, did ya?"

"No, I didn't know he passed until I arrived," she whispered.

"Glenna and I discussed it, and the arrangement still made sense," Holt added.

"A marriage of convenience," Gunner nodded his understanding.

"Mutually beneficial," Glenna added softly, wishing it didn't sound so much like a question.

Five

Holt sighed, rolling from his back to his side. Sleep had been elusive. He could not remember the last time he'd slept through the night. If he was, to be honest, from the moment Clint had passed, it had been impossible to truly rest. Added to that was Glenna's arrival and all that had come with it. He had worked hard all day, hoping to drop into bed, unable to keep his eyes open. The plan had failed.

Sighing, Holt pulled himself up as he tossed the quilt to one side, bare feet hitting the floor, his elbows resting on his knees, head hanging, shoulders dropped. All the things that kept eating at him during the daylight hours now plagued him all hours. Clint's death was still so new, raw.

Only weeks ago, Holt was not the sole owner of his family's ranch or their cattle business. He wasn't the guardian of two young children. He wasn't a married man. He also wasn't being kept awake at night wondering why his brother had kept Glenna a secret from him or why he had been acting so strangely in the weeks preceding his death.

It had never settled well with Holt when Clint had suddenly grown easy to anger, acting out of character. On more than one occasion, Holt had stumbled upon Clint muttering to himself while pouring over some papers, just to have Clint hurriedly put them out of sight.

Everyone had seemed satisfied with the idea that Clint's death had been a tragic accident… everyone aside from Holt. Nothing about it settled well with him.

Clint's behavior could have been chalked up to lack of sleep; Clint had moved his bed into the kids' room after Gracie passed to be nearer to them when needed, or perhaps the stress of raising the children with little help and running the ranch had made him irritable.

Holt had thought Clint had truly forgiven him. He had welcomed him home. Had Holt been wrong about that as well? Why wouldn't Clint tell him he had intended to marry? Why hadn't he confided in Holt about anything that had been going on? And suddenly he was gone.

Questions. That's all he had now. Questions, not all of them, about Clint. Things had moved so fast that Holt hadn't stopped to think about what he was doing, not really. He could have walked away, sent the little ones off to live elsewhere, sold the cattle and the property, and cut out cash in hand. Why hadn't he?

The answer had appeared suddenly at the front door. Her shabby grey traveling dress, wrinkled, tiny carpetbag as light as a feather, fear, hope, strength, and determination equally mixed in each expression that crossed her lovely features. Glenna.

Holt cursed himself as she dominated his thoughts repeatedly. She had only been part of their lives for a few days, and in those few days, everything had changed. Holt had changed.

Unable to keep his mind quiet enough to rest, Holt stood, running a hand through his hair. Lighting the lantern wick, he reached for Clint's box and sat at the edge of the bed. Lifting out the letters he knew to be from Glenna, his fingers reached those he had thought were less important at the bottom. Taking the first letter he had yet to read, Holt wasted no time opening it.

> *Mr. Sterling,*
> *I have received your inquiry and will look into*
> *the matter immediately. Any information that I am*
> *able to gather will be forwarded per your*
> *instructions.*
> *Cordially,*
> *Mr. J. Burke*
> *Burke and Olson Office of Inquiry,*
> *New York, New York*

Holt read the simple letter another two times before folding it up and setting it aside. There was a similar one from a solicitor Holt had never heard of. Looking for more information on both, he went on. Digging through more papers and letters, nothing else caught his attention until he reached a small ledger and pulled the cover open.

On the first page, Clint had drawn the Crossroads cattle brand in perfect detail. The ledger held herd numbers going back at least five years, though these numbers were not the ones Holt had become familiar with.

Without comparing the two books side by side, he couldn't be certain what was off about the ledger, nonetheless he knew in his gut that something about it was wrong. Turning toward the back where Clint had scribbled some incoherent notes, Holt squinted at them and tried to make out the meaning as a slip of thin paper fell from the book and fluttered into his lap.

Carefully, he lifted it into the light to see a second brand sketch, this one slightly larger than Crossroads, with oddly similar lines. He turned the paper in the light, holding it at different angles. The brand was one he knew, but who owned the rights to it was alluding him.

Why would Clint have thought having this sketch would be important? Why a second ledger? Again, nothing save more questions! Feeling a rush of anger and betrayal, Holt replaced the loose paper and snapped the ledger closed. Only one more item lay in the bottom of the box, folded once to fit.

Unsure that he now cared to add the mysteries Clint left behind, Holt dropped the ledger back into the box, not bothering to examine the last items. Then, tossing in the letters and other papers, replacing the lid, he tucked the box back away. Everything he had read only added to his insomnia.

Taking the lantern with him, Holt crept as quietly as possible down the stairs. He noted the soft glow of firelight coming down the hall from the kitchen and his ears caught the sound of Glenna's voice. Holt hesitated. What could be keeping her up this late in the evening when he was sure everyone had already retired? Had one of the children woken up and he hadn't noticed, lost in his mental torment? There had been no reply to her soft voice, and he concluded she was alone and addressing only herself.

Suddenly torn between wanting to make sure she was alright and retreating to his room, Holt felt the tug of hesitation. As if his body had made the choice before his mind was able to process it, his feet were moving in the direction of the kitchen.

"I thought I was the only one awake at this hour..." Holt started as he rounded the corner and stopped dead, mouth snapping open in a dumbfounded gesture.

"Oh!" Glenna yelped and, jerking in surprise, made a wave of water crash from the tub over the side and soak into the floor.

Although Glenna had set up the privacy screens, drawn the curtains closed, and taken all other precautions for decency, her figure was still visible from his vantage. Overcoming the shock, Holt pivoted and turned his back to her.

"I — I'm sorry. I should have told you I was planning on bathing before the Sabbath," Glenna rattled.

Holt closed his eyes tightly and pinched the bridge of his nose. "It's alright, Glenna. I think we were both just a bit surprised, is all."

She didn't respond. Then he heard the sound of suppressed laughter as if she had clamped her hand tightly over her mouth. Shaking his head, Holt could also see the humor and grinned to himself.

"We do seem to find ourselves in some singular situations," Glenna whispered finally.

"You should have told me you intended to bathe. I would have hauled in the extra water for you and — made sure to stand watch from a proper distance. You do live on a ranch with four men; privacy is a luxury," he said, turning his head enough she could hear him, just not far enough to make her uncomfortable.

He could hear the movement of the water as it lapped at the sides of the tin tub, the sound destroying any traces of levity Holt had felt, leaving a very peculiar feeling in its place he was unwilling to examine further.

"I will gladly take you up on your offer in the future," she said, followed by more sounds of water than an odd silence.

Holt fought the temptation to glance over his shoulder. Clutching the lantern he still held, he resisted and stood fast, taking a few deep, steadying breaths. Whatever he had expected from this day, coming upon Glenna in such an innocent and vulnerable situation, had been the farthest thing from his mind. However, he was sure it would now be impossible to remove the image from his memory.

"You may turn around now, Holt; I am quite decent."

Still unsettled, it took a few moments for him to comply. Glenna had indeed dried herself off and dressed, her long dark hair now being held over one shoulder and combed. Holt stood, marveling at its length as he had not had the chance to see the long dark locks untethered. She didn't lift her eyes, but continued to comb out her hair as he stared at her.

The air in the room smelled sweet of rosemary, black tea, and lavender. She had used the soap he had gifted her. The thought made him feel oddly dizzy and warm. Swallowing hard, Holt chided himself, he wasn't a boy of fourteen! He could be in the presence of a woman, not just any woman, his wife, without becoming disconnected from his senses.

"You were unable to sleep? Would you like a warm cup of milk?" Glenna asked, setting aside the comb as she started to work her hair into a long braid. Small ringlets of natural curls framed her face.

"I am not sure it would help," he said honestly.

Glenna finished her braid, took up the bucket she had used to haul water inside, walked around the screens she had put in place, and dipped the bucket into the bathwater, filling it.

Holt dashed forward around the tub and reached for the handle of the bucket. "I'll drain the water, Glenna," he insisted.

She was close, her hand trapped under his as they both still grasped the handle, the bucket swaying between them. Again, the sweet smell of lavender filled his nostrils. Glenna blinked once and tilted her face up just enough to look him in the eye.

His willpower slipped and Holt tugged the bucket toward him, her hand still trapped by his fingers, forcing her to move closer. There was no one to distract him, no child's cry to interrupt. If he dropped the bucket and reached for her, would she pull away from him or…

"Very well." It was barely above a whisper. Slipping her hand out from under his, she stepped back a fraction of a step, paused, and under his watchful eye, moved to gather her things.

"Good night, Holt." She offered a shy-looking smile.

"Good night."

———————————

Sunday morning dawned bright and early. Glenna had come down early to prepare breakfast. Standing at the threshold of the kitchen, she looked around the space. No physical signs of her late-night bath remained, yet Glenna could feel the rush of color that danced into her cheeks at the memory.

Their unexpected encounter the previous night was still fresh in her mind. Bare feet, suspenders hanging uselessly next to his legs, shirt untucked and more than half open, hair tousled, Holt had looked handsomely disheveled when he suddenly appeared in the kitchen doorway.

The sight of him had startled her temporarily, and her pulse quickened. As he turned his back on her, Glenna realized instantly that if she had been able to see him so clearly through the gap in the privacy screens, that Holt, in turn, was able to see her. She had been thankful for his gentlemanly discretion as he allowed her to rinse, dry off, and dress before laying eyes on her figure.

It hadn't been her figure that Holt hadn't been able to remove his eyes from. His gaze on her face had felt as real as a caress to the skin. Meeting her eyes, darting to her lips. For an instant, it had seemed that he might lean down and claim her mouth in a kiss. Glenna had shivered in anticipation of the promised contact, then had shrunk away from it, breaking the connection with her exit.

The night hours had tortured her once she had retreated to her room. She had let down her guard. Feelings were never supposed to be a part of the arrangement. She had suffered the hurt and crushing disappointment of loving someone who did not love her back once.

90

No matter how pleasant it might feel to share a tender embrace with the man she called her husband, she also knew that physical closeness did not equate to emotional intimacy as well. Glenna would not... could not allow her heart to be trifled with in any manner. Even if that wasn't Holt's intention.

Just as she drifted off into a restless sleep, Glenna had resolved to keep her heart at a distance. Clinging to the things about her new life that made any sort of sense, Glenna would be the very best caretaker to the children, the cook, and the housekeeper she was capable of. Yet a true wife to Holt? Was such a thing even possible?

Glenna had worked through her tumultuous thoughts and soon the fire was stoked, fresh biscuits cooling from the oven as thick slices of ham, fried next to a pot of simmering beans. She was thankful to have something else to occupy her when the cowhands all clambered inside, bleary-eyed and ready for a cup of coffee.

Finn bounded in minutes later, Holt carrying Daisy soon followed. He greeted her as usual and placed Daisy in her chair before retrieving himself a cup from the cupboard. Glenna noted how well he looked, rested, and — washed.

It was clear he had taken advantage of the bath full of warm water before draining the tub and placing it on the hook where it waited for its next use. She smiled a little at this. The leather and sage that was his normal scent would be intermixed with lavender, rosemary, and the black tea she had used in her hair.

"Mornin'," he nodded to her as he poured the dark liquid into his cup.

"Good morning."

He seemed at ease, and that put her at ease. There was no unnecessary awkwardness between them, and Glenna breathed a sigh of relief.

"Eat up boys; we need to get a move on if we're all gonna be ready for church on time," he announced, taking his place at the head of the table.

"It's my Sunday to stay put," Bowen announced after a long drag of coffee.

Holt nodded as Glenna started to serve the food, making sure to keep Daisy out of reach until the beans had cooled. Everyone bowed their heads while Holt offered a blessing. Then, as if by magic, the food disappeared. Chairs squeaked along the floor as one by one Gunner, Bowen, Decker, and Holt all excused themselves from the table once their plates had been scraped clean.

Finn had tried to keep up with the men. Ending up with a mouthful of half-chewed beans, a roughly cut piece of ham dangling from his fork as the last rattle of the screen door sounded.

"It's alright, Finn. You still have time to eat and see that your morning chores get done," Glenna assured him as she spooned some beans into Daisy's waiting mouth.

He nodded, slowed his jaw, and swallowed carefully. "I suppose the eggs aren't goin' anyplace."

She smiled at him as he drank heavily from his water cup and set to work on his ham. The boy was determined to grow up as fast as possible. She must encourage his natural curiosity and instill a love of learning that would grow to be as feverish as his desire to help his uncle on the ranch, making him a well-rounded man.

Once Daisy was full, Glenna set to work cleaning her up. Finn had also cleaned his plate, and after asking to be excused, dashed out to feed the chickens and collect eggs.

"You haven't touched your plate, Miss. Cold beans ain't any good. Take it from an old cowhand that has spent plenty of time eating 'em on the range." Bowen had come back into the house, reaching for the slop bucket, and noticed her untouched plate.

"I suppose if I had eaten cold beans as many times as you allude to having them yourself, I wouldn't care for them either," she said kindly.

His knowing eyes scanned the scene. "You do us all a kindness by ensurin' we have been seen to before takin' care of yourself; the littles, to be sure, need the extra attention. But if you don't mind my sayin' so, you'll have less and less to give to others if you do not also take care of yourself." He touched the brim of his hat, and the slop bucket, now in hand, left the house.

Glenna thought about his comment. She was so accustomed to not having another living soul care for her welfare; it felt odd to have multiple people seeming to.

<hr />

Hattie waved enthusiastically, Theo standing near her, a welcoming smile on his face as their wagon rolled to a stop. Holt jumped down and secured the horses, and the pair approached.

"It's wonderful to see you, my dear," Hattie gushed as Glenna was helped down from the wagon seat. "Oh my, what a lovely broach!"

Thanking her for the compliment, Glenna's hand fluttered over the broach. She had worn the very same dress on the day of her wedding, including the broach.

Hattie relieved Glenna of Daisy and placed a kiss on the child's cheek. "You look very pretty today." Daisy giggled.

"What about me?" Finn had rounded the corner of the wagon and stood for inspection.

Hattie looked him over. "You make a very handsome picture of a young man, Finn."

"I combed my hair," he said proudly.

Hattie smiled. "And washed behind your ears?"

"Auntie Glenna made sure to scrub my neck too."

"Good, no dirty little boys in our pew," Theo swatted at Finn with his hat, Finn dancing out of reach, laughing.

Theo strode to Hattie, offering her his arm and leading her up the steps and past Pastor Joseph, who was greeting his congregation as they filtered in. Finn was on their heels, Decker and Gunner followed suit. Holt stepped next to Glenna and took her arm. She was grateful for the friendly greeting of the Pastor and that the church was not yet full. They slipped into the pew next to Hattie and Theo.

With each new wave of churchgoers, Glenna knew the interest in who she was had mounted. Of course, she suspected that everyone already knew. There was little doubt that Mrs. Carson had shared the news of Holt taking a bride with more than a few townspeople. Perhaps even Rachel had eagerly told friends of her being the first to visit and welcome Glenna to Buffalo.

Hattie leaned close to Glenna and patted her hand, giving her a knowing smile. Daisy whimpered and reached for her; Glenna gathered the little girl to her. She had already grown accustomed to having Daisy close by, and it gave her the comfort she hadn't realized she required.

Soon, Pastor Joseph had closed the doors and taken his place at the pulpit. He was a commanding speaker, his bold voice reverberating in the space. His words rang of Christlike behavior, and he admonished those in attendance to be honest in their dealings with one another, with those not in attendance, and to act as the Lord would have them toward their fellow man.

94

The sermon was punctuated with music and the sharing of scriptures. He ended with a reading from 1 Peter, chapter three, verse eight, "Finally, all of you, be like-minded, be sympathetic, love one another, be compassionate and humble." He ended in a prayer of thanksgiving, and the congregation joined their voices in song.

Glenna had been so involved in the powerful words being spoken, she hadn't noticed time had slipped by so easily. Even the children had seemed to be captivated by Pastor Joseph, as Finn had sat listening to each word. Daisy had quieted in Glenna's lap, as if his words had also touched her, compelling all to listen without interruption of any manner.

Slowly, those seated on all sides of them started to stand and prepare themselves to leave the chapel. Pastor Joseph had taken his wife's arm and together walked to the large double doors, and stood shaking hands with each member that passed them, thanking them for their attendance.

When Holt and Glenna reached him, he shook both their hands with great vigor, "I am glad to see you both, Holt. Mrs. Sterling." He smiled at them both. "I hope the sermon didn't disappoint. All of this must pale in comparison to services in places like New York and London."

"There is no comparison." Glenna shook her head a little. "In one session, you have surpassed all others I have ever attended."

Pastor Joseph beamed, "I thank you for such a glowing review, although I doubt you will feel the same each Sabbath."

Rachel leaned forward and gathered Glenna into a friendly embrace, working around Daisy who was clinging to Glenna's side. "It is wonderful to see you, Glenna."

"And you, Rachel." She meant it. There was something so genuine and cordial about the woman that one couldn't help but feel welcome when in her presence.

Regretfully, they had to take their leave as others pressed behind them. Almost the moment her feet left the last step, Glenna found Holt and herself encircled by a throng of townspeople.

"Congratulations are in order, I hear," one man said while slapping Holt on the shoulder.

"Sheriff," Holt greeted him and turned to introduce him to Glenna, "I'd like you to meet my wife. Glenna, this is Frank Canton."

Further rounds of introductions took place, making Glenna feel as though her head were spinning as she attempted to retain as much of the information as possible. After each introduction, she felt obliged to apologize if in the future she would need to be reminded of their names. This caused more than one woman to laugh and wave off her concern.

Every new introduction came with a hearty handshake or a warm hug, accompanied with well-wishes for a happy marriage. A few scolded Holt for keeping Glenna such a secret and insisted that he allow her ample time to accept visitors in the next week, as each wanted to come by and give her a proper welcome. Holt assured them he had no intention of monopolizing all her time and that they were welcome.

Glenna knew without a doubt each woman who had made such a comment would indeed grace the house within the next week. A few appointments were enthusiastically made and invitations were made by others eager to include Glenna in local events, a sewing circle, and preparations for the Church's Harvest Festival.

"I believe my wife is becomin' a bit overwhelmed with all these invitations and introductions." Holt had pulled away from his conversation and moved to slip his arm around Glenna's shoulders.

"We'd better take our leave." He tipped his hat to each of the remaining well-wishers.

Turning from the crowd, he guided her to the wagon, where Decker and Gunner were waiting with Finn.

"Hattie and Theo already left; Hattie said she'd have supper started by the time we made it home," Gunner called to Holt.

"We always have a family meal on Sunday. It's been a tradition for as long as I can remember," Holt explained further when he noted Glenna's look of confusion.

"I like that you have family traditions." She shifted Daisy's weight as he helped her into the wagon. She hadn't noticed it with all the intermixing scents inside the small building, yet, out in the clear air, she caught the unmistakable scent of lavender layered under the more masculine fragrances of leather and cologne that were distinctly Holt.

Glenna smiled knowingly just as Holt caught her eye. As if it was possible to read her very thoughts, he shrugged. "It was about time I had a good scrubbin' myself."

A flush of heat touched her cheeks as Holt swung up into his seat and took the reins.

"Pie or sweet bread with cream?" Finn bellowed.

"Cobbler?" Decker countered.

"Carrot cake or her dutch oven chocolate?" Gunner added.

"They are placin' bets on what dessert Hattie will have prepared for after supper tonight," Holt told her as the wagon headed out of town.

"Do you join in?" she inquired, glancing at him.

"No." His jaw worked into a hard line. Then noticing Glenna looking at him, Holt seemed to relax a measure, "I've learned to just enjoy whatever marvelous confection she has made."

"Holt isn't a man of speculation," Decker grunted with a snort. "Even for sport. What about you, Miss? Want to place a bet for a bit of fun, is all?"

"No thank you, Decker. I have no taste for betting." Glenna tried to sound lighthearted, nonetheless there was a pit forming in her middle that felt heavy.

"I know meetin' half the town was a little overwhelmin', but how did you like the sermon?" Holt asked her, changing the subject as if Decker had never said a thing from the back of the wagon.

"Much more than I expected to," she said with candor.

"Pastor has a way with words."

"I was impressed by his poignant take on the gospel. It left me with the impression I will hear many more thought-provoking sermons in the weeks to come."

"That's Pastor Joe for you. Always makin' ya think," Gunner added to the topic.

"The true sign of a persuasive and inspirational teacher." Glenna nodded.

"Uncle Holt, would you play checkers with me when we get back home?" Finn had stood up, pushing his way in between their shoulders, and was looking up at Holt.

"Yes, after you've had your lunch and all that needs doin' is done, I would like to play checkers with you."

Finn grinned. "Do you play checkers?" He was now looking at Glenna.

"I have never attempted the game."

"I can teach you if you'd like." Finn was bouncing on the balls of his feet with excitement, keeping his balance only by bracing himself on the shoulders on either side of him.

"That sounds very nice. Thank you, Finn."

Finn extracted himself from them and plopped back into the bed of the wagon, chattering to Gunner and Decker about the games of checkers he had lined up for the afternoon. For their part, the two men took his jabbering in stride and didn't once belittle the boy or shame him into silence.

"You seem very far away. Somethin' on your mind?" Holt leaned closer to her side with the question.

"I was just listening to Finn."

"And what could he be sayin' that would cause such a look of melancholy to cross your face just now?"

Glenna hadn't any idea that her expression had changed. "Not melancholy. I was just marveling at how Finn is treated. His free way of speaking with all of you. It is refreshing."

"I suppose that comes from my grandfather. He taught my Pa that his thoughts mattered, and he wanted to hear 'em. It was not the popular approach as young ones are to be seen and not heard. I guess Pa's lesson passed on, stuck with Clint and me."

Glenna mulled this over in her mind. Was the concept exclusive to the males, or would Daisy also be encouraged to know her mind and speak it? Glenna thought of Hattie, and the idea that Daisy would be stifled or treated inferior seemed ridiculous.

"And now you smile," he observed.

"I was just thinking about what the house will be like when Daisy is as talkative as her brother."

Holt gaped at her before letting out a laugh. "I expect there will never be a dull moment for any of us between the two of them."

Glenna shared his smile. Her gaze dropped to the little girl seated comfortably in her lap. Smoothing her fine hair, she studied the cherubic little face.

"They have a way of claimin' your affection, don't they?" Holt's voice was low, his words only meant for her to hear.

Daisy's hand curled around two of Glenna's fingers. "I have grown fond of children under my care in the past. However, I didn't realize how much I would feel for — how soon I would come to care deeply —" She paused in search of the right words, "I cannot imagine what life on the ranch would be like without them."

———————

Holt watched as Finn, who was acting the perfect student, attentive and focused, patiently set up the checkerboard and went over the rules with Glenna. The book in his hands had been forgotten as the scene played out across the room from him.

Hattie had shooed them all from the kitchen after lunch had been served. She insisted on Glenna enjoying herself and banned her from helping with the evening meal. This left Glenna open to become Finn's next opponent.

Theo rested in a large, leatherback chair, his head drooping to one side as sleep threatened. He, Decker, Bowen, and Gunner had all worked extra fast on the Sunday chores so each could rest up and spend time doing what they pleased with the remainder of the day.

After a few games, Glenna finally won, and Finn celebrated with her, considering the success due to his teaching rather than Glenna's skill. Daisy crawled over to the chair Glenna was seated in, leaving her toys, and tugged at Glenna's skirts with a yawn.

"Another game will have to wait. It seems your sister is ready for a nap." Glenna reached down and took Daisy into her arms.

"I'll play with you," Theo offered, rubbing the sleep from his own eyes.

Holt watched her leave, then tried to refocus his efforts on absorbing the words from the page he hadn't turned despite staring at it for several minutes.

"It — seems to me that we have a good stretch of time between now and supper. Why don't you see if Glenna would like to see some of the property?" Theo said over the checkerboard, not looking directly at Holt.

Mulling over the idea for a minute, Holt rubbed the palms of his hands over his knees.

"Ya' think Glenna would like to?"

"Would I like to do what?"

All eyes turned to Glenna, who had descended the stairs in virtual silence and entered the room.

"Go for a ride with Uncle Holt," Finn blurted.

Her dark eyes turned to Holt as he stood. "Theo suggested that you might like to see more of the spread 'sides just the road to and from town."

"I would." She smiled.

"Do you — do you ride?" He wondered, realizing that there had been no occasion to ask her before now.

"Yes, aside. Do you have a sidesaddle?" She asked with just as much trepidation as he had wondered about her ability to ride at all.

"I do; it belonged to Grace."

"Well, it's settled." Theo also got to his feet. "You go saddle up while I get myself beat by Master Finn here."

"I'll go change," Glenna announced, half-turned away from them, stopped, hesitated, decided something internally, and finished her exit, retreating up the stairs.

As Holt was leading the mounts from the barn, Glenna was stepping out of the house and onto the front porch. She had changed out of her pale purple dress into the same dress he saw her in every day; her bonnet hung at the nape of her neck, ribbon tied loosely around her neck. Spotting him, she left the porch and headed in his direction.

"Who do we have here?" she asked, holding out her hand so the horse nearest her could smell her palm.

"This is Ranger,"

"He's your horse." It wasn't a question. The buckskin quarter horse nuzzled Glenna's hand, then dipped his head and sniffed at her skirt. She laughed and reached into the pocket of her dress. "You're a smart one." Retrieving an apple, she held it out for him to take. Ranger wasted no time taking the offering and allowed Glenna to stroke his nose and between his ears.

"You've made a friend," said Holt, observing the exchange.

"He's very handsome."

"We've been through a lot together this ornery cuss and I." Holt laughed and patted Ranger on the neck. He had to admit the animal was a good-looking one. His light-colored body made a striking contrast with his thick, coal-black mane and tail.

Glenna moved to greet the second horse; another apple appeared in her hand as she greeted him, "Hello, what's your name?"

"Copper," Holt answered.

"Named for his reddish coat," she observed. Copper turned his head a little to get a better view of the newcomer and dipped his

102

head, placing it under Glenna's hand; she laughed and stroked his nose, then down his neck. "Friendly."

"Needy," Holt said with amusement. "Copper was used to a lot of fussin' over him."

Glenna understood this was the horse Gracie had bonded with and used for all her rides. Copper was used to the weight and hand of a woman. He also knew that a female rider could mean extra brushing or treats.

"There is nothing wrong with a little extra attention, is there?" Glenna asked Copper, who was enjoying having his neck rubbed.

"I thought he would be good for you — we have others, of course. Scout, Rosie, or Big Red."

"I think Copper and I will get along just fine."

He handed her Copper's reins. "Let's get them to the fence." Leading Ranger, Holt struck out, Glenna close behind. Once there, he draped Ranger's reins over the top rail, and knowing that the horse wouldn't bolt while he helped Glenna into the saddle, he made no effort to tie him down.

Stepping to Copper's left side, he waited for Glenna to finish tying him off. "Would you like a box to stand on?" he asked.

"I think you and I can manage," she answered, to his surprise.

Glenna turned her back to him, reached up, and took the saddle horn in one hand; with the other, she took up her skirts just enough to place a foot in the stirrup without the skirts becoming tangled. Holt felt his lips twitch with amusement. He had thought she would be a bit more demure about mounting her steed, though as he placed both hands at her waist to lift her into the saddle, he couldn't deny that he preferred this method to her standing on a box.

She bounced on the balls of her feet twice, using the momentum of her movement and his strength; Glenna was easily lifted, her foot catching the other stirrup just as his hands slipped away from her. She twisted gracefully just at the apex of the ascent to seat herself comfortably in the saddle.

Glenna adjusted her other leg, arranged her skirts and pulled the bonnet from her back to her head, tying it in place with a bow tucked under her chin.

Untying Copper, Holt handed her the reins and pulled himself into the saddle. Turning Ranger toward the eastern patch of the property they started off at a slow gate. Glenna looked at home and had no issues matching Copper's gate to Ranger's stride.

"Are we riding to anyplace, in particular, today?" she asked, once the homestead had dissolved into nothing more than a bright patch in the distance.

"Sort of." He watched her from the corner of his eye, "I'm going to take you by Theo and Hattie's spread. I thought maybe you'd like to know your way to their place."

"I would. Thank you."

By and by, he found himself watching her. Glenna rode with her head up, eyes scanning all sides, taking in every aspect of her surroundings with an air of confidence. She seemed genuine in her interest in everything her gaze touched.

"Do you often spend Sunday afternoons in this manner?" she asked after a long stretch of silence.

"No," Holt shook his head. "It's been — years since I rode the property just to look at it."

"I know you must have a great many demands on your time; I am grateful you could take the time to show me some of your home. It's very beautiful."

Holt tore his eyes from her and looked out over the multicolored, slow-rolling hills that resolved themselves into long stretches of flat grasslands only to rise again, the reds and browns of earth mingling

104

with a variety of greens from vegetation. All of this was dotted with small groves of trees, beds of wildflowers, and streams cutting their way through the landscape. It was beautiful!

Was it truly possible he had entertained the idea of selling the place after losing Clint? The idea seemed ludicrous now. He wondered to himself when was the last time he had looked out over the property and truly saw it? How many other things in his life did he look at and not genuinely see them for what they were?

"I realize it has only been a few days, nevertheless I thought living on a cattle ranch, I would have seen more cattle than just the milk cows," Glenna teased as they came up a rise, the homestead now in view.

Holt smiled at her. "The herd is out in the summer pasture grazin' before the snow falls. We will bring them closer to home durin' the winter months, and you'll be plenty sick of their bellows and stink by spring."

She returned his smile, then looked back over the terrain they had covered on their ride.

"It really is so beautiful."

Glenna watched Holt for a few breaths as he gazed across the landscape. Each time she looked at him, she was struck by his strong, handsome features and easy smile yet, this evening he looked cold and distant, the same look she had seen after he told her of Clint's death, and she knew where his mind had wandered.

"Holt," she breathed. "Tell me what happened."

"To Clint, you mean." It was not a question.

"Yes," she said simply.

He turned in the saddle to look at her. "No one but God and Clint know what really happened that day."

She watched, feeling uncomfortable as his square shoulders slumped forward a bit under the weight of what he was saying. "He had acted out of character, becoming short-tempered, always distracted. I thought it had more to do with the stress he was under. You see, after Grace passed, Clint had to find a wet nurse for Daisy.

"The woman was a local mother. She soon wasn't able to keep up with the demands of two hungry children. That's when Clint bought that blasted milk goat, bringin' Daisy home permanent at the same time. She didn't thrive as expected, always fighting us on eatin', cryin' all hours of the day and night. It's hard to think of it now, as she is such a happy little thing."

"He mentioned her trouble with gaining weight in one of his early letters," she remembered.

"Daisy has always been small and slow to hit milestones; in comparison to what it had been like with Finn. Clint was sure it was the lack of a mother and being brought up by two cowboys that was holdin' her back." Holt seemed to realize something, and his expression changed, softened a little.

"Months back, she took a turn for the better. Clint changed how he held her when she'd be bawlin' somethin' awful, and it helped quiet her. He changed up how he was feedin' her and insisted on a routine for her sleep times. That was you, wasn't it? Those things he changed came from your suggestions."

"I relayed to him that children thrived with structure and how to cradle an infant in order to relieve digestive discomfort," she acknowledged. "I worked as a nanny for a time, learning a lot about the care of children." Glenna explained.

106

"It's no wonder Clint wanted you out here!" Holt shook his head, a knowing smile crossing his lips. "It did help and changed a lot for both of us. For a time, Clint was more relaxed, and I thought happy. In the weeks before his death, the stress had seemed to return, but I was never able to ascertain its cause."

"There was no indication in any of his letters of anything amiss."

"I had stayed in that mornin' to look after the children and go over the ledgers. Clint had said he wanted to ride out and check on the herd. The boys were out looking for stragglers, and I had assumed he would be riding out with them."

Holt paused, his eyes dropping. "Hours later Scout came amblin' back to the homestead, Clint riding slack across the saddle. I — I ran out to see what was wrong. When I reached to help Clint, he was — cold, a large gash to the side of his scalp. The injury hadn't been instantly fatal. He had bled out trying to make it home."

"Oh Holt…"

"When the boys got back, none of them had seen him all day and had no idea where he was when it happened. I hadn't seen from which direction Scout had come — we all could make guesses as to where he really had been riding to that day, but no one knows for sure." His voice hitched.

"What do you believe happened?"

"I — I don't know. Sheriff Canton did a brief investigation as a favor, and ultimately, his death was recorded as an accident. It could have been. I can't help but think his mood beforehand has some connection to his death, that maybe Clint had been caught up in somethin'." Holt paused. "He was an experienced rider — on the other hand, it could be possible he was thrown. It just doesn't add up for me. If Scout had been really spooked, he would have bolted, leavin' Clint."

"Are you saying you believe Clint may have been attacked?"

"I don't want to believe it. Maybe… maybe he exchanged words with someone over grazin' or stumbled onto somethin' he shouldn' have. I can't prove foul play, except somethin' in my gut tells me chalkin' it up to an accident isn't right."

Glenna chewed her lower lip. "Have you searched through all his things? Perhaps he left a clue."

"I haven't — yet. The weeks after his death are such a blur — a whirlwind that I hardly remember most of it. Before I could take a breath — you knocked at the door, a whirlwind of another kind." He was smiling at her, this one with a touch of sadness to it.

"I am sorry. I can hardly imagine what all of this has been like for you. In truth, I have been feeling very selfish as my thoughts have tended to on my own troubles."

"There is no need to be sorry, Glenna." Holt sat straighter in the saddle, the homestead growing larger with every hoofbeat. "Your arrival was a surprise. That doesn't mean it was unwelcome."

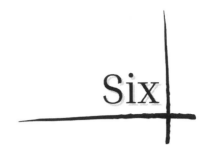

Six

"Why don't I fetch the feed for the hens while you gather the eggs?" Glenna presented the option as she, Daisy, and Finn headed out toward the chicken coop.

"I can do that." Finn skipped off as Glenna made her way to the barn to retrieve the food, Daisy pointing out a variety of things, pronouncing them happily in her own particular language.

When Glenna returned to Finn, a particularly cantankerous hen was refusing to leave the nest. She watched the power struggle with humor. Finn won out and retrieved the eggs she had been protecting.

"That's the last of them," He pronounced.

"Ready for your morning lesson?" she asked as Finn took up the now full basket of eggs and together they walked into the house.

Finn set diligently to work, giving Glenna his full attention. They started with basic addition and subtraction. To add a bit of fun to his lesson, she had spilled a handful of dried beans onto the tabletop. Finn would carefully count out the beans into piles, adding them together or subtracting them to match Glenna's instructions. He would write the numbers out or trace the ones he didn't already know on his slate.

Once this activity had grown tiresome, Glenna moved on and they began working on his letter recognition. With only one full month's worth of schooling under his belt, Finn was progressing far better than she had expected.

"Can you tell me what these letters are?" she asked, pointing to each one in turn. Finn was delighted with himself as he got each letter correct.

"That's right, and do you know what that spells?"

"It's my name," he beamed.

"Very good Finn." Glenna beamed at him. "Do you think you'd be able to trace them and write your name all on your own?"

"Yes," Finn grinned back at her and, wiping the slate clean, started again. Carefully writing the letters as he said each one, "F. I. N. N. Finn."

"Finn!" Daisy echoed loudly from her place on Glenna's lap, clapping.

"That's right, Daisy." Glenna bounced the little girl on her knee. It had been clear in the first few days of lessons that Finn was a very quick learner and eager to lap up every bit of knowledge he could. Now, weeks into their lessons, he was identifying many more letters and recalling their sounds, although he was still mostly fascinated by his name.

"Are the two of you ready to spend some time outdoors? We need to take advantage of the good weather and gather some things out of the garden for supper."

Finn forgot all about writing his name and dashed from the table. "I'll get the vegetable basket."

Glenna laughed and moved to put away the school supplies and went to join Finn outside. Blu greeted her, yipping and licking at her hand. "Come with us and keep an eye on Daisy for me, will you?" she asked the dog, who always seemed to understand what Glenna was saying and settling down, walked next to her toward the garden gate.

Finn was already tugging away at the carrots, his favorite vegetable. Glenna put Daisy down and shut the gate behind her. Blu lay down next to Daisy, allowing the toddler to crawl on him, followed by a squeal of delight as her face was thoroughly licked in return.

"Good boy!" Glenna smiled, setting to work digging at some potatoes.

Lost in the work, she started to hum a favorite childhood song to herself. The humming soon turned into soft singing.

"That's pretty."

"Thank you, Finn. It's a song my mother sang to me when I was your age. The Lass of Richmond Hill."

"Would you sing it one more time?" he asked, bringing the basket and handful of carrots closer to listen.

Glenna obliged, trilling softly the familiar melody.

On Richmond Hill, there lives a lass
More bright than May-day morn
Whose charms all other maids' surpass
A rose without a thorn.
This lass so neat, with smiles so sweet
Has won my right good will
I'd crowns resign to call thee mine
Sweet lass of The Lass of Richmond Hill.

Sweet lass of The Lass of Richmond Hill
Sweet lass of The Lass of Richmond Hill
I'd crowns resign to call thee mine
Sweet lass of The Lass of Richmond Hill.

Ye zephyrs gay that fan the air,

And wanton thro' the grove
O whisper to my charming fair,
"I die for her I love."
This lass so neat, with smiles so sweet
Has won my right good will
I'd crowns resign to call thee mine
Sweet lass of The Lass of Richmond Hill.

Sweet lass of The Lass of Richmond Hill Hill
Sweet lass of The Lass of Richmond Hill Hill
I'd crowns resign to call thee mine
Sweet lass of Richmond Hill.

"My Ma used to sing to me too," Finn remembered when the last of the chorus died away.

"Do you remember much about your mother, Finn?"

Finn nodded, "I 'member both him and Ma. Daisy won't," he added, and it tugged at her heart. Glenna patted Finn's cheek.

"Daisy will know them both if you tell her stories about them. Things you loved about them, things you remember. She will know them through you and your Uncle Holt. Perhaps as we work on your writing, you can even write things down to keep forever. Would you like that?"

Instantly, Finn brightened. "You mean like you do in them books?"

"My journals, you mean. I write my memories in them, things I want to keep a hold of forever. Would you like to have a journal, Finn?"

"Yes, Ma'am. I would write stories about Ma' and Pa' to tell Daisy," he stated faithfully.

112

"I would like to hear about them, too. Could I listen to the stories as well?" Glenna asked.

Finn's face lit up. "Sure!" Then he seemed to think of something else; his brow furrowed, he chewed on his bottom lip before asking, "Miss Glenna, do you miss your Ma and Pa?"

Glenna paused a heartbeat before answering, "I do."

"We are kind of the same, aren't we?" Finn asked, rushing on, "Both of us bein' orphaned."

The expression that crossed Finn's face was one of such deep sorrow it cut into her.

"You know my parents passed away?" she asked.

"It's how you look sometimes, smilin' but sad all at once. I feel that way too," he said simply. "Were you sad when your Ma and Pa died?"

"Yes," she answered simply and honestly.

Finn stepped closer to her and flung both arms around her neck, giving her a tight hug. He stepped back, took up the basket, and started toward rows of onions. Glenna was still crouched down, resting on one knee, watching Finn for a few heartbeats. Dragging the back of her hand across her face to remove the evidence of tears that had escaped, she took a steadying breath and set back to work harvesting a few more potatoes.

"I think we have enough for supper. It's time to get Daisy down for a nap. Would you like to stay outside and play with Blu Dog?" Glenna asked and picked up the full basket of vegetables.

"Can I work on my letters some more first? I want to show Uncle Holt when he gets home."

"Of course, Finn."

"Heard Carson's daughters have come back home from visitin' their newly married cousin down in Cheyenne," Bowen commented as the chorus of "Amen" rang out over the evening's supper.

"The Carson girls…" Gunner said wistfully.

"Patsy, and what's the younger sister's name? Eddie — or Elaine?" Bowen asked between bites of food.

"Edith." Decker chimed in. "Edith Carson."

"That was it, Edith. Pretty little redhead if I've ever seen one," Gunner pronounced around another bite of food.

"She also had a temper, if I remember," Gunner commented.

"A man could put up with a temper for a face like Edith Carson's," Decker mused over a large piece of bread slathered with butter.

"She had her eye on you, Holt, as I recall." Bowen grinned.

Glenna felt the rush of disappointment at Bowen's words. Although their marriage had only just lasted just a few weeks, she felt herself protective of the fledgling relationship, to speak nothing of her budding feelings in regards to Holt. She supposed that was only natural, after all, to feel a pull toward the man that she now shared a name with.

"I doubt either of ya knuckleheads will ever have the pleasure of findin' out anythin' about Edith Carson's temper, as I am sure she won't give ya the time a day," Bowen laughed around a full bite of stew.

"Well, now that Glenna has taken Holt out of the runnin', why not?" Gunner grinned across the table at Glenna and gave her a wink.

114

"Yes, thanks for that, Glenna." Decker nodded his agreement. "You've made things a might easier for the rest of us by tyin' Holt down."

Glenna ducked her head to hide the blush that spread across her cheeks, finding the conversation almost unbearable to listen to, let alone be the subject of.

"I suppose this is the proper time to say 'you're welcome?' " she managed. This elicited a roaring laugh from each of the men, save Holt, who grunted.

"I'm gonna ask her, Edith, to dance at the Harvest Festival," Decker announced.

"Be prepared to be left without a partner if I get to her first." Gunner jabbed Decker in the side with his elbow.

"Why not ask Miss Patsy? She is a fine-lookin' woman." Bowen grinned.

"Everyone knows Patsy is bein' courted by John Helm," Gunner said, as if this truly had been a widely known fact.

They continued to go a few rounds of speculation on who would get to seek out Edith's approval first or which one of them she might agree to share a dance with. All the while, Glenna focused a bit too hard on making sure Daisy was eating the food in front of her.

"Do I have to dance at the festival?" Finn asked, his nose scrunched upward in disgust.

"You don't want to?" Holt wondered.

"No, I'd rather play jacks or marbles with other boys. Dancin' is for girls and old men." This made everyone at the table laugh; Glenna cracked a smile as well.

Once this new round of levity had died down, Finn looked across the table at Glenna and added, "Unless you want a partner, Auntie Glenna."

"That's very thoughtful of you, Finn." She smiled at him. Already the gentlemen.

"I think you are probably safe from dancin', Finn." Holt reached over and tousled Finn's hair, adding, "Your aunt already has a full dance card for the evenin'."

Glenna's spoon stopped halfway to her lips, and she was unable to lift it any further, as it had suddenly grown quite heavy.

"You're goin' to dance with her, aren't you?" Finn asked, patting his hair back down.

"Yes, I am," Holt declared.

The stew had been forgotten. Talk of the Harvest Festival hosted by the Mayor and his new wife, held on her parents' property, as they had a very large barn to accommodate dancing after a picnic, had started to circulate during her visits into town. It was a topic discussed anytime someone from the area had stopped by to welcome her to Buffalo, or the few times she had taken tea with Rachel. It was all anyone could seem to speak of as the October date loomed ever closer.

She knew Holt was looking at her; she could feel the pressure of his gaze without returning it. The spoon slowly finished its ascent and Glenna pushed the food past her lips in the most casual manner possible, hoping that everyone else seated at the table hadn't noticed her discomfort.

The conversation didn't waver as it changed to the topic of when to move the cattle to closer pastures for the winter months. Soon the dishes had been emptied, and everyone went their separate ways.

Finn dashed out the back door, ready to take full advantage of the warm evening air; Blu bounded out after him, barking happily. Daisy cried out after them and pointed with one stew covered hand in the direction her brother had disappeared.

116

"I know, sweet girl, you want to go run and play too." Glenna took a washcloth to Daisy, who protested being cleaned. "Alright, why don't you play while I clean up, and then we can go join Finn and Blu Dog together?"

Daisy squirmed in her arms. Glenna placed her near a basket of blocks and Daisy instantly reached for the lip of the basket, pulling it towards herself and tipping it over, spilling the blocks around her legs.

Glenna made short work of the dishes and had the kitchen ready for the next day's cooking just as Holt appeared at the door. He swept off his hat and let the screen bang closed behind him.

"Tell me what's eatin' at you, Glenna." Holt's request was softly spoken.

Wiping her hands dry, she turned from the washtubs to look at him. "I'm quite well."

Holt let his eyes drop to the Stetson hanging from his lean fingers. "I know I have a lot to learn 'bout you, still I can already tell when you are holdin' back. Somethin' at supper bothered you, and I want to know what it was."

Glenna felt her mouth open in protest. No sound escaped.

His eyes lifted and studied her face. "I can't help fix what troubles you if you won't talk to me, Glenna."

She felt bewildered at his statement. When was the last time anyone cared enough to ask about her feelings? Who was the last person to have observed her close enough that they could see past the face she presented? Was it possible to recall anyone offering to help fix what troubled her, as he put it, before this very moment?

Realizing he was still waiting for some kind of answer, Glenna pulled herself back to the present. "Thank you for being concerned, although truly, I am well."

Holt narrowed his eyes, his jaw working as teeth ground together.

Glenna took a deep breath. "I — I didn't want to. It is utterly unimportant and should not cause you any amount of distress." She shook her head and waved off the topic.

"There is somethin' botherin' you," Holt said with satisfaction.

"I had planned on asking Hattie or Rachel, then time got away from me. I thought perhaps you might not wish to and I would be saved from the embarrassment."

"What on earth are you goin' on about?" Holt sounded puzzled.

"I — I have no idea how to dance the Two-Step or Square Dance, or even what a Square Dance might be for that matter," she said finally. "There wasn't any call for me to attend dances in New York and I am unsure how similar things are to the balls I attend after my coming out. I was hoping that perhaps I would not be required to — dance."

Glenna was in no way prepared for Holt's reaction to her confession. At first, he looked at her, blinked a few times, his mouth twitching. Then suddenly, as if it was bubbling up from inside with great force, Holt roared with laughter, doubling over, and slapping his hand on his leg, shoulders shaking.

She stared, flabbergasted at his reaction. "It is a silly thing to worry about, I know." Glenna pulled at the strings of her apron and tugged it loose, yanking it over her head carelessly, the loop catching and pulling at her hair. Finally wrestling the thing off, she tossed it onto a nearby chair along with the dish towel and bent to gather up Daisy, retreat her only goal.

Holt's hand caught her wrist. He pulled her up and toward him at the same time. Caught off guard, she stumbled a few steps before regaining her footing.

118

"I'm sorry I laughed." He was grinning at her, her wrist still held tightly in his grasp, as if once he removed his fingers, she would again attempt to flee. He would be right. Feeling ridiculed, she had no desire to stay and tugged at her trapped arm. Holt held fast and waited for her to look up at him.

When it was clear that he wasn't going to relent or release her, she did meet his blue eyes with an air of defiance. The Stetson had been discarded in his fit of laughter, leaving his other hand free to reach over and tuck a curl that had come loose behind her ear.

"I didn't mean to upset you. I was relieved that it wasn't somethin' much worse."

"That was you being relieved? What on earth did you think I was going to say?"

His grasp on her arm fell away as the humor drained from his eyes; what replaced it was darker, leaving a shadow over Holt's features. "Then you aren't unhappy here?"

"No."

"I — er — saw you with Finn in the garden today and it looked as if you were upset — he seemed melancholy as well — tonight at supper, you seemed distant and distracted."

Glenna recalled her conversation with Finn and the hated tears that had escaped. "You misunderstood what you witnessed. Finn and I were discussing our similarities as orphans. He misses his parents terribly."

"We all have that in common, I suppose."

"Oh, Holt!" Glenna felt awful that she had not once thought of his loss, both his parents gone, his only brother and sister-in-law, both taken long before their time.

"I'm glad he opened up to you about it. Finn hasn't talked to anyone about Clint or made mention of his mother in all the time they've been gone."

"I didn't know," she said sadly. "I assumed he had confided in you, Theodore, or Hattie. The poor boy."

"Everyone deals with loss on their own terms."

Glenna nodded her understanding.

A hint of a smile had crept back into Holt's features. "Can you forgive me for laughin'?"

Glenna paused and attempted to look thoughtful. "I suppose I could be persuaded. " She folded her arms across her middle in an attempt to look severe.

He eyed her, his head slightly cocked to one side. "You truly never went out to any of those fancy dance halls in New York?"

Glenna thought briefly of what her life in the city had been like, arriving friendless, and terrified. Not at all prepared for the challenges that she would face or the life she would find herself living in this foreign country.

Should she tell him about the fear she had endured? The long, cold, seemingly endless nights. The bone-weary days marked by hunger and exhaustion? Would he be shocked to hear the things she had witnessed and heard living in the boarding house that led to her sleeping with a carving knife under her pillow? It all seemed like such an awful dream now. That life hadn't lent itself to the carefree joviality of dances, laughter, or companionship she had known in her youth.

Unable to form an answer, Glenna finally simply shook her head.

"Come with me." Holt bent, scooped up Daisy in one arm and his hat in the other. Glenna didn't have time to question him and curiosity had her following him out into the yard.

120

He sat Daisy down and, placing a hand to his mouth, gave the loudest whistle she had ever heard. All three hands appeared from various directions.

"Boss?" Glenna could hear Gunner's question as Holt approached the others.

Glenna stood apart from the foursome as Holt addressed them, unsure of her role, as Decker and Bowen stepped away and headed toward the bunkhouse.

"Finn, can you and Blu Dog keep an eye on Daisy for a minute?" Finn nodded and sat down near his sister. Blu followed suit. Holt stepped back to where Glenna stood.

"Come here." He directed her to stand facing him across a few feet of open space. Bowen returned with a banjo and Decker with a harmonica.

"What are we doing?" she asked, fearing she already knew the answer.

"Givin' you a dance lesson."

Gunner began to call out orders as Bowen strummed a jovial tune, Decker adding to the tune. She watched Holt for cues and repeated his movements. She was pleasantly surprised at how easily she picked up the motions; the dance having similarities to the ones she had learned in her youth; rows of women on one side, men on the other, listening to the caller, moving to the music as they did his bidding.

She was laughing and out of breath when Gunner had called his last, and the music stopped.

"Square dancin' is simple enough. It has roots that speak back to ballrooms of all of Europe. As this country was settled, all those that came brought their traditions and dances along, music and dance a common ground, so to speak. The caller gives order to the chaos."

Decker plucked a light tune on the banjo strings, sounding the start of another dance.

"The Two-Step is a bit different," Holt said and stepped a bit closer to Glenna. "It's more like a lively version of the waltz."

His right hand slipped around her waist, his left holding her hand. Glenna rested her free hand lightly on his shoulder. With a kind of hop and skip, the dance commenced. She found herself clinging to Holt and laughing until she was unable to catch her breath. The dance was cheerfully animated with large, exaggerated steps and body movements.

There was little that reminded her of the structure of a waltz. The only comparison to the dance she knew was his hand at her back and the other cradling hers, the pressure of his lean fingers leading her in the sudden changes of direction or speed.

The music stopped and the world with it, as she stood, still caught in Holt's grasp. "Was that enough instruction?" he asked with a teasing glint in his blue eyes.

"Am I to expect every dance to be as spirited as this?"

"Cowboys don't do nothin' halfway." He grinned and squeezed her fingers before dropping his hands away from her and stepping back.

Holt swept off his hat and shut the front door behind him. The morning chores hadn't taken long, and he wanted to speak to Glenna about accompanying him into town as they needed to visit the blacksmith and pick up an order from Carson's. He also admitted to himself that he hadn't stopped thinking about dancing with her and kept being drawn back to the house for little things just to see her.

122

He could hear Finn chattering away in the kitchen as he came down the hall.

"Auntie Glenna, why don't you ever wear nothin' else?"

"What do you mean, Finn?" Glenna questioned in a soft voice.

Holt stepped forward a little and leaned his shoulder on the wall just outside the kitchen doorway; he was able to see them from his vantage point, yet was left unseen himself.

"You always have this one on, 'sides Sundays, I mean." Finn indicated the dress Glenna now wore. "Don't you have no other dresses?"

Glenna gave Finn a half-smile. "Is there something wrong with my dress?"

"No — one of the ladies at worship last Sunday, she said that you must have had a lot of pretty dresses before you came to the ranch," Finn commented innocently, "I wondered why you don't wear 'um, is all."

"She is right; I did have a few very fine dresses. However, some things are more important than having a closet full of fine clothes," Glenna offered.

"What happened to them? Couldn't you bring 'em with you on the boat?" Finn asked, scratching out something on his slate.

Glenna crouched next to the table, so she was looking the small boy in the eyes. "I had some. They became of little use to me, so I sold them. Do you have more questions?"

"I do. I also know some about ya already. I know you are English; that's why you talk funny." Glenna smiled at this.

"Quite, what else?"

"You lived in a big city back East."

"I did."

"I don't think I'd like the city. I like it here."

"I like it here as well," she smiled.

Finn shrugged. "I was sad when I thought I would have to leave Crossroads after Pa died. I'm glad you and Uncle Holt decided to keep us here. What was your home in England like? Are you sad you had to leave it?"

Glenna looked at him, thoughtful for a moment. "I lived in a very large estate before I came to America. There was a grand house, very fine furnishings, brightly colored tapestries, paintings on every wall, and shelves that reached to the ceiling filled with the best books. I adored my family's home." Finn nodded his understanding, but kept quiet as he waited for her to continue.

"Well, when I set sail, I was only able to bring one trunk with me, forced to leave all else right where it was. Once I reached New York City, the only things of value that I still owned — the items that had yet to be bartered away, the necklaces, and other jewelry, hats, shoes, gloves, and dresses, they all had to be sold to pay for a room at the boarding house where I lived. I learned that you can be very happy with less; now I have a work dress and one for the Sabbath."

"I have some good work clothes," Finn said with pride, adding in a slightly sadder voice, "I would like a nice shirt, though. Somethin' like my Pa used to wear."

Holt stood up straight, pulling himself away from the wall. He stole into the kitchen with a smile and ruffled Finn's hair. "Are you lettin' Glenna get anythin' done?"

"Uncle Holt! I have somethin' to show you." Finn jumped up and down excitedly.

"Oh?"

"Watch this." Finn tugged at his hand and demanded his attention. Holt sat next to him on the bench.

Slowly Finn worked out the letters of his name, saying each letter as he wrote it, and proudly held up the slate for Holt's inspection.

"That's great!" He patted Finn on the shoulder and pulled him in for a hug. "You have been workin' hard and I am very proud of you. How 'bout we take the rest of the mornin' off and go into town?"

———————

Finn had bolted the instant the wagon had come to a stop. Bowen jumped off the back of the wagon and strode into Carson's after the boy with a lazy gate. Holt gave Glenna his hand as she stepped down, balancing Daisy in her other arm.

"I need to make a stop at the blacksmiths. Get anythin' you need for the house. Bowen will settle up with Carson, and I'll meet you back at the wagon."

"Alright," Glenna strode into the store. Finn had already attracted some attention at the counter, two very pretty women, both with deep auburn colored hair, fussing over him.

"Oh, Master Sterling, how grown you have become while we were away," one of them said, beaming down at him.

"A whole summer's growin' and I turned five and one half."

"Almost six years old already! No, how can that be possible?" The other acted surprised in the most dramatic manner.

Bowen grunted and moved farther down the counter from the scene with a roll of his eyes.

"We were both so sorry to hear about your father," the taller of the two women commented, her face grave.

Finn didn't respond to the topic.

"Yes, our deepest condolences go out to all your dear family. How is your uncle?"

"He's well," Finn offered just as his gaze caught hold of Glenna. "May I have a butterscotch drop, please?"

Both women turned their attention in the direction Finn had asked, and Glenna felt the atmosphere in the shop change instantly.

"I think that would be fine," Glenna addressed Finn.

Mr. Carson, who had been watching the exchange, cleared his throat. "Please, allow me to make introductions." He stepped out from behind the counter with a flourish. "These are my two daughters, Patsy and Edith. Girls, I'd like you to meet Mrs. Glenna Sterling, Holt's new wife."

"Pleased to make your acquaintance," Patsy said with true warmth, her green eyes sparkling. Glenna felt an instant liking for her.

The shorter of the pair, the one Glenna now knew as Edith, stepped forward a bit with what was clearly a forced smile. Her darker eyes narrowed while taking in Glenna's appearance, sweeping from her auburn locks to the ill fitted gray dress down to the worn boots. Glenna tried not to show her discomfort at the other woman's assessment and kept a kind smile on her lips.

"You aren't at all what I expected." Her sister seemed surprised at the boldness of Edith's statement. "Taller, to be sure, a bit more natural elegance than described. Not at all what... well, Holt's tastes must have changed drastically indeed. I suppose that is bound to happen when you feel as though you have no choice in the matter." She added with a flippant laugh.

Glenna noted that Patsy seemed to want to interject, except she was being abruptly cut off from doing so. The elder sister would open her mouth to speak, and Edith would rush forward, hardly

126

giving Patsy time to breathe. Glenna wondered if this was how it always was with the sisters.

"You are just as I was led to believe," Glenna said with all honesty and a touch of malice. It was unfair of her, she knew, yet Edith's open disapproval of her gave rise to a heat in Glenna's veins that drove her to speak the truth, even if it was a bit unkind.

Both sisters were stunning beauties, she had to admit. Seeing them in person, she understood more acutely the interest in the topic from supper. It was no wonder Gunner and Decker had argued over Edith. Although both sisters were very attractive, it was Edith's air and forceful nature that set her apart from her more reserved sister.

Edith's expression gave away her pleasure. "You have heard of me, then? I confess we have heard of little else outside of the new Mrs. Sterling, in the short time we have been home. Your unexpected arrival so soon after the loss of Clint gave everyone something new to talk about. Of course, everyone seems taken with the new — until the newness fades." She added the last with a curl to her upper lip.

Glenna was keenly aware that Edith was not complimenting her. "I hope the reports have been favorable." She attempted to be civil, for Holt's sake, if nothing else. It would not do to have tales of his unruly wife upsetting him.

There was an audible intake of breath from Patsy, who was shaking her head with a small smile forming on her lovely face, and again, before she was able to speak, Edith already gave a slight giggle and pressed on.

"They have not done you justice, I assure you." Edith said with a deliberate attempt at a smile that looked reminiscent of a grimace.

Glenna bristled, "Neither have yours."

Edith disliked her. That was clear. She meant to shame Glenna by her comments and looks. Glenna felt sure that she had much more experience with women who used false kindness to put another in their place than Edith had ever experienced. After all, it was she, not Edith, that had watched these same tactics used in polite society all her life.

"I do hope to have every opportunity to become better acquainted with you in the future. Now you'll have to excuse us; my sister and I were just off to take tea with the Mayor's wife, Clara. She has long been expecting us." Edith gave Patsy a clear look of warning not to make a comment and reached for her sister's hand.

"By all means, do not keep Mrs. Burritt deprived of such company any longer." Glenna stepped to one side to open a walkway for the Carson sisters.

"Please, give my old friend Holt our warmest regards," Edith said pointedly. Glenna knew it was not meant for Holt, but for her alone. She was an outsider, an interloper into their lives, and Edith wanted her to feel it.

Edith started to drag Patsy by the hand out of the store, saying a loud farewell to their father, and made a show of leaving. Poor Patsy looked a bit embarrassed by Edith if Glenna was reading her expression correctly. In their absence, the shop had grown very quiet. Glenna sighed inwardly; she would have to guard herself in the future against allowing Edith to antagonize her into pettiness.

Glenna had expected Holt to be waiting by the wagon when she and Bowen exited the store with their purchases a quarter of an hour later, there was no sign of him. Bowen began to load the flour and oatmeal into the wagon box as Glenna let her eyes scan the surrounding area for any sign of him.

Bowen relieved the last purchased items from Glenna's grasp, freeing both her arms to wrestle with Daisy, who was growing restless.

"Where is Uncle Holt?" Finn asked as he kicked a few stones into the street from the boardwalk.

128

"He had some things to attend to." At that very moment, her eyes caught sight of Holt; he was in conversation with a man she didn't recognize, his back to them, his stance hard and unyielding.

"Who is that man Holt's talking to?" she asked Bowen, taking an instant dislike to the small, dark-haired man.

Bowen spit into the street, "Silas Landry. He and his brother Tripp run the spread that borders the northern patch of Crossroads."

"Holt looks displeased with the conversation." He had moved so that he was now in profile, arms crossed over his chest and looking down at the shorter man.

"I expect he is. The Landry brothers aren't exactly on friendly terms with anyone in these parts. Clint and Holt have had their fair share of run-ins with the pair over the years."

"Uncle Holt!" Finn called out, spotting him, and before Bowen or Glenna could stop him, he darted away straight for Holt.

Glenna sighed and rushed after him.

Finn stood next to Holt, looking up into his face with admiration and excitement.

"Auntie Glenna, let me get a butterscotch drop!" he said and waved the sweet in the air as proof.

"That was kind of her." She heard Holt respond attentively to Finn, although the lines of his face hadn't softened.

"I apologize for the interruption," Glenna rushed to explain and reached for Finn's hand. "Let's let your uncle finish his business in peace."

"Holt, have you forgotten all your manners?" the man she knew as Silas Landry said, with what she was sure was meant to be a charming smile, except it gave her a shiver.

"Silas, this is my wife." Holt gave the introduction, his stance still stiff.

One thin, greasy-looking eyebrow lifted. "Pleased to meet you."
Glenna only nodded her response.

Silas' lip twitched as he took in Glenna with a dramatic sweep of his coal-black eyes. The effect gave her the same reaction as being dunked in frigid water, and she wanted to recoil from his gaze.

"Well — well — Holt, it seems you're doing better than you let on. A new wife, and a right pretty one, at that." Silas smirked, making Glenna feel uncomfortable. "I'm starting to understand now why you refused my offer. It didn't make sense when Clint passed it up — all alone out there, but I'd hold out on selling the place as well if I had someone with a voice as sweet as fresh honey, whispering in my ear, and warming my bed each night —"

Holt's fist plowed into Silas' jaw with such force that it knocked the other man off his feet, leaving him sprawled out on his back in the middle of the dusty road.

"Take care Silas, that tongue of yours will get you in more trouble than a busted lip one of these days!" Holt said harshly.

Glenna looked between both men in pure shock. Silas rubbed his chin, touched the back of his hand to his bloody lip, and shot Holt a look of pure venom.

"What's the trouble?" A taller, thinner version of Silas had appeared suddenly and stood between Holt and Silas as the latter dusted himself off and got to his feet.

Bowen had also rushed over, standing near Holt, shoulders squared as if he was prepared to jump into a brawl.

"No trouble, Tripp. Holt and I were just having a friendly discussion." Silas muttered, his hand still pressed to his lip.

"Why do so many of your friendly discussions end with a tussle, Silas?" Tripp Landry glanced over at Holt. "I suppose my little brother owes someone an apology."

130

"You might want to teach him how to hold his tongue when in the presence of women and children."

"My most humble apologies, Ma'am. My brother has yet to learn how to act in polite society." Tripp tipped the brim of his hat to Glenna.

"You might want to rein him in on a few other matters as well." Holt snorted, and with one hand taking Finn's and the other placed at Glenna's elbow, he led them away from the Landry brothers to the waiting wagon. Bowen followed.

"What was that all about?" Bowen dared to ask, lifting Finn into the back of the wagon.

"Just teachin' Silas a lesson on keepin' his foul tongue in his head," Holt growled.

"He insulted Miss Glenna?" Bowen looked between the space that now separated them with a deadly glare, "Does the man have a death wish?"

"It appears so." Holt turned away from Bowen to help Glenna into the wagon seat, his eyes on her face, searching.

This was not the first time she had been witness to violence, as fights would periodically erupt outside the boarding house when men stumbled home after a night of drinking. However, this felt much different to her than any of those had.

Holt swung up into the wagon seat next to her, Bowen settling in the back with Finn and the supplies, tipping his hat over his eyes and laying back on the large bag of flour in an attempt to ride more comfortably as Finn chattered excitedly to him.

The town grew ever distant, and Glenna was glad to see it go. The more space that was put between her, Edith Carson, and the Landry brothers — the better.

"Are you alright?" Holt worried. The question was little more than a whisper spoken between them.

She shifted Daisy on her lap and took a few deep, steadying breaths.

"I am sorry you had to witness that, Glenna. I don't lose my temper easily — but when I do…"

"There is no apology necessary, Holt," she assured him.

"That coward — that no good — he was out of line!" Holt seethed with anger, sitting rigidly next to her.

"You will not hear an argument from me on that point." She assented, whispering over the top of Daisy's nodding head. The degrading manner in which Silas had ogled her, coupled with his insinuation, had made Glenna's skin crawl.

As if of its own accord, her mouth began to curl upward at the corners, "I do believe the image of you sending him into the dirt will stay with me for a very long time." This was followed by what could only be described as a giggle.

Holt glanced at her, clearly surprised. His mouth also lifted and a low rumbling laugh erupted. "It did feel damn good," he confessed.

All seriousness returned. "I've set your life spinning into chaos, Holt. That much is clear."

"Sometimes it's the chaos that makes life worth livin'," he answered. "But I get the idea you are referrin' to more than Silas' bad behavior. What happened I'm not aware of?" He was able to read her too easily.

"Mr. Carson introduced his daughters to me." She watched for a reaction to the statement.

"And why would makin' their acquaintance make you believe that you somehow added to the chaos of my life, as you put it?"

132

"— Miss Edith Carson was not friendly in the slightest. She indicated her utter surprise at our connection and asserted you had perhaps put feelings aside for another to sacrifice for the good of your niece and nephew — of course, that is not wholly off the mark. However, it brought to mind the fact that you never commented on the topic of her at supper the other evening."

"And you to conclude — what?" he coaxed.

"That, perhaps you — might hold some regret where she is concerned." The words slipped from between her lips before Glenna was able to stop the thought from filling the space. "I'm sorry, I have no right to pry," she rushed on, feeling foolish.

"If you haven't the right, then who has? You're my wife after all." There was humor in Holt's tone. Glenna couldn't bring herself to look over at him.

Nerves gripped her tightly, making her stomach twist. "Did you — have eyes for her?"

"You know the answer to that already," he professed. "You asked me if there might be anyone other than you I'd make an offer of marriage to. Do you recall?"

Suddenly remembering their first conversation regarding marriage, she wondered at her assertiveness in regards to the questioning of a man she had known only a few minutes and his personal history.

"I was quite bold, wasn't I?" She smiled.

"Still are."

Glenna blushed. He was right, of course.

"You had every right to be bold. Do you remember what I told ya?" Holt wondered.

"Yes."

"Have I given you any reason to believe otherwise?"

"Holt, I was not questioning your integrity," Glenna agonized.

"Only my honesty?"

Glenna started and her eyes flew to his face, "Oh, Holt, no!"

His handsome face split into a wide grin. "I'm teasin' you, Glenna, but if I didn't know better, I'd say my wife of nearly five weeks was a touch jealous."

Relief intermixed with embarrassment. Reaching inside herself to access the same reckless courage that had seen her through the first days after arriving at Crossroads, she smiled back. "I prefer the term — apprehensive."

"Territorial?" he offered with a grin. "Or could it be possessiveness?"

"Protective, perhaps," she allowed, punctuated with an eye roll, "Although that might even be a stretch of the imagination, let alone vocabulary."

"And do I need to be *protected* from the likes of Edith Carson?" He was laughing at her, she knew, but didn't mind in the least.

"Yes," she chortled. "I believe you do."

"I'm sorry Edith was rude durin' your meetin'; there was no call for poor conduct. She may have once had designs I was not aware of," Holt shrugged, "for my part, there was never anythin' in it. She was not for me."

"You have put all my anxieties to rest," Glenna said, resolute.

"Good, because I don't believe green is your color," he teased her. "It would seem we would have both been better suited stayin' home today." Glenna seconded Holt's sentiment.

"How was her sister, Patsy?"

134

"I cannot answer that honestly. The poor woman only said a total of four words in greeting before Edith railroaded right over any comment she could have made."

Holt gave a short chuckle. "Patsy might be the elder sister, but Edith has all the brash and brazen of the pair. I would have a great deal of trouble rememberin' the last time I heard Patsy say more than a full four words to anyone without Edith speakin' up for the both of them."

A new silence fell over them for a few moments, in which Glenna considered her feelings. Holt had answered her honestly when he said there was no one else he would have preferred to make an offer to. It didn't matter that Edith Carson may think otherwise. He hadn't given her any indication to the contrary and so did not deserve to be censured or upbraided.

"It will come in time, Glenna." Holt's words shattered the silence.

"What will?" She wondered.

"Trust between us."

Her first instinct was to argue with him. Protest the assumption that she did not trust him when she had displayed a lack of confidence in his word by asking him about his possible feelings for another. She bit her lip to keep from speaking untruths.

"It must have been hard fur ya, not bein' able to believe whomever it was in your past that made a practice of lyin'. I don't expect you'll believe much of what anyone says without actions to back it up." He was looking over at her. She knew the distinct feeling of his eyes on her.

"Am I that transparent?" Glenna felt her heart fall at his assertion regarding her past.

"Am I wrong?" he pressed.

"No," she whispered.

"All jestin' aside," Holt went on when Glenna didn't elaborate on her answer, "I aim to earn your trust and deserve it."

Seven

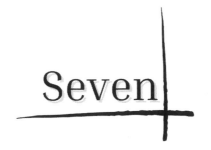

"Glenna? I didn't mean to interrupt you.'"

Glenna laid her pen aside and looked over at Holt, who had just come from upstairs.

"It's quite alright," Glenna waved off the show of concern. "It can wait."

She noted that he glanced over her shoulder to look down at the open journal briefly.

"You are almost out of pages," he observed.

"I keep meaning to look for another when we are in town, however, I often find myself distracted by other things." He gave her a knowing look at this comment.

"Why don't we go into town early, before the picnic starts and see about orderin' you one? Somethin' quality."

"Thank you. I would like that very much."

"It will also give you a bit more time to be social and the like."

"I think our last trip was quite enough socialization for now, don't you?" Glenna smiled, remembering the uncomfortable encounters of two weeks past that she was glad had not been happened again. Rachel and Patsy had been by for tea, thankfully without Edith, and there had been no sign of the Landry brothers.

Holt returned her smile. "You have me there."

"We do not need to make trips into town for either of us to be more social. I feel as if we have had no end to the sudden and unexpected drop by visits of well-wishers in the last month. So much so that I am quite certain to have met or taken tea with every last woman that lives in town and the surrounding ranches or farms."

Holt dropped his eyes a little and chuckled. "You have had to field a great deal of those visits alone, and I am sorry for that."

"Insignificant small talk does not seem to suit you, Holt. I doubt you would have welcomed the distraction those visits bring to the middle of a workday."

Glenna enjoyed how his responding smile reached his eyes, making the blue in them deepen with levity.

"With that being said, you came in with a purpose and I have distracted you from it," she went on.

"I'm not — I hope you don't — could be oversteppin' but," stammering, Holt stopped abruptly and ran a hand through his hair, leaving it ruffled. He seemed flustered in a way she hadn't seen as he tried to articulate his thoughts. The effort it was taking him to find the right words showed clearly on his face.

"I overheard your conversation with Finn the other day," he finally blurted out.

Glenna's brow furrowed. "And something that was said upset you?" She wondered what he could have overheard in any of their conversations that could have been weighing on him.

"Yes — no —" Holt quickly averted his eyes, as if looking directly at her would only lead to more stuttering. "Would you come up to the attic with me?"

Holt didn't wait for her to answer, turned and started up the stairs. Glenna followed. He was quiet while passing the children's

138

room where Daisy was napping and stopped to pull open the door that led to the attic storage area.

The attic space was only a small room with a single window on the far end where they both stood. Glenna let her eyes roam over the collection of old furniture and trunks that sat scattered around the floor. Holt stepped around a broken rocking chair and made his way to a large trunk sitting close by.

Glenna moved to follow him into the dimly lit room.

"I want you to have these," Holt stated, and bent to lift the lid on the trunk.

Glenna bent, lifting the linen that hid the contents from view. A dress, shawl, bonnet, and stockings lay with care atop what she could only assume would be much more of the same. Instantly, she lifted her gaze to find Holt looking back at her with a softness in his expression that made her catch her breath.

"Apparently, I am not as observant as a five-year-old." He smiled sheepishly. "Please take them and remake them to suit you."

"These were Gracie's things." It was not a question.

"Yes," he nodded, "And a few belonged to my mother before her. You're the lady of the house and now — they belong to you."

Glenna blinked hard a few times and stood, "Holt — I —"

"You aren't about to argue with me, are you?" he complained, arms folded over his chest.

She knew, of course, that Holt was being practical, just as he had when he showed her to the unused former bedroom of Clint and Grace. However, it was hard to recall the last time anyone had offered her anything of this kind. Here were functional items that would also bring her some comfort and ease. It was made even more meaningful that these items belonged to those he had cherished.

Holt let his arms drop to his sides and shifted his weight from one foot to the other. "I've offended you? I know it's — they are secondhand and if you'd rather have new — I just —" He was stammering.

Glenna moved a fraction of a step nearer to him, "Thank you," she said in a whisper. "I was going to say thank you."

"Oh!"

"I am honored that you would like me to have anything that once belonged to your mother or sister-in-law."

He suddenly looked even more uncomfortable than he had previously.

"Well — I'll leave you to it," Holt managed. "I'll be gone for the rest of the day, helpin' Theo find some missin' cattle." Glenna watched him go before turning back to the opened trunk.

He'd been worried about insulting her, and it had made him nervous. He had not been nervous when they had discussed the proposition of marriage. His nerves had not betrayed him at the altar. She wasn't sure she had ever witnessed him in such a state previously. What had caused this change?

He cares about how you feel.

The thought came as clearly to her mind as if it had been spoken aloud. It startled her a little. The idea that Holt could care about her feelings captivated her and sent a flutter rustling through her middle.

———————————

Seven short weeks… seven weeks had come and gone from the time Glenna had come into his life. He was amazed at the transformation Daisy had made in that time. His niece had put on much-needed weight under Glenna's care. She had also added new words to her vocabulary and every day she grew stronger.

Finn was also flourishing in her care. He had taken to his schoolwork under her supervision and was very proud of his accomplishments. Glenna was working with him on his letter and number recognition, something that started with his mother but had been lacking from the time of her death. Clint had tried to keep up with Finn's schooling as best he could during the evening hours and read to the boy every night, nonetheless Finn needed a dedicated teacher, and Glenna filled that roll effortlessly.

The boys had also taken a liking to Glenna aside her cooking and caretaking. Gunner and Decker acted as if she was a sister to them, seeking advice and always playful with her. Bowen engaged her in genuine conversation almost every evening. This surprised Holt as Bowen, although knowledgeable about a variety of topics, was usually a man of few words and little conversation. Hattie and Theo had, from their first meeting, been supportive and treated Glenna as family.

"Your mind is wanderin' off — it's back home. Isn't it?" Theo interrupted his musings.

"Sorry, Theo." Holt shook his head. Glenna seemed to always be in his thoughts, even when he was trying to focus on other things.

Theo laughed heartily. "It's alright, my boy. Ridin' out after my runaway milk cows doesn't make for a rivetin' conversation topic."

"I just have somethin' on my mind."

"You mean *someone*," Theo corrected.

"Is it that transparent?" Holt worried.

"You're bound to think of her."

Holt grunted at Theo's comment.

"Did — did somethin' happen between you two? Is that why you were so quick to come help today? You had to get away from home."

"I'm always willin' to help you, Uncle," Holt countered, then sighing, relented, "nothin' happened, but I did need to get away for a few hours. Clear my head."

"What has you so troubled, Holt? Is it the fact you find your feelin's are growin' for her or that you have them at all?"

"Feelin's?"

Theo tossed his head back and laughed, "It's clear as day, Boy!"

"This might make me sound like a madman, but even from our first meetin', I felt a connection. Somethin' inside me is drawn to her — I have a drivin' need to be around her —" Holt snapped his mouth closed.

Theo chuckled, "You should be talkin' to her, boy, and not me."

They rode in silence for a stretch before Holt asked, "How was it with you and Hattie?"

"Oh, I knew right away she was made for me," Theo said with conviction.

"How?"

"She told me so." Theo shrugged.

It was Holt's turn to laugh. "That sounds like Aunt Hattie."

"She strode right up to me, finger pokin' me in the chest and demanded that I stop pussy-footin' around and propose to her. I almost swallowed my tongue as I stuttered over my immediate agreement and attempted to rectify the oversight I had made in not proposin' to her already."

Holt was still laughing when he asked, "How long had you known each other by then?"

Theo spit and scratched his head. "Oh, about five or six weeks, I'd say."

Holt whistled, "Well, I guess when you know somethin's right, you just know."

"Yes, sir," Theo agreed, adding, "or if you are too slow to catch on, don't worry; womenfolk have ways to remedy it for ya."

Holt removed his hat, swept at his brow with a handkerchief, and shoved his hat back on. "What if — if it's one-sided?"

"Do you believe it is?"

"Feelins were never supposed to be part of the deal. Glenna — Clint — me — all of this was never supposed to happen."

"Holt, you know Clint would never begrudge you happiness."

"Uncle — I — anytime Glenna comes to my mind, all I can think of is how things would be if Clint was alive. She'd be his wife. It makes me think that — whatever is happenin' — that it shouldn't be."

Theo didn't answer for a spell, and the silence unnerved Holt even more.

"Livin' in the what if's of life is a sad and dangerous place to live. Ain't no good can come of it. I can't tell you what to do, my boy, but I stand by what I believe, and that is, Clint would want you to be happy."

"I don't know. Sometimes I think maybe she sees me the way I see her — other times she says things that make me think she regrets it wasn't Clint who answered the door that day. And what if," Holt paused, finding it draining to put his feelings into words, "What if it's all a matter of convenience, proximity, or availability?"

"You mean, you think you could be talkin' yourself into feelin' somethin' that isn't real because Glenna — is what? Easily accessible?" Theo said with a touch of indignation in his tone. "That ain't how love works, my boy. You can't talk yourself *into* or *out* of it. Either you fall in it, grow in it, or get slapped upside the head with it."

Holt gave an exasperated sigh. "Love — is that what this horrid feelin' is?"

"Better be. There isn't anythin' else in the world worth gettin' so worked up over."

Theo chuckled and reached across the space that separated them to give Holt's shoulder a sound slap. Then he added thoughtfully, "Life can set you on a path to a place you never imagined. This doesn't mean that you ain't endin' up right where you belonged all along."

Glenna surveyed the effects of her hard work in the mirror. The pale blush-pink skirt paired with a cream-colored blouse she had chosen to makeover for herself had turned out well and took little time as they needed the least alterations of all the items Holt had gifted her with.

Grace had been close enough to her height that nothing needed to be let down or taken up. However, Glenna had slightly shorter arms, so the cuffs needed to be altered and several inches leaner so the waist band had to be drawn in. Addressing these issues took up any spare moments she could scrape together.

The clothing needed no detail work, as the style was still in fashion. This made Glenna think that perhaps these items had been some of the very last Grace had made for herself prior to learning she was expecting Daisy.

Having to settle for her own well-worn shoes rather than the boots she had found in the trunk, as Grace had worn a smaller size that would only pinch at Glenna's toes, she was glad the skirt was long enough that it mostly hid her feet.

She turned, one hand pressed to her middle to quiet the butterflies that had taken up residence there, and nodded her approval at the overall effect. The tattered dress she had worn every day lay rumpled in a heap on the floor where she had stepped out of it thirty minutes earlier. Sighing, she moved to it, lifted and draped it across the back of a chair.

"We have been through a lot together, you and I, haven't we?" she said with an air of sadness. It had been an odd mixture of joy and hesitation as she dressed for the Harvest Festival.

The gray dress had been somewhat the same as a suit of armor to her. Tattered, dirty, worn, much too large for her, made from a sturdy material that had lasted her through many months of hard work, Glenna could always guarantee she could blend into the background wearing such a garment. She could fade away in it and go unnoticed, or so that is how it had been on the dank streets of New York.

Once she had arrived at Crossroads, the dress had become something else entirely. She knew when she was seen wearing the dress, as visitors stopped in or on trips into town, many of the looks she had been cast were ones of ridicule and judgment. Although most were kind and welcoming to her, she still felt a slight sting and had made a practice of never removing her apron or shawl whenever possible.

She knew, of course, becoming uncomfortable about her appearance in those instances was only brought into sharper focus by her insecurities, feelings that she had been plagued by in the months following her arrival to America, causing forced isolation.

Now, her hair freshly pinned, neck and face washed, and dressed in something that fit properly, Glenna had to admit that she thought she looked well. This made her more nervous than going out once more in her gray dress. There was only one good opinion she wished to procure: Holt's. The knowledge of it sent her emotions into a whirlwind.

"Auntie Glenna," Finn's light tapping came at the door, pulling Glenna from her thoughts.

Scolding herself mentally for being so silly, Glenna reached for her shawl and stepped to the door, pulling it open.

"Are we ready to go?" she asked.

"Seems so." Finn had dressed in what was his Sunday best shirt and set a comb through his hair. "You look pretty."

"Thank you." She offered him a warm smile. "Why don't you head down while I tend to Daisy before we leave?"

Finn dashed down the steps two at a time while Glenna turned toward the children's room to gather Daisy.

She hadn't expected to come upon Holt tying Daisy's bonnet into place and stood still, watching the sweet exchange. He was talking to her softly. "Well now, don't you look pretty?" Daisy reached both hands up, begging to be swept up into his arms. Holt obliged and gave her a hug before fully turning toward Glenna, who was standing in the doorway.

146

His eyes caught sight of her, and his forward momentum halted abruptly.

"I was just coming to dress her; it seems I am too late," Glenna commented nervously as the butterflies fluttered madly in her middle while Holt stared openly at her.

Drawing in a breath, one side of Holt's mouth twitched upward into a crooked half-smile, "You look — not that your Sunday dress isn't — or that you don't regular look —" He stumbled around the compliment. "You look very fine."

Glenna blushed. "You look very dapper."

She smiled as Holt glanced down, as if he had forgotten what he was wearing. It was impossible not to notice it's deep blue, bringing out the color in his eyes. "It's too nice for a work shirt and too bright to be proper for worship." He shrugged.

"Holt," Daisy added enthusiastically in her little voice.

"Let's show Auntie Glenna what we practiced with Finn." Holt addressed Daisy as he crouched down, placing her little feet firmly on the floor so she was facing Glenna. Slowly, Holt removed his hands as support and Daisy stood freely on her own.

Daisy teetered a little, arms out for balance, one foot shuffled forward a fraction of a step. Glenna dipped low and held out her hands. "That's it! Come on Daisy." Holt stayed where he was, hands at the ready in case Daisy started to tumble. With her round blue eyes locked on Glenna, Daisy took another wavering step in her direction, then a third.

Her little legs wobbled unsteadily, and Daisy tilted too far forward to stay upright. Glenna reached out, grasped Daisy before she fell flat on her face, and pulled her into an embrace.

"I'm so proud of you!" she exclaimed, placing a kiss on her soft cheek.

"She took a few steps for Finn. I expect we will have a runner on our hands any day now." Holt said warmly.

Glenna looked at Holt, still crouched down, their eyes level with each other over the top of Daisy's head. She felt a lightness in her limbs when he used words such as "we" and "our" including her in his statement in a way she hadn't expected. It was impossible to deny that she delighted in the way it sounded and the effect it had on her emotions.

"I suppose it's about time to head out." Holt stood.

Glenna followed suit. "I'll fetch the picnic basket," she said and handed Daisy to him, then, remembering an earlier thought, turned back to Holt. "Before I forget to ask you, would it be permissible for me to ask for one of Clint's shirts?"

Holt seemed to freeze, as if turned suddenly to stone. "One of Clint's shirts?"

"Yes. Finn mentioned that he would like a new Sunday shirt like his father would wear. I thought it would be fitting to make him one out of his father's things."

His stance instantly relaxed with her explanation. "I think Finn would like that." Nodding his approval, Holt walked to the trunk at the end of the single bed she knew had once been where his brother slept. "His things are still in here. Take what you'd like."

"If you wouldn't mind, I'd like it if you chose. It would mean more if it was a shirt his father favored, and I have no knowledge of such things."

"It's a very kind thing you would be doin' for him." He observed, pulling the lid open and rummaging through a few items.

"You and I both know what it is to lose a cherished parent. This is a small token… a way to keep those happy memories close." Glenna had thought about wearing her mother's broach, only worried it would be lost while dancing.

Shirt in hand, Holt turned to face her. "You do a great deal for the care and comfort of the children. I am grateful for it." He handed her the shirt, a red that was once a much deeper color, now faded and worn with time. Holt didn't relinquish his hold on it right away, the garment in a state of suspension between them, until she met his gaze. "I'm grateful for you as well."

———————

Daisy had already lulled herself to sleep in Glenna's lap from the swaying of the wagon as the wheels turned toward home. The little girl had been up long past her usual bedtime. The added excitement of the Harvest Festival had worn her out. Holt could tell by the sound of snores that Finn was also fast asleep in the bed of the wagon.

Finn had avoided being roped into dancing once the picnic was over by playing games with a few other school-age boys; while Daisy spent much of the evening bouncing on Hattie's knee, clapping happily to the music.

Glenna's shoulder collided with Holt's as the wagon wheel dipped into a rut on the road, throwing them both a little off balance. She pushed herself upright and attempted to hide a yawn.

"Tired?"

"It has been some time since I have been so wonderfully exhausted."

Holt looked over at her, able to make out her features clearly under the light cast by a full fall moon. "Wonderfully exhausted?"

"Yes." He could hear the smile in her tone. "One can be just ordinarily exhausted, mentally exhausted, or even emotionally exhausted. Why not wonderfully? I had a marvelous time," she added, punctuated by another yawn.

"I'm glad," Holt said with feeling.

"And you? Did you enjoy yourself?" Glenna asked just loudly enough for him to hear.

Her question brought to mind the disappointment he felt each time a song ended, as it meant Glenna would be pulled away from him to visit with someone new. Although he had been good on his word and made his way back to her side each time a new song was announced.

A smile touched the corners of his mouth, remembering how not once had Glenna shown signs of tiring, her smile as bright as it had been during the picnic, her steps as light as when the dancing had first started. He had relished the feel of her in his arms, her hands held in his.

"I did," Holt finally answered, clearing his throat.

He was sure a lifetime could pass and he would still remember the way laughter and merriment had sparkled in her eyes, cheeks rose-kissed from exercise, and dark auburn locks that escaped to curl about her face by the end of the night.

"I find myself once more indebted to you. It seems to happen so often that I feel as though the words, "thank you", are no longer enough."

Holt's brow furrowed. "There is no debt between us."

"Our arrangement was presented in equity, however, the scales have not been in harmony for some time. You and I are sorely out of balance, I'm afraid. I owe you more than can ever be repaid." There was a pause in which Holt heard Glenna let out a long breath. "It seems several lifetimes past that I have had an evening so carefree and full of levity, and although I am thankful for it, I am even more grateful for each quiet, pleasantly peaceful day in which we pass company."

Something in her voice tore at Holt's insides as if he was being clawed at, turning him inside out.

His mouth opened; silence followed.

"Before my arrival — before resolving to answer Clint's advert, I had not allowed myself to hope for such things as peaceful days."

"What had you hoped for?" Holt managed.

"I only wished that he would not be a cruel man… one that would raise his hands to me in anger." She paused as if to gather her strength to continue.

Holt stayed quiet, allowing Glenna the time with her thoughts without interruption as his mind had been sent whirling, analyzing each word. She had put her faith in a stranger, someone she knew nothing about besides a few lines scribbled on paper. She had traveled across the country to yolk herself to him, raise his children, and her only wish was that he wouldn't abuse her. Holt swallowed back sickness at the thought of anyone harming Glenna.

"Finding your brother gone — my circumstances not permitting my return East — the children — and *you*. Oh, Holt, can you not understand?" She was looking up at him, her eyes catching the glow cast from the moon. "When I agreed to marry you, to stay here — I had never dreamed of being treated so kindly. I thought perhaps you would be detached, unsympathetic, indifferent even. I would be tolerated because of what I could offer. That is a life I could have accepted without anguish or regret, one that made some sort of sense to me."

Holt's grip on the reins had become slack as he listened to her, unable to take his eyes from her. His team slowed only a little; eager to return home, they kept moving even without his guiding hand.

Glenna sighed, "You have instead — at almost every moment, proven my assumptions utterly wrong. You commented today that I do a great deal for the children and expressed your gratitude. It is I that should be grateful, and I am far more than I can express."

Finding his voice, Holt spoke, "You are givin' me too much credit." The words sounded feeble, even to his own ears.

"Words are just that in the end. Words. It is in someone's actions you learn who they truly are. You are not a cheat, or a liar, a drunk, or ruled by your temper. You are a good man, Holt Sterling."

The feeling of being torn asunder was suddenly replaced with something else, an emptiness that was deeper and filled with more inky blackness than any starless night. His grip tightened on the reins, and he looked back to the road.

"Not every pacifist is a good man. Just as not every man who drinks is a cheat or a liar, and every man has a temper." He ground his teeth together. "You need not fear that mine will be used to cause you or the children harm."

152

"I never meant to —"

"I know," he cut her off, "and I appreciate your thoughtful words. I am in a position to give what worldly goods you lack is all, bein' kind to another livin' soul is Christian and right. Our arrangement is intact; there is no imbalance between us." Holt snapped his mouth closed. He cursed himself silently as he felt Glenna stiffen in the seat beside him and shift slightly away from him to lean more heavily on the rail.

"I apologize if I have offended you." As she spoke, Holt felt a powerful twinge of sorrow.

Glenna had opened up, opened a door to him that held a glimpse into her feelings regarding her life at Crossroads, about how she possibly felt toward him, and he had effectively rejected it with one thoughtless statement, slamming the door closed. Would he ever be able to help her understand why? Or even understand it himself?

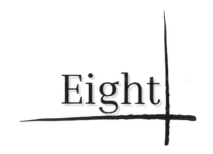

Eight

"We're goin' to have a storm," Theo said after sniffing the air.

Glenna glanced at him from her spot on the front porch, forgetting momentarily about the sewing in her lap. Hattie cast her eyes between the two of them and smiled knowingly.

"Theo believes he can taste the rain in the air."

Glenna looked out over the horizon. It was clear, the sky a light crystal blue without a cloud in sight.

"Don't trust your eyes, Glenna girl." Theo waved a finger at her, bringing her attention back to him. "It's going to pour." He punctuated this statement with a wink, and Glenna wasn't able to stop herself from smiling.

"Mind if I borrow Glenna for a minute?" Holt asked, stepping out onto the porch from the direction of the barn.

"Who are we to protest?" Hattie laughed and waved them both off, taking the mending from Glenna. Blu lifted his head and watched her, jumping to his feet when Glenna rose to hers.

"It's okay, Boy; you can stay here." She patted his head affectionately and walked down the porch steps.

"I wanted to walk you through a few things before the round-up starts," Holt explained.

Glenna nodded. "Of course."

"The boys and I will be leavin' in a week or two, dependin' on the weather, to bring the herd down from the mountain. I like to keep the cattle close to home for the winter months and calvin'," he explained, and she nodded her understanding.

Something had shifted after the Harvest Festival between them. Their day-to-day interactions still held the same easy manner as they worked with and around each other. The time spent with the children in the evenings or when everyone gathered around the supper table, all felt the same. However, she could feel a slight strain that hadn't been there previously that hung between them whenever she found herself alone with Holt, as if each of them had something very important they wished to say though continued to leave it unsaid.

"When we go, you'll have to take over milkin' the goat and cows. Finn can help carry buckets and pen Lady in the milkin' stand, but his hands aren't strong enough to do the milkin'."

"Milking —" Glenna repeated as if she had not heard properly what Holt had told her.

He stopped walking and turned to look down at her. "Yes, twice a day, every day, until we get back."

"How long will you be gone?" She asked, as if it had anything to do with the cattle and not her heart sinking in her chest.

Turning fully to face her, Holt planted his feet in a wide stance. "Depends on how scattered the herd is, mostly. A week — maybe longer."

Glenna swallowed.

"You aren't nervous about bein' here alone?" Holt asked, his blue eyes narrowing ever so slightly as he surveyed her. "I'll be sure to have Theo stop by to check up on ya." He went on, as if he had resolved any discomfort she might have. Holt nodded once, turned, and started toward the barn.

"I'd like you to teach me to shoot."

Her request brought another abrupt halt to his steps as he rounded on her.

She rattled on. "I was an excellent markswoman with a bow. I have a steady hand for it — I just need some basic instruction." Squaring her shoulders, she looked Holt straight on. "I have the right to know how to protect those I care for, don't I? To protect my home," she added.

"Yes, you do," he agreed.

"If we are to be left alone, I would prefer not to feel defenseless." She went on. It was clear she had given the topic some thought.

Holt's lip twitched. "No one that has ever known you would describe you as defenseless."

"Deflecting will not dissuade me. I am determined, and you are not the only man living here that knows how to shoot." Glenna raised her chin in defiance. "Shall I ask Bowen to instruct me?"

"I'm not opposed to the idea. Every frontier woman should know her way around a rifle, and no one but me will be teachin' you." His voice was authoritative.

"Alright, when?"

"Milkin' first," he said, tipping his hat in the direction of the barn with a teasing look.

"Milking first," she agreed.

"Come on. Finn has been waitin' for us."

She fell into step next to him and followed him to the side of the barn that faced the kitchen door. Glenna had, of course, become very familiar with the area as she and the children often found themselves with the chickens kept here, however she had never paid much attention to the structure they now approached.

"This is the milkin' stand," Holt said as he took the lead rope from Finn, who was standing waiting for them with patience far beyond his five years. The goat, Lady, as she was called, was a fine-looking white animal in contrast to her looks. She was ornery and had a temper. Up to this moment, Glenna had never wished to get very close to her. At their first meeting, Lady hit her so hard in the legs with her head to leave bruises.

Glenna watched closely as Holt led Lady onto the platform that made up the stand and toward the gate-like structure at one end. Once there, he made sure her head went through the opening. On the other side, a small feeding trough was attached with its bottom full of what looked like oats and molasses.

Holt slipped a secondary board into place at the top of the gate, effectively trapping Lady's head in place as she could no longer back out. Glenna was sure Lady did not mind, as she was no longer paying Holt any notice, nibbling away at the sweet treat.

"Once you get her into place, Finn can hand you the bucket." Before Holt was able to finish his sentence, Glenna felt Finn pushing the handle of the milk bucket into her hand.

"Now, pull up this stool and seat yourself at her side." He waited for her to get into place, making only slight adjustments to her placement. Glenna was aware enough to know where to place the bucket and did so without instruction. Holt leaned over her shoulder and demonstrated how to express the milk and direct the stream into the bucket.

Glenna placed her hands and tried squeezing and pulling. The stream of milk missed the bucket, skipping across the rim and splashed onto the hem of her dress, soaking it. Pursing her lips together, she tried again, this time working to angle the stream. Lady stomped her back leg at the same time Glenna pulled. The bucket tipped, dumping out what little it held right over the top of her boot. Finn giggled.

"Alright, Lady, let's give this another try." Glenna cooed in a soft voice while righting the bucket and starting over. Going slowly, Glenna began a rhythm. Lady calmed and stood still. Soon Glenna sat back, rolling her shoulders, and surveyed her work.

"You did well," Holt said. "Now let's see how you do milkin' a cow." She could hear the laughter in his voice.

The infernal cow had not only kicked at her twice, but during her last fit had landed her hoof right into the bucket, spoiling all the milk. Not appreciating her hoof trapped into a bucket she kicked out, the bucket, had been sent flying, spilling the ruined milk all over Glenna. The cow shivered and stomped, knocked into Glenna and sent her sprawling to the hay strewn ground.

Unable to contain it a small yelp escaped.

"You alright, Auntie Glenna?"

Opening her eyes, she looked up into Finn's and Holt's faces. "Yes, Finn, I am alright. That bloody beast has it out for me is the problem."

"Her name is Buttercup, and I'm fairly sure it's not personal for her." Holt laughed and held out his hand to help her back to her feet.

"You'll get the hang of it, Miss." Glenna heard Bowen's voice and knew that the audience to her humiliation had just widened.

"Yeah Glenna, don't let her best ya." Decker grinned.

Now returned to her feet, Glenna surveyed the damage.

"She won't get the best of me," Glenna muttered and picked up the milking stool, ready for another round. Everyone stepped back and allowed Glenna to retrieve the milk bucket, planting herself at the animal's side. "Alright Buttercup, let's do one more round of practice for today."

Petting Buttercup's flank, she warmed her hands and made another attempt, this time with firmer motions. The cow was used to having a man with much larger and stronger hands relieving the pressure built up from milk production, so Glenna needed to mimic this as well as she could. A jet of warm milk splashed into the bucket, then another; Buttercup swung her head to look at Glenna, made one half-hearted stomp of her back hoof, and went back to chewing quietly while Glenna finished the milking with no further troubles.

"We knew you would get the hang of it." Bowen grinned at her when she had turned to face what was now a crowd. Holding the bucket out for Holt's inspection, he relieved her of its weight. He, Finn, Bowen, Decker, Hattie, and Theo, holding Daisy, had all appeared in the barn at some point and now stood on all sides of her.

"I appreciate your vote of confidence, Bowen. I was less sure." She smiled back while picking straw from her hair and tossing it to the ground.

"What's everyone doin' in here?" Gunner called out from the barn door while leading his horse inside.

"Glenna was givin' us a demonstration on milkin'," Decker laughed.

"Sorry I missed it." Gunner grinned.

"Don't worry, Holt said shootin's next, and I don't think any of us would miss seein' that lesson for nothin'," Decker informed Gunner.

Gunner looked over at Glenna as she pulled odd strands of hay from her hair, and took in her milk-soaked appearance with a humorous sweep.

"Well, if it goes as well as it looks milkin' went, I'm sure we are all in for a great time."

"All right, all right, that's enough." Holt shook his head. "I'm sure if Glenna was teachin' you cusses how to cook an edible meal, we would all be laughin' at your expense instead." The group all chuckled and started to disperse.

"Hey Boss, I grabbed the mail while in town." He passed Holt a few large envelopes.

"Why don't you take this inside for Glenna?" Holt handed the milk to Finn, who started toward the house after Hattie, Daisy, and Theo. Bowen and Decker left with Gunner to unload the saddlebags and see to feeding and watering the animal.

He turned back to Glenna, "It will get easier over time."

She looked at him. "I didn't mind the teasing."

"I wasn't talkin' about the boys." He stepped closer to her, stuffing the envelopes into his front shirt pocket as he did, and took her left hand into both of his. Until his touch stopped the motion. She hadn't noticed she had been kneading her hands tightly together. Holt set to work on the tender muscles her palm, down each finger, rubbing out the soreness and cramps that had formed. Letting go of her hand, he took up her right and started the process over.

"I was foolish to think my hands held any sort of strength up to now. How you do this twice a day every day is a wonder."

His fingers were still working away at her palm. Looking up at him, she found his eyes on her face. The pressure of his fingers on her hand wavered as his eyes caught hers.

160

Her ear, more keen, caught the sound of his breath. Or was it her own that sounded so short and raspy?

He grunted and abruptly released her hand. "We'll leave shootin' for another day."

"Of course." Glenna rushed to leave the barn and the heat of the barn for the much more comfortable climate and fresh air found outside. Halfway to the house, she realized she had been holding her breath and clutching her hands together tightly, her skin still warm and tingling from the contact.

Holt thoughtfully touched the stack of letters in his pocket and, letting out a heavy sigh, made up his mind. Supper was over, the evening chores had been taken care of, and the children would be down for the night. There was no putting it off any longer. It was time to do what needed to be done.

"Night boys, " he called out to no one in particular and turned his footsteps toward the house.

"Tell Miss Glenna good night from the rest of us, won't ya?" Decker grinned.

"She doesn't want to hear any sweet talk from the likes of you, Decker." Bowen laughed and tossed a handful of fresh hay in Decker's direction.

"Tellin' someone kind to ya to have a peaceable night ain't sweet talk." Decker snorted in protest.

"Even if you did try sweet talk on her, it would do no good. Miss Glenna only has eyes for the boss." Gunner put in his two cents from the hayloft while leaning on his pitchfork.

Holt knew all three men were now looking at him. "You ugly cusses better get done with the work and catch some shut-eye. Tomorrow is goin' to come fast and we can't burn daylight."

"That ain't a denial." Gunner noted, grinning.

Holt didn't respond, pushing open the barn door and left the three hands to their speculation.

Blu yipped at his heels. "Come," Holt commanded, Blu padding along at his side.

The walk to the house seemed longer than usual, and he could smell the rain in the air; the ground would be soaked by morning, he was sure. When he reached the porch, Holt hesitated. Feeling a peculiar kind of tiredness he wasn't able to explain, he sank work-weary bones into a chair, giving himself time to think of how to approach the topic with Glenna.

Blu sat near Holt's side, seeming to feel the tension pulsating from his master. The dog cried a little in a low whimper. Holt patted his head. "It's okay, boy."

Sitting there, he felt the weight of the letters in his shirt pocket as if it was burning a hole right through it and leaving him scorched. The heaviness had increased with every passing hour as he agonized over what to do with them. Had it only been earlier that day that the mail had been handed to him? Or that he had first laid eyes on their contents?

Feeling as though it would be better off as kindling for the fire, the heavy envelope left his pocket and appeared in his hand. Turning it over to look at the address, he reassured himself it was, in fact, from the same inquiry agent Clint had employed to contact Mr. Perry's solicitor. There was no doubt. Finally deciding on his course of action, Holt started to slip the letter back into his shirt pocket.

"I apologize. I thought I heard Blu Dog; I did not mean to interrupt your letter reading." Glenna had stepped out onto the porch and, catching sight of Holt so engrossed, had started to retreat into the house.

"Don't leave," Holt called her back.

Glenna allowed the screen door to shut behind her as she pulled a shawl closer around her shoulders. She hesitated, walked to the seat opposite him so they would face each other. Blu instantly jumped up and moved to sit at Glenna's feet. He was rewarded with a friendly scratch behind the ears before curling himself as close as he could get to her and laying down, head resting on his paws.

"Is something bothering you?" she asked, concern etched into her delicate features.

Resolute, Holt cleared his throat, "On the day you arrived you offered up the letters from Clint as evidence of the truth of your story. I declined them. Now I feel that I should tell you I found the correspondence you sent to my brother and have read your early letters to him." He waited for her reaction.

There was none. Her face didn't show any sign of misgivings at his news.

Holt reached across the space that separated them and held out the stack of letters to Glenna. She looked from his face to the letters and slowly reached to accept them.

"At first, it was just a means to understand, Clint — and you. After a time, I realized somethin'. There ain't nothin' in these that I cannot learn from the woman herself. I much prefer that method myself."

"I prefer that as well," she answered softly, not lifting her eyes to meet his.

"There's somethin' else." A letter appeared from his shirt pocket, and he held it out for her to take. "It's addressed to Clint. It took some time to reach us out here and just arrived today."

Glenna placed the old letters in her lap, took the one Holt now offered, and lifted her eyes to his. "Has its contents upset you? You do look as if something is weighing on your mind."

"It's contents — I haven't inspected all of it. The first few lines held enough for me to decide the letter rightly belonged to you." He said, unable to take his eyes from her face. She looked uncertainly at the thick parchment before pushing back the broken seal and opening the letter.

A smaller, tightly folded letter that had been placed inside the larger correspondence fell out into her lap as she did so. She ignored it. Holt watched closely as her eyes roamed over the parchment. Keenly aware of the almost imperceptible change as it swept over her. The line of her lips becoming thinner and the controlled intake of a deep breath betrayed her tenuous emotions to his watchful eye.

Not finishing the letter or bothering to look at the second one, she hastily folded it back inside the first and let her hands drop to her lap with a defeated sigh.

"I didn't know Clint had — that he had sought out such in-depth information regarding my family's past."

"I knew he had secured the services of an inquiry agent from some of the things I found after his death. I didn't know why," Holt admitted.

Glenna finally lifted her eyes to meet his gaze. She had a look of determination on her face he had never seen her express. She held out the letter for him to take.

"He went to a lot of trouble to gather this information. It might as well be of some use — to someone."

"What use is it to me?" Holt questioned, not bothering to take it from her.

She blinked a few times and cocked her head to one side, as if trying to understand something very perplexing.

Taking the letters from her lap and setting them aside, she stood, rousing Blu, and walked a few paces away from Holt. The dog followed and once she had stopped, eyes locked some place in the distance, Blu sat next to her, ever vigilant and protective.

"There is no doubt in my mind of what is contained in those letters. They most likely weave a very heady tale of a man who inherited, upon the death of his grandfather, by all accounts, a very large estate, with it all the wealth and privilege connected to becoming a landowner. It will go on to tell the reader that he was soon married, most advantageously, to a woman with a sizable dowry.

"They would have a single child, a girl. In her youth, the girl would lose her mother very unexpectedly to a sudden illness. After which the daughter would be reminded daily what a disappointment. It was she had not been born a son. Without the right of inheritance, she would be left to the murices of a good match if one could be made. Only a dowry to call her own."

Holt watched Glenna pull the shawl tighter around her shoulders as the night air brushed past her; small tendrils of hair that had once been put up neatly now danced at the nape of her neck and brushed her cheeks.

"The child grew, and lived what seemed a very charmed life—for a daughter, the very best finishing schools, the kindest nurses and governesses, the most fashionable dresses, lovely holidays spent in pleasant diversions and frivolity, all the while, not knowing she was living in her father's lie." Her voice had gone hard and emotionless.

"A father should love his wife and children above all other things. This man did not love either. He only had a stomach for drink, and an eye for speculation, cards, and the heavy perfume of dimly lit rooms where men put their livelihoods on the table, making them reckless and foolish with the thought of winning." She shivered slightly now as the breeze rushed between them. Holt felt a heaviness settle into the pit of his stomach.

"The passages in those letters will recall how this man lost everything, no doubt. Wealth first, over time as it dwindled, he would place his future and that of his daughter on a wager. His lands, holdings, inheritance, house, all gone. All the while, his daughter was kept blissfully unaware."

Holt's eyes didn't stray from Glenna as she talked. Her face was lifted high, her gaze locked on some distant point in the darkness that had fallen so completely, the night so black it seemed to have swallowed the distant mountain peaks; their only light came from inside the house, spilling out of the window to splash onto the porch and turn everything it touched a muted imitation of its daytime counterpart.

Holt hated the pain he could hear in her voice when she started to speak, wishing he could erase it from her tone. However, he did not comment, making no attempt to stop her from continuing.

"There was a letter sent to the daughter as she was away from home on holiday with a dear friend visiting London for her first time. This letter painted the most beautiful and intoxicating descriptions one could imagine of an adventurous expedition with her father.

"The lines beckoned her to return from London with haste, as they would depart almost immediately. All the proper arrangements had been made, and before she knew it, she had been whisked away on a grand adventure. That moment, the cusp of her seventeenth year, would be her very last of proper innocence." Glenna flinched as if she had been struck, then rushed on, anger now lacing her words.

"He had panicked when the debts had been called in, debts he could not pay because the fortune was already gone. This coward ran, taking his child with him, only to die on the journey across the North Atlantic, leaving her destitute — alone — friendless, at the mercy of strangers, and headed to a foreign country."

Glenna folded her arms over her middle, the shawl slipping from one shoulder went unnoticed. "That is what information Clint sought when he contacted my father's solicitor. That is the sad story of *my* family."

"That is not where your story ends," Holt ventured quietly.

She laughed, a laugh full of raw emotion, biting at the edges, "You are very right Holt, my story did not end there. You see, I had the education for the life of a Lady and no practical skills for the life I had been left to."

Holt left his seat and moved to close the space between them. Blu didn't give up his claim on Glenna and stayed close to her, "Glenna, I didn't mean to upset you."

Glenna sighed heavily. She lifted her eyes to meet his gaze, "No, of course, you did not. That kind of cruelty isn't in you." Her eyes fell away from his with a forlorn look. "I should not have tried to hide my family's dealings from Clint... or from you, and perhaps he wouldn't have felt the need to seek it out. I am ashamed. For you to find out in this manner, only turns me into a liar as well. No better than my father. I should have known his disgrace and ruin would forever follow me, no matter how I try to leave it behind."

No longer able to stand the hurt he saw in her eyes, Holt reached out and grasped her by the arms, turning her, forcing her to face him. "You are no more your Pa than I am my brother. We each make our own choices."

"If that is true, why did I have to pay for my father's? Each family member takes part in the ruin of a family member so I could not return home — if there had been something to *return* to. I would have been shunned by all who knew me, cast out, and as alone there as I was here." She looked pale and drawn. Her lips quivered slightly.

"Did Clint's inquiry agent know that my father hung himself like a coward from the handrail of our ship, I wonder? Did he mention that our passage was not paid for when we boarded, and I was propositioned very improperly by the captain to *pay* for my continued presence on the ship now that my only protection was gone? Does the letter contain that it took every bit of my father's belongings and many fine pieces of my jewelry to subdue his lust and secure my safety? Do the lines on that paper speak of those things? What an end my father's choices had led me to?"

"Glenna... " Holt felt sickened by what he had just heard.

"You may as well know the rest," Glenna shuttered under the pressure of his grip, and Holt realized he was still holding her forcefully in place. His grip loosened, though he did not remove his hands from her arms as she continued, "I found a boarding house that

168

would take me. I had to barter the last of what I had been able to keep, the very clothes I wore. Faster than I dreamed possible, all I owned was gone. I held back only one piece, my mother's broach.

"I begged for work in order to not be cast out on the street. I knew what other girls were doing. Selling their flesh for the amusement of men. I was never able to even contemplate resorting to — I could not bring myself — even as starvation loomed." She paused as a shutter ran over her, either from the cool night air or the memories he wasn't sure, the action made Holt want to draw her into him and hold her until the shutters stopped. Until the memories had been forced from her mind for good.

"Instead, I sold the only thing I could in good conscience, my ability to sew. It wasn't enough to sustain me in the boarding house and I found myself in a poor house… my time there is best forgotten. Those skills I did not possess I learned by taking any job I could: cook, laundress, maid; it didn't matter the hours or the pay as long as it was honest. I lived like that until I could earn enough to once again find a room in a slightly more respectable place."

She turned her face away just as he saw moisture glistening in her eyes, glinting in the dim light. "This, of course, led to more opportunities, and I was able to work in the boardinghouse kitchen. I learned every useful thing I could and saved up for the day I would leave. I hired out on my off-hours to local shops and ladies who needed mending done or children tended. All I wished was the chance at something better — then the ghost of my father found me."

"How do you mean?" he wondered as she pulled out of his grasp.

"I had come of age to inherit my dowry, a modest future set aside by my mother's family in my name upon my birth. It would be mine to lay claim to upon my nineteenth birthday, preceding that event, it would have been kept out of the clutches of my father." Glenna let her head drop a little, "It seems that in one way or another we all suffer and pay for the mistakes of others. Anything that wasn't lost in his gambling was sold off after his death, still it was not enough.

"Shortly after receiving word of the dowry, I was contacted by my father's solicitor regarding his debtors, and they were kind enough to relieve me of the inheritance. With it gone, so were my prayers for a better life. My hopes had been shattered. Dreams dashed. Each gray day melted into the next as time slipped by in a fog. Then one day, as if by a miracle, I saw Clint's advertisement, and there was salvation in it."

Looking suddenly right at Holt, she gave him the saddest of smiles. "Can you now understand my feelings when Theodore pulled up to *this* place? To *this* house? It was heaven on earth to me. More wonderful than any description your brother had given during our correspondence. My need to stay overwhelmed all rational thought. I couldn't allow you to send me away — to send me back." Holt had to restrain himself from reaching for her a second time.

Glenna looked toward the mountain range in the distance.

"I have felt safe here, under this roof. This place is filled with laughter and happiness. The daily reward of hard work and honesty. You were very blessed to have the parents you did. To have your brother, whatever his faults may have been. I cannot help but envy you, Holt, and the life you have led."

Holt willed his mouth to open, to express his sorrow for the trials she had suffered, to tell her that he would never judge her for the actions of another, that he admired her determination and strength. He wanted to argue with her and tell her there was nothing to envy

170

because she too could make this place her home, that he wished nothing else except to have her as his wife in more than name only, and that he also had secrets in his past, things he wished had never happened. With so many thoughts racing through his brain, he found it nearly impossible to form anyone thought into a coherent sentence.

Glenna moved suddenly, walking back to where she had left the letters and gathering them up, including the one Glenna had refused to open. She held them out to him. "Please. These do not belong to me. I want nothing to do with them."

This time, he allowed the letters to be placed back into his hands.

Blu suddenly lifted his head, looked in the direction of the house and whimpered.

"Daisy must be awake," Glenna whispered and patted Blu softly. "Good boy." She turned slightly, as if to leave. Her delicate face turned upward, catching the light from the window, making her dark, mesmerizing eyes dance, as a ghost of a smile crossed her lips.

"Goodnight, Holt," she whispered and was gone.

Holt stood, feeling desolate, staring at the spot he had last seen her long after the sound of her footfalls had dissipated into the cold night air, only to be replaced by the sound of the soft patter of rain as it started to fall. Holt felt a suffocating tightness in his chest at the thought of what Glenna had just revealed, of all that she had been through, and a more primal urge to ease her pain. Turning over the letter, she had yet to open, Holt dragged his thumb over the wax seal.

Glenna sat in the rocker, holding Daisy, who was finally calm enough to drift off into slumber, while listening to the sound of the promised rain pouring down outside. She had found a strange kind of solace in cradling Daisy close to her as she fought back the torrent emotions raging inside of her, as if the little girl brought healing to her fragile heart.

It wasn't until Daisy had started to fall back into a peaceful sleep that tears stung the backs of Glenna's eyelids. All the things she had tried to rid herself of had found her, followed her across the distance. She hated her father for all that he had done and now hated herself for still allowing it to harm her—anew.

A new ache was welling up inside her breast. As the hours turned into days that passed into weeks, she found it even more impossible to imagine what her life would have been like if she hadn't been brave enough to answer the advert. Being with Daisy and Finn, the playful banter of the cowhands, visiting Hattie and Theodore, being in company with Holt, it all seemed like a dream. One that she would surely wake up from.

There had been firm footing when Clint had offered her his hand, a future. Suddenly there was nothing — nothing turned suddenly into marriage to another.

She had formed attachments to the children — to Holt. Her feelings betrayed her even now, as the very thought of him sent her heart racing. It was always quickly followed by sharp disappointment. And now? Now, what would he think of her? Would she ever be anything other than the disgraced daughter of a drunk gambler?

Daisy snorted and moved restlessly in Glenna's arms. Glenna lifted her and placed her back into her crib. She pulled the covers back up over her and checked on Finn before slipping out of the room.

The house was quiet, aside from her movement. Grateful, she retreated to the safety and solitary space of her empty room. Lighting a lamp, Glenna drew near her desk, ready to let all the turmoil of her feelings out into the pages of her journal, when a slip of paper caught her eye.

Placing the lamp on the tabletop, she lifted it.

> *Glenna,*
> *This belongs to you, and I am honored to restore*
> *it to its rightful place.*
> *Yours,*
> *Holt*

Her fingers trembled as she reached for the letter, laying with the seal now broken. The moment it was lifted, something slipped from it, wrapped in plain brown paper. Glenna took it up, laying the letter aside, and unwrapped it slowly.

"It can't be!" she breathed.

Glenna collapsed into the chair, grasping at the locket with both hands and pressing the treasure to her breast. The chain was impossibly thin, the oval shell inscribed with tiny roses. So many memories flooded through her mind at the sight of it.

Sucking in a breath to steady her hand, she opened the locket and stared in wonder at the miniature portraits of her mother and father.

The images were impossibly small yet captured them both so beautifully, her mother's lovely, delicate features and her father's handsome face. Tears blurred the faces momentarily and Glenna brushed the away with a brush of her fingers. How was it at all feasible? Eager now, she fumbled with the letter in her haste to read its contents.

April 12, 1884

Mr. C. L. Sterling,

I have received word from your inquiry office regarding one Miss Glenna Eleanor Perry and am sending word in return via the same office you have procured to research the matter.

I had the great pleasure of working with Miss Perry's family for nearly thirty years, first for her maternal-grandfather and after her mother and father. Her mother did indeed die suddenly when Miss Perry was very young. The death of his wife left her father, Louis Perry, a bitter and broken man who found solace at the bottom of a bottle and often at the gamblers' tables.

As you can imagine, that style of living is not sustainable and Mr. Perry lost all that had been left to him or inherited upon his marriage. I advised Mr. Perry to economize, and in time, his debts would be paid off, leaving something for his daughter to live off of when he was gone. As you must already know, he did not take my advice.

Over the years that followed the death of her father, I have often wondered what became of Miss Perry. My only contact with her was very brief, just after she became of age to inherit the dowery left by her mother's family. Sadly, that too did not end well, and I lost contact with Miss Perry, after which it was

174

rumored that she had been found in a poorhouse. I
am pleased to know she is alright and in your care.

It is my hope that you will be so kind as to pass
this small memento on to her. It was entrusted to me
by her father shortly in advance to their departure as
a safeguard that it would once again be returned to
its rightful owner.
Cordially,
Mr. S.C. Lyman, Solicitor

Could it be true? Her father had ensured the locket was returned
to her. The idea softened her a little to his memory. Had he known
she would one day need it and the comfort it would bring to her? The
man had not been as selfish and heartless as she had believed him to
be. He had thought of her in this one instant at least, and for that she
was thankful.

The strength Glenna had been clinging to faded as the air seemed
to rush from the room. The letter and locket lay forgotten on the
tabletop as a wave of emotion overtook her. Standing, she paced
back and forth until no longer able to bear another moment trapped.
She turned and fled from the room, only to slam right into the solid
wall of Holt standing right outside her door.

"Oh!" His hands reached out to catch her as she stumbled
backward a step and held on as she regained her balance.

"I'm sorry," he whispered. "I wasn't tryin' to startle you."

Glenna felt her throat close, and she was unable to speak.

"I heard you restless and thought maybe you'd need —"
Whatever Holt was going to say was lost as Glenna started to sob in
earnest.

Holt stepped closer, pulling her to him, cradling her in the circle of his arms, grief and sorrow pouring from her.

"Shhhhhh, it will be alright," he hushed.

"It was easier to hate him. To believe him every evil thing. I can't reconcile the man that took his own life rather than face his wrongs with the man who saved that locket."

"It is possible for a man — any man to have made mistakes once thought unforgivable, to change — to grow — to seek forgiveness." Holt's words seemed to reach her and the tears lessened some.

"The idea of change is splendid to imagine. How many times have I wished he could have exhibited the strength needed to be a real father to me, yet I never saw it — never experienced it. After my mother died, he sent me away, and he became a fleeting figure I shared a physical resemblance to, nothing more. He was always passing me on to someone for a holiday, so he didn't have to be responsible for my care." She choked back another sob, holding onto Holt for support as her knees grew weak. "Why? Why did he abandon me? Why wasn't I enough to fight for?"

"I'm sorry he wasn't strong enough to be there for you." Holt silently cursed a man he had never met.

"He and I are more alike than different, for I am not as strong as I pretend to be," she cried.

"No one is; we just strive to be, I suppose," he muttered next to her hair.

"You are," passing a hand over her face to remove the last of her tears, Glenna pulled back from Holt, not breaking the full circle of his arms yet no longer clinging to him as she had.

The lamp, still burning low in her room, cast its light into the hall and over his features.

176

"You are the most honest and genuine person I have ever met. That is strength beyond strength, to be holy yourself with no airs."

Holt abruptly dropped his arms from around her. "Glenna — I'm just a man tryin' to be better today than I was yesterday."

Going from the warmth of his embrace to the coolness that accompanied the absence of his touch made Glenna shiver as they stood, not speaking as she attempted to gather herself back together.

"Thank you for leaving the letter for me. It means a great deal." She managed to say after a time.

Holt nodded, and she watched him shifting his weight from one foot to the other uncomfortably.

"I'm quite all right now." Glenna whispered, willing it to be the truth.

"Goodnight, Glenna." Holt shuffled backward into the hall.

"Goodnight," she whispered back as he pulled her door closed behind him. Glenna took a few steadying breaths, sinking onto the edge of the bed. Thoughts of her father, mother, her life at Crossroads, and Holt danced inside her head. Too much had transpired, too much to process. Sleep would not come easily.

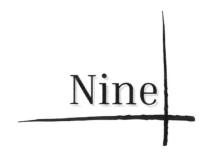

Nine

"Are you goin' to fill us in, Glenna?" Decker asked as soon as everyone had sat down at the table.

"Fill you in?" she asked with one eyebrow raised, knowing full well what he was referring to.

"Yes, we've all been waitin'," He insisted.

Glenna gave a knowing smile and took a mouthful of potato soup, chewing slowly rather than answering.

"Oh! This is maddenin'! Holt won't tell us nothin' and now you are stonewallin'. I knew one of us should have come out with ya." Decker tore apart a biscuit and dipped it one chunk at a time into the stew, sopping up the broth, then shoving it into his mouth.

"He's not wrong," Gunner commented. "We've all wondered how the shootin' lesson went, and Holt here hasn't said one word."

"It went well," Glenna answered, feeding Daisy a few carrots and potato chunks.
The three hands had gone quiet, and all eyes were on her.

"Well now, that wasn't much of an answer," Bowen laughed.

Glenna spooned out a little more for Daisy and gave a little cough. "I outshot him."

"I'm sorry — did she just say?"

"I outshot him," Glenna said again with fervor.

178

Bowen's upper lip twitched. Gunner was grinning from ear to ear. Decker who outright laughed, slapping his knee.

"Serves him right for forcin' you to sit through two days of safe gun handlin' before even gettin' a chance," Bowen laughed.

"Hey now! In my defense, you can't teach anyone to shoot when it's pourin' outside like the end of days. Sides, she wanted to learn to shoot; safe gun handlin' is a necessary part." Holt protested.

"I feel like I need more details," Decker pressed.

Holt put his spoon down and sat back in his chair. "Glenna has a keen eye. She was able to hit the target — dead on — every time."

Glenna shook her head almost imperceptibly. "None of today's targets were moving, so it's hardly a fair assessment of my abilities. As I have said, I had years of practice with a bow, and although a rifle is different, the idea of lining up a target is primarily the same." She rolled her shoulders a bit and took another bite of her supper.

"I'm guessin' the bow doesn't have the kick a rifle has," Bowen smirked.

"Only the first few rounds got the better of me. After the proper adjustments, my shoulder was fine."

"Can we all come next time, Uncle Holt?" Finn asked, looking up from his supper for the first time since grace had been said.

Holt reached over and ruffled his hair. "Why? You wantin' to see Glenna best all four of us?"

"You think she'll outshoot all of you?" Finn asked with clear skepticism.

Glenna acted as though she didn't notice the way Holt glanced over at her or that all sounds of eating had stopped at the supper table.

"I think Glenna is capable of anythin' she puts her mind to."

"The roads are dried out a good bit and packed well enough to hitch the wagon for a supply run. How does a trip into town sound?" Holt asked as he stomped the snow from his boots after stepping into the kitchen.

"A welcome distraction," Glenna greeted him warmly. "I'll get the children bundled."

"I'll hitch up the wagon and be back for you."

Glenna hurried to ready Daisy and Finn for the ride into town, and rushed to pull on her shawl.

The trio stood at the front door, Blu joining them when Holt pulled the wagon to a stop. Jumping down, Holt dashed to help Glenna load Finn into the wagon box, then gave her his hand.

Soon Daisy was fast asleep, and Finn occupied happily with Blu. It was the opportune time to discuss her plans for the children.

"I've been meaning to speak to you. I was wondering, did Grace or your mother keep a sewing box? I can't seem to find even a simple needle and thread in the house. My meager supply has been taxed to the point of extinction since my arrival."

He seemed to think over the question. "Both my mother and Grace did fine needlework, but if I remember correctly, the sewin' box my mother kept went to Hattie when — when Clint needed patchin', he took his things to her from what I remember."

"I suspected as much. Would it be permissible for me to pick out some spools of thread? I'm at a standstill working on that project we spoke about before the Harvest Festival."

Holt stiffened next to her. "Are you askin' my permission?"

"I suppose I am. I've already exhausted my funds. Perhaps a small stipend could be considered?"

"Good heavens, Woman!" The effect of his tone had Glenna clamping her mouth closed with a snap; Daisy whimpered in her sleep. Glenna set to work calming her as Holt went on in a much softer voice. "Have you forgotten you're my wife?"

She looked over at him quizzically. "Of course not."

"You never need to ask permission for those things needed to run your household as you see fit. Askin' permission makes me feel like a tyrant. Have I made you feel all this time that you couldn't ask for things you needed? Things for the house, the children, or yourself?"

"No," Glenna sputtered.

"This is my fault. I'll admit my oversight at not noticin' your need for a few extra dresses and things until I heard Finn askin'." Holt shook his head, scolding himself.

"Holt, please."

"There will be no more talk of stipends," Holt went on. "You aren't a nursemaid, Glenna. You're a Sterling, the children's aunt, and *my* wife. That means you are entitled to everythin' that involves. Isn't that what you expected of Clint? A home, a family, and all that comes with it?"

Glenna blinked rapidly, taking in the full force behind his words.

"I have no idea what being a wife involves," she admitted softly before rushing on. "Tending to the children is easy. Their needs are clear. The housework is simple to understand: cook, clean, tend to what needs tending. Being a wife — that is complex beyond comprehension.

"You and I, we share space in the house, yet nothing beyond that. I am still desperately attempting to gain my footing, in this place, by your side, and what any of it means to myself or to you. " She stopped, remembering the feeling of his strong fingers working the soreness from hers after milking, the pressure of his skin on hers, the way he had held her as the walls she had built crumbled into sobs, the multiple tender and thoughtful gestures that had kept her up with thoughts of him.

How it all tossed her emotions into fits of confusion as she tried to interpret their meanings. Biting her lip, Glenna pushed the thought aside. There was enough confusion in her own emotions. She didn't need to wonder about Holt's.

It was his turn to stay mute as she rushed on softly. "I do not think you are a tyrant, Holt. Quite the opposite, in fact. As I have previously stated, you are a good man. I will be more open in the future in my requests."

Holt stayed quiet, his jaw clamped shut as he set to work grinding his teeth. Glenna could see the muscles tightening under the slight beard that had started to grow.

Not wanting to upset him, Glenna thought it best to keep the rest of her thoughts to herself. He had, after all, been avoiding the possibility of finding himself alone with her the past few days, as if he was afraid she would toss herself at him in the throes of an emotional break down. Something about the truths she revealed to him had put a wall between them. She did not understand how to deconstruct.

Was it possible he found her repulsive, or perhaps he now resented her for their abrupt marriage and his entrapment? Could she blame him if he did? After all, she had admitted to him that she would have moved heaven and earth to stay at Crossroads after arriving. How could she have acted so brazenly? So desperately? Glenna was sure he thought very little of her and the idea sent a painful wave coursing through her, filling her limbs with tension.

Soon enough, the wagon stopped outside Carson's, and Daisy was roused. Holt helped them all down and muttered something about needing to see the blacksmith.

182

"I'll be back soon; get whatever you need while I'm gone," He commanded without meeting her eyes. Glenna sighed and toted Daisy inside with Finn at her heels.

The warmth of the store's interior was pleasant and welcome.

"Well, good Monday mornin', Mrs. Sterling. Daisy. Finn," Mr. Carson greeted them.

"Good morning," Glenna nodded to him, then addressed Finn. "Would you like to get a basket?"

Once Finn had the basket in hand, Glenna went over the mental list she had made and gave Mr. Carson her request for oats, barley, and flour before she turned her attention to the small items on the shelves.

"Come, Finn, help me decide on thread colors."

Overjoyed to have something he could finally put into his basket, Finn skipped alongside her to the corner of the store that housed the sewing items.

The bell over the front door rang, and a gaggle of townswomen entered the store. Glenna could hear them, though, was obscured from their view by the shelves that separated the sewing items from the larger open floor of the store. The party stopped near the soaps and perfumes, chatting merrily.

"Do you have a preference?" she asked Finn, indicating the small selection of thread colors.

"Brown, maybe?"

"Brown would be just the thing. Thank you, Finn." She handed him the spool. "I'll need white —" She placed another spool in his hand.

"What about buttons?" he asked, looking at the display.

"No, I have buttons to use. I do need a new needle and thimble. Would you be able to find the thimbles? I need a few to choose from. A thimble must fit properly." Finn nodded and started to rummage for thimbles. Once he chose a few he thought suitable, Finn presented them to Glenna. She shifted Daisy into the other arm and took each one in turn to inspect them.

"This one is perfect! You did a very good job," she reassured the boy.

"May I pick out a taffy now?" Finn grinned at her.

"One." She nodded, and while swinging his basket, Finn skipped off to the front of the store and Mr. Carson's sweets counter.

"— poor Holt. He looked quite put out just now." The woman's conversation rang out clearly in the space as her own conversation had paused.

"Well, why wouldn't he? With all the talk about his wife, I suppose he is regretting his choice very much indeed." Glenna stiffened, unable to stop herself from practically holding her breath in order to catch what might be said next.

"Talk?" another voice pressed.

"Oh yes! Well, I heard it from Marcie, who you know is a very reliable source, that while in New York, Glenna was a woman of ill repute — you know, a painted lady! Of course, Holt knew nothing about this when she tricked him into marriage."

Glenna felt the blood in her veins boil at the lie.

"Oh no, I don't believe that at all. Glenna has always seemed to be such a godly, Christen woman." Glenna felt a ray of recognition at the sweet voice of Rachel defending her.

"You can pretend to be anything if it suits you," one of the others retorted.

"Well, I don't believe it. It sounds like idle gossip to me."

"Oh, Rachel, you'd love to believe the best in everyone. On the other hand, what do you really know about her? About her past? Or her intentions?"

"What do you really know? What proof does Marcie have for that matter, and what right do you have to spread such damaging stories? I thought better of you, Edith Carson." Rachel must have

184

had enough of the conversation because, at that very second, Glenna heard rushed footsteps, and the bell over the door chimed.

"Well, there was no reason for her to storm off as she did," one voice accused with a hint of self-righteous indignation. She knew eavesdropping was wrong and she should move to make herself known, however, the next words spoken kept her frozen in place, as if held there by some mystical power.

"Even if Glenna is the picture of Christian femininity, she has to be some sort of ninny to have come all this way just to yolk herself to a gambling drunk." Edith's voice dripped with disdain.

"I thought you fancied Holt at one time, Edith." the other voice laughed and sounded a bit closer.

"When I was young and foolish. Now? I'd rather never settle down than marry someone silly enough to spend so much time chasing the bottom of a bottle as Holt Sterling did. It's no wonder Clint kicked him off the place."

Just as the last word left her mouth, Edith Carson appeared in Glenna's view. She stopped so suddenly that her companion, a woman Glenna had never met, ran right into the back of her.

"Edith! What on earth?" The second woman looked around Edith and caught sight of Glenna. Her mouth fell open into a silent gasp of horror, yet it was Edith's face that Glenna couldn't remove her eyes from.

Edith's had gone white at the sight of Glenna. Her lips trembled, moving as if she wanted to speak, yet was unable to form a sound. Glenna didn't lower her gaze or feel flushed with embarrassment. She stood tall, giving the two women a small smile and a nod her of the head.

"Lovely to see you, Edith. I do hope you are well." Glenna managed to keep her voice light and even. There was no point in allowing them to know they had been overheard, or that it had rattled her. She would regain power by kindness, not by slighting the other women.

"Glenna — I — we —" Edith finally managed.

"If you'll excuse me, I believe my shopping is done for the day." Giving the duo a second nod, she turned and walked to where Finn and Mr. Carson were haggling over the size of the taffy Finn would be taking home with him. The bell rang again, and more customers began to mill around the neatly stocked shelves.

"Would you add this to the total for today, Mr. Carson?" She handed him the needles, thimble, and thread.

"Of course. Did you see Edith? I believe she and a few other ladies slipped past me into the back. I'm sure she'd enjoy catching up with you while I finish calculating your total."

"I did see her. Thank you. Although, we will have to catch up later. The children and I need to make a stop at the post office. We will be back shortly to settle up the bill."

"Can I take the taffy now? Or do I have to wait until we come back?" Finn wondered.

"I'll remember to write down the amount. Take the taffy." Mr. Carson rumpled Finn's hair.

Finn grinned and accepted. Removing one glove, he took the taffy and started to bite off tiny bits, making the candy last as long as possible. Just as they made to pass through the door, Patsy pulled it open, almost running into Glenna.

"Oh! I am so sorry. I was in a hurry and didn't see you," Patsy apologized in a soft voice.

"It's quite alright, I was not paying attention." Glenna tried to sound much kinder toward the woman than she currently felt being with anyone. After all, it was not Patsy who had joined in on the gossip; it was not this sister that seemed to want to slander her name or that of Holt's.

186

Patsy stepped aside, leaving the path open for them to pass. "I hope you have a wonderful day." She gave Glenna a genuine smile, one that touched her eyes and lit up her face. Why was this sister so different?

"You as well, Miss Carson."

Glenna walked slowly toward the post office. The conversation she had overheard weighed heavily on her mind. She knew that if Holt had been the one to hear it, she would have wanted him to disregard the slander and gossip for what it was, yet those things said about Holt's past clung to her consciousness, unwilling to slip away or be pushed aside.

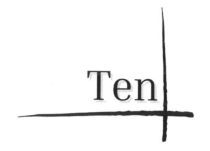

Ten

"What are you readin' with such interest?" Holt asked after watching Glenna from the doorway. She had been staring at the same piece of paper for minutes without moving.

"It's just an invitation for tea." The note was folded and placed in her apron pocket.

"From?"

"Rachel."

Holt noted the touch of sadness that crossed her face after the name had been spoken.

"You look upset. What could be so bothersome about an invitation from Rachel?" he worried.

"Nothing," she protested with an attempt at a smile.

He cocked his head to one side and eyed her. "Glenna."

"I think I have perhaps a touch of melancholy. It will pass." Glenna shrugged a little.

Blu barked happily as Finn squealed in delight in the yard, drawing both of their attention to the window for a minute. Holt looked back over at her; she was smiling at the scene, yet something in her gaze still spoke of sadness.

"There has been somethin' off for the last few days." As he said this, a realization came to him. "Something happened when we went to town, didn't it? Glenna, please, what is weighing on your mind?"

"It would do no good," was the only answer she gave.

Glenna stood, moved to the window, and watched Finn wrestle a stick away from Blu and toss it as far as his arm could throw. Holt watched this exchange from over her shoulder. She sighed heavily and leaned on the window frame.

"I don't believe I have ever cared for anyone as I do these children." The smile reached her eyes this time, and Holt was glad to see it.

"It's clear the feelin' is mutual," he said as his heartbeat sped up a fraction.

"Do you really believe so?" she asked with a quiet hope lacing the words.

"You bein' here — it's the first time since the death of my parents and since Grace left us that Crossroads has felt like home for any of us. For me especially," Holt said, looking behind where she stood to see Finn bound after Blu with relish, the dog now rushing away with the prize stick firmly clutched in his jaw. Giving up the chase, Finn sat on the edge of the porch, pulling off his hat to swipe at the beads of sweat that had formed on his brow.

"Have you hated it here so much?" Glenna asked softly.

Holt sighed and cleared his throat. "I remember my father buildin' that porch." He nodded out the window to where Finn was now happily swinging his legs off the edge. "Mother always wanted a place she could come to watch the sunrise and sunset each day. Between the two of them, this house, the ranch, the whole place was an act of love. They loved each other; they loved this land, and together they turned it into a home.

"Before I knew it, everythin' that signified this place as home to me was gone. Again, I felt the itch to be away, always workin', and the loss of Clint only compounded the feelin'. My childhood home was nothin' more than a graveyard. I didn't want that for myself or the children."

Holt felt the air rush from his lungs as Glenna turned from the window to face him.

"And now?" she whispered the question. His chest tightened as if a band had been placed around it.

"Now, it feels different with you here. There's laughter, light, and hope. You've changed this place and us for the better."

He wasn't able to pull his eyes away from her.

"You ready to head out, boss?" Gunner called from the kitchen.

Holt sighed, the spell broken. He stepped back from her. "I'll be right there," he called back, and the sound of the door banging shut rang through the space.

"I — um — wanted to check that you have everythin' you need before we head out."

"Yes, I believe we do," she said, her eyes not quite meeting his.

"You remember how to hitch the wagon?"

"Of course."

"Where the extra rounds are kept?"

"Yes."

"I should have made sure you had more firewood in case another cold snap hits." He slapped his hat against his thigh.

"Holt," she called his name as if waking him, "we will be alright. I promise." She punctuated this statement by meeting his gaze.

He nodded. "Well, I'd better go before we waste any more daylight."

"Be safe," she breathed, the sound of her voice making him hesitate. There was a long breath where neither moved. Coming back to himself, Holt took a few meaningful steps away.

"We'll be back in a week's time." He didn't wait to hear what she might have said, rather moved swiftly out the door and down the porch steps, shoving his hat on while he went.

"Uncle Holt!" Finn called out when he caught sight of him.

"Finn, you take care of Daisy and your Auntie Glenna while I'm away."

Finn had rushed to follow in Holt's footsteps and just caught up with him as Holt reached for the reins of his horse.

"I will," Finn said faithfully.

"Good man." Holt laid a hand on his shoulder and pulled him closer for a quick hug about the shoulders. "I knew I could count on you, Finn."

The sound of wagon wheels made her pulse jump. Gathering up her skirts, Glenna hurried to the window. There was a wagon pulling up to the house, not one she recognized. Feeling the sting of disappointment, she gathered up Daisy and made her way downstairs to greet the unexpected guests.

"Hello!" Rachel called, waving enthusiastically as her husband helped her from the carriage.

"Good afternoon, Rachel. Pastor Joseph." Glenna greeted them both just as Finn skidded around the corner of the house.

"Oh, I thought you were Uncle Holt comin' home," he said with a touch of sadness.

"Will I be forgiven for not your uncle if I tell you that I brought you some fresh sweet bread?" Rachel said, holding up the basket she had just retrieved from the wagon bed. Finn's eyes grew wide, and he licked his lips, nodding.

"Mrs. Sterling, if you don't mind, I have to make a stopover at the next ranch, and when Rachel found out I'd be passing, she insisted I bring her for a visit," Pastor Joseph explained.

"Yes, of course. I couldn't pass up the chance to come and see you before winter set in. I hope you don't mind." Rachel made her way up the front porch steps as she addressed Glenna.

"It's a welcome diversion." Glenna smiled.

"Well, I'll leave you to your sweet bread and visiting." He smiled and tipped his hat, climbed back into the wagon and pulled away from the house.

"I'm so glad to see you, Glenna. I wasn't positive I'd be welcome after you said you couldn't come to tea."

"I'm so sorry Rachel, I didn't mean to give you any reason to believe such a thing. It's just with all the men being away from home, my daily chores have doubled, and I wasn't able to take half a day to come into town. I hope you didn't feel slighted. That was never my intent."

Finn bounded up the steps. "I'll take the sweet bread into the kitchen for ya," he offered, and held out his hands for the basket.

"That's very kind of you, Finn." Rachel gratefully handed it to him, looking back at Glenna. "I know you overheard Edith; I thought maybe — you were angry with me."

"How did you — why would I be angry with you?" Glenna stammered in confusion.

"I saw you leave the store not long after I did."

192

"Well, that explains how you deduced I overheard any of Edith's conversation, however what on earth would make you believe I would be upset with you?"

Rachel grabbed Glenna's free arm. "Oh, Glenna, I am so frightfully sorry I allowed her to bend my ear. I knew it was wrong, and I didn't put a stop to it as soon as I should have. I have been feeling so awful and — when I received your note, I was certain that I had lost a friend."

Glenna felt a rush of kinship flood over her, "Rachel, you must stop. There is nothing to fret over. You have not lost a friend."

Rachel's eyes blinked rapidly, "Truly?"

"I am blessed to call you friend," Glenna said honestly. "We should go inside, open some apple preserves to have with your sweet bread. That is, if Finn has not polished it all off already." Together they laughed and, arm in arm, went inside.

Glenna handed Daisy to Rachel, who had her giggling in a matter of minutes and set to work putting on the kettle and pulling out a small bottle of preserves. Finn almost wiggled out of his seat with all his bouncing as he tried his best to sit and wait for the treat to be served.

"When do you expect them back?" Rachel asked as she stirred a lump of sugar into her tea.

"Uncle Holt said he'd be home in seven days. It's been eight days," Finn said around a mouthful of sweet bread.

"We expect them any moment. However, he did warn me it could take longer than expected if the herd was scattered," Glenna added.

"Eight days — I hate it when Joseph is gone for more than a day seeing parishioners. You must miss him something terrible," Rachel observed.

Glenna thought about it. The first day she had passed the time by being as busy as possible. Once the daily chores had become more routine, her mind wandered more than she would have liked and Holt was often in her thoughts. Although the prospect of seeing him warmed her, it also pulled at something deeper, a fear that wouldn't fade.

"I do look forward to having them all home soon," she responded.

"May I have another slice?" Finn asked, his plate cleaned.

"One more, I don't want you to fill up before supper," Glenna said as she slathered a second piece with preserves. Finn dove in without hesitation, and in an instant, half the serving was gone.

"I believe that is the best compliment I've ever received on my sweet bread," Rachel said happily.

"Daisy likes it too," he pointed out. Daisy had bits of bread all over her face and smeared into her hair. The treat hadn't lasted long in front of her either.

Setting her tea aside, Glenna stood to start cleaning the matted clumps from Daisy's hair when the sound of horses approaching reached her ears.

"Oh dear, that couldn't be Joseph already? I had hoped for a bit more time."

"No — it doesn't sound like a wagon." Glenna strained to hear. "I'll go see who it is. Would you mind keeping an eye on the children?"

She didn't wait for Rachel to answer, and rushed into the hall. Riders. It was most definitely horses and riders coming up to the house. Perhaps Holt, Decker, and Gunner had come ahead of the wagon? Glenna knew the moment she saw the two horses, one without his rider just outside the house, that it was not Holt or any of the hands.

"Mrs. Sterling," Tripp Landry drawled slowly, catching sight of her.

"How can I help you, Mr. Landry?" Glenna asked, trying to sound as if his appearance hadn't offset her in the slightest.

His dark eyes narrowed and peaked at her from under the brim of his hat. "I came to speak to your husband." Tripp drew out each word in a low drawl.

"He ain't here," Silas announced triumphantly as he suddenly appeared from the direction of the barn. "No one is," he added, and spit a mouthful of chew.

Tripp tilted his head to one side, his eyes never leaving Glenna's form. "Is that so?" He leaned forward on his horse. "I suppose that means we should be talkin' to you."

"Any business you have can be taken up with Holt. As for now, I have company and must ask you to leave until a more appropriate time can be arranged for a discussion." Glenna crossed her arms and addressed him coolly just as she felt both sets of black eyes on her, making her skin crawl under their gaze.

"Company you say? I don't see anyone but us? How about you, Tripp? Do you see anyone — anyone at all?" Silas had stopped and stood at the bottom of the porch steps, his lips turned into an ugly sneer.

"Not a soul," he answered in a way that made Glenna feel ill. Why had she thought of Tripp as the kinder of the two when they had met in town all those weeks ago? He was just as repulsive as his brother.

"Well, then, why don't you invite us inside for some refreshment? After all, it's the neighborly thing to do," Silas said while advancing up one stair.

Glenna forced herself not to retreat or show her repulsion.

"Must feel pretty good about being the mistress of such a fine house." Tripp seemed thoughtful while he took in the breadth of the house. "If Holt had taken my offer, this fine house would have been mine. I suspect right around the time you showed up, in fact." This was the second time one of the Landry brothers had made mention of Holt selling Crossroads.

"That's right, Tripp. Come to think of it, maybe Mrs. Sterling would've become Mrs. Landry instead. It's all just a matter of convenience, after all."

The insinuation that Glenna would have married either of the two men made her skin crawl. Silas sneered and went on, "Or dumb luck in Holt's case. After all, if we hear it right, you were bought by Clint, but he went and died, leavin' you no other choice."

"I was not purchased as you so callously put it," Glenna bit back, unable to hold her tongue.

Silas raised both hands. "Didn't mean no disrespect."

"You know, Mrs. Sterling," Tripp said, drawing out the name between clenched teeth, "before your arrival, that husband of yours was all set to sell this place, cut his losses, and move on. It is too bad he changed his mind so quickly. Ranchin' life is hard — and dangerous. This is no life for a refined lady such as yourself. I'd hate

196

to see Holt go the way of his brother — leavin' you a widow and those little ones without any kin." Tripp's voice was full of mock concern.

"He's right, anythin' tragic like could happen —" Silas added. There was no concern in his tone, mock or otherwise. Silas was still sneering in a half-grin, taking another step up.

Tripp gave her what she could only assume was meant to be a charming smile and sat up tall in the saddle. "You have his ear. Why not encourage him to finish what he started and sell the place? It is no place for women and children — so far from town — or help of any kind." Tripp's cold insinuation sent a shiver down Glenna's spine.

Had the Landry brothers just threatened her? Holt? The children?

"Thank you for your concern. However, we are very well and not at all alone." Glenna squared her jaw and stared down both brothers. "Now, I had better get back to my guest and ask you both to leave."

"I don't feel like goin'. D'you, Tripp?" Silas was laughing at her, taking another step in an attempt to make her give ground, to show some weakness.

"Glenna, is everything alright?" Rachel called from the hall, her voice carrying out onto the porch. Glenna didn't blink as she watched the Landry brothers. Silas froze in his advance and looked at Tripp. Rachel pushed open the door and stepped out.

"Well good afternoon, Mrs. Joseph." Tripp touched the brim of his hat and nodded.

"Is there a problem?" Rachel looked between Glenna and the two brothers.

"No problem. We came lookin' to speak to Holt, but it seems we will have to come back," Tripp said with what Glenna was sure was meant to be a charming smile that only came off as smarmy.

"I think that would be best," Rachel muttered.

"Sorry to deprive you for so long of Mrs. Sterling's company. We'll be leavin' now." Tripp tipped his hat.

"Think on what we said. Help Holt to see reason. It would be best for everyone." Silas spat out another bit of tobacco, then grinned up at the two women with grayish teeth as he backed off the steps and returned to his horse.

Glenna didn't take a full breath until the pair had become nothing more than a speck in the distance. Rachel must have been able to feel the unease as she didn't leave her side.

"As a Christian woman, I don't like to speak ill of anyone, however —" Rachel bit her lip.

"I feel as though you and I have the very same sentiment about the Landry brothers." Glenna was glad to get back indoors and to the children.

"Auntie Glenna, a wagon is pullin' up."

Glenna moaned inwardly, "Finn, please stay with your sister while I see who today's unexpected visitor could be." Finn nodded and moved to sit down next to Daisy who was grabbing balls of yarn from the basket and tossing them around the floor.

Two days had passed since the unfortunate visit by the Landry brothers and the stress of what had been implied was wearing on Glenna. She felt a cloud of unease settling itself over every moment;

the weight crushing her slowly. Although she was sure the Landry brothers wouldn't return by wagon, after two nights of no sleep, Glenna wasn't in the mood for any more unexpected visitors. Stepping to the front door, she recognized Theo's tall frame. Hattie's voice carried over the distance and sounded like music to Glenna's ears. She rushed out to greet them.

"Oh, it is so good to see the two of you!" Glenna flew from the porch steps and warmly hugged Hattie. Relief washed over her in waves, followed by such deep exhaustion her bones felt weary.

"What a greeting! You can't have missed us that much. We stopped by not four days ago." Hattie pulled back to look at Glenna. "Are you alright?"

"Please, tell me you'll be staying for supper," Glenna implored.

"We finished our chores, so we are at your disposal for the rest of the evenin'," Theo said as Hattie turned Glenna back toward the house. Once safely inside, Glenna watched Hattie give Finn a warm pat to the crown of his head.

"Finn, why don't you help Theo unload the wagon?" Hattie gathered Daisy up and tossed a few wayward skeins of yarn back into the basket as she did.

Finn dashed outside, glad to have something to do.

"Glenna, my girl, you look positively worn out," Hattie fretted.

Glenna groaned, "That's because I am. I didn't get a wink of sleep last night or the night before last."

"Little Miss Daisy having trouble sleepin'?"

Glenna was saved from having to sidestep questions she wasn't ready to answer as Theo and Finn walked in, both grinning madly.

"Look who we found!" Finn practically jumped out of his skin with excitement as Gunner walked into the kitchen behind them.

"Boy oh boy, is it good to be back!" Gunner grinned.

"He said Uncle Holt, Decker, and Bowen are a few hours behind." Finn was smiling and bouncing up and down.

"They are gettin' the herd into the winter pasture. Holt asked me to ride ahead and let Glenna know to expect us," Gunner explained. "It's wonderful to see the two of you here," Gunner added and placed a kiss on Hattie's cheek.

"We'd better get a move on supper," Hattie laughed, waving him away.

The kitchen turned into a flurry of activity, making it impossible for Glenna to analyze her reaction to the news that Holt was coming home. Hattie had her and Finn set to work peeling and chopping potatoes while. Daisy happily practiced her walking between a chair and Glenna. Theo carried in water and set it to boil while Gunner got a head start on the evening chores.

Before Glenna knew it, supper was ready and the sounds of the men laughing floated into the room from the direction of the kitchen door. Her head swam a little, vision blurry at the edges. Unable to determine if these symptoms were due to her sudden case of nerves or if she was falling asleep on her feet, Glenna rubbed her eyes and tried to slow her pulse. Daisy wriggled in her arms and tried to turn in the direction of all the activity.

The door swung open, and almost en masse the men filtered into the kitchen.

"It's about time. Now get washed up; supper is ready, and if you let it get cold after the work we put into it, I will never forgive any of you," Hattie snapped.

"Yes, Ma'am," Decker said with a smile and headed right for the washbasin. The moment Holt crossed the threshold, he stole a glance at Glenna, catching her eyes on him. The corner of his mouth twitched upward into a crooked grin, his gaze lingering.

"It's good to have you home, my boy." Hattie smiled and gave him an affectionate pat on the arm. Finn had rushed to attach himself to Holt's side and was rewarded with a hearty squeeze.

"No place I'd rather be," he answered, never taking his eyes off Glenna.

"Smells like heaven," Theo said with a dramatic flare as he walked to his wife and pressed a kiss to her lips. "Supper smells good, too."

"Oh! You old flirt. Go and wash up," Hattie laughed and swatted at him as Theo did a sidestep out of her reach, laughing.

Holt slipped off his hat, banged it once on his leg to remove the dust and nodded to Glenna, "Hello."

"Hello," she returned the simple greeting.

"You've been well, I hope," he wondered. Glenna noted that the room had gone quiet as all eyes turned toward them, rapt attention at the exchange.

"I have," she nodded, not ready to discuss the Landry brother's unpleasant visit. "The children have kept me quite occupied." Glenna added, hoping it would divert their audience and Holt's focus onto someone other than herself.

Holt moved around the table to draw closer to where she stood, Finn at his heels.

"And you, Daisy, did you miss me?" he coaxed and laughed when she reached for him, wrinkled her nose and hung onto Glenna instead.

"I'm guessin' the scent of livin' in the saddle for over a week doesn't much agree with Miss Daisy," Gunner quipped.

"I don't blame her; it's a good thing Theo thought ahead and hauled in water for the lot of you to take a proper bath," Hattie informed them. "First supper, then you can all get cleaned up and set those clothes aside for washing. Now, enough chatter. The biscuits are warm. Let's eat!"

The room started to fill with normal sounds of movement and in no time at all everyone had washed and seated themselves around the table; the ruckus of their conversation and tones of deep rumbling laughter as cups clattered was music to Glenna's ears.

"Alright — alright, let's say grace," Holt called over the chaos and everyone grew quiet. Glenna slipped Daisy into her seat and took the hands of those seated on either side of her. All heads bowed as Holt said grace.

The wonderful sounds of chaos filled the space as, "Amen." sounded.

After promptly cleaning his plate, Bowen leaned back in his chair and patted his middle in satisfaction. "Very fine vittles, Miss," he nodded slightly to Glenna.

"I'm glad you enjoyed it." She smiled at him. "The credit goes to Hattie this evening. I was just doing as instructed."

"Well, I thank you both. Gunner's chuckwagon cookin' can't hold a candle to freshly churned butter and warm biscuits," Decker added, and everyone laughed in agreement, all except Gunner, who protested the insult with a touch of humor.

Many around the table helped themselves to seconds, and soon all the biscuits were gone and the cups drained. Slowly, each of the men took their leave, each to his task, and shortly, Hattie and Glenna found themselves alone with the children.

Glenna noticed the older woman moving a little stiffly as she gathered the empty bowls.

"Hattie, I hate to impose on you further. Finn's studies have been sorely neglected these last few days. Would you mind reading him a few passages? I can manage very well in here."

"I can't leave you alone with this mess," Hattie objected.

Glenna took the bowls from Hattie and placed them near the already filled washbasin. "I insist. You have been an angel; thank you. Now go put up your feet."

Hattie gave her a warm hug. "These old bones could use a rest. Come along, Finn. Let's see what adventure awaits for you tonight." She shook her finger at the boy, who rushed to go with her, glad to not get roped into cleaning.

Glenna set to work washing the dishes and clearing away the remains of the meal, Daisy playing happily at her feet. Soon, a pleasant melody entered her mind, and Glenna hummed along to it.

"I've missed that."

Glenna jumped a little at the sound of Holt's voice. She didn't turn to look at him though and focused harder on scrubbing the supper bowls.

"What is that?" she asked with a nervous tremble in her voice.

"The sight of you — in here — with Daisy," he said and stooped to scoop up Daisy, who giggled with joy at the action, wrinkling her nose at him.

"You talk as if you had been gone for months rather than just days," Glenna said, attempting to sound unaffected.

"When you are out on the range with just the cowhands as company and hardtack for meals, you tend to get a little nostalgic for the simple comforts of home, I suppose."

Daisy giggled, and Glenna turned a little to see Holt tickling her. The sound was musical, and she smiled at the two of them. Holt's eyes lifted and Glenna felt the weight of his gaze on her.

To cover up the rush of feelings that had swept over her with just his glance, Glenna refocused on the task at hand. She was grateful for the support of the washbasin, as each breath seemed to drain more energy from her. Glenna could hear him moving behind her and his steps sounded in the hall, moving away from her.

She glanced over her shoulder to find the kitchen empty. He had taken Daisy with him. Glenna forced out a breath, not realizing she had been holding it in, and wondered at the sense of disappointment that had overtaken her.

Footfalls sounded, telling her that she would no longer be alone with her racing thoughts.

"Daisy is enjoyin' story time with Hattie and Finn." Holt said in way of announcing his presence, clearing his throat he went on, "If you don't think I'd be in the way, I'll move a few things and get the bath brought in."

"Of course." She nodded and went back to scraping any leftover bits into the slop bucket.

The sound of chairs being dragged across the floor kept Glenna keenly aware of each of Holt's movements, making it hard to concentrate on what she was doing nearly impossible. The door creaked as he stepped outside, then again as he reappeared with the tin tub and set it near the fire. It was when the rickety cloth and board privacy screens started to appear and blushed while remembering the last time she and Holt had been alone in this room with those same items.

How profoundly different her feelings were now than what they had been that night. She had felt a pull between them, yes, mutual respect growing, yet something more had developed around her doubts, growing deep inside of her in his absence.

She had missed him, missed his presence in the house, the heavy sound of his boots on the wood floor, the sound of his voice, and how his low rumbling laugh made her insides churn. How she had longed for his conversation, longed to have him near.

Extraordinarily, Glenna was able to admit to herself how deeply she cared for him, much more than she could have imagined. She was decidedly glad he was home. The truth of it emerged so suddenly and rushed over Glenna with such force it momentarily pushed the unrelenting fatigued she had been living in to the background.

"You and the children seem to have kept the place runnin' without a hitch." His observation caught her off guard, and she shook off her thoughts to acknowledge him.

"Finn was a great help, and I don't know if we could have done half of what needed to be done without Theodore's visits." She pushed her hands deeper into the water and started a search for any cutlery that had been missed.

"I — worried about you — you all," he confessed.

Glenna turned to face him more fully, biting down on her lower lip, wondering if this was the time to bring up the unpleasant call she had received from the Landrys.

"I'm relieved to have you home," she admitted in a small voice.

Holt strode toward her from where he had been arranging the screens, leaving the job half done and forgotten.

"What happened?" Although it was a question, it sounded more like a demand, his voice carrying an edge of urgency.

She blinked slowly and with real effort to reopen her eyes, the fuzzy feeling stronger now, hands dripping wet, hanging useless at her sides, and looked at him. His care and worry filling the space with the safety that had been missing. Holt was here; he was safe; everyone was safe.

Whatever she had imagined the Laundry's could possibly do fled from her mind, and the last vestiges of strength she had been clinging to seemed to rush from her in a great wave. Holt caught her about the waist just as her knees gave way.

Instantly, he was depositing her into a chair.

"Hattie!" Holt called out.

"I'm fine," Glenna protested.

"What is it?" Both Hattie and Theo rushed into the kitchen.

"Nothing. I had a slight dizzy spell."

"She just drained of all color and pitched to one side. Somethin's wrong," Holt said, ignoring Glenna.

"Holt, the poor girl hasn't had a wink of sleep. She's dead on her feet. I should never have left all this for her to clean up," Hattie chastised herself.

"No, no, I'm alright." Glenna protested.

"What's kept her awake? The children?" he asked Hattie.

"Please don't — don't speak about me as if I'm not here," Glenna insisted.

Theo pushed a cup of water into her hand. "Take a drink," he said simply, and Glenna obeyed, sipping on the cool liquid until the dizzy feeling in her head started to dissipate.

"Glenna needs rest," Hattie insisted and took her by the elbow, directing her out of the room. "Answers can wait."

206

Eleven

Glenna blinked. The room was awash in light. It was a sudden shock to her system, and she bolted upright in bed, feeling disoriented.

Tossing off her covers, she noted that she was still in her dress from the night before; vague memories of Hattie forcing her to lay down started to resurface. The old shoes had been untied and tossed to the side. Neither had wanted to bother with washing or undressing.

The quilts hardly crumpled state meant that she had not only fallen right asleep but hadn't moved during the much-needed rest. The house was silent, yet she could hear activity outside. Taking the time to redress and wash up, she went to the kitchen to answer the demands of her stomach.

"Good mornin'," Holt quipped from his spot at the kitchen table. Daisy's seat had been pulled up close to him and he was in the middle of feeding her when Glenna entered. "How do you feel?"

"Like my old self," she answered.

"It's not nearly as edible as your usual fare. I saved you some eggs and toast." Holt stood, took a covered plate from the warmer above the stove and set it at the table for her.

"Thank you. I'm sure it's delicious." She took the seat. "I'm feeling a bit silly sleeping so late." Glenna sheepishly took a bite of the eggs.

Holt offered Daisy another bit of bread soaked in milk and molasses. "Would you like some tea?"

"Tea sounds heavily," she admitted. Her eyes followed Holt as he moved around the kitchen, grabbing a kettle and a cup while preparing the tea. Once it was set in front of her and the now-empty plate removed, Glenna sipped at the hot liquid with relish.

"Holt, there is something I feel that you should know," she said after a few long moments of quiet. It was clear from his expression he had been waiting for her to be ready to speak.

Glenna took another sip, holding the cup with both hands, her eyes locked on the amber liquid inside, set about retelling her encounter with the Landry boys, why it had bothered her so and kept her awake all hours of the night out of fear.

"At the time, I was still so taken back by their arrival, the way Silas kept inching closer, that I didn't react to the thinly veiled threat in their words; however, it was impossible not to continually revisit what they said once I was left alone."

Holt cursed, leaving his seat, and began to pace angrily about the room.

"It's no wonder you haven't been able to rest with all this on your mind and my bein' gone," he seethed. This was followed by more cursing and pacing. Glenna pushed back from the table, leaving the forgotten tea behind, and walked to stand in his pathway.

"Holt?" The sound of her voice seemed to draw him out of himself. "You do not believe we were in any real danger, do you? I had thought the attempt at intimidation was only meant to unsettle me, and of course you, once you learned of it."

"I never believed those two snakes would be so bold — so incredibly idiotic as to —" Holt bit back the last of his words in anger.

208

"It's the second time one of them mentioned you selling Crossroads. Is that a possibility?" She hadn't meant to sound so accusatory and snapped her mouth shut.

Holt ran a hand through his hair. "There was a time after Clint passed. I thought this place would be too much for me to run with, keepin' the kids here as well, even with the hands. Of course, Hattie and Theo are a help, but they had already taken a hit to their earnin's by takin' off so much time from workin' on their own place to help me out both after Grace passed and Clint."

She watched Holt paused, looking at Daisy. "Hattie acts boisterous and energetic, however her heart is weak. Adding an infant full time would have been a death sentence. Askin' them to take on the littles — just to keep a handle on Crossroads, it didn't feel right. Sendin' them away didn't either, so when Tripp proposed to buy me out, cattle and all — I can't say I didn't entertain the idea. I only gave it a thought for a few days before turnin' him down. Not a full twenty-four hours later, you showed up knockin' at my door."

He looked directly at her. "You said once that the need to stay at Crossroads overwhelmed all rational thought. That's exactly my feelin'. I knew I had to stay, had to try to keep the family together, and you made it possible in a way I hadn't even considered. Once you agreed to stay as my wife, I never looked back or gave another thought to his offer."

"I am happy to hear it." Glenna wasn't able to express the overpowering sense of relief his words had given her. It was impossible to imagine leaving this place even after the short time she had been there.

"Somethin' more is eatin' away at you," he insisted.

Glenna didn't rush to answer as his statement was broad and could have encompassed so much of her feelings at the moment. One worry did push itself to the forefront, pressing down on her.

"Did one of those cusses say somethin' else?" Holt pressed, adding in a softer tone, "Won't you talk to me, Glenna?"

She blinked rapidly. "There is nothing to discuss."

"You're lyin' to me." Holt didn't back down or step away from her, keeping his eyes locked on hers. After a few breaths, Glenna sighed and her shoulders sagged.

"It was nothing, just some idle gossip," she relented and wished all the more she had never made mention of it.

"Gossip? What gossip?" His demand for an answer was clear and Glenna hung her head a little, eyes cast away from him.

"I didn't mean to eavesdrop on a private conversation. However, when I heard our names, I felt frozen, as if my feet had been rooted in place." She bit at her lower lip. "I suppose it is better you hear it from me. It seems there is talk that I was a — that while I was back East, I worked as a — harlot." She spat out the word with venom. "There is no truth to it, of course. Nonetheless, I once had the impression I could be friends with these women; I find myself in their company at church and social gatherings. Now, how can I look at them?"

Holt didn't speak for a moment, as if he needed to mull over what she had shared with him. With each passing second, she felt more and more the weight of his continued silence.

"Those small-minded — cruel — that sets my blood to boil!" He stopped short with a start, his gaze softening with understanding, "Glenna, you didn't think I would have believed such a thing, did you?"

"I hoped if it reached your ears you would come to me first, as I should have with you. I am sorry for not being brave enough to speak about it before you left on the drive."

"I'd take your word over any other's." This bold declaration of trust made a lump of emotion form in her throat that made it difficult to swallow. Holt studied her. "That wasn't all you overheard, I take it?" His arms folded across his chest.

"No, also, it was said that I tricked you into marriage with false pretense."

Holt swore under his breath, "The only two people that need to know how or why this marriage came about are right here. The rest of them be damned."

Glenna flinched. "I can understand why those who care for you may wish to believe this falsehood. You could very well have married any of the eligible women from town to keep your family together, yet you yolked yourself to a stranger. Someday you may very well come to regret your rash choice, Holt."

"I don't believe I will have cause to." There was such certainty in the statement it surprised her. Glenna's gaze lifted, her eyes searching his face. Something flashed in the depths, then was gone.

"Was that all you overheard? The jealous rantings of a few silly women?" He demanded.

Glenna sagged, shrinking a little under his gaze. Taking a few breaths giving herself time to find the fortitude to continue.

"I am — it seems, just as weak minded. I could not as easily dismiss the things they said regarding you as you are of those things spoken about me."

"What did they say?"

There was no use in hiding anything from Holt. He was able to read her too clearly to even attempt such a thing.

"That I married a man with a constitution not unlike that of my father's," she said softly.

There was a sound of air rushing out from between clenched teeth. His silence felt as a confirmation of her worst fears. A painful knot formed in her middle and Glenna focused on Daisy rather than Holt and waited a breath before forging on.

"I wished rather than believed this wagging of tongues to be more lies, yet doubts have plagued me. I lost everything to my father's gambling and drinking, the entirety of my life stripped away by his choices. For years — alone in that city, forsaken. I wondered why he could not stop? Why my mother and I could not be enough for him?"

Glenna stopped to look up at Holt, daring him with her gaze to tell her the truth, as somber resolve had replaced the sorrow.

"Tell me, Holt, tell me that my fears are unfounded. That the children aren't doomed to the same ugly fate I suffered. Tell me it was also a lie and I'll believe you."

"I can't." The pain in his voice tore at her insides and Glenna felt the world around her shift and become unfocused. Those two simple words felt like a physical blow, and her insides ached. She pushed the chair out from under her and stood. Needing to put some distance between them.

Holt reached for her, stopping Glenna from rushing from the room. "Please, let me explain. What I mean is that it's not all a lie. There was some truth to what you overheard, but it's also not what you think." She could hear the desperation in his tone.

"Boss, Decker needs ya in the barn," Gunner said as he jerked open the kitchen door. "Beg ya' pardon, I didn't know you were havin' a discussion."

"No, it's quite alright Gunner, Holt was just leaving," Glenna answered back and pulled her arm from Holt's grasp.

"Alright, I'll let Decker know you're on your way." Gunner backed out, leaving them alone.

"Glenna, you have to understand it's not — you need to hear the full story and then you can make up your mind. Please, just give me the chance to explain."

"I will hear you out," she said stiffly.

212

He shook his head a little. "Now isn't the time. Will you walk with me after supper? I promise to answer any questions you have."

"Alright," she answered simply.

———————————

Glenna pulled the wrap around her shoulders as she stepped out onto the porch. The early evening was still warm enough to forgo her heavier coat, and she relished the feel of fall that hung in the air, everything so clear and crisp.

She had noticed that not long after the mid-day meal Holt had left with Gunner. The two of them returned not long after, Gunner sporting a fat lip and Holt with a welt on his jaw that was turning shades of red and purple. No one had said anything about either injury during the evening meal. Supper had been painfully awkward.

Holt had only spoken enough to ask Decker to sit with the children while they went for an after-supper stroll. He had fallen silent. It seemed to be his way, retreating into himself when there was something troubling him. He often grew quiet and withdrawn when presented with an issue on the ranch, taking his time to mull over the answer. She wished her own thoughts didn't make her so tense or cause the slight pounding that throbbed at her temples.

Now, Holt was in the barn helping with chores and giving last-minute instructions to Gunner and Bowen before he would meet her. She was glad for the minute of peace that retreating to the outdoors alone offered.

Blu's happy yelp cut into the stillness as the dog rushed out of the barn in front of Holt. Glenna watched as the duo walked toward her. As they grew closer, Blu left his master to run full speed at the porch, jumping over the stairs to rush Glenna and greet her with a wet nose. She obliged with a scratch behind his ear.

"Hello, Boy." The two-toned eyes looked up at her as his tongue lolled out.

"Blu Dog insisted on joinin'. I hope you don't mind."

She shook her head. "Of course not."

Leaving the porch, she moved to stand near Holt, Blu at her heels, and together they started a slow amble away from the house.

"It's best to stay on the path. It's still rattler season and it will be easier to see them than in the brush." Holt mumbled to her. It was then Glenna realized they were on a path, not a wagon path, but one just wide enough for two people to walk comfortably side by side. It was a well-worn path, used by the ranch's horses often, she was sure.

Blu padded a few feet ahead of them as Glenna waited for Holt to say something more... to say anything. For several minutes he just walked at her side, aloof and detached. Every so often, he would kick at a stone or remove his hat, smooth his hair back and replace it.

After what seemed to be an age, the sound of cattle lowing started to fill the air around them. Blu bolted ahead and over a rise, and was gone. Glenna felt the ground under her feet tilt upward as she too reached the rise. She was at the crest, a low valley stretched out in front of her like a giant serving bowl crested at the edges of sweeping hills. The valley was lush with wild grasses, a small stream cut through it, and dotting the scene where several hundred grazing cattle.

"I didn't realize the herd was so close." A slight breeze rushed past her shoulders, pushing past her to wind down into the grassland.

"The homestead is up wind. When that shifts, you'll know exactly how close the herd is." His voice held humor and Glenna relished the sound of it. "Do you believe people can change, Glenna? That they can find redemption?" The question took her back.

"Yes, if the repentance is true, so will the change be and in that change lies redemption." She said simply.

214

"When I was no more than seventeen, I was sure I knew — well, everythin'." This statement was followed by a chuckle.

Glenna didn't respond, unsure of what his teenage self had to do with their earlier conversation.

"In my arrogance and foolishness, I fancied myself in love." He shook his head in disbelief at his own words. "I knew I was too young to marry or even court her. So I set out to work, save my earnings and prepare to strike out on my own. All things that would make me a more suitable husband.

"That winter, a fever swept through the territory — Clint was the only one that didn't get struck down with it. Both my father and mother seemed to recover quite well, but for some reason, it held on to me. I remember little of that time, though, to hear Clint speak about it, I was in the throes of death, to the point that my parents were preparin' to lose a child."

She looked over at him, his hands stuffed deep into his pockets, head down, as if studying his feet.

"The fever left me alive but took a toll on my strength, leavin' a lingerin' cough that tore at my lungs for months. It wouldn't be until the summer thaw that I would be back to a semblance of my old self. The months of illness could have taught me a few humblin' lessons about life. All I saw was that it had kept me from reachin' any of the goals I had set up for myself."

"Did the fever claim any lives?" She asked, finding her voice.

"Yes."

"Was one of them the young lady you had feelings for?"

"No." Holt shook his head slowly, seeing where her thoughts might be taking her. "Her father, the postmaster, had fallen very ill, and she nursed him. While doin' so, she was often put into the company of the doctor. They married that spring."

Glenna thought of doctor John Tillman; she had met both the man and his wife, Tennie, during her first few weeks on the ranch as they had called on her to welcome her to the area. Both had seemed very fine people and had a small brood of adorable, fair-haired children that she often found herself admiring during Sunday worship. Was Tennie Tillman the very same woman Holt was talking about now? She thought better of asking. It no longer mattered.

"I blamed the illness for my bad luck. It had set me back, removed the possibilities of those things I felt I had a right to and it made me angry and bitter. I started to make it a habit of goin' into town once or twice a week to sample whatever horrid drink was being offered at the bar. It dulled the disappointment —"

Holt's shoulders sagged. "At the time, we didn't know how the fever had damaged my mother's heart. She was never quite the same — and two years later, when we lost both our parents. Ma went and then Pa as if he couldn't live without her. After that, I attempted to drown my sorrows at the bottom of a bottle."

A flash of memory blindsided Glenna's senses. The thick stench of alcohol and the sight of her father passed out on the low sofa near the fire. This was often how she found him after the supper she had eaten alone. She hadn't been aware of his gambling, yet there was no possible way she could have been oblivious to his drinking. The drinking had escalated after the death of her mother, so much so that a night seldom passed that she didn't find him in the very same position.

Holt drew her back out of her thoughts by speaking. "Clint tried to make me see reason. He was about to be a married man and didn't want a drunk around his wife or their future children. I resented him for his happiness in the midst of my pain. There wasn't enough beer or whiskey to fill the gappin' whole that had been created inside me."

Glenna wrapped her arms around her middle. She knew all too well how looking for peace in drink only led to more regret.

216

"Clint thought perhaps givin' me more responsibility could somehow snap me out of it and pull me back to reason. He was the kind of man that always saw the best in someone, even when there was nothin' there to be redeemed or respected. At twenty, I was an even bigger fool than I had been at seventeen."

Holt paused, taking in a few deep, cleansing breaths. It was clear that the things he was sharing caused him pain.

"Clint trusted me with funds to make a large cattle purchase — all the ranche's savings, except a little set aside for immediate use. The heifers would be good breedin' stock and would have built up a fine herd. I went with the hands to Cheyenne and did well at the auction. To celebrate, I took them out to the local waterin' hole and got myself good and drunk. The hands made their way back to the hotel — I — well, in a haze of alcohol-infused bravado, I thought it was a good idea to join a poker game."

Glenna unfolded her arms, wrung her hands together and waited for his next sentence, although she felt in her bones she knew what he was about to tell her.

"I lost. I lost it all. I lost the cattle that had been purchased. The money that was left. Gone in the course of one night. I had signed a promissory note for the lot and tossed it into the pot, letting it ride on one hand."

"Oh, Holt." She wasn't able to stop the gasp.

"The next mornin', I sent a telegram to Clint. Like the coward I was, I couldn't face him with what I had done. I hadn't just gambled away part of our future, I had broken his trust —"

Glenna dared to look at him. Her heart ached for the misery that was etched into his expression.

"Glenna," He caught her eye, his look pleading. "I have never had another drink. That day was the last time I allowed anythin' stronger than lemonade to pass my lips. I haven't set foot in another bar or picked up a set of cards either."

"I believe you." She breathed softly. His stance changed at her words. He became visibly more relaxed and the lines of worry that had etched his face softened.

"You'll never know how much that means to me." The statement seemed to come as a surprise to both of them for Holt cleared his throat and pressed on with his story, "I — I spent the next several years workin' any job I could get, sendin' the money home to Clint to make up for what I had lost. After a time bouncin' around, I settled in with an outfit for a few seasons. It was then I finally became brave enough to send a letter to Clint along with the money. He responded in true Clint fashion, all warmth and forgiveness. He told me about the birth of his son. Then invited me to come home and meet Finn."

"Did you come?"

"Yes," Holt murmured, "It was hell."

"Was Clint very hard on you?" Glenna wondered.

"No, that was the crux of it. He was — just as I had left him, only much happier. He welcomed me home with open arms, as did Grace. Both insistin' I should stay, work the ranch with them and make this place my home. He said he needed my help more than my money."

"He missed you. Why not stay? It is clear that Clint had forgiven you."

"I tried to stay. I wanted to stay, to belong to this place. Then the longer I was here, the more I knew I had to leave. I couldn't live with myself after disappointin' Clint — and myself without tryin' to make amends. I hadn't earned all the money back. Cattle hands wages aren't much to live off and still put somethin' away. Somethin' deep inside told me that Clint didn't care, but I did."

Holt took a half step closer to where Glenna stood. "Bein' here, seein' Finn and bein' around Clint and Grace, taught me that not all

218

my goals had died. I wanted to be a man deservin' of a life like his. I wanted to be the kind of man he was. Someone worth my word."

Glenna understood, "You had yet to forgive yourself. That is why you asked me about redemption."

"I didn't rush right home. No, I still had a lot of work to do. It took several long years, however, I found firm footin'. Regained my faith, I had felt the power of forgiveness and I came home again, meanin' to work that last of my debt off here, workin' for Clint." Taking a pause, along with a deep breath, Holt continued.

"Towns like Buffalo have long memories and they do not forgive so easily as blood. I've worked hard to regain respect and good workin' partnerships with people around these parts. I'm not that same man Glenna, I'm no longer that drunken clod and I won't ever go back to bein' him."

One of her hands slipped out from under the shawl and came to rest on his arm. "I know."

"Can you — forgive me?"

"There is nothing to forgive, Holt." Her fingers slid from his arm, only to be caught up in his grasp.

"Glenna, I wasn't tryin' to hide my past mistakes from you. Just as you didn't mean to hide your past from me. Neither of us wanted to live in them is all. That it's no rightful excuse, us gettin' hitched in such a rush — but honest, it didn't seem important at the time. So much has happened in the between to put it out of my mind. Yet, when I learned about your father's past, I should have told you instead of you bein' blindsided —"

"I can understand why you didn't rush to divulge it. I must not have made it easy with my venomous talk about my father." Then something occurred to her. His past must have been the catalyst for his reaction to her comment the night of the Harvest Festival.

"I knew I should have told you that I had a history with drink and about the gamblin' after learnin' about your Pa but I held my tongue — worried you'd lose all respect you had for me. I acted out of selfishness."

His thumb made a lazy circle across her knuckles as her hand still rested within his. "I didn't want to see that in your gaze and know I had caused it. I was actin' ungenerously and thinkin' about myself only — my comfort." Holt let out a derisive laugh. "You and Clint had so much in common you never even knew about."

Glenna applied a small amount of pressure from her fingers to his, "I was frightened today when it seemed you had confirmed my worst imaginings. However, Holt, you should know that is no longer the case. I apologize for the insinuation that you could be anything like my father, especially without knowing any of the details. You are right, Clint and I would indeed have had a lot in common, yet it is the differences that signify."

Holt gave her an inquisitive look and Glenna pressed on, "I am in awe of you. You faced a refiner's fire, walked through it, and came out the other side tempered — stronger. That fire consumes lesser men, destroying them utterly. For me, personally, I know that promises and fanciful words mean little when actions do not follow. You are a man of action. A man of change and growth — of honor. These things are to be respected."

She watched the effect her words had on Holt's conscience. The strength and confidence she had always associated with him started to return. His shoulders squared, the line of his jaw tightened. Holt stopped walking, turning to look at her.

"I care nothin' for the good opinion of those you overheard talkin' but it bothered me somethin' awful to think, even for a short time, that you thought ill of me."

Glenna blinked, processing Holt's statement.

"I am proud to be your wife and I will never allow groundless chatter to so easily shake my faith in you." She said with certainty.

"— I would like to know if one of the Landry brothers gave you this though," Glenna added, lightly touching the dark patch of his jaw line where a fist size bruise was visible even in the dying light.

Holt gave her a wry smile, "Oh, this ain't nothin'. Those two got worse than they gave."

Twelve

"Auntie Glenna?"

"Yes, Finn." She didn't look up from her sewing.

"Why don't you ever talk about your Ma? Don't you miss her?"

The needle prick was hard and Glenna pulled her thumb back sharply. The question had surprised her so that all thoughts about the current task had been forgotten.

Finn looked up at her from his spot on the floor, blocks now forgotten, "I have been thinkin' about my Ma — missing her. I wondered if you missed your Ma too?"

Glenna let the fabric fall to her lap, and she looked hard at Finn. "I do. Very much. I miss her every day. There isn't a moment that I don't wish she was here. I want to share so many things about my life with her. I know she would have loved to hear all about you and your sister." Glenna smiled a little to herself at the idea. Her mother would have indeed loved the two darling children.

"What else do you remember about her?" He wondered.

"Oh, where to begin?" Glenna sighed, smiling warmly, "She smelled like the flowers of a lilac bush. Her hands were soft and kind. She always had a sparkle in her eye, an air of mischief, and loved to laugh. The sound of it was infectious.." Glenna had to stop as the well of emotion inside her threatened to overflow.

"She sounds like my Ma." With this simple comparison, Glenna felt her heart swell. Here she sat, with someone who could

222

completely understand the depth of her loss. An orphan, like herself. She had something he did not, years and years of memories of those that she loved most.

"My Ma smelled like warm grass and honeysuckle. I loved her smile. Dad used to say she was bright like the sun because everyone always looked to her for warmth. I didn't understand why he said that until she was gone —" Finn said, and desperate sadness touched each word.

"Stay here Finn, I'll be right back." Putting the mending aside, Glenna slipped into the house and hunted for the items she wanted. Returning, she sat at the small table that looked out over the side yard and motioned for Finn to sit near her.

"Tell me your favorite memory of your mother Finn," she sat, journal open to a blank page, posed to write.

"But, what about your sewin'?" He asked with concern.

"There are more important things in this world."

Satisfied with her answer Finn made himself comfortable, Blu yawned and curled at Glenna's feet as Finn started to recount a memory.

Time seemed to fly by as story after story poured out of Finn and onto the pages of the journal. Soon Daisy's voice could be heard calling out from her crib.

"Finn, that was a very good start. Thank you for allowing me to learn more about your parents today." Glenna set the pen down.

Finn stood next to her, his eyes hungrily devouring the lines on the page that stood open to his gaze.

"You'll read these to Daisy, won't you?" He asked.

Standing, she placed a hand on his shoulder, "I will, but not before you tell them to her yourself."

Glenna squeezed his shoulder and went to fetch Daisy, who was now crying a bit more loudly.

"Hello sweetheart, I'm sorry it took me so long to come to fetch you. Let's get you changed and a bit of bread. How does that sound?" Glenna chattered on as she lifted Daisy from the crib.

"Auntie," Daisy's soft voice floated over as she pressed herself into Glenna's arms, laying her head down, small arms encircling her neck.

Glenna breathed deeply a sigh of warm satisfaction. Her arms cradled Daisy a little closer. There was something so natural about the toddler's embrace, and she allowed herself to revel in it a minute longer before changing her.

"Alright little one, it's time to start preparing for supper." Glenna hummed as she left the children's room. She yelped, running right into Holt's soiled frame.

The books and papers Holt had been holding slipped from his hands and scattered along the hall floor.

Glenna went to her knees alongside Holt and, angling Daisy away from the mess, started to gather the papers with one hand.

"I am so sorry, I wasn't paying attention —"

"It's alright Glenna."

She pulled a few of the scattered pages toward her. "I've seen this image." Lifting the thin paper, she looked at it, turning it slowly. "This is the Crossroads cattle brand," Glenna said with recognition.

"Yes, I found it in Clint's things." Holt picked up another slip of paper and held it up. "Along with this one, I don't recognize it." His brows knit together. "I've been trying to make heads or tails of the ledger I found in Clint's things- all of this was with it." He motioned to the scattered items.

"This one I do not recognize." Glenna looked at the second brand. Placing the first into the pile Holt had created, she looked carefully at the second.

"And now I've made such a horrible mess you'll have to start over with simply organizing it. Please, may I help?"

"To tell the truth, I think I could use a second pair of eyes, I've been starin' at this mess for so many weeks I'm not sure what I'm even lookin' at anymore." Holt seemed relieved at the offer of help.

The brand images forgotten Glenna reached for the leather-bound book. It fell open easily; the ledger was a bit unorganized with added columns running down the right-hand side of each page, numbers placed in all three with little notes scribbled into the margins.

"I'm no expert, though just glancing over this ledger, it would appear that Clint was attempting to account for some discrepancy."

"That's what I thought as well. This line, it matches the Ranch books kept in my father's desk." Holt pointed to the first of the three lines. "I was takin' them down to run some comparisons. See if I could figure out why Clint was keepin' a second book, one that he kept hidden."

He seemed to hesitate, as if he wanted to continue, but was waging some kind of internal battle that had yet to be decided. Glenna shifted Daisy on her hip and, placing the book back into Holt's hands, touched his arm with light fingers.

"Talk to me Holt, what about all of this is weighing so heavily on you?" Glenna could feel the stress pulsating off of Holt in waves.

He was staring at her, his eyes seeming to look at her and through her at the same time. She watched with dismay as his shoulders sagged. "There are a lot of things that have been weighin' on me since his death. I feel certain his gettin' shot was no accident."

His blue eyes cut into her and she was sure of his meaning. "You think Clint was killed over something in this ledger?"

"In it or his papers. I aim to find out either way. How he died never sat well with me. But investigatin' took a back seat to runnin' the place, the kids and —"

"And my arrival." She finished for him, holding Daisy closely now with both arms. "Holt, if your bother was murdered, couldn't you also be in danger?"

He nodded solemnly, "Possible if whoever wanted to keep Clint quite learns I'm lookin' into things. I haven't talked to anyone else about my suspicions as of yet, and the idea of puttin' the children or you in harm's way — it makes me ill." He added with a whisper.

Glenna nodded. She understood he was trusting her with something he had yet to tell those closest to him, men he had worked and lived with far longer. It was both a very heady honor and crushing responsibility at the same time.

Holt looked thoughtful, "I am a bit worried about what I'd find, somethin' that could toss Clint into a bad light or spell ruin for the Ranch. Maybe whatever Clint was mixed up in is better off being buried with him." He whispered.

Glenna's hand found its way to his forearm, drawing his attention back to her and out of his darker thoughts, "Holt, I cannot tell you what to do. Nor, in this instance, would I pretend to know your feelings on the matter. However, if discovering what really happened to Clint is somehow buried in these pages, the risk is worth it — for myself, at least." He didn't answer her or try to

226

contradict her statement. Rather, Holt took a deep breath and waited as Glenna rushed on.

"I — my situation is not the same, yet, learning the truth about my father — although hard and bitterly disappointing, was preferable to continuing to live in his lie."

"And are you sure about that, Glenna?" Her hand slipped from his arm, coming to rest on Daisy's back. The little girl seemed to sense Glenna's emotions curled into her as little arms clapped around her neck.

She blinked at him a few times. "I'll admit that it did affect me negatively, in more ways than I can count. Sent my world spinning in some strange topsy-turvy manner as I lost my footing — my beliefs were shaken, my faith lost." Unshed tears stung at the back of her eyelids. "It also shaped my life into something new. That newness could have been dark and joyless. Instead, it brought me here." She held Daisy even tighter.

"You — don't regret it? Losin' your life in England. All that followed?"

"I will always feel loss and sadness over the parts of my past I was not able to control, although I have not regretted my choice to come West. It brought me to you — to you all." It was a bold statement, but a true one.

She wanted to tell him not to worry, that they would face it together, yet kept this thought to herself. A long stretch of silence followed, where they both seemed to realize they were crouched in the hall. Only half the mess gathered up and the heaviness of the conversation hanging over them.

Working together, they finished gathering up the scattered papers. Glenna stood, stretching out her cramped legs, "I'd better get back to Finn."

Holt also stood, his eyes not leaving her face, "For what it's worth, Glenna, I'm sorry for what you had to face. Yet, I can't say I'm not glad your path led you here."

***

"Hey boss, the boys and I finished up the chores. Headed to the house to see about talking Miss Glenna out of a slice of that cake she was baking before we have supper." Gunner announced and slapped Holt on the shoulder.

" I'll second that." Theo licked his lips.

Hattie had been keen on spending as much time as possible helping Glenna prepare for her first Wyoming winter and although they had done plenty of canning just after the harvest Hattie had come out the last few days to teach Glenna about drying the meat and using the smokehouse.

Holt and the boys had spent the better part of the previous day helping Theo on his spread. A fence had gone down and needed replacing, as well as a few wayward goats and milk cows that needed rounding up.

Theo, in true fashion, had insisted that if Hattie was there helping Glenna, it was only right for him to repay the favor and help Holt get the barn ready for calving season. With the extra pair of hands, the work had flown by.

The flurry of activity had also meant that Holt hadn't had one moment to look over Clint's books. The very disorganized stack of papers and ledger had been all but forgotten in the chaos of everyday life.

"I could use some cake." Gunner rubbed his middle as they all headed to the house.

Glenna was quick to oblige their requests and soon everyone sat happily on the porch with cake in hand. Conversation, teasing, and laughter flowed easily between them all. Holt wondered if this was what his mother had in mind when she had insisted on such a large porch. A gathering place where memories were made.

Glenna laughed openly at something Decker had said, her shoulders shaking with levity, the sound washing over him. She had such a bright smile, one that reached her eyes and lit up her face. Holt liked how the laugh had erased all lines of care and worry away from her face.

Hattie nodded, "Holt, I was chatting with Glenna and she tells me you have not taken her out on a horse ride in a spell. Theo and I aren't in a hurry to be leavin' and still need to load up. Why don't you take her on a ride before supper? Everything is already prepared and it won't take nothin' for me to get it on the stove alone."

"It is a rare moment to have not only cake to ruin our appetites, but so much time to while away on such a fine day," Theo added with a lifted eyebrow.

" What do you say, Glenna? Would you care to join me for a ride?" Holt asked pointedly. Not caring that they had an audience for her answer.

" Yes." she answered warmly.

Soon he had Ranger and Scout saddled and Glenna, who had changed into her riding dress and wearing a bonnet, walked toward him from the direction of the house.

"Where's Copper?" She asked.

"Copper threw a shoe. Decker will take care of it while we are gone."

"Ranger has a smoother gate, I know he is a bit larger, but you won't regret ridin' him." He said, handing her the reins to his horse.

Leaving the road, he led her past the old homestead cabin and out into a large open patch used to winter the cattle closer to the main house. It was the perfect place to try out a gallop. Glenna wasn't deterred by this and matched his speed. Ranger pulled ahead by a nose, a neck, a torso, leaving Holt staring at the horse's tail. Her bonnet went flying off her head and bounced behind her as the wind danced through her hair.

The race had been short and left them both laughing when Holt caught back up with Glenna, who had slowed Ranger to a walking pace.

"You were right. I do not regret taking your mount. He is magnificent." She leaned low over Ranger's neck and patted him affectionately.

"He is." Holt agreed.

"Will you show me more of the property? This is as far as we have been on any of our previous excursions in this direction."

He led them farther away from the Homestead. The ranch was a mixture of low flatlands and grassy rolling hills. All of these stood in contrast to the distant mountains and blue sky that always seemed to call him back home, no matter how far he wandered. Seeing it through Glenna's fresh eyes had brought a new appreciation.

Her comment of being envious of him, of his life, had struck a cord deep inside. He was as much a part of the land as it was a part of him. It ran in his blood, seeped into his bones, and he knew he wouldn't ever feel the wanderlust of his youth again.

After a time, they had left the rolling hills and low flat stretches behind them for more rocky terrain. A unique mixture of red clay, sandstone, and mountain rock marked the area.

"Before coming out west I was certain that those who talked of colored cliffs were mad." Glenna mused as they rode through an area with deep reds and startling purple bluffs dotted with sage.

"I thought men were mad when they told me of buildings that touched the sky." Holt smiled over at her.

" I prefer the mountains to anything I left in the city." Holt looked over at her and felt a familiar band tighten around his chest, constricting his breathing. With each day that passed, his feelings for her grew stronger and harder to ignore.

They rode for a while in companionable silence. Holt stole another sideways glance at Glenna to find her eyes on him as well.

Looking back out over the landscape, she said in a wistful tone, "I've never met anyone quite like you, Holt Sterling."

Holt felt a smile pulling at the corners of his mouth. "Not much call for cattlemen in New York City, I suppose."

Glenna laughed. The sound of it, unrestrained, bright, and bubbly, did indescribable things to his pulse.

"You have a rare combination of very admirable qualities that speak to the strength of your character. If my own experiences as a beneficiary of your thoughtfulness and generosity were not enough to prove your singularity, the many other instances I have witnessed would. "

"All of that is very high praise and wholly undeserved. You make it sound like I'm some kind of saint." He shook his head.

"Perhaps we can withhold bestowing sainthood. I have witnessed you work small miracles in the lives of those around you.

Taking food to widow Jensen. Giving that young boy an extra penny for candy when you thought no one noticed. The number of times you have proved my words correct is countless, no doubt." Glenna paused and swallowed hard, rushing on, "You make a difference."

———————

Glenna gratefully sat under the shade of a tree close to the edge of the stream where they had stopped to water the horses. She quite liked this patch of the property. Large trees lined the banks, giving protection from the hot sun and variety to the sparse patch of sagebrush they had been riding through. It also reminded her a little of the trees she used to visit growing wild on the edge of the property of her childhood home.

Holt filled his canteen and moved to stand close to where she had chosen to rest and held out the freshwater for her. She took the offer with a smile and drank deeply, handing it back to him.

"Do you believe Theo is right? Is this is one of the last days of fair weather before winter settles in?" She questioned.

"Theo is right more often than he is wrong. The daylight hours are shorter and nights cooler. Yet, there have been many a year that winter seems to have set in when suddenly all the snow melts and weeks of warm weather pass just as you saw this last week."

"From what I gather, winter in Wyoming is not like any I have yet experienced." Glenna mused.

"I expect not." Holt gave a low, rumbling laugh. "When it does set in, you might question your choice to stay."

"Winter in New York was quite cold and with snow that ground city life to a halt at times."

232

"I've never experienced winter in the city. You'll have to let me know how it compares."

"Do you really spend months with no contact outside of those in your home?" Glenna said with a little hesitation.

"Yes. Even when the snow lets up, the wind grows so cold it can freeze man and animal in their tracks if caught in it too long. Some months the snow will pile so high we won't be makin' any trips to town. Then just when you are thinkin' you might go mad from the isolation, the sun'll come out to melt the snow just enough to make a soupy mess of mud that soaks into everythin', makin' travel possible but miserable."

"You have given me so much to look forward to." She said with a smile.

"It isn't all bad," He chuckled. "Did you ever take out a toboggan on fresh snow drifts?"

She looked at him, brow furrowed.

Laughing now, he shook his head. "I'll take that as a no. You'll have to remind me to take you and the children this winter. It is a good way to spend an afternoon."

"I'll remember the offer. Tell me, if it is that cold and travel is hampered, how do you get your work done during those months?"

"We'll move the herd close to home. Many will be ready to calve soon and we'll need to keep an eye on them. You'll see much more of us, I'm afraid."

Glenna bit on her bottom lip. She had wondered what changes winter would bring to their daily lives but had not expected to be in daily close quarters with Holt in the same way she was now alone with the man. The idea made her feel slightly lightheaded.

" A while ago you made mention of something — Elmer's something or other?" She asked, looking for a change in the subject.

"Elmer's Gulch." Holt nodded as he removed his hat, dusted it on his thigh and mopped at his brow with the back of his sleeve, squinting out over the horizon.

"No one knows why the place is called Elmer's Gulch. When my grandfather set roots down, the stretch had already gotten the moniker."

Holt moved to the tree trunk and sat down near Glenna, leaning on the tree and stretching out his long legs with a sigh. Glenna took a steadying breath as his arm brushed hers.

"My Pa hated that place. He called it all kinds of creative names that would infuriate my mother." Holt laughed at the remembrance, and Gianna was unable to stop her smile. "He said that when he was a boy, the cattle would wander down into it and get themselves good and stuck after a thaw or hard rain. He cussed about having to try to get them back out. The gulch rises on both ends to meet the surrounding land, in the middle is wide and deep enough to swallow four or five heads of cattle standing shoulder to shoulder."

"I enjoy hearing the stories you tell of your parents." She said in a wistful tone.

"They were wonderful people." Glenna could hear the smile in his voice without needing to look over at him. "Both would have been taken with you. Ma especially." He added.

"I would have liked to have known them." She answered softly.

"Crossroads has seen a lot of loss — it's also born witness to a lot of life, most good and filled with love and laughter."

For a few minutes, neither pushed the conversation forward. Holt sighed and got back to his feet.

234

"We'd better start back or we'll miss supper." He slipped his hat back on and turned, offering Glenna a hand. She looked at it, remembering how he had taken the same hand as they walked only days ago. A gesture that, although, had yet to be repeated, had kept her sleepless for thinking about the feel of his touch. She took it, slipping her delicate fingers into the warmth of his grasp. Holt pulled her to her feet in a swift motion that took her a bit off balance.

She braced herself just before colliding right into him and regained her footing. Although she had avoided crashing into Holt, Glenna had found herself standing so close to him that her every breath took in his scent. An intoxicating mix of masculinity, earth and the remains of the cologne she only associated with Holt.

Her eyes lifted to explore the expanse of his shoulders, slowly arcing up to become transfixed by his clear blue gaze that held her captive until the whinny of Ranger shattered the spell and Glenna dropped her eyes. She noted Holt's mouth was set in a tight line, the muscles of his jaw bouncing as if he was grinding his teeth.

The pressure of his fingers still holding hers tightened for a split second before he dropped her hand and stepped away, turning to un-tether the horses. Glenna felt as if she was able to expel her first full breath and it came out as a shutter. She couldn't be sure. Perhaps she had just wished it to be there, yet, for a moment, there had seemed to be something in the depths of his eyes — something pulling her closer to him — drawing her in.

Thirteen

Holt cursed under his breath. He had wanted to kiss her. The idea had crossed his mind repeatedly over the weeks that had rushed by since their wedding. The mixture of her hand cradled in his with the look in her eye had made him forget himself and long for something he knew couldn't be.

Glenna wasn't his. Not really.

Of course, he had thought about what she might feel like pressed to him. Holt thought of little else when around her than sweeping the feisty English brunette into his arms and kissing her until both of them had been left breathless. There had been no occasion to even attempt such a brazen act until that very day.

Holt's thoughts tortured him constantly with reminders that regardless of his own feelings, Glenna had almost been his sister-in-law, his brother's wife — his brother's widow. It was easier to convince himself that she could never feel anything for him past a polite tolerance, regardless of the fact she now shared his name. She had never been intended for him, and he did not deserve her.

Over the weeks he had become quite good at brushing off the glances, the way her cheeks turned a shade darker when he looked at her longer than necessary, the times their fingers had brushed during everyday tasks, her attention to the meals he enjoyed, the deep and meaningful conversations they had shared, or the feel of her hand clasped in his — each thing that would have given other men the right to hope had become the very same things that had built up a

236

wall between himself and Glenna. A wall of protection that had kept Holt safe from his feelings.

In that moment of weakness, it had all come crumbling down.

What could he be thinking?

Grunting something unintelligible, he handed Glenna the rains to Ranger, who greeted her with a friendly neigh.

They each mounted and Holt took the lead, pulling his horse back in the direction of the homestead.

He took notice of Glenna. She seemed distracted, as if her thoughts were weighing on her heavily. Cursing to himself, Holt could only imagine what could be going on in her mind. What could she possibly be thinking of him right now?

Distracted by his line of thought, Holt almost missed seeing the glint of sunlight bouncing off something in the distance. For a split second, it blinded both him and Scout, who tossed her head as if shaking off bothersome flies.

The unmistakable sound of rifle fire rang out. Holt yelped as Scout shook, stumbled, and the horse's legs crumbled underneath him. They both went crashing to the ground. Holt kicked his feet from the stirrups and used the momentum of the fall to push himself away from the dead animal, escaping her weight coming down on his leg, pinning him to the ground.

He could see from the corner of his eye Glenna, fighting to keep Ranger, who was frightened, under control. Before Holt was able to scramble to his feet, a second rifle blast rang out.

"Glenna!" He shouted as a terror such as he had never known rushed through his veins.

It was too late. Ranger had reared up on his back haunches and with a loud trumpet, he slammed his front hooves back into the ground with the force of over a thousand pounds of pure muscle that was being driven by adrenaline-laced fear. This jarred Glenna and he could see her grip slip on the reins. Ranger kicked out with his back legs and lost his rider as Glenna was flung into the air.

The sound of her startled cry was cut short by the sickening sound of her body making contact with the ground with a kind of dull thud.

Ranger was gone, bucking wildly between spurts of erratic running. Holt kept himself flat to the ground as he half dragged himself and half crawled toward Glenna. He had to make sure she was alright and get them to cover.

Reaching her side, Holt pulled himself close to her, her deep brown eyes were open, locked on the sky, her mouth gaping open and moving with silent cries. He knew that look. The wind had been knocked from her and she was unable to draw breath.

Doing something he had witnessed his mother do when he and Clint were children, Holt leaned over her and blew a strong puff of air right into her face. She had started to turn an ill sort of purple-blue color, but when Holt's breath swept across her face, Glenna blinked and suddenly sucked in a painfully short breath. He waited for the space of a heartbeat, repeating the action. She seemed to scramble for more air and took several fast gulps in rapid succession. Then, painfully, she was able to draw in one long full breath.

His eyes scanned her face. "Are you alright?" One hand never leaving his pistol, the gun wouldn't be a match for the longer range of a rifle. Even so, the feel of the cool metal under his fingers gave him some sense of control over this sudden madness.

She took another shuddering breath, nodded, looking unsure of her answer. "Glenna, you landed pretty hard,"

"Nothing seems to be broken." The sound of her whispered assurance was music to his ears. Unable to take the time to process the powerful sense of relief he felt, letting eyes scan the horizon in the direction he was sure the gunfire had come from.

"It's too exposed here. Can you move?" He asked, wishing he could give her more time to recover, but knowing he also had to keep her safe.

"Yes — Yes." She repeated, taking another deep breath.

"Good, we are going to head back toward the stream. We can use the trees for cover."

Glenna didn't wait for further instruction and making small sounds of pain rolled to her side. In one swift move she was on her feet and running, skirts held up to allow faster movement. Holt followed closely, and neither of them stopped until they were back in the cover of the trees.

Glenna was leaning on a tree, taking deep breaths, one hand pressed to her side.

"Glenna, are you sure you're alright?" Holt was standing in front of her, assessing any possible damage.

"My ribs hurt a bit and my vision is still blurred." She confessed with a grimace. The reality of their situation seemed to set in and she rushed on. "Who was that? Why did they shoot at us?"

Holt was preoccupying himself with looking her over, noticing the small cuts and bruises forming on her hands and wrists from the brush grabbing at her during the fall. His mind was also listening to every little sound, searching for any signs of danger.

"Holt?" Her hand shot out and grabbed his forearm. "Are *you* alright?"

He looked into her face. All color had drained from the normally rose cheeks and apprehension had replaced the mischief he was accustomed to seeing shining in her eyes.

"I'm alive. I think that's more than was expected." He said finally.

"Clint." Glenna breathed as her hand slipped from his arm. "You told me when he was found it was ruled an accident. That someone probably mistook his horse for a buck from a distance. What is the likelyhood of that happening twice?" She finished with incredulity.

He shook his head, "Whoever was doing that shootin' was well within my property and knew he wasn't aimin' at a pair of bucks — and after findin' Clint's second ledger I'd say it's pretty clear someone wanted my brother dead. I just need to figure out why." He wanted to add that his own life counted on it as well. Holt cursed under his breath. It wasn't just his life anymore, it was hers, the children. This thing was bigger than just him.

The fear he had glimpsed early on her face was gone. Her deep brown eyes shown nothing except for clear concern coupled with a fierce resolve. Glenna was stronger than he had given her credit for. He knew little about her time in New York save what she had shared with him, although he imagined that the experience had been the refiners' fire for her. She had been tempered. Using the same analogy she used to describe him seemed fitting.

Standing there, in the cover of the trees, looking into her face, something he had forgotten was pulled to the forefront of his mind.

"One of the last times Clint and I talked, he told me some cattle had gone missin'. He was sure the discrepancy in numbers wasn't due to sick cattle being picked off or wanderin' too far from the herd in the winter and freezin'. There was no way to prove either of the theories."

"You didn't agree with him?" She wondered.

"There aren't many reasons for men to go about killin' each other around these parts anymore. But our livelihood, cattle would be one of them."

Glenna could hear the bellows of a few of the cattle in the distance and wondered absentmindedly how close the herd was to their current location. The thought slipped from her mind as a sharp pain protested her jarring footfalls. Glenna was starting to feel the effects of being thrown from her horse and held a hand to the stitch in her rib as her side throbbed. Holt took note of her slowing steps.

"I'm sorry Glenna, I wish we could take this slower." He glanced at her while his eyes kept scanning the horizon. "I can't help but feel exposed this far away from the Ranch. It's making me a mite jumpy." He linked his arm with hers, giving her something to lean on as they returned to the pace he had set. Glenna felt herself rushing to keep up with his long strides.

"You think whoever shot Scout is still out here?" She asked, unable to keep the unease from her voice and her eyes scanned the area around them as well. They had waited for some time in the cover of the trees to venture out. Dusk had started to settle and Holt had wanted to use its cover to their advantage. She agreed, moving toward home would be best. Doing so in the dying light made her nervous.

Holt squinted in the direction they had come from and frowned.

"Right now, all I can think about is gettin' you safely back home." He cursed. "I would feel better with more than just my pistol."

"Holt —" Glenna paused, "I've been thinking about what you said — if cattle are the reason and Clint felt you had been losing more than the expected numbers due to natural cases then... perhaps, are you thinking theft is the cause?"

"It's common, illegal and deadly, yes, but common all the same."

"How is it possible? I thought all your cattle were branded."

"When I was workin' in Colorado, another rancher was caught leadin' young calves and their mothers away with feed. Brandin' the young ones with his own and releasin' the mothers to wander either findin' their way back or dying. He had been doing it in small numbers, but enough that it had become suspicious. The thief was caught and charged with rustlin'."

"Do you think something similar could have been taking place here and Clint caught wind of it?" She waited for Holt to respond.

"The answer to that has to be in the second ledger."

"If Clint had suspected theft or perhaps caught them red-handed, it would make some sort of sense that they felt his death was necessary. I am trying to make some sort of sense of it and I can't seem to." She was confused. "How could killing Clint be a benefit?"

"The workin's of some men's minds will never make sense, Glenna. Those that kill for their own gain or to cover actions they have made are no kind of men you should want to understand."

She knew he was right. Another thought persisted. "Why would anyone take such risks? If caught and tried, wouldn't the thieves lose everything?"

"Out here cattle is king. The more head you run, the better off you are. Crossroads is located in a prime location. We have freshwater year-round, good grazing, healthy land for crop grown'. It's enough to tempt any man."

"Could whoever is doing this also covet Crossroads and not merely the herd?" She thought of the house, outbuilding, and barn. Those alone would be something to covet.

"I expect so and I have an idea of who it could be, course I can't prove none of it — yet," Holt said in a low voice, then continued, "My family has worked generations buildin' up the herd. We are careful what bulls are brought in for breedin', and they produce some big, healthy calves. Any of them would fetch a good price. But to take over the herd all together would be a life-changer. If Clint hadn't put my name on the deed before he passed, we might have had the place sold out from under us by the bank."

"If they are after the whole place, you coming home to help run the ranch and becoming co-owner might cause them to act desperately." She said with understanding. Holt nodded, looking thoughtful.

"I doubt whoever it is knows about the deed. No one outside Clint, myself, and the banker knew about the changes."

"When the ranch didn't get put up for sale, someone must have figured it out. You are the sole owner, Holt, and someone wants you gone." She said soberly.

His steps slowed only a fraction, and Holt caught Glenna's gaze. "I would never put you in danger knowingly and I'm sorry you are caught up in this mess."

He looked away from her face just as fast and back out toward the setting sun. Glenna felt a flutter in the stomach that had nothing to do with the heaviness that had settled there.

"You are not going to send the children and I away, are you?"

Holt didn't answer for several strides, and she wondered if he had heard the question.

"No, I won't." Glenna glanced up at him from the corner of her eye and noticed the look of determination on his face. "I won't send you or the little ones away. I can't risk puttin' any of you in harm's way, either. I'll work it over and come up with a solution.

The conversation stalled as the sun quickly set. The large Wyoming sky seemed to blaze for a few minutes as darkness descended, like a blanket covering the land.

"We are still quite a ways away, aren't we?" she dared to ask.

"Yes." He growled. Glenna left sure that they were far from being lost, Holt knew the ranch better than anyone, she had also noticed landmarks that had caught her eye earlier in the day and could still hear the sound of cattle, although they seemed to be closer than they had been.

Up ahead, she could make out the deep gulch that they had ridden past earlier.

"We will save time if we cut across here rather than walk around. Are you alright to climb down?"

"Let's go," Glenna gritted her teeth and took her hand away from her side, gathering up her skirts, making the slow trek down easier. He had let go of her arm to take the lead and she kept close to Holt, who was testing each step for loose ground. They reached the bottom and started to cross the wide gap to the opposite bank.

It wasn't hard to imagine this place in the spring. The gulch was longer than she remembered from their passing earlier and at either end slopped up gradually, an easy place for cattle to wander down into. Earth walls rose feet higher than Holt stood. The idea of attempting to coax a muddy bawling heifer back out would be quite the chore indeed.

The walls rising on either side of her were dry, hard-packed clay. The ground under her feet felt as solid as rock. The incline they now would attempt to climb seemed much steeper than the bank they had descended.

"We need to move farther down the gulch to get good footin'."

She followed without a word. The deep of the night seemed to thicken with every step she took behind him. The inky blackness was only cut into by the rising of the moon. Full and bright, it was their only source of illumination.

244

Her legs started to ache and Glenn felt the last of her energy seep out of her as her foot slipped, her knee hit the ground with a thud. She leaned into the earth, catching her breath.

Holt had stopped moving, standing like a statue just a little to her left.

"I'm alright." She assured him.

"Shhhhh." He hissed.

Unease settled in her bones. Something was wrong.

Glenna held her breath and strained to hear what Holt had already sensed. She was able to make out the oddest sound, a cross between a primal cry of a wild animal and a popping. Both sounded out of place amidst the normal sounds of the night's symphony. That was the second thing she had noticed. All the other night sounds had stopped, now replaced with the unmistakable sound of pounding hooves.

The ground under her palm was vibrating. Suddenly the air above them was rent with the cries from what sounded like hundreds of heads of cattle.

Holt was beside her in an instant, grabbing her roughly around the upper arm and yanking her up and after him.

"What?" she gasped, stumbled, as a sound like thunder grew louder.

"Stampede." He breathed and the blood in her veins froze. It was hard for her to make out shapes in the moonlight. The mass of blackness that was storming toward them from one end of the gulch was unmistakable.

Holt stopped abruptly and the next second Glenna was shoved harshly against the hard clay wall, a small outcropping of earth obstructing her view, blocking out the image of the cattle and offering her some protection. She knew there was no time to climb their way out. The stampeding animals would be upon them in seconds. She also knew that Holt wouldn't risk pushing her to climb when there was any risk of her slipping. The mental image of falling into the mass of raging cattle was enough to make her stomach lurch. This dry clay wall was their only hope.

The ground under her feet shuttered as if the earth was alive. Holt pressed himself into the outcropping with her, standing directly in front of her, pinning her in place with his body. Glenna wished she could block out the cries and hoof beats as the sound exploded around them.

Holt braced himself, pressing his body along the length of hers as he held tightly to the outcropping with one hand, the other reaching out and above them to grasp at a tree root that had been exposed sometime past.

All at once, the wave of heat and deafening noise slammed into them as the cattle started to rush past their hiding spot. She was instantly thankful for the protective wall the outcropping offered.

Dust filled every breath Glenna took. She could feel it clogging her throat and coating her mouth. Glenna could feel dirt and rocks pelting any exposed flesh. She turned her face into Holt's shoulder, eyes tightly closed.

Glenna felt rather than heard herself cry out as a jarring impact to Holt's back drove him into her. Clutching at him, she willed herself to sink further into the incline at her back, to keep him out of harm's way. His feet moved next to hers, digging in the hold they had on the trembling earth beneath them. A prayer welled up inside her and propelled itself to the heavens just as Holt grunted in pain, taking another blow.

For a nightmarish instant, Glenna felt one of her feet slip a fraction from its already precarious perch with the slide of earth tumbling under it. "Holt!" Glenna felt his every muscle coil and harden to stone around her, keeping her from sliding further by the sheer force of his body covering hers.

His head now bent low over hers as rocks, shaken loose, started to rain down over them from above. For several heartbeats, the world had gone mad. Exploded into something unrecognizable.

Holt kept his place for a long while even after the shaking underfoot had subsided and the last of the cattle had rushed past them and out into the darkness, their cries growing ever more distant.

His ragged breathing slowly started to come in more even puffs. Glenna dared to open her eyes. The moon, a small sliver of white light that penetrated the gulch and illuminated their surroundings. She was amazed at the thick veil of dust that still hung heavily in the air, shafts of moonlight curling into the clouds as they started to settle.

Holt took a tentative look over his shoulder, pulling himself away from her ever so slightly as he did so. It was then that Glenna realized her hands were still clinging to Holt's shirt front in tight fistfuls. His arms tensed as he moved back to press himself closer against her again, head bent low, his mouth close to her ear.

"Don't move," He whispered. Her hold tightened once more as a new sound reached her ears. The slow pace of what was unmistakably the gate of a horse.

It was difficult for her to gauge how close the horse was to them as the sound bounced off the walls around her, perhaps a few yards away or just above her. There was no way for her to be sure. The hoofbeats slowed and stopped altogether. A new kind of dread was spreading over her. A horse — a horse meant a rider — that explained the strange noise she had heard just before the cattle stormed toward them. Someone had started that stampede.

Glenna pressed her face into Holt's shoulder, attempting to hide the sound of her shallow breaths in the folds of his shirt. It seemed as though Holt had stopped breathing altogether as she didn't feel him draw breath until the sound of hoofbeats broke the silence, slowly growing distinct.

She dare not move, focusing only on controlling her breathing and slowing her wild heartbeats. They had survived the stampede, only thanks to Holt's quick thinking. They had survived two attempts on their lives in one evening. The thought sent a shudder coursing through her limbs.

Holt shifted his weight slightly. The arm that had been holding to the outcropping threaded behind her back, wedged tightly between Glenna and the wall behind her, holding her to Holt in a very different way. His other hand had given up its hold as well and was now caressing her hair softly. He was muttering something, so low it was almost inaudible as they stood on the precarious footing, leaning into the wall of the gulch and clinging to each other.

"It's alright, you're alright." She heard the words, yet was unable to process their meaning.

Glenna felt all dignified propriety leave her as she allowed Holt to hold her in such a familiar manner, his arms the only thing keeping her from slipping to the ground in a heap of raw emotion. She knew a few tears had escaped, feeling the sting of them on her cheek.

"Shhhhhh — you're alright." The reassuring sound of his voice seemed to cut through the fog of dread that had its grip on her. She shuttered, took a deep and steadying breath, allowing her senses to return.

Fourteen

Holt could feel a change in Glenna as her hands released their hold of his shirt. Her small frame became rigid in his arms. The mutual comfort they had sought with each other had passed. He allowed his arms to fall away from her, taking a steadying breath, Holt stepped back and away from her.

The shared venerability had taken him by surprise. He had thought of nothing else outside their immediate safety when the stampede had been rushing past them and in the tense moments as the rider had looked for signs of their survival. It wasn't until she had shuttered next to him that he had softened and gathered her into his arms.

She had responded to his touch, melting into him. That single act shook him to the core. They had clung to each other, offering solace and strength. It may have been just a reaction to the stress of the situation that had pulled them together in such a manner nevertheless he was sure that the feel of her in his arms, her face pressed to his shoulder, her soft hair brushing along his jaw, even covered in a layer of earth, wouldn't be something he would easily be able to put out of his mind.

"Glenna," She had yet to move from where they had stood, "Glenna, are you injured?" Like waking from a dream, she started at the sound of his voice, flinching visibly.

"No — I don't believe so." She shuttered, "Holt, are you alright?"

Pushing away from the wall, she moved to him. Her hands reached for him, tentatively touching his arm.

"I'm a little banged up." He answered.

"A little — Holt, you — you were hit!" Unable to finish, anyone thought Glenna let out a strangled sob as her knees gave way. Holt caught her, softening the fall as they sank together to the ground. Glenna allowed herself to be pulled into the circle of his arms.

"Glenna?"

"We could have been killed." She finally breathed.

"I believe that was the idea." He muttered.

Glenna pulled out of the embrace and looked up at him, her face bathed in white moonlight, "They knew you would take the shortcut through the gulch rather than risk a longer walk that close to nightfall with me in tow. One horse was dead and the other runoff. Whoever it was must have known you wouldn't risk losing time getting back home. Holt, this is someone you know and knows you well enough to guess at your behavior."

"I thought the same thing." He agreed.

"Who can we trust?" She voiced with deep concern.

Holt wished he had an answer for her.

"Theo will have sent someone out lookin' for us by now. Let's get out of here." He stood and took her hand, helping her back to her feet. She did not object to keeping her hand in his and allowed him to help her up the side of the gorge. The contact didn't last as she pulled her hand back to wrap both arms around her middle as they reached the crest and the ground leveled out.

Keeping pace with her, they walked slowly, with a sense of urgency in each step. Neither spoke as they traveled. He wanted to reach for her hand each time she stumbled, however her arms never left her sides, giving him the chance to take it. His body was sore, pain shooting through his back with each step. A broken rib, some bruising, but he would mend. The physical wasn't half as bad as the mental torment he felt thinking that he had almost lost her twice… twice in one evening.

He wasn't sure how much time passed or how much ground they had covered when the welcome sound of Blu's bark sounded. The dog brushed right by Holt, bound at Glenna's heels. She laughed a little and rewarded Blu with an affectionate welcome as she went to one knee and wrapped her arms around the dog. Blu answered the show of affection with a lick to her face, creating a clean spot in the dust that covered her from head to toe.

"Hello boy! Oh, I am so glad to see you." Blu yipped happily. Horses with riders weren't far behind Blu and the sound of their approach gave a sense of relief to their predicament.

"Holt!" It was Decker's voice.

"Here." He called back as a light bobbed in the distance.

Soon the lantern light reached them, the horses stopping and the riders dismounting. Decker, and Bowen, who were leading a horse with no rider.

"I've never been more happy to see your ugly mug!" Bowen slapped Holt on the shoulder.

"When Ranger came runnin' into the barn and with no rider, we knew somethin' must have happened," Decker added.

"How long ago did Ranger show up?" Holt asked.

"Not long after dusk. He was all lathered up like he had been runnin' hard. We waited for a spell to see if you'd make it back on Scout. However, after a stretch Hattie couldn't wait another minute and set us out with Blu Dog to look fur ya."

"Scout's dead," Holt answered the unasked question. "She — slip busted her leg. I had to put her down. Ranger spooked, and he threw Glenna." He hoped Glenna wouldn't contradict his version of events.

"You alright miss?" Decker addressed Glenna with concern.

She nodded, "I believe so." The moon was bright and overhead, casting enough light that it was easy to see her expression. One of weariness, Holt noted.

"You look plenty dirty for just footin' it home," Bowen observed.

"Our adventure didn't end there." Holt spat. Both men started to ask questions one over the other in rapid succession.

"There was a stampede." Glenna said softly. The statement caused the men to fall silent, looking at her, then at Holt, who raised a hand, staving off more questions.

"I'll tell ya everythin', but first let's get home —" Holt bit off his sentence."Where's Gunner and Theo?"

"Gunner is still in the stables with Ranger givin' him a good rub down. Theo stayed with Hattie to put the littles down for the night. They are all worried somethin' awful about ya both." Decker said.

The look that passed between Glenna and Holt went unnoticed by the other two men. He knew she felt the same rush of relief at knowing none of the men that worked for him had not been the man that had shot at them or turned the cattle down the gorge. The burden

252

of suspicion had weighed heavily on Holt, and the wash of relief that spread over him was a boon to his soul.

"Well, let's get you both back to home before Hattie sends out a second search party," Bowen said and swung up into his saddle.

"Here Holt," Bowen moved to offer him the fresh mount. Holding it steady so he could help Glenna into the saddle.

He tried to help her, but she stepped back. "I think I'd better walk the rest of the way. I'm still a little sore from being in the saddle."

Holt stepped closer, taking her by the elbow, maneuvering Glenna to the side of the horse. "It's better to get back in the saddle after bein' tossed in the dust."

"I — can't—"

Holt didn't let Glenna finish her protest and cut her off by hauling her up close to him, his lips pressed next to her ear, "In one night you have been fired at, lived through a cattle stampede, and you're gonna let a little thing like fallin' out of the saddle to stop you? You didn't strike me as a weak woman."

That did it. Glenna pulled herself free from his grasp and grabbed the saddle horn, firmly planted her foot into the stirrup and started to swing her other leg up and over the back of the horse. Holt placed his hands on her waist, giving her a boost, careful of the side she had been nursing.

"We'll take it slow," Holt reassured her as he swung up behind her, arms coming around her to grip the reins. His back had protested the move, and he held in a groan of pain with gritted teeth.

"By the looks of it, both of you got your fair share of bruises." Decker commented, as he mounted his horse, thought to add, "How did y'all manage to do so well durin' the stampede?"

"Luck and the grace of God, Decker — it was close." Holt answered. "Blu Dog, lead the way home." He ordered and the dog, who had been sitting patiently waiting for instructions, jumped up and started to move in the direction he had come from.

Glenna felt herself fading. A kind of deep exhaustion had her in its grip and relentlessly pulled at her. Soon it was too much to fight it and her eyes closed. Head bobbing, she felt Holt's guiding hand leading it to rest on his shoulder. Unable or unwilling to lift her head from its new resting spot, she allowed herself to drift off into sleep as Holt held her between his arms, the horse's slow even gait rocking her. The night sounds a lullaby.

"Glenna, sweetheart, we're home."

She knew he was talking to her, yet couldn't for the life of her understand how they had already reached the homestead when her eyes had just closed.

"Already?" She moaned.

"I'm sorry. I know you're tired."

Rolling her neck a little, she tried to lift her head and forced her eyes to open despite their protest. The warm glow of lights from inside the house called out to her.

"Home — " she slurred.

The horse stopped, Decker holding his head.

"I hate to ask you to move even an inch more, but I can't dismount — "

She blinked, trying to discern his meaning, realizing she was still leaning on him, and sat forward, her hands finding the saddle horn for support. Once Holt was down, he reached for her. Glenna did not argue and slid into his waiting hands, grateful for the strength they offered as her legs betrayed her and were of no use for a moment.

"Come on, sweetheart, let's get you inside." He said softly and with his arm encircling her shoulders, guided her up the back steps as Decker and Bowen led the horses back to the barn.

The kitchen was awash in light and warmth. Glenna had to close her eyes, as it was almost too bright for her.

"Holt! Glenna!" Hattie cried and fell on them, kissing them both on the cheeks, tears streaming down her lovely face.

"You have anticipated our needs, I see," Holt said with affection. It was then Glenna noticed the bath screens had been put up.

"I — thought maybe Glenna would appreciate a soak — first I think you both should take a moment to eat while I warm some more water for the tub."

Glenna allowed herself to be led to the table and slid into the chair carefully, feeling the soreness she had tried so hard to ignore. The noise that slipped from her was involuntary and she bit down on her lip to stop a second from escaping.

Holt sat next to her, leaving his usual seat at the head of the table empty. Hattie fussed over them, placing bowls of potato soup on the table next to several fat slices of bread and fresh butter. Holt gulped the glass of cool water she had poured for him. Glenna tried to drink. She tried to take a bite of delicious soup, except her stomach turned.

"Try the bread, no butter, it might help," Holt said softly and placed a large chunk into her hand.

Glenna nibbled on the bread. Slowly, the churning in her middle started to fade, and she took another sip of water.

"Thank you,"

Hattie stopped bustling around as suddenly the room began to fill. Theo, Bowen, Decker, and Gunner all standing around the table, looking at the pair of them, questions clear on each of their faces.

She watched as if in a daze as Holt placed his soup spoon back on the tabletop and, taking a breath, addressed the room as a whole. It was bewildering listening to him recount the events of the evening. Or the events in their altered form. His horse suffered a broken leg. Holt put the animal out of its misery. Their untimely trek into the gulch. She listened as he left out the horse and rider. Letting the listeners believe something unknown, perhaps a coyote, had spooked the herd, sending them down the gulch.

Each of the audience gasped, cursed, or spat at different spots but never interrupted or asked questions until he had finished. Holt never once mentioning Clint or his suspicions that this could be connected to his brother's death, his brother's murder.

Glenna trembled at the thought — Clint had been murdered.

"That's enough for one night. These two need to get cleaned up and go to bed." Hattie ordered.

"Holt — one bit is botherin' me more than the rest." Theo said, undeterred by his wife. "The herd — they shouldn't have been that close to Elmer's Gulch in the first place."

Holt sighed, "I don't have an answer for that, Theo. When we moved them down to the winter pastures, we didn't have them in that area. That's true. Although the herd does what it wants sometimes."

Theo didn't look convinced, but didn't press the issue.

"I'll go out tomorrow and retrieve the saddle." Decker assured Holt.

"No, that's alright Decker. I'd rather do it myself." Holt countered. Glenna knew it was to keep anyone from finding a horse with no broken legs. Her stomach did a flip. She had forgotten about the dry bread and tried another bite.

Part of their earlier conversation replayed in her mind, *"Holt, this is someone you know and knows you well enough to guess at your behavior."*

"I thought the same thing."

"Who can we trust?"

He had never gotten around to answering the question she posed and now she knew it was because he had never planned on telling any of them the truth. Lifting her eyes, she took in the surrounding faces. No, there was no possible way that one of them could be involved? The idea made her stomach turn violently.

"Alright, alright, it's time for you four to get out of the kitchen and let these two finish eating." Hattie shooed them out of the room. She fussed over the water on the stove before excusing herself to gather some clean clothes for Glenna.

Glenna tried to eat, sipped at her water, then gave up on the food.

Seeming to understand that something was weighing heavily on her, Holt leaned closer and spoke low so that his voice did not carry,

"I had to do what I thought was best. The lie wasn't so much because I don't trust them — I don't want to get the boys or Theo and Hattie involved unless I have to. It's bad enough you are in danger. I couldn't add them into the mix until I have a better handle on what's going on."

Glenna shifted in her seat. "I do not like being blindsided by the decision. I am just as much involved in this as you are, regardless of your wishes to the contrary — and I have just as much to lose." She added, emboldened by fatigue.

He looked taken aback. "I should've told you how I was going to explain it to them. That wasn't fair to you." He answered, covering her hand with his as it sat on the table.

The feel of his touch sent a jolt through her and all weariness fled from her bones. Jumping up, Glenna pushed back from the table as if she had been kicked. Her heart had started to pound in her ears as an uncomfortable heat overcame her, as if the room had suddenly become several degrees warmer. On her feet, she abandoned the untouched meal and, much like a caged animal, began to walk the floor.

"I — know logically that I should be in some sort of shocked state." She wrung her hands together, feeling the layer of grit that still clung to her skin. "I should be undone — perhaps even in hysterics over the fact that not one, but two attempts were made on my life tonight —" Pausing in her pacing, she looked in his direction without lifting her eyes to meet his.

"I know I should be focused on the who's and the why's of it all. That, as you surmised, I should be more bothered by the lies — yet — I find myself only reliving one moment repeatedly with brutal clarity."

"Glenna — " Her name was no more than a breath in the air between them as Holt got to his feet.

"Please, allow me to finish or I fear I will never have the strength to speak of it again." She begged, lifting her eyes to hold his gaze.

He nodded for her to continue.

"I thought you had been killed, Holt. When I heard the gunshot and your horse began to fall — " She paused and swallowed hard, attempting to control her emotions, "I thought I had lost you. I've never known terror like that. Ripping at my insides. It was as if time had slowed and thousands of thoughts rushed through my mind all at once — each one of them of you and you alone. Regret washed over me for being so cowardly at not speaking the truth. For wasting so much time holding my tongue — out of fear."

A dull pain welled up in her chest, acting as if she had been caught in a vice, compressing her lungs until she could only gasp for air as she rushed on in a stutter, "I am not asking you for anything more than what you have already committed to between us. I have no expectations. I would not presume to believe your feelings — that you would — return them — yet I cannot go on acting as though I don't feel deeply — passionately — for you — "

Holt had crossed the space between them in one stride, and whatever she was going to say next was swallowed up in his kiss. The kiss was savage, ardent, and almost painful in its intense urgency. Holt was mindful of her injured side as his arms slipped around her. Holding her close in a tender embrace, he continued to kiss her with such passion that overwhelmed Glenna until she was left utterly weak and trembling.

"I love you, Glenna. It's only ever been you — I have never loved another." Holt said a little breathlessly once he had pulled back enough to capture her eyes with his. When Glenna remained frozen he laughed, a dazzling smile spread across his handsome face, "Didn't you know? I've been desperately in love with you for so long now I can't put a finger on when it started."

"I wanted it to be you — " she whispered, as if confessing something very different. His arms now encircled her, pulling her closer to him. "The instant you opened the door, I wished it was you — my intended. Just as swiftly, I suffered a disappointment that turned into such guilt when you told me of Clint's passing. I do not believe I have ever suffered such a torrent of emotion in such a short amount of time before."

"I wrestled many a month, feelin' as if I am betrayin' Clint by lovin' you as I do." Holt moved one hand from her back to hold Glenna's cheek, tilting her head up so that her gaze stayed locked on his. "Then a very wise friend pointed out the error in my thinkin'. There is no use in livin' in the 'what could have been' when it wasn't. What's meant to be will be and you and me, Glenna — are meant to be. I've never been more certain of anythin'."

Glenna reached up and tentatively touched the line of his jaw with her fingertips; the feel of a thin layer of earth covering both his face and her fingertips. She wound her hands around his neck. "I love you, Holt. Completely — utterly — with everything I am." This kiss wasn't unexpected, still its effect on Glenna was just as powerful and startling as the first.

She was lost in all-encompassing happiness. It washed over her as bright as the rays of the morning sun bathing the mountains in its warmth.

Fifteen

Finn beamed, looking at his reflection in the small round mirror as he turned slightly, viewing himself from the side. The new shirt looked to be the perfect fit.

"It turned out wonderfully," Holt said with a meaningful smile as he caught Glenna's eye.

"The color suits him," she nodded, brushing off the complaint.

"It's not just the color Glenna." He argued, "You have real skill. I would never guess this was Clint's shirt remade."

"This was my Pa's?" Finn asked, spinning on the spot.

"Yes," Holt grinned, "And Daisy's new dress was once your mother's blouse."

Finn flung himself toward Glenna, grasping her about the waist and crushing his cheek to her middle with enough force she almost toppled over.

A gush of air rushed from her at the contact. The surprised expression on her face quickly changed to one of joy and she wrapped her arms around Finn's small shoulders, her head bent low to place a ghost of a kiss atop his head.

"Thank you," Finn muttered.

Daisy burbled happily in his arms, drawing his attention. She looked bright and happy in the light green dress dotted with small white flowers along the hem. He knew Glenna had taken great care to reuse every bit possible of the clothing in the gifts. Each button had been taken from the original, the cuffs and sleeves tiny copies of the former.

"The snow has stopped. Do you think the roads will be passable soon — maybe by Sunday?" Finn had moved back and was admiring himself in the mirror.

"Can't wait to dash off to town and show off your new clothes?" Holt asked with humor.

"Yes," Finn answered with some humility, his eyes cast down.

"It's alright Finn, wear it with pride." Holt reached out and clasped him on the shoulder.

"I'm going to go take it off now." Finn said, sounding unsure of himself as he glanced at Glenna. "I don't want to get it dirty before Sunday service." He explained.

Glenna beamed at him, "Of course,"

To give some privacy, Holt and Glenna went out and started down the stairs. Once their feet hit the landing between floors, Holt reached for her hand, spinning her in place to face him.

The newness of their relationship still hung in the air around them. It screamed in his nerves at being so close to her and spoke of his attraction to her as his heart raced. Impossible to deny himself the simple pleasure of stealing a moment. He searched her eyes for a second, leaning in and brushing a kiss across her lips.

"Mine." The word split them apart and Daisy repeated the word as she reached for Glenna squirming out of his grasp.

Holt burst into laughter. "Can we share?"

Daisy pushed out her bottom lip. "Mine." She repeated and cuddled close to Glenna.

"Well, I'm not sure I can argue with that." Holt said with a grin, but leaned in to steal another kiss. Relinquishing his hold on Glenna, and said with some reluctance, "I better go get the boys movin' for the day."

"The children and I have a full day as well. Will I see you at lunch?" Glenna said softly. A touch of pink lit her cheeks as it did any time he showed her affection. The blush only highlighted her attractive features and made him want to kiss her all the more. Still, he tore himself away from her and started down the last of the steps.

"I'm not sure how long it will take to round them all up and move them closer to the homestead." He said thoughtfully. Holt knew that she also had a long day's work ahead of her now that the weather had begun to clear a bit and everyone was taking advantage of the sun while it lasted and didn't want to add more work to her load. He and the boys could survive on some dry tack for lunch with the promise of a home-cooked supper on the horizon.

Just as his feet hit the bottom step, he looked back at Glenna. He noted how she had stiffened slightly, her head inclined to one side, her lips set in a thin line. Holt opened his mouth to speak to her when he too heard it. A distant sound — a bark, followed by a voice — someone calling out — a voice sounded, pulling at Holt and forcing him into action.

"Holt!" It was Decker. His large bulk was easy to recognize, even from a distance. Blu was leading the way, racing through the snow toward the house, baying mournfully.

Decker was riding as hard as he could in the snow that was now slowly melting into slush. A wet and ragged looking bundle sagged in his lap, the bulk of it clutched tightly to his chest with one massive arm.

"What?" Glenna had come to stand beside him. As soon as the question slipped from her mouth, her hand had found Holt's forearm in a farce grip. She drew in a sharp breath, "Good Lord."

They had both seen it in the same instance. What had looked like a bedraggled bundle had materialized into the form of a human, a woman, covered almost completely by Decker's coat as it had been wrapped around her. Holt bolted off the porch and ran toward Decker, who was pulling back on the reins to slow the horse enough not to trample Holt as they almost collided.

He didn't ask questions, just reached his hands up to take the bundle from Decker, who was already reaching toward Holt before his mount was able to gain sure footing and come to a full stop. Neither man exchanged words. It was clear in Decker's stricken expression this was a matter of urgency.

Holt spun, rushing back toward the house. Glenna stood, holding the door open for him. He noted that Daisy was absent from her arms and knew that she had anticipated his need for her help and had possibly handed her care off to Gunner and Finn.

"Take her to my room," Glenna ordered and he could hear her racing up the steps after him.

Without any ceremony or qualms about propriety, Decker had followed as well. Glenna raced around him and tore at the quilts on her bed, tossing them to the foot, making space for Edith.

"Lay her here," Holt didn't question the command and deposited the waterlogged bundle where she had indicated, getting his first real look at the woman's face.

"Edith?" He was unable to stop the sound of surprise he made as recognition dawned.

"Holt, I found her — found her wanderin' — she was mutterin' about the wagon and her father. I didn't catch much —" Decker swallowed hard. "I had to bring her here before lookin' for her Pa." He rushed to explain.

"You very well may have saved her life." Glenna said in a rushed but kind voice, then added, "Holt, you need to get the others and go look for her father."

She was right; he knew. Edith had felt bitterly cold in his arms and much heavier than a woman her size had any right to, and the few moments he had carried her had left him chilled. He knew that meant she had probably been out all night, if not longer. Snow turning to water, soaking the fabric of her dress and coat.

Holt didn't contemplate about what had to be done next. Didn't stop to ask himself what on earth Mr. Carson and his daughter had been doing out right after a storm but ran two steps at a time down the stairs, hearing as he yanked the door open the sound of Glenna directing Decker to stay and help her.

———

"We need to get these wet things off." Glenna had already set her fingers to work on Edith's coat buttons. When Decker didn't move, as if he was glued to the spot, she almost shouted at him from over her shoulder, "Help me, Decker!"

He just stood still, his face stricken.

Spinning, Glenna grabbed at Decker, forcing the large man to look into her face. He blinked, trying to focus. "Decker, we have to get Edith out of these wet things before she comes down with a fever. We need to get her dry and bring her body temperature up."

She pleaded with him to understand the seriousness of Edith's situation and added softly, "Please, I need your help... her life depends on it."

He nodded once, his jaw set. "What do you want me to do?"

Decker took instruction, his fingers flying over the loops of Edith's boots as he worked to remove them from her feet. Glenna set back to work, pulling at the buttons of the coat. Edith's coat, hidden under the layer of Decker's coat that had been wrapped around her. Next, the heavy scarf wrapped first over her head to cover her ears, then down around her neck.

Glenna set to work on the strings of her woolen cap hiding under the scarf. The material was frozen, making horrible cracking sounds as she pulled it away from Edith's skin. Glenna stopped when Edith's right ear stuck to the fabric, frozen to it. Knowing time was of the essence and also not wishing to cause further damage, she glanced toward Decker. "Poor me some water on that cloth."

He did as instructed and handed the damp cloth to Glenna. She leaned in close and pressed the cloth to the area, allowing the water to soak into the material fully before attempting to remove it. The work went slowly and required the cloth to be dampened several times.

"That water ain't warm, won't it hurt her more?"

"You must be careful when warming up someone suffering from frostbite. Rubbing or chafing the skin will only cause more damage. Slowly warming up the body with tepid water and dry clothes is much better than setting someone directly into a hot bath or in front of a roaring fire. It seems counterintuitive, nevertheless you can not rush the process."

266

Decker was gingerly pulling off the second boot when Glenna started to roll down the gloves covering small hands. Glenna groaned inwardly at the sight of her fingers.

"Decker, I'm going to need you to help me get her out of this dress."

Decker shot to his feet, "Oh, I can't —"

"There is no time for decorum! I can not tend to her hands until she is out of this dress. She may lose her fingers if we don't hurry." She knew her tone was bitting and filled with frustration. "Now, sit behind her, just there, supporting her head and shoulders." Decker moved as she had directed, averting his eyes as Glenna worked to remove Edith's frozen dress.

She didn't stop to try to make Decker more comfortable but did, for Edith's sake, cover her with the quilt, as much to keep her modest as to retain what little body heat she still had. With each passing minute, it became harder and harder as the fabric went from stiff to soaked and stuck to her skin. Lastly came her under clothes and stockings. Glenna said a silent prayer. It was disjointed, rambling, and at times incoherent when she pulled the stockings away from her toes.

Dashing to the dresser to retrieve one of her nightgowns and a shawl, Glenna instructed Decker to cradle Edith, holding her steady as Glenna worked the dry clothes over her head and down her body under the cover of the quilt.

"Can you move her here?" Glenna asked, indicating the head of the bed. Decker lifted Edith and placed her ever so softly into the middle of the bed. Glenna pulled the quilts up over her and tucked them under her chin.

"Fetch me two towels, would you?" She asked Decker as she set to work unpinning Edith's hair. He hesitated only a second and was gone in a flash. Glenna felt her fingers burn from the extended exposure to the cold. She cringed, thinking about how impossibly cold Edith was to the touch.

"Here," Decker pushed the towels toward Glenna and she set to work rubbing at Edith's hair, trying to dry as much of it close to the scalp as possible. Edith moaned, her eyes fluttering open for a moment, unfocused. They closed once more.

"Decker, I need your help with her hands. Fetch two shallow bowls from the kitchen and the kettle from the stove. Hurry."

For all his bulk, the man moved faster than Glenna would have expected and was back in an instant.

Glenna poured a small amount of the hot water into each bowl followed by a more generous amount of the cooler water from her wash bowl pitcher until the water reached the temperature she desired.

"Place this bowl right under her hand so that her fingers dangle into the water." She told him, handing over the bowl. Decker did and cringe visibly when Edith gave a pitiful moan.

"You must keep her fingers in the water. Hold her hand in it if you have to." Glenna instructed sternly and again the big man paused, looking a bit scandalized, "The water will help slowly bring the heat back. Her hands and feet are the most vulnerable to damage from prolonged exposure." Glenna explained while placing her own bowl under Edith's other hand.

Decker didn't argue, just set his lips into a thin line and, sitting next to the bed, pressed her hand into the water with a light touch. Glenna noticed his every movement made with a single-mindedness and done with great compassion. Edith moaned, muttering something Glenna couldn't quite make out.

"It's alright, you're safe Edith," Glenna said in a low soothing voice, contenting to work the water from Edith's locks.

Her blue lips split apart. "Papa?" It was barely a breath.

"Holt has left to collect him. Don't worry." It was all Glenna could manage as she took the second towel and wrapped Edith's hair into it, covering her head and praying they were doing enough to save her life.

"Decker — I need to set some more water on to boil. We will need to continuously add small amounts to these bowls. Stay with her, keep her fingers submerged. I'll be back soon." She reassured him, dashing out of the room.

Gunner lifted his head from the story he had been reading to Finn and Daisy, Blu resting next to the fire, as Glenna passed the front room headed to the kitchen. She gave him an appreciative look. He nodded back his understanding.

"Holt and Bowen are out lookin'. I stayed back to help with the youngin's." Gunner answered the unasked question.

"Alright, I need to make some warm broth and heat water for Edith," Glenna said and glanced over to the children.

"These two are fine with me. Do what you need to for her."

Glenna set to work as the trio delved back into their story. She felt as though hours had gone by before she could return to the room. Decker had moved to the other side of the bed, working on Edith's opposite hand.

"Has she said anything else?"

"No, just some sounds from time to time," Decker said with worry.

Glenna rushed to get the bed warmer, fill the pan with embers from the fire and lifted the blankets at the end of the bed and placed it as close as she felt comfortable next to her feet. Edith whimpered slightly, shivered, her teeth chattering.

Decker looked at Glenna. His expression was one filled with such concern it tugged painfully at Glenna's heart.

"Shivering means her body is trying to regain the heat it's lost." She reassured him.

It was something she had learned during the bitterly cold winters after the death of her father. The rooms at the boarding house had never been warm and felt as though the winter winds past right through the walls. Using the bed warmer had helped. Still there were nights when the winter chill had felt as though it would shake her beyond the point of breaking. Glenna pushed past the memory.

Blu whimpered from the door, drawing both their attention. "You want to help, boy?" Glenna whispered and beckoned the dog to come closer. Blu never came up the stairs, and it was odd seeing him here now.

With permission Blu padded into the room and without further prompting made his way to the foot of the bed, up onto the chest that sat there and taking soft, deliberate steps made his way onto the bed, stretching out his length next to Edith's side as if he knew she could use the added heat that his body could offer. Watching this made tears sting the backs of Glenna's eyelids. Decker, too, looked as if it had suddenly become harder to swallow.

"I didn't find her like I said." Decker's voice broke into the silence. "It was Blu Dog. He was right there with me, then suddenly he bolted. I called him to come back, but he just dashed over the rise and was gone. I heard barkin'. He wouldn't stop. So I followed the fool dog, wonderin' if he had found a dead yearlin'. My heart dropped out of my chest when I saw her. Nearly collapsed to her knees, huggin' Blu Dog."

He let his head drop a bit. "I wasn't to take him this mornin'. It was just a quick ride to check on the main road condition. If Blu Dog had stayed home like Holt had told him to, I'd never have found her."

Glenna blinked back more tears and reached over to scratch Blu just behind the ear. He didn't lift his head, but opened his eyes to look at her.

"Good dog," she whispered as emotion caught her voice, causing it to crack. "I'm going to fetch another quilt." She said, attempting to regain her composure. Decker didn't lift his head or acknowledge her statement.

He was still holding Edith's hand nearest him, pressing her fingers into the bowl, head bent low. As she passed, Glenna could hear the soft sound of Decker's voice. He was reciting scripture, or perhaps it was prayer. She felt like an intruder listening and slipped out of the room.

***

"What do ya reckon happened?" Bowen inquired as he and Holt followed the winding path Edith had cut through the snow. It was easy to see where she had slowed, stumbled, fallen and regained her footing as the snow told a clear story of her travel.

Holt shook his head. "I can't say, but if I venture a guess, I'd wager Carson was makin' some deliveries up the way."

"The roads have been passable the last few days... with a light wagon, he shouldn't have run into any trouble." Bowen added thoughtfully.

Simon Carson was a good man, he was a transplant to Wyoming, but had been in the area for most of Holt's life. The man knew just as well as Bowen or Holt when the roads would be good for travel.

He was also known to make deliveries to a few families needing supplies before the snow became impassable at the foot of the mountains. There was a fair chance that was what had taken him out with Edith. Whatever had stranded them and why Edith had been found wandering alone was another matter altogether.

Holt pulled back on the reins as they came to the road that led to town.

"With all this fresh melt in the ruts, I can't tell what direction she came from," Bowen huffed.

He was right. The warmer day had melted a good deal of snow and the runoff had filled the wagon ruts, washing away evidence of her footfalls. "We need to split up."

Bowen nodded, turned his horse toward Buffalo, and set out at a slow gate, his head on a swivel looking for signs Edith had passed that direction. Holt did the same in the other direction.

Bowen disappeared over a rise. Holt could still hear his call for Simon as they took turns calling out for the man. His eyes trained on any small sign that Edith had come this way, any small disturbance in the snow. She hadn't traveled towards the home-place on the road his wagon used to meet the main road, rather stumbled in the direction Decker had found her walking in from nowhere near the well-worn road.

It made Holt believe that Edith had used some of the landmarks beside the main road to know what general direction she needed to take. What mad kind of fear had driven her off the main road? Daring to take what she must have thought was a shortcut to the nearest house.

The choice could have left her stumbling about until the cold halted her footsteps forever. With a second snowfall, her path would have been lost and any search for her would have been fruitless. Edith was unbelievably lucky to have been found at all.

"Simon… Simon Carson." Holt called out as the road curved and the grade steepened. There was no reply. Pulling back on the reins, he held Ranger a moment and let his eyelids fall shut, the blanket of snow bleaching all color from the landscape also stung his eyes.

Ranger pulled on the reins, "Alright boy," Holt clicked his tongue. Minutes ticked by as he desperately looked for any signs that Edith had passed this direction. Ranger swung his head, snorted with impatience. His ears flickered forward, then back rapidly.

"You hear somethin' don't you?" Holt patted him on the neck, "Go," he whispered and Ranger bolted forward, his hooves finding purchase on the soft earth.

Holt held on, leaning low over Ranger's neck as the horse bolted down a long stretch. Mud and water sprayed up from his hooves, soaking Holt. Another slight curve lay up ahead and Ranger slowed to round it, pulling up short with a nicker. The small wagon sat just in front of them. Laying on its side, the yolk pulling on the horse still strapped to it. The animal was laying at an odd angle, chest heaving, head laying in the mud.

Holt dismounted, gave Ranger one thankful pat on the neck as he approached the wagon, hands up, slow movements and speaking softly so that he didn't spook the other horse. It was clear as he drew closer the hind leg was broken. There was nothing he could do for it.

"Simon?" He left the animal and started around the wagon, noting the broken axle, a sinking feeling settled in, knowing what he was going to find. Simon Carson lay trapped from the mid-chest down under the side of the wagon, the contents spilling out around him, his skin ashen gray, his left arm lay pinned between his chest and the edge of the wagon, clearly broken.

Eyes looking unseeing at the sky, dried blood stained his mouth and chin. A buffalo hide had been placed haphazardly over him. Perhaps the man had still been alive when Edith had gone for help?

It was clear he was dead now. Holt noted the indentation in the snow in the exact shape of someone curled up, pressed close to his side. The sight was startling on a level he wasn't expecting. He had known, of course, that Edith must have stayed next to her father during the night, but to see the evidence of it shook him.

It also gave him an unexpected timeline. The ground under the indentation was clear of snow... how long had they been exposed to the elements? Holt swept off his hat and went down on one knee, a prayer for peace and rest slipping from between his lips.

Sixteen

"Has she woken?" Glenna asked, setting down a warm bowl of broth next to the bed.

"No," Decker answered, sounding a bit lost.

"She's been through an ordeal. It may take some time." She tried to sound reassuring. "I'm going to try to feed her a bit of broth. Would you mind helping?"

Decker, who had been sitting next to the bed, still holding one of Edith's hands, nodded and tucked her hand back under the warmth of the covers.

"Just hold her head up a bit." She instructed and, taking up the bowel, attempted to spoon a small amount of the liquid in between her lips.

The broth started to dribble back out of her pale lips. Glenna was quick to mop it up with the corner of a washrag. The second attempt yielded the same results. Glenna felt worry tightening in her chest as Edith's lips closed as tightly as her eyes.

She moved the spoon closer and, taking up a small amount, lifted it to Edith's lips, pressing the tip of the spoon to her bottom lip and waited for any sign of response. Her lips stayed closed.

"Edith, you need to drink the broth." It was Decker's voice. Low and smooth, coaxing Edith to drink.

Edith seemed to respond to the sound of his voice and her lips parted, allowing Glenna to tilt the spoon and the amber liquid trickled between her lips. Edith sputtered and coughed, the broth being expelled.

"May I try?" Decker took up the small decorative pillow that had been in the chair he had taken up residence in and tucked it behind her head, freeing his hands for the bowel. Glenna passed it to him and watched as Decker worked, with care and patience, to get Edith to take a few spoonfuls.

Edith moaned and turned her head from the spoon. Decker didn't push, just handed the broth back to Glenna, and gently slipped the second pillow out from under her head. Edith made a soft sound, then fell silent.

Glenna met Decker's eyes across the space. She could read the unspoken words held in his gaze. She nodded her understanding. He would stay, watch over her. Glenna took up the bowl and turned to leave the room.

Just as her feet hit the hall, a knock sounded at the front door. She rushed down the steps just as Gunner pulled open the front door.

"Sheriff?" Gunner moved back, allowing Sheriff Canton and a second man Glenna didn't recognize to step into the entry, sweeping off his hat.

He nodded at Gunner, turned to Glenna, who hadn't yet made it to the last step. "Mrs. Sterling, this is John Helm," Glenna recognized the younger man as Patsy's beau.

"You're looking for Mr. Carson and Miss Edith." She cut him short. "Please, come with me." She waved at them to follow her up the stairs. He looked taken aback, started after her, leaving the second man with Gunner.

276

Glenna walked into the bedroom. "Decker, Sheriff Canton is here."

Decker stood, "Hello Sheriff."

Frank Canton looked from Glenna to Decker. His eyes landed on Edith. "How is she?'

Glenna swallowed. "It's a bit early to tell."

He tore his gaze from Edith. "Mrs. Carson rousted me out of bed this morning in a panic. She thought maybe Mr. Carson and Edith had stopped to stay with someone when the snow fell earlier than expected, but when the roads became passable and there was no sign of them, she began to worry. Patsy's young man," He inclined his head toward the stairs to indicate the young man he had left with Gunner. "He was ready to go out looking to help quell the fears of his new sweetheart. That's all I know… now, fill me in on what's been happenin' here."

"I went out with Blu Dog early, checkin' on some of the cattle, when he bolted. I followed. He led me to Miss Edith. I brought her right here." Decker offered up the information.

"Holt and Bowen left right away to look for her father," Glenna added.

"Has she said anything that might help in locatin' her Pa?"

"No," Glenna said with regret. "I'm afraid she hasn't been coherent enough."

Sheriff Canton asked a few more questions before he seemed satisfied. He nodded to himself as if he had made up his mind about something. "Alright, I am going to head out and see if I can meet up with them, help with the search. Mr. Helm will get word back to her Ma' and make sure to send out the Doc. Thanks for your help, Mrs. Sterling." He bowed out of the room and Glenna moved to follow him, noticing Decker had sat back in the seat near Edith's bedside out of the corner of her eye.

Once he was within speaking distance to John, he gave the firm order for the young man to head back into Buffalo, send Doc Tillman out, and go right to Mrs. Carson. With as much politeness as it was possible to muster, the young man dashed out of the house with only a nod in Glenna's direction. The poor young man looked white from stress. She felt for him. He was about to deliver distressing news to those he cared deeply about.

"— I didn't pass anyone on my way here. That tells me I need to head toward Hardin's." The Sheriff was saying to Gunner. Daisy had left where Finn was still sitting with a book laying open on the floor between them and was now tugging on Glenna's skirt. She bent and scooped up the little girl.

"Gunner, you should ride out with him," Glenna said softly, interrupting their conversation. Both men turned to look at her and she cleared her throat. "That is… we aren't sure what state you'll find Mr. Carson in — you may need an extra pair of hands." Thinking of the condition Edith had been in, Glenna rushed to gather up Holt's bedroll and pressed the items into Sheriff Canton's hands upon her return.

"You might need this as well." She said in a small voice. His eyes grew soft as he took the items and nodded.

"That's very thoughtful of ya." With that, he stepped outside. Gunner at his heels.

Holt walked slowly back to Ranger, who was now tied securely to a nearby tree, and slid the rifle back into the scabbard suspended from the gullet. He leaned on Ranger's neck and patted him lightly, speaking nonsense in a reassuring voice. It was clear Ranger was nervous after the sound of gunfire coming so near him after the last close call. He dug at the thawing ground beneath his hooves, snorted and pulled hard at the reins.

"It's alright boy, you're alright — it's over."

Ranger nickered in protest, kicked up more earth, before starting to calm. Holt stayed probably longer than necessary, thinking over his next move. The wagon needed to be lifted. Simon needed to be taken home.

Holt turned just as a whistle ran out, Gunner. He knew the sound of it from many days in the saddle and gave his answering whistle and rushed back to the road to meet him. Moving toward him, Holt saw Gunner and Sheriff Frank Canton riding toward him. Both men urged their mounts faster at the sight of him — at the sight that lay behind him.

The moment their boots hit the ground, Holt started talking. "Simon — Mr. Carson, he's gone. Passed probably sometime early this mornin'."

"We heard the rifle — you had to put the animal down, I'm guessin'." Frank said and Holt nodded.

The three approached the wagon, Frank looking closely at every angle, assessing the horse, the axel, finally moving to crouch near Simon. He had started to mutter to himself, stood up, and cussed loudly, throwing his hat to his feet.

"I'll have to wait to get the full story from Edith — assumin' that she will recover — but I think I have a pretty good idea of what happened." He said, finally breaking the silence. "Let's get him home to Phyllis."

Holt went to work unhitching the wagon from the horse. "Are you ready for this?" Frank asked somberly. He and Gunner had moved to lift the end of the wagon, leaving Holt to pull Simon out from under it. Holt took a long breath, plunging both hands into the snow beneath Simon's shoulders and grasping the man just under each arm. His body was stiff and cooler to the touch than the surrounding snow.

The wagon lifted, and Holt tugged backward. For an instant Holt worried that Simon's body might have frozen to the road under him. Readjusting his grip, Holt pulled hard, digging his heels in and gaining purchase. Painfully slow, Simon's lower torso appeared out from under the side of the wagon. It took a few more sharp pulls before his legs and feet had cleared the space.

"I have him," Holt called, and the wagon slammed back down into the mud with a thud. Gunner and Frank both appeared next to Holt just as he lay Simon back down.

"Damn," Gunner breathed, looking over the crumpled body. It was then Holt realized this was the first thing he had said.

He wasn't able to keep his eye from surveying the damage. The wagon, although not as large as some, was still heavy enough to do considerable damage. His arm shattered, chest collapsed inward at a nauseating angle, leaving an almost perfect impression of the wagon's edge.

His right leg had a matching dent and bent at an odd angle. It was clear that the collapse of the wagon wheel had caught him by surprise, its sudden tip toward him catching Simon off guard and giving him no time to jump out of harm's way.

280

Frank walked back to where they had left their mounts and unstrapped a bedroll from the back of his saddle.

"Your Missus was good enough to send this." He said, returning with Holt's bedroll.

Moving quickly, they wrapped Simon in the heavy fabric and slung his body across Ranger's back, strapped just behind the saddle.

"Let's pack up what we can in our saddlebags to take back to Phyllis," Frank instructed.

Gunner went to work. There wasn't much left in or around the wagon. There wasn't any sign that food had been in the wagon on Simon's return trip to town. He must have made all his deliveries before the accident, Holt surmised. The only items scattered around were a collection of buttons, ribbons, pins, thread, a few tins of salve, pipe tobacco, a bottle of some tincture, and a box whose lid had shifted, showing small scraps of fabric. All items those not able to travel to town might require during the long winter months. He must have thought to bring them with him to offer for purchase at his scheduled stops.

There had been no more words spoken between the men. There was no need. What they had come to do was now done, and the task ahead would be one much more unpleasant. Death was a fact of life. Lord knew they had each seen their fair share. Nevertheless, telling a woman she was now a widow, hearing her cries of despair and sorrow, was never something any man was prepared for.

Glenna fed the children, attempting to listen to Finn's chatter and answer his questions even though her mind was not where it ought to be. He was fascinated with the prospect of having Edith in the house and was speculating on the why's and how's of it all. It was a bit trying to her, nonetheless Glenna bit back her annoyance and answered him with kindness in her voice.

"I am sure your uncle will be back soon and we will have more information. I need to take some food up to Decker and check on Miss Edith. Finn, could you keep an eye on Daisy for me? I won't be gone long. Just give her a bit more bread if she finishes. Alright?"

Finn nodded and hopped into the chair nearest his sister, pulling his plate along with him. Glenna felt a swell of thankfulness well up and she bent to place a kiss on his brow.

"You are such a wonderful help, Finn. Daisy is lucky to have such a charitable elder brother." She meant it.

Decker was just as she had left him. Seated next to the bedside, his hand holding Edith's in the water. Glenna set down the tray of food and went to the foot of the bed to remove the bed warmer that was now cool to the touch. Tucking the quilt back in place, Glenna grazed her hand across one of Edith's feet. This action incited a painful groan. Decker and Glenna glanced at Edith, exchanging a look between them.

Not wishing to say anything alarming as thoughts about what the exposure might have done, Glenna pushed Decker to eat. With some reluctance, he lifted his hand from Edith's and reached for the tray.

Blu lifted his head just enough to sniff at the food and lap up the morsel Decker offered, then laid his head back down on the quilt, eyes closed. It was in this moment of utter silence she heard the sound of horses and rushed to the window that looked out over the front of the house toward the road.

"It's Doctor Tillman," she felt relief at the sight of him. Something else caught her gaze and her heart stopped. Three riders converged with him on the road from the other direction. Three riders, only three.

She swallowed hard. "Holt, Sheriff Canton, and Gunner are almost home as well."

"Do they have Carson with 'em?"

She blinked and turned to Decker. "I — I can't tell from his distance." She lied, not wishing to say anything upsetting in case Edith was lucid enough to hear her.

Something unspoken passed between them, Decker looking from her to Edith. The reluctance to leave her side was written in his expression. His strong features softened slightly as his gaze lingered on her a moment longer. When he drew his eyes back to Glenna, it was clear that Decker knew what she had been thinking. It was not the time for talk of Edith's father. She was in no condition to hear news of his fate or their speculation of it.

There was no need for an explanation as Glenna left the room and made her way to the kitchen to check on the children. Her path led her to the front porch to meet the men.

Doctor Tillman was the first to reach the house and dismount, unhooking his medical bag from the saddle as he did. Gunner and Sheriff Canton jumped from their mounts as well. Glenna saw all of it without taking her eyes off Holt and the bedroll strapped to the back of Ranger. The air was full of their voices, inquiries followed by explanations.

Tillman and Canton walked around Ranger and disappeared behind his flank, inspecting the contents of the bedroll. Something was addressed to Holt, who nodded his acknowledgment, turned Ranger back toward the road.

"The poor man," Doctor Tillman sighed, coming up the steps.

"If you don't have anythin' else for me, Doc, I think it best I go back to town with Holt. I'm afraid he'll need help with breakin' the news to Mrs. Carson." Sheriff Canton pulled himself back into the saddle.

"That might be best. I asked Mrs. Carson to stay at home until I had examined Edith. She was in a state of terrible shock when John delivered the news." The doctor said with sadness.

Canton tipped his hat to Glenna in farewell, spurred his horse to make up the distance already between him and Holt. Glenna turned and led Doctor Tillman inside.

Seventeen

Holt attempted to fold himself into the smallest corner of the Carson family home after he and Sheriff Canton had delivered the news. Phillis and Patsy did not need an audience to their grief, and he itched to leave them to those better equipped to offer consolation than himself.

However, after he and John had carried Simon in and laid him out on the long kitchen table as requested Phillis had broken down into a fit of sobs and was caught up by her youngest daughter, the two of them lost in their sorrow had also blocked the only exit to the room.

He noted that young John also looked a mite uncomfortable and unsure of what should be done or said. The sheriff was the only one who seemed to keep his head. Crouching near the pair, he started to talk in a low tone to Phillis, who soon quieted, dried her eyes, and seemed to steal herself. Holt wondered what the man could have possibly have said to her to stop her sobs.

She lifted her eyes, now red-rimmed, and looked right at Holt. "Thank you for bringing my husband home."

A lump formed in his throat, preventing Holt from giving her a response, and he simply nodded.

She allowed herself to be pulled to her feet and Patsy followed, suddenly looking very aware of the surrounding company, she dried her tears. Phyllis wrung her hands hard and walked to the head of the table. Her chin wavered however, she kept her jaw locked as she looked down into Simon's face.

Suddenly remembering herself, she turned sharply from her husband just as Holt took a side step toward the door, stopping him in his tracks.

"Edith! Oh, my darling girl."

"She is in good hands, Phyllis," Sheriff Canton reassured her.

"We should have her fetched home as soon as possible." She pressed.

"Doc Tillman is at Crossroads now," Holt finally ventured to comment.

Phyllis blinked as if he hadn't spoken. "She would do much better at home, I'm sure,"

"Ma, perhaps we should wait to have her moved until we have talked to Doctor Tillman," Patsy said in a clear and steady voice. "Edith's health should be our paramount concern, not her location."

Holt was mildly surprised by this declaration and stole a glance in her direction. For the first time, he saw Patsy Carson as a young woman and not the child sister of Edith's. He had always known her as. When her elder sister wasn't doing the speaking for her, Patsy, it seemed, had a mind of her own.

"Yes, of course," her mother nodded. "John, would you mind calling for the Pastor and — we need to have him measured for a coffin — I'll need to press his Sunday best and — and —" emotion clogged her throat and the room fell into silence. John had taken her instruction to heart and slipped from the room.

Patsy stepped over to her mother's side and put a hand on her shoulder, "It's alright Ma, everything will get taken care of." Phyllis leaned into Patsy's side, drawing up her shoulders in a show of

286

strength. Patsy leaned in and said something too low for the sound of it to carry to Holt's ears. Feeling his unintentional intrusion, Holt moved toward the exit.

"Mrs. Carson, Patsy, I wish I had the right words to say — somethin' to comfort you — you will be in my prayers and please let me know if there is anythin' we can do to help. Anythin' at all."

"Thank you, Holt," Phyllis said with unshed tears brimming her eyes, "You and your Missus are taking care of our Edith, we are so thankful for that —"

Holt was left with not being able to respond as John walked back into the room with the announcement that Pastor Joseph was on his way. Sheriff Canton was offering assistance, and John was doing his level best to console Patsy, while Holt made to leave. Canton caught his eye, and the two men exchanged a nod of sober understanding.

Holt passed through the storeroom and out into the open shelves of the shop. The closed sign hung limply in the window and a small crowd had formed on the walkout front, frowning at the locked doors.

"Holt!" Patsy called after him. "Please, would you take something to Edith for me?"

"I would be glad to."

"I'll be just a moment." She flew back through the storeroom and was gone.

True to her word, she did not leave him standing there long, rushing back a small book and folded a bit of paper clutched in her hands.

"I think Edith would feel a bit more at ease —" She pressed the small bible reader and hastily placed the note into his hands. "The note is for your wife. I know Ma didn't say — she should have thanked your cattle hand as well for saving Edith, for finding her. Please tell him I am grateful beyond expression. We owe you all a great debt."

"There is no debt between neighbors, Miss Patsy." Holt reassured her, "But I will pass on your thanks to Decker and don't be too hard on your Ma'. Her life — your life and that of Edith's has suddenly changed forever. She is facing a great and difficult new chapter without your Pa."

"Is that what you felt when Clint passed?" She asked, her green eyes swimming with emotion.

"And my parents." He nodded.

Patsy mulled this over, "You are a good man, Holt Sterling," Patsy blinked a few times, "I'm afraid we were not very neighborly when it was your loss. We could have done more for you after all your loss. Shown more kindness and understanding about the ways your life changed suddenly. I know for my sister's part she was not very — forgiving when it was known you had suddenly married." Patsy's face went a little pink as she sputtered. "The coldness toward your wife was uncalled for. As was the lack of empathy shown toward you by any of us."

"Miss Carson, there is no ill will between our families." Holt said thoughtfully and meant every word.

"I am relieved to hear it," she smiled, this time a tear slipped from her eye. She was quick to brush it away. "If we are welcome, I know as soon as possible Ma' would like to see Edith. I am not sure — when that will be possible — there is so much to arrange for Pa." Patsy's voice broke and she clamped her mouth closed.

"Our home is open to you and your mother at any time."

"Thank you." Patsy said around a sob.

There was a tap at the door behind Holt. Both turned to see Pastor Joseph and Rachel standing outside the locked doors.

Patsy rushed to unbolt the door and allow them to slip in. Holt took this opportunity to leave, promising to deliver the reader and note to Edith and send Doctor Tillman back straight away with word of her condition.

Holt tucked the reader and note into his saddlebag and suddenly bone-weary slumped a bit once he had pulled himself up into the saddle as if all his energy had swept out of him in one great motion.

"Come on little miss, you are going to come to help Finn and I get some chores finished up." Gunner swept a bundled up Daisy into his arms and she giggled with delight. Glenna gave him a grateful look as the trio slipped out to head to the barn, Blu taking up the rear. It would be better for Finn and Daisy to play in the dry, warm straw rather than in the house.

Gathering up her strength for what was coming, she pulled the pot of hot water off the stove. Moving as fast as she was able without spilling the water, she made her way back up to the bedroom. Decker looked ashen, his face a pained, sickly gray. Dr. Tillman directed her to put the water on the bedside table where he had laid out his tools already.

"You did well Mrs. Sterling. The damage would have been much worse if not for your fast action."

Glenna only gave him a tight-lipped curt nod. It was not the first time she had seen the effects of frost bite nor her first time helping to treat it.

"I've given her a sleeping draft. It should help to keep her calm for what's coming, but that isn't a guarantee she won't thrash, the two of you will have to help hold her. Decker, I need you to sit behind her and hold her arms. Glenna, would you mind helping me lift her?" Dr. Tillman asked and took up one of Edith's shoulders.

Glenna moved to do the same, supporting her head as much as she was able; they lifted Edith until there was enough room for Decker to slip behind her. Laying her back into the wall of his waiting chest, Decker gathered her up, holding her a bit loosely as he looked uncomfortable though determined at the same time. The conflict of emotions was something she had not seen the man express, and it contoured his normally pleasant features into something unrecognizable.

Doctor Tillman took up both her hands, bending Edith's arms at the elbow and draping her arms crossed over her chest. "Good, now Decker. You'll need to hold her arms down, like this." Decker obeyed and his large arms encircled Edith, pressing her arms close to her torso, immobilizing them. She was almost fully enveloped in his arms, disappearing into Decker's embrace. Head lulling on one of his shoulders.

"Glenna, I need you to steady her legs, I need to remove these toes and she must stay still." Glenna kneeled at the edge of the bed, her arms and upper torso laying across Edith's legs, pinning her in place. Edith didn't stir at the pressure.

From the corner of her eye, she watched with a dull horror as Dr. Tillman took up a small bone saw. Sucking in a deep breath, she stilled her resolve, eyes closed she turned her face away and wished she could cover her ears as the sounds burrowed into her brain.

290

After a few moments, Edith's body jumped. She began to writhe and scream. The sound of it tearing from her throat was beyond excruciating, and Glenna felt hot tears stinging her cheeks. Edith tried to bend her knees, pulling her legs away from what was causing her pain, forcing Glenna to flatten herself, pinning Edith's legs to stay where they were.

Logically, Glenna knew the dead tissue and bone wasn't causing any pain in the removal process. She also knew the pain Edith was experiencing was from the necessary removal of some healthy bits along with the dead to stop the flesh from becoming necrotic and the damage from spreading. It was horrific to know Doctor Tillman was forced to cut away undamaged portions to insure healing long term.

Edith cried out and jerked hard, sobbing, "Stop! Please stop!"

It was then she heard a new sound, a soft and reassuring noise, and realized that Decker was speaking to her. His tone even. His voice resonated low.

Edith's erratic movements quieted. The crying continued overshadowing the sound of the saw. Glenna felt the pull to look, to witness the magical effect Decker seemed to be having. Not wanting to break the spell he had put Edith under, so she kept her eyes closed.

———————————

Holt wavered, pushing open the kitchen door and stepping inside, unsure of what he would find. Gunner sat at the table with Daisy and Finn, who all turned to greet him.

"Uncle Holt!" Finn bounded toward him and hugged both his legs, arresting his forward motion. Holt patted him on the head.

Daisy also called for him but was prevented from toddling over to him by Gunner, who was wrestling with the little girl to get the food off her face.

Gunner gave up, cleaning her off and let her go just before she started to cry. Holt bent and embraced Daisy, whose steps were still a little wobbly. "I take it things here haven't been goin' well." He said, taking in the state of the kitchen.

Gunner, looking somber, just tilted his head toward the upper level of the house.

Holt gave Gunner a look of gratitude over the top of Daisy's head, passed her back to Gunner, and addressed Finn. "Why don't you help Gunner finish cleanin' your sister's mess? After I check on Miss Edith you can help me start the evenin' chores?"

"Ok, Uncle Holt." Finn nodded faithfully.

Just as Holt walked into the hall and right into Glenna. She let out a little yelp of surprise as a hand flew to cover her mouth in an attempt to stifle the sound. The sight of her sent a wave of relief pulsing through his veins.

It was impossible to tell who reached out first, but in a blur of movement, she was suddenly in his arms. Glenna clinging to him, his arms crushing her to him painfully. For a brief moment, the others, only feet away in the kitchen disappeared, there was nothing save the two of them, giving the other comfort. He kissed the top of her head softly and with his lips still pressed to her skin. Holt sighed as he breathed her in.

Uncurling her fingers from his shirt, Glenna composed herself and stepped back a fraction, still encircled by his arms. "Poor Edith lost three of her toes, a finger, and part of her right ear to frostbite. Doctor Tillman isn't sure she won't still suffer some damage to her chin, cheeks, or nose from exposure as well. He is still with her."

292

Holt felt his stomach drop. "Has she talked yet? Told what happened?"

Glenna shook her head, "No, she just cries out for her father." Her lower lip trembled slightly as he pulled her back into an embrace.

The sound of footsteps above them and a woman's sob pulled them apart.

"I should get back." She stammered and brushed the evidence of tears from her cheek. Holt noted the remains of blood smeared and dried to her hands. The sight had Holt rushing to encircle her in his arms, blocking the sight from view.

"I just came to grab some freshwater and towels." Glenna muttered, her head buried in the crook of his neck.

"I'll fetch the water, love, go where you are needed." He said, reluctant to let her go. Turning, he rushed to fill and carry up the pail of water and tried not to spill any when Dr. Carson indicated where he should place it once he entered the room. As soon as it was set down, Carson started to do a fast rinse job on his tools and casting instructions over his shoulder, addressing the extended care expected.

With one glance, he took in the rest of the room, his eyes unable to stop from taking in the state of Edith. The bandages already soaked with blood, nightgown sodden with sweat, and blood spatter across the quilt lying beneath her made for a disquieting sight. For the space of one blink it was no longer Edith but the form of his mother in the bed, gray and still.

Slowly, the apparition of his mother dissolved back into the younger woman. The floor seemed to pitch drastically under his feet as the image dissolved back into a painful memory. Holt swallowed hard, bringing himself fully back into the present, his eyes finding Glenna, steadying him.

Glenna was fast and efficient. New quilts and bed-clothes appeared as if from thin air. Holt was moving. The action registered in his mind, going to her side. As if his feet and hands acted out of their own accord he and Decker worked in tandem taking instructions, holding what needed to be held, pushing or pulling when bid to do so, soon Edith was dressed in a fresh nightgown, her modesty preserved by Glenna's careful hands.

The sullied items discarded in a pile at the foot of the bed. New, dry quilts pressed close to Edith's side, the chair pulled close to the side of the bed, Decker seated himself in it, looking as if he was in a daze.

Remembering himself, he handed the book and letter to Glenna. "Patsy sent this." She looked at the reader, pocketed the letter and held out the book to Decker with the order to read it aloud. He looked relieved to have been given the task.

"I'll be back in the morning to check-in." Doctor Tillman announced, seeing himself out of the house.

Glenna stooped to gather the soiled linens as Holt stepped forward and took them from her arms. She gave him a tired yet grateful smile. "There is an empty washtub in the kitchen,"

He hadn't even made it down the stairs when voices sounded, "— where have you been all this time?" Holt recognized Gunner's voice as footsteps sounded in the kitchen.

"Doing my job, boy, and it seems everyone else's to boot," Bowen responded none too kindly. "I knew there was no use for me to keep looking for Carson by the time I returned to the Homestead so I set about gettin' done all that needed doing. Not everyone gets to

294

stay holed up, warm and all cozy while playin' nursemaid." Bowen snorted.

Holt didn't bother waiting to see what else would be said and stepped into the space. "Thank you for doin' what needed done Bowen, I know the work was badly neglected today, but that ain't no reason to take out your frustrations on Gunner."

"Oh, boss, I was just joshin' with him." Bowen hadn't looked at all surprised by Holt's sudden appearance or the armfuls of bloody linens.

Gunner, on the other hand, had a look of clear irritation on his face. Holt emptied his arms and picked up Daisy, who had toddled over to him. "Let's get some supper started." He said, addressing only the two children.

Eighteen

The kettle whistled shrilly before Holt could pull it from the stovetop, desperate to silence it, praying the noise hadn't roused either Glenna or Edith. He hurried and pulled it off the hot cook top. The effort proved fruitless when Glenna came into the kitchen a few moments later. She looked worn, her hair and clothes rumpled. Clearly, she had not slept well. Glenna affectionately greeted Finn and Daisy, sinking into a chair with a sigh of weariness.

Holt kissed her brow as he placed the tea kettle and a fresh cup in front of her. "I'm sorry. I didn't mean to wake you." He handed Daisy a slice of buttered bread and Finn a fat slice of bacon, sitting himself.

"Sadly, I have been up for hours." Glenna reached over and took his hand in hers, stopping Holt from moving too far away, "Thank you for the tea." She mustered a tired smile.

"Do you feel up to some breakfast?" Holt asked, squeezing her hand.

"Perhaps I will feel up to some food after tea. Has everyone else already eaten?"

"Yes," he hesitated a moment, "How is Edith?"

She sipped at her tea, answering. "She is finally resting." After another sip of her tea, the liquid was abandoned in favor of laying her head across folded arms over the tabletop, her eyes drooping shut.

Moving as silently as he could, Holt dressed the kids up warmly and took them out to gather eggs. The weather was again on the turn; the snow melting away, leaving giant puddles. Blu barked and rushed up to greet the trio, making a mess of himself in the process. Finn laughed, pushed the wet dog away from him after a few friendly licks to the face and falling in step next to Finn.

"Uncle Holt… do you think Miss Edith will be alright?"

"I hope so, but it's in God's hands now." Holt paused, then added, "Some hurts run deeper than the skin. The best thing we can do for her now is to be kind."

"The way everyone was kind when Pa died?" Finn asked.

Holt swallowed hard, "I suppose so,"

Finn kicked at a clump of melting snow. "I — I didn't much care for it — "

"Why's that?"

"Every time someone would hug me, pat my head, or look at me all sad like, it just made that feelin' right here worse." Finn hit himself in the middle of his chest with great emphasis.

Reaching the hen house, Holt shifted Daisy so he could unlock the door. Finn had scrunched up his nose in thought and with a sigh of defeat he shrugged his shoulders, "I guess there ain't much anyone can do — her Pa is still gone, same as ours."

"Bein' a friend to someone who's hurtin' can help." Holt pressed his hand to Finn's chest. "We never stop missin' those we have lost, nor should we. The hurt that seems sharp can dull with time and love can help heal, even those hurts on the inside."

Finn nodded his understanding.

"We better get a move on. There's a full day's work ahead of us as well as seein' to your schoolin'." Holt said, waving away the chickens still seated comfortably over their eggs.

"Can't see to schoolin' if Aunt Glenna is still asleep at the table." Finn countered.

"There isn't any gettin' out of your responsibilities today, young man." Holt sounded stern but gave Finn a wink. "If your Auntie is still sleepin' when we get back, I'll shoo her up to her room."

Finn placed two eggs into the basket. "It will make Aunt Glenna happy that I didn't let my work slip while she was helping Miss Edith."

"It will, Finn. It should also make you happy. Learin' is a tool you will never regret havin' sharpened."

Glenna sat upright, suddenly roused from her sleep. Blinking to adjust her eyes to the dark, she shook the last vestiges of sleep from her brain. It took several breaths for her to remember where she was and what had taken place in the previous two days.

Extracting herself from the quilt, she pushed up off the mattress set on the floor near the foot of her bed, which was still occupied by Edith. The day had been long, as Edith was in and out of fitful bouts of sleep. When evening had come, it had brought word from town. Mr. Carson would be laid to rest the next morning. After which, Edith's mother and sister would come to collect her.

Getting quietly to her feet, Glenna wondered what had roused her from sleep. Her ears strained to hear the sound of the other woman's breath while holding her own. The sound of her heartbeat

298

seemed much louder in her ears than it ought to be. Risking waking Edith, she crept to the edge of the bed and leaned close.

There it was, an intake of breath, a low shallow sound that sent a feeling of alarm rushing through Glenna. Something was wrong, something had changed. Her hands shot out, finding and pressing to Edith's skin.

Glenna bolted from the room and dashed across the hall, not caring for any sort of propriety she threw open the door. "Holt!" She blurted into the room.

The bed creaked its protest as Holt left it, "Glenna?" She could hear him fumbling in the pitch. A single light blazed up as he lit a match, holding it to the candle at the table near his bed.

"Edith has caught a fever."

Holt was shoving his arms into his shirtsleeves as he grabbed his boots. "I'll fetch Doc Tillman."

She took the candle from him and retreated to her room. Now able to see her charge, Glenna felt her stomach drop. Heavy beads of sweat pooled on every inch of exposed skin, with the nightgown laying heavily on her soaked through. Hurrying to grab a strip of bandage, she dipped it in the water left in the basin and started to mop Edith's face.

"Edith — Edith —" she called softly. There was no response. Just another shallow breath. Glenna pulled the quilt off and continued to bathe her face and neck in cool water. All the while saying a prayer. Prayer, something so natural and yet so foreign to her. Her mind had turned to God after all this time of believing he no longer cared or listened to her. Using the conduit to beg for his intervention in the life of another. Desperate for a benevolent response.

The effort to cool her down felt counterintuitive after working so hard getting her body warm after her exposure. This had Glenna hesitating. The only constant was the continued prayer that didn't falter until she heard the sound of hooves outside the house. Saying Amen just as Holt led Dr. Tillman into the room along with the added light of a lantern.

He sat his bag down and leaned over the edge of the bed, listening to Edith's breath, eyes on his watch as he checked the pulse at her wrist. Glenna noted his grave look and said nothing. He went about the rest of the examination and looked under each of her bandages as well as lifting her eyelids to study her eyes. Finally, doing a cursory glance at her bedpan, turning to Glenna.

"I see no signs of infection. You are using the camphor I left on her wounds, I see."

"Yes, of course."

He nodded. "There is a risk of infection, so keep her bandages as clean and dry as possible." He rummaged in his bag and pulled out a folded parchment, handing it to Glenna.

"I need you to mix this powdered willow bark in with her tea or in a broth, a spoon full, once a day, no more. Try to keep her drinking room temperature liquids, a little at a time. You can continue to bathe her face and neck in cool water, and I recommend a light quilt for the time being."

He turned sharply to Holt, "I also recommend the removal of both children from the home until Edith's fever has broken. I can not discern its cause and therefore can't rule out the possibility of it being infectious."

"I'll take them to Theo and Hattie."

300

"Holt." She reached out and gripped his shirt sleeve. He understood the implications.

"It's alright, love. Hattie is tough enough to watch over them both for a few days."

There was no need to discuss the preparations that needed to be made, Holt rushed out of the house and headed to hitch up the wagon as Glenna lit a second lamp, pulled out her carpetbag, and went right to the children's room, leaving Dr. Tillman to give Edith her first dose of willow bark.

The introduction of light in the room didn't rouse either of the children. Quickly she filled the carpetbag with clean clothes, fresh napkins, and wool covers for Daisy, then moved to gather items for Finn. Being quiet and efficient didn't seem to go hand in hand. Finn sat up in bed, rubbing his eyes.

"What — what's goin' on?"

Glenna paused in her frantic packing and knelt next to him. "Miss Edith has developed a fever. So, you and Daisy are going to go stay a few days with Hattie and Theo." She explained, pushing his sleep damp hair out of his face with one hand.

"Daisy can go, but I could stay, help look after Miss Edith, and do chores."

Glenna felt a swell of emotion build in her chest. "You are always a very good helper, except I do not need help with Miss Edith. Hattie and Theo do, however, need help with your sister."

Finn thought about this for a moment. "If Uncle Holt is stayin' to do all my chores, I think I can go to look after Daisy."

Glenna pressed a kiss to his temple, "Daisy is lucky to have such a good big brother. Now, why don't you grab your boots and bundle up while I finish collecting your things?"

Finn didn't need to be asked twice and clambered out of bed.

The night was fading into the cool light of dawn as Holt pulled the wagon up to the house. Finn sat next to him on the seat, the carpetbag placed near his feet, Daisy bundled warmly in a quilt tucked neatly in one of Holt's arms. They exchanged a look as the wagon pulled away that held all they were unable to say aloud.

Holt glared from Decker to Bowen then back, "Get, go cool off." Decker's stormy gaze didn't leave Bowen as Holt offered him a hand, helping him off the barn floor where Decker's right hook had landed him moments before.

"It's alright Holt," Bowen rubbed his already bruising jaw, "I probably deserved worse."

Holt put out his hand. "I'd let the two of you duke out your differences if I didn't need you to get some work done. Now get out and feed the herd before I lay you both out flat on your asses."

Decker clenched and unclenched his fists, clearly still trying to regain control, but relented with a nod. Bowen bent and took up his hat that had flown off when Decker's fist had plowed into his face, slapping it across his hip to dust it off, slapping it atop his head, leaving the barn.

"You want to tell me what the hell that was about?" Holt spat at Decker when Bowen was out of earshot.

"Just a disagreement." Decker also stormed away.

Holt turned to the only one left. Gunner, who had been standing back away from the action, shook his head. "Bowen made an off-color comment about Miss Edith not pullin' through. It didn't sit too well with Decker — he's quite taken with her."

Holt felt his jaw clench a little tighter and noted the pain in his back teeth. He had been grinding them a bit more than usual the last three days. Edith's fever had held steady despite the day and night efforts of Glenna and Dr. Tillman. There was a good chance she wouldn't pull through.

Gunner shook his head slightly. "How is she today?"

"No change." Holt admitted sorrowfully.

"I'm not tellin' ya what to do, boss, but I'd either say something sharp to Bowen about his lip or separate him from Decker until Edith is — gone from Crossroads."

———

"— Pa? Pa? No! Pa!"

"Shhhhh, it's alright. Shhhhhh." Glenna mopped Edith's forehead with a cool cloth. Her eyelids lifted, pupils unfocused.

"May I come in?" Decker asked from the doorway.

"Would you read to her? She seems to rest more deeply when you do." Glenna asked, waving him into the room.

Decker took up his spot near the head of the bed, took up Edith's reader, and opened it to where he had last left off. Glenna dipped the cloth in the cool water, rung out the excess, and brushed it along Edith's arms, neck, and face.

"It's my fault Pa's gone." The statement brought all movement in the room to an abrupt standstill. Glenna noticed that Edith looked more coherent than she had in days, her eyes suddenly clear and bright, locked on a spot across the room.

"Edith, it was a terrible accident." Decker protested, the reader in his hands all but forgotten.

Edith pressed on in a weak voice as if Decker had not spoken, "I wanted to order in some new material to have a dress made up. Father said he would need to wait until some of his larger accounts had been made current. I insisted we make the deliveries and collect payments that day. Almost that very moment." Her voice broke with emotion.

"I chastised him for allowing people to abuse his good nature and always having their accounts unpaid. That it was important for him to be seen as a strong businessman, one that commanded respect. I bullied him and made him feel small for being kind." Tears had started to roll down Edith's pallid cheeks.

She did not attempt to brush them away or hide the emotion in her trembling voice. "He packed up the wagon without complaint as I demanded to go along to ensure payment was made. He would have waited the week if not for my selfishness. My thoughtlessness over a frivolous and unnecessary expense. He would have waited — perhaps even discovered the issue with the axle before attempting to make the deliveries — he would have waited for the weather to clear and he would still be alive."

Glenna watched with a great weight in the pit of her stomach as Decker leaned slightly forward, one hand raised to cover Edith's. Brushing his fingertips across the back of her hand, Edith snapped it out from under the light pressure as if the contact caused her pain.

"Do not offer me comfort. Whatever horrible events took place only transpired because of me, and I ought to feel the full weight of it."

304

Nineteen

The sound of paper rustling and light filtering out into the hall from the half-open door drew Holt's attention. It was well past midnight, and he had been sure both women had long since gone to sleep.

Glenna was seated on the floor of the room, her back pressed to the wall, skirts gathered around her, a lamp burning low close by, surrounded by papers and two ledgers laying open across her lap, a quilt drawn around her shoulders.

"What has been keepin' you from sleep, love?" He asked softly, not wanting to bother Edith.

Her head darted up, her dark eyes bright. "I think I found something." She waved him over to her.

Holt stole a glance toward Edith, who seemed to be sleeping peacefully for the moment. Blu Dog stretched out along her right side. As quietly as the floorboards would allow, he made his way to her and crouched down as close to her as possible, careful not to rustle the papers.

"You should be gettin' some rest."

Glenna shook her head and waved off the comment, "Holt, I've been poring over the discrepancies between the ledger you found in Clint's room and this one." She indicated both of the books. "In this one, the cattle numbers match what you and the boys have been reporting. This one, however, shows many more recorded births over the past three seasons. Taking into account the number of newborn deaths that seem to occur and the occasional loss of sick or old animals, you are still looking at numerous unaccounted for missing cattle from this second ledger. You already figured that part out."

He nodded.

"Well — I've been sorting through some of the correspondence you found within Clint's hidden ledger. He was in contact with the Brand Inspector. Your brother was convinced someone was stealing the cattle and rebranding." Glenna handed him one significant letter dated just weeks previous to Clint's death.

It was a short message. One stated the Brand Inspector would be willing to look further into Clint's suspensions, but only once he had an idea of the culprits, there wasn't the manpower to inspect every ranch in the area for possible rebranded cattle.

"I don't think Clint had the chance to answer this letter with one of his own."

Glenna handed him a folded sheet. Across the top was the Inspector's name, a brief greeting, and the date, nothing more. It was the date that was significant, the day Clint had died.

His knees weakened and Holt lowered himself so that he too was seated on the floor, not bothering to sweep away the papers now trapped under him.

"I believe your brother was in the process of writing to the Brand Inspector that he had found proof of cattle theft. He was interrupted from writing the rest of the letter but not hiding it away. If I am right — and you are right that Clint wasn't just thrown from his horse — it's what got him killed."

Holt felt his head swimming. "What in all of this makes you believe that."

"Because I found it, I found the rebranding designs as well."

Glenna took up the two brands that had been sketched out onto separate loose pages. Lifting the Crossroads brand image to the light, she held the page steady and slipped the second paper in front of it, both showing clearly with the lamplight shining behind them as she turned the second page until the lines matched up, creating a third familiar brand.

Holt reached out and took the two sheets gingerly, making sure not to move either.

"That's the Landry brand."

"Clint must have been suspicious that the Landry boys were taking cattle from your herd, not enough to be easily noticed, and rebranding them. Perhaps for years. It wasn't until the last few seasons that the discrepancy was large enough to be noticed."

"I wouldn't put it past the Landry brothers to rebrand rather than build their herd honestly, sadly a few sketches aren't enough to prove anything. It isn't enough to kill for either. If Clint had some kind of proof, it was larger than anything he left behind in that box." Holt muttered.

Glenna's brow furrowed in thought, "Holt, how would one go about rebranding?"

"You have your brand registered to prevent cattle theft. The only way to rebrand is to cover the original with a new one as seamlessly as possible to avoid questions."

"So a brand, it's cut on one solid branding iron?"

"Yes,"

She reached across her lap, taking his hands in hers, and dragged them away from each other, separating the two sheets of paper. "In order to create the Landry brand using the already existing Crossroads brand, they would have to have made a second branding iron with just this symbol alone. If Clint was able to find that brand or the person who created the brand for the Landry's, would that be enough proof?"

"It would have been enough to get the Landry's investigated for rebranding and cattle wrestling." He agreed.

Glenna held up a small stack of papers, "Clint had written to and heard from several blacksmiths," Holt grasped them, "There isn't anything promising in those Holt." She said sadly.

Holt still looked over the names on the return addresses just to put treasure himself of their contents.

"Would Clint have had another place where he kept important correspondence?"

Holt sat upright at her comment, and forgot about the letters in his hands, got to his feet and dashed from the room. Blu raised his head at Holt's abrupt departure but laid back down, restful when he returned.

"When you told me about your letters to Clint, I went lookin' for them. He kept them in this box, along with some other things I didn't think much of, outside his letters from the solicitor I have not looked at anythin' in here."

Together, they started to scour through each scrap of paper. Holt felt a rush of anticipation with each rustle. Several minutes passed with both lost in their search.

"Holt —" Glenna breathed, holding a letter tightly between trembling hands. She pressed it into his hands, urging him to read it and she waited with baitd breath.

> *Mr. Sterling,*
> *I made that very cast a few years back for a bloke who paid handsomely for my craftsmanship and discretion. You paid a bit more for my candor.*
> *-Elden Dawson*

308

She was being a bit silly; she knew. Holt would be gone only a short time, however, after the revelations of the past few days being apart, even a little while, loomed over her like forever. In anticipation of his departure, Glenna leaned into the embrace, holding onto Holt longer than necessary, relishing the feel of his arms around her.

The past weeks' stress and sleepless nights causing her to succumb to her emotions rather than her reason. Holt pressed a kiss into her hair and settled into the embrace, resigning them both to a much-needed reprieve from all that had taken place.

"I'll be home by nightfall, if not just before." His voice was soft and reassuring.

"Please give the children my love." She answered.

Edith's fever had broken during the night. She was coherent, although still weak and in need of extended care. Glenna wasn't sure it would not be another week until the children could be sent for and her heart ached for them to return.

Knowing it was time, Glenna slipped her arms from around his back and pulled away just enough to step back and look up into his face.

"I'll send Mrs. Carson out to see Edith as soon as I reach town."

"And the sheriff?" She worried.

"I'll go see him as soon as I get this letter off to the Brand Inspector. I have to be careful how I go about it so as not to tip my hand."

Glenna suppressed a little shiver. If their suspicions were correct, the Landry brothers had somehow orchestrated Clint's death because he had found them out. Assuming that they could so easily end

Clint's life, there was nothing they wouldn't do to Holt. The idea of losing Holt, someone she cared for so deeply, made her stomach lurch.

"It'll be alright." He reassured her, as if he was able to hear her thoughts. "You'll see."

Holt leaned in, drawing her to him, and kissed her. It was impossible to focus on anything outside, the pressure of his mouth moving over hers. All her worries fled in this singular euphoric moment.

With bitter reluctance, she let her hands fall away from him as Holt stepped away. She watched him leave, then retreated into the warmth and comfort of the house.

It took her several minutes of inner debate between using her time to fret over all possible outcomes to their late-night discovery or to busy herself. Now that Edith was no longer suffering from fever, Glenna felt that she could leave her for longer periods and tend to some of her badly neglected housework.

Settling on attending to the mending, she set to work patching a shirt. It felt wonderful to do something so ordinary as pulling a needle and thread through the weight of the fabric. It soothed her and some of the tightness in her shoulders eased with the repetitive movement.

The morning seemed to rush by. Only three shirts had been mended and she checked in on Edith twice before it was time to lay aside the mending in favor of preparing the noon meal. Right on time, Gunner, Bowen, and Decker all trickled in.

"Saw Holt ridin' out early." Gunner commented while seating himself down at the table.

"Yes, he went into town to take word to the Carsons about Edith's improvement. He will head over to check on the children on

310

his way home." Glenna confirmed as she set up a tray to take to Edith.

"I expect you will be relieved to have Miss Edith gone and the children underfoot again." Bowen drawled.

"I look forward to having Finn and Daisy at home. Edith, however, is welcome to stay for the duration of her convalesce if necessary."

Glenna took up the tray as Bowen snorted, "You'd be asking' for trouble if she did."

The threatening look Decker cast in his direction wasn't lost on her. Glenna stopped, pivoted, and held the tray out toward Decker, who had yet to sit down.

"Would you mind taking this upstairs for me? I'll be right there. I need to gather up some fresh bandages and salve, however, Edith has waited long enough for this broth."

Decker gratefully took the tray from her and left the kitchen. Glenna waited until the sound of his footfalls moved to ascend the stairs. She rounded on Bowen, fire in her gaze.

"I don't care to know what issue you have with the late Mr. Carson, his wife, or daughters, that poor girl is a guest in this house and your disparaging comments in regard to her are doing more harm than good."

Bowen, who had clearly not expected to get a tongue lashing, stared back at Glenna, a full bite of food forgotten in his mouth.

She didn't wait for him to respond. "If your remarks are meant only to raise Decker's hackles, you have met your mark and need not press further with such juvenile behavior."

Bowen didn't bother chewing the rest of the food but swallowed it whole before attempting to speak. "I am just teasing the boy. No harm meant." He croaked around the swallow.

Glenna narrowed her gaze. She was fully aware of the comments made in the barn and why Bowen was sporting a yellowish-purple fist-sized bruise.

"I believe it's time to find a new topic of discussion with Decker." She said pointedly.

"Yes, Ma'am," Bowen said darkly, clearly displeased.

Glenna had just finished redressing Edith's foot when the sound of horses drew her to the bedroom window.

"It appears you have a visitor." She smiled and returned to clear away the old bandages.

"It must be Patsy with Ma," Edith responded. "I'll be out of your hair by the end of the day."

Glenna chose to ignore the comment and rolled the last of the soiled items into each other and placed them in a basket to be taken to the kitchen for washing.

Once that task was done, she hurried to remove her makeshift bed from the floor, fluff the bed pillows for Edith to sit more upright, and rearrange her quilt. Just as she lay the cloth gingerly over Edith's injured foot, the knock at the door sounded.

"Miss Carson, Mr. Helm, please come in." Glenna beckoned the chilled looking pair into the house.

"Mrs. Sterling." John Helm tipped his hat to her, then removed it entirely. "I am glad to meet you again under happier circumstances."

"As am I." She nodded and turned to Patsy. "You must be anxious to see your sister. Please, follow me."

She noted that John didn't move and added, "Mr. Helm, please make yourself at home."

312

Patsy practically fell over herself in her rush to reach the edge of the bed once inside Glenna's room.

"Oh, Edith!" She breathed and pressed a kiss to her sister's forehead. The tender exchange made Glenna feel a rush of tender feelings for both women.

"Where's Mother?"

"She — wasn't able to come."

Feeling very much the intruder Glenna made to bow out, "I'll leave you two alone, please let me know if you need anything."

Patsy turned a little, removing her gloves as she did to address Glenna before she could fully extricate herself from the room. Her mouth opened, though it was only Edith's voice Glenna heard coming from behind Patsy, cutting off what she was about to say.

"Please wait Glenna, with both of your help to dress, I should be ready to go in no time. Where — where are my things, Patsy?"

Patsy closed her eyes briefly and drew in a long breath, turning back to Edith, "I — I am not here to take you home."

"Patsy! You can't leave me here." Edith bawled, sounding more like the petulant young girl Glenna had met in town than the contrite and more mature woman she had come to know during the duration of her convalescence and fever.

"Edith, please be reasonable. You aren't fit to travel. Even the distance from Crossroads into town. It is under the recommendation of Doctor Tillman that you remain here to rest and regain more of your strength." Patsy sounded weary, tugging at Glenna's heartstrings.

"You can't leave me here!" Edith said with a bit more force.

"I know what it is to long for home, yet, until you are well enough to travel, you are very welcome to stay." Glenna offered in an attempt to defuse Edith's apparent frustration.

"You don't have any idea what I long for." Edith bit back. Tears glinting in her eyes.

"You and I are more alike than you think," Glenna said, feeling frustration at Edith's blunt distaste for the hospitality shown to her.

"You and I are nothing alike." Edith retorted fiercely.

Drawing a steadying breath, Glenna lifted her chin. "You may well believe that. Yet, I too lost my father in an unexpectedly violent fashion and only a few years after the passing of my mother. So I do understand what loss is and that not all scars are visible." There was nothing more to say, and Glenna left them both staring after her.

She stopped on the landing to gather herself. There was understanding and deep sympathy for what Edith had lost, burning inside her. It had been easy to extend kindness and empathy to another, yet incredibly hard to do the same for herself.

Watching someone else suffer a loss had forced Glenna to be introspective about her own life. It brought understanding that forgiveness for her father, for his choice, was still some time away. With this came the realization that she still loved him, despite his leaving her willingly. Glenna also knew that she still believed in God, that her Christian faith had not died with her father.

Indeed, God had been there for her even when she had denied him during her darkest days. The realization had hit her when prayers for Edith, others of thanks for Holt and the children, and so many others had started to pour from her amid life's chaos.

Now she uttered another silent plea for her heart to be filled with compassion, and for fortitude in the face of adversity. She believed the words she had spoken to Bowen. Edith was a guest, however unwilling on her part, and Glenna would continue to treat her as such.

A second knock sounded on the door just as Glenna closed out her prayer and she moved down the last of the steps to answer it.

314

Surprised to see Pastor Joseph and Rachel bundled up standing on the porch, hands ladened with food.

"Oh, my! Please come in," Glenna stepped aside and waved the pair inside. Taking a covered dish from Rachel in the process.

"My mother taught me it was impolite to arrive empty-handed when visiting a home where someone has been ill." Rachel offered as an explanation,

"As soon as we chatted with Holt this morning, I was informed by my wife we must prepare ourselves and come out right away."

"I am glad you did. I'm sure Edith will find comfort in the presence of friends. Her sister is with her now," Glenna explained. "I hope you don't mind waiting until Patsy has been able to spend time with Edith?"

"We are at your disposal," Rachel commented while she removed her gloves, unwrapped her scarf, and shed her coat, taking the food items from her husband and following Glenna into the kitchen, leaving her husband to greet John.

"It's not much. Ham and bean stew, cornbread, and butter."

"It is heavenly! I am so grateful for your thoughtfulness." Glenna reassured her, beginning to transfer the food into her pots. It was a kindness to have a meal brought in. It was rude, however, to keep another's cooking utensils.

Glenna's hands stilled over the food.

"Glenna, are you alright?' Rachel asked, a wrinkle in her brow.

"Yes, it's been a day of revelations. I just thought of these dishes in terms of mine, not that they belonged to the house or someone else. It struck me as odd."

"You are truly settling into your life here. That is wonderful." Rachel beamed, adding wistfully, "I am certain Grace is very happy to see you here, to have you loving and caring for her children. Making this home your own."

It was an impossibility for Glenna to do more than stare at her. Of course, Rachel had known Grace. The two women must have been friends. She had spent so much time focusing solely on what she had lost, on what Holt had lost, and what the children were missing in their lives and she had forgotten about all the other people that had known and loved both Clint and Grace. How the loss of them had impacted their lives.

"I apologize. It must be difficult seeing me here, in Grace's home."

"Not at all. It's wonderful, in fact. Certainly, I miss my friend, that is a constant. Yet, I have gained another in her sister-in-law. That joy is only added to by witnessing Holt's feelings for you. He is a good man and deserves all the happiness you have brought into his life."

Glenna felt uncomfortable with such praise. Although it was pleasing to know those that had known and cared for, Holt approved of the match.

"John and I are headin' out to split and carry in some firewood? I noticed you are low." Pastor Joseph announced, entering the kitchen, John close behind him.

"That would be wonderful, thank you."

"We'll have something hot for you both to drink when you are finished," Rachel promised.

Left alone, Glenna and Rachel finished transferring the food, giving Rachel's dishes a quick wash before setting out to make tea. The conversation strayed to less emotionally charged topics such as last week's sermon and the fine gingham fabric Rachel had just acquired to make herself a new dress. The company drove all melancholy from Glenna's mind.

316

The sound of footfalls on the stairs sobered both women, bringing their minds back to the present. Patsy appeared, wearing what was clearly a carefully constructed smile. Glenna felt a pang in the pit of her stomach.

"I'm sorry for interrupting — I was looking for John."

"He went out to split some fire wood with Joseph. I'll fetch him for you." Rachel said and rushed to get her coat.

"Patsy, please sit down, have a cup of tea." Glenna moved to take down another cup.

Patsy blinked and shook her head. "Thank you for the offer. Regrettably, my visit today can not be extended. Mother took to her bed after we buried Pa and hasn't been able to leave it. I can't be away from her for long." Patsy wrung her hands. "I do hate to impose on you any longer. However, I don't think I can look after both Edith and Mama on my own."

"Of course, Edith is welcome to stay here as long as she needs. Perhaps your mother will rally now that she knows that her daughter is on the mend." Glenna offered in the way of comfort.

"I feel that it will help her as well to know Edith's been so well taken care of." Patsy stepped around the table, drawing closer to Glenna, "I am sorry for what Edith said to you. She's always had a tongue full of venom. Regardless, her treatment of you has always been regrettable. I am sorry for my part. I should have set her right long before now. I hope, in time, you can forgive us both."

"It is all forgotten." Glenna waved off her concern.

Patsy gave Glenna a pointed look. "I believe, given time and a change of my sisters' actions toward you, that can become a true statement. Edith was too much indulged by both our parents, a child never given to consequences, yet, she is at her core a good person. I have to believe that God has given her this second chance to prove just that."

Twenty

Satiated, Holt dropped his spoon into the empty bowl and leaned back, resting the breadth of his shoulders on the high back of the chair. With a sigh that held equal parts weariness and contentment, he pulled Glenna's hands into his from across the table and pressed a kiss to her fingers. Her dark eyes softened with the contact.

"How was today, love?"

"Busy. Patsy came, of course. That was difficult for Edith and Patsy. Their mother has taken to her bed, and Patsy has been left to tend to the store and her mother alone. She mentioned that John has been a great help when he has the time to spare."

"I heard as much from Sheriff Canton. Poor Patsy is bein' run ragged." He confirmed.

"Although I know Edith wishes to be home, I assured Patsy that she is welcome to stay. She then had a visit from the Pastor and Rachel. They were kind enough to bring out a meal and fill our wood boxes."

Holt lifted an eyebrow. "That was kind of them."

"I believe Pastor Joseph was giving John Helm something constructive to do while Patsy visited with her sister. He had been previously abandoned to his own devices." She freed one of her hands to lift her cup of tea to her lips then continued, "After Patsy and John took their leave, it was the Pastor's turn to see Edith. He and Rachel prayed with her. I did not stay to overhear any of their

318

discussion, but the sound of sobbing from time to time reached me even down here. When I said my fair-wells, Rachel confided that there had been council given on the subject of her father's death and her apparent second chance that struck a deep cord with Edith."

"All of this was before Doc Tillman showed?"

"Yes. He came just thirty minutes after everyone else had left. Doctor Tillman was very pleased with her progress. She is weakened from the ordeal. Still, he thinks her fighting spirit will pull her through to full recovery."

"Fightin' spirit?" Holt lifted an eyebrow. "That is a delicate way of puttin' it."

"Be kind." Glenna scolded him. "Once he was gone, Decker came to read to her while I checked her dressings. She was so tired from the day's events she fell to sleep straight away. Now, tell me, how did your meeting go? How are the children? Were you able to get word off to the Brand Inspector?"

"Slow down!" He laughed. "Things went a bit more smoothly than I had expected. By the time I reached town, I had made up my mind to see the Sheriff before postin' anythin' to the inspector. It turned out to be a good choice."

"Do not leave me in suspense!" Glenna protested when he stopped to draw a breath.

"I presented all we had found to Canton. He came to the same conclusion we had. Rather than mail off an inquiry to the Brand Inspector, he had a telegraph sent and locked up all the evidence in his safe. That meetin' burned up a good deal of sunlight. Once I was satisfied there was nothin' more to be done in town, I went to see the children."

"How are they?"

"Both are healthy, no signs of fever. They miss you somethin' awful."

"Oh, how I miss them. When do you think we can bring them home?"

Holt felt a rush of emotion drawing him nearer Glenna and he drew her face to his with one coxing hand. Placing a tender kiss on her lips.

"I told Theo and Hattie it would only be a few more days at best. I know they love havin' both Daisy and Finn there. They also have never had both children at the same time, not with Hattie's health bein' what it is. She would never admit it, but I think she is lookin' forward to a full night's sleep."

At the mention of sleep, Glenna yawned and nodded her understanding. "We should not speak about sleep. I don't think either of us has had a full night's rest in quite a while and poor Hattie. I have been worried about her."

Holt nodded. "As have I. She insisted she is feelin' fine. Yet, the sooner we can bring the kids home, the better off I think she will be. She looked a bit — haggard."

"You had better never repeat that sentiment, or Hattie will have your hide!" Glenna giggled. No matter how her heart had weakened, Hattie was a force to be reckoned with.

Holt grinned. "You are right about that." He kissed her again, lingering longer this time as she answered his kiss with one of her own. Then, with great reluctance, he pulled away, "Go, rest while you can."

Glenna smiled past her tiredness and softly dragged her fingers over his jaw, "I love you."

"I do not believe that I will ever get tired of hearin' you say that." Holt smiled. "I love you too."

"I've brought you something a bit more substantial for breakfast today," Glenna announced, finding Edith awake, her eyes fixed on some point on the ceiling, studying it with real interest. "Shall we see how you do with a good cup of tea, eggs, and a bit of bacon?" She said encouragingly.

"I'm sorry about your parents," Edith said without ceremony.

Glenna felt a jolt of surprise, hurrying to place the food tray on the bedside table before it could slip from her hands, "I'm sorry about your father. I did not know him well, however, I will always remember his kindness."

"Pa was a kind man. He treated you — treated everyone, as I should have. I hated you without reason." Edith risked looking over at Glenna, then snapped her gaze back into place.

"It's all right, those things are in the past," Glenna reassured her.

"No, it's not all right. I was cruel and petty, with no justification. Although there is never a justification to treat anyone with the animosity, I showed you. You had something I felt I deserved, yet never really wanted." Edith peeled her gaze from the ceiling to meet Glenna's.

"I was never in love with Holt. I suppose I talked myself into some type of affection because it was expected. My mother, although well intended, had always pushed the idea on me. He was from a family that had wealth and influence, with good prospects for the future, a comfortable home, a stable living, and at his core, Holt is a good man."

"Edith, you do not have to explain yourself to me." Glenna countered, "I am the last person that should judge another."

"Perhaps not explain myself to you, although I do need to ask for your forgiveness."

The inner battle Edith was waging was evident in her expression as she waited for Glenna to answer, "You have it."

"That easy?"

"You sound disappointed," Glenna almost laughed. "You and I do not have to be at odds, Edith. We can be friends."

"I think I would like that. To be your friend." Edith looked over at her, eyes glistening with unshed tears.

"I would like that as well." Glenna smiled with real honesty.

"Am I interruptin'?" Decker asked from the doorway.

Edith seemed to stiffen at the sound of his voice, her cheeks suddenly flush with color.

"I — thought I might read with Miss Edith before ridin' out this mornin'." He explained further when neither woman answered.

"Oh, um, yes, of course, Decker. First, would you give me just another few minutes alone with Edith first?" Glenna asked sweetly.

Decker nodded and retreated. The instant he was gone, Glenna went to her closet and pulled out one of Grace's pretty pale pink shawls. Tossing it over her arm, she freed her hands to take up her brush, comb, and one silk ribbon.

Edith made no protest to having her hair brushed, the long tawny locks pulled into a tidy braid that lay prettily over one shoulder, the ribbon tied into a bow at the end adding a touch of delicacy. Glenna helped Edith to a full seated position, arranging the blankets around her neatly, adding the shawl to her slim shoulders.

Edith and Glenna shared a meaningful look full of understanding once Decker reappeared. She noted the healthy flush that darkened Edith's cheeks at the sight of him.

"I have a few chores that need tending to," Glenna started, then let the words fade to silence in her mouth, realizing that she was only speaking to herself, and slipped from the room. From the cover of the hall, she stood a few moments longer than necessary, guiltily listening to the painfully awkward conversation happening.

"I — you look improved," Decker said with a stammer.

"Thank you,"

"Should we — should I start from the beginnin'? I — I am not sure if you could hear me. Do you want me to pick up from where I felt off or?"

"I was able to hear you," Edith said in a soft voice. "There were times it seemed your voice was the only thing that penetrated the darkness."

Glenna tiptoed away, smiling.

———

"I am very happy with how you are healin'. There are no signs of infection to any of the amputation sights and the skin is healin' nicely. Your nose and cheeks are a healthy pink. You are very lucky."

Edith pushed herself up straighter in the bed, "How is Ma?"

Glenna started gathering up the newly discarded bandages for washing.

"Your mother is doing better, you could go home as early as tomorrow. Mr. Helm is taken' on more responsibility at the store and Patsy is capable of takin' over changing your bandages."

"I see." Glenna noted the furrow to Edith's brows. She seemed to struggle with something for a breath, clearing her throat. "Doctor,

I'm still feeling a bit weak. I think — maybe — I should stay a few more days before burdening Patsy."

Doctor Tillman looked from Edith to Glenna.

"She is more than welcome to stay. Our home is open to her as long as needed." Glenna reassured them both.

"Alright, another week would put your mother to rights," He turned to Glenna. "She needs to get up and move. A little at first, every few hours."

"Of course."

"Be patient with yourself, miss Edith. It's going to take time to trust yourself on your feet. Don't be too proud to take help when offered."

Shutting his bag, Doctor Tillman took his leave.

"Glenna," Edith called, "Would you stay a moment?"

Glenna shifted the bundle of bandages in her arms. "Yes."

"Thank you for everything." It seemed that Edith wished to say more, however raw emotions kept her from being able to force the words out into the open.

"I'm going to set these to soak and I'll be back to get you up and test your strength. How does joining all of us for the midday meal sound?"

"I would like that, although preferably not in a nightdress." Edith smiled.

"I have something I worked up that would look very well on you, I think."

Glenna backed out of the room and almost skipped down the stairs. Her heart was lighter than it had felt in days as the children would be home soon, her relationships blossoming, and those things that had plagued Clint coming neatly to a resolution that seemed certain, leaving her in a very good mood indeed.

324

Added to that, Edith and her mother having both turned very important corners in their health battles, Glenna hoped they would also find peace in the mental anguish that accompanied such a loss as theirs.

Reaching the bottom of the staircase, Glenna caught sight of the figure of a man bent low over something, holding his attention on the sitting room desk.

"I thought you were out spreading feed this morning." She quipped. It was not Holt that turned to face her, rather Gunner, who startled at the sound of her voice, dropping the stack to papers, sending them fluttering across the floor.

"Glenna, you spooked me."

"Was there something particular you were hoping to find among Holt's papers?" She asked in a steady voice, hoping she didn't betray her sudden suspicion that she had walked in on something she was not meant to see. "Did he send you to fetch something I can help you locate?"

"I was — just — I was trying to find — somethin' for Holt," Gunner stumbled over his words while rushing to clean up the papers, stuffing them back into the drawers of Holt's desk with haste.

"Oh, alright. Let me set these bandages down and I'll be right back to help look." Glenna said, trying to sound as carefree as possible, Gunner was acting quite odd and she didn't want to let on that she was in any way suspicious of his reasoning for being in Holt's papers.

Fear had started to creep into her mind, taking hold as the idea formed, and refused to let go. She needed to talk to Holt, and soon. Tossing the bandages into the laundry pile, she rushed back to the sitting room. Soaking would have to wait.

Gunner was gone and there was no way of knowing what he had been after or what he might have taken.

Holt led the round of cheering and applause that erupted around the kitchen as Edith hobbled in, favoring her bandaged foot, leaning heavily on Decker's arm. She blushed and smiled, waving away the attention. Blu followed the pair into the room, looking like he was herding them to the table.

"We are mighty glad to have you join us for supper." Holt said when the ruckus died away and she had been seated, Decker took great care to scoot her chair in. Blu, satisfied his job was done, curled up near the hearth, relaxed, and almost instantly fell asleep as if dealing with the humans in the house was purely exhausting.

"Thank you," Edith said softly as everyone else also took their seats, "It's nice to be out of that room — not that it isn't a perfectly lovely room —"

"We understood what you meant," Holt reassured her. He said a prayer of thanks over the food.

"You look much recovered, Miss, how are ya feelin'?" Bowen asked as the meal started in earnest.

"I feel — much better if not a bit unsteady. Thank you for asking."

Holt noted this was the most polite he had ever heard Edith in any of her encounters, over all the years he had known her. He wondered at the change. Could it be due to feeling the loss of a loved one? The physical changes she had so painfully undergone, the fever, the kindness of a woman she had treated badly, or the effect Decker was having on her? Perhaps a combination of all of those things had left Edith forever changed.

Bowen nodded politely. "I suppose that will come with time."

"What has Decker here been readin' to ya all this time?" Gunner pressed between bits of bread.

"My bible reader. I am afraid your friend wasted much of his time during my fevered days, as I was in and out of wakefulness."

"Are you certain it was the fever? I think I would block out the sound of his voice on purpose. Dull and uninspirin', if you ask me." Gunner said dryly.

Holt marked Glenna's scrutiny of the look of confusion that crossed Edith's expression.

"Gunner is teasin' Decker at your expense. Pay him no heed." He explained as Decker kicked at Gunner under the table, clearly making contact with a shin as Gunner grunted and jumped.

"Yes, sorry Miss Carson, I was just joshin'. I'm sure the dulcet tones of Decker's melodious voice made it rivetin'," Gunner corrected, leaning over to rub the offending area on his leg that was surely now throbbing.

The supper conversation continued with the joviality that had been missing over the past weeks. Edith too joined in on the good-natured ribbing, her laugh infectious. All too soon, the interaction had tired her out and Glenna was ushering her out of the room, insisting she rest for the remainder of the evening.

"Alright boys, let's get a start on those evenin' chores," Bowen growled and pushed back his chair.

Gunner and Decker moved to follow him out the door. Decker paused long enough to glance in the direction Glenna and Edith had disappeared, pulling on his coat and stomping out after the other men.

"I can see to that." He hadn't expected Glenna to return so soon and the sound of her voice sent his pulse racing in a manner that was not at all unpleasant. Glenna brushed past him and was reaching for her apron when Holt seized her by the arm, spinning her around and hauled her toward him.

Glenna let out a little squeak of surprise as his lips crashed into hers, swallowing the sound. She was smiling, lips upturned under his, as her arms slid around his shoulders, fingers tangling in the hair at the nape of his neck.

"No pleasantries? No preamble? No pretense? Is this what we have been reduced to, desperate interludes in the middle of a dirty kitchen?" She laughed once the kiss had ebbed.

Holt only pressed her closer to him. "Woman, you have turned my whole life upside down and inside out. I used to be a rational thinker. Able to do a task with my mind unbothered by the thought of you." Dropping his head low to her neck, he breathed deeply of her scent.

"And now?" She breathed.

"Now? Now I can't think of nothin' else but you. Like the way you always smell of lavender soap — *my* lavender soap — taste of honey and tea. My mind wanders, makin' work near impossible, and you want to waste time with pretense? Pleasantries?" He drew in another long breath, "Preambles be damned." Holt kissed along the length of her neck, across her jaw, and calmed her mouth again.

Glenna was kissing him back until they were both gasping for air.

"And how was your day?" He muttered next to her mouth once he was able to regain any semblance of rational thought. "Will that do for pleasantries?"

Her softness turned ridged in his arms. Hands sliding to his shoulders, she pushed back from him enough to look him in the eye.

"Something a bit odd happened I think you should know about."

328

"Somethin' you didn't want to mention in front of the boys I gather." Holt frowned. The stolen moment shattered as he was forced back to reality, although he refused to let her move farther away, arms still firmly linked behind her back. "Tell me."

She blinked. "After Doctor Tillman left today, I came down to find Gunner going through papers from your desk."

Holt took this in. "Did he say what he was doin'? Give you any reason?"

"He stumbled over the explanation. That he was looking for something for you, yet couldn't come up with what specifically." Glenna shifted slightly, "He was nervous Holt, clearly he hadn't expected me to stumble upon him and he bolted at the first chance."

Holt cursed under his breath, "I — don't want to suspect — there is no reason for him to be lookin' for —"

Glenna put one hand on his cheek, holding his gaze, "I did not want to upset you, and I am not accusing him of anything. I thought you should know, in case it has any significance."

Holt felt the inner battle raging. She wasn't the only thing that had turned his world inside out. Dropping one hand from her waist, he pulled out the small slip of paper from his shirt pocket and handed it to her. Glenna took the missive and read it quickly.

"As early as tomorrow?" She breathed. "I did not expect the Brand Inspector to arrive so soon."

"Sheriff showed up today with that telegram. It seems Crossroads isn't the only one having issues with unexplainable cattle losses in the area. According to Canton, the inspector has heard from a few spreads. It wasn't until I showed up with Clint's records and brand sketches that he felt there was enough to start a full investigation."

Twenty-one

"There," Glenna said and stood back to survey her handy work.

Gazing at herself in the mirror, Edith turned her head, her upswept hair twisted and pinned to perfection. At her request, Glenna had worked to cover the missing bit of Edith's ear with some effort and was pleased with the results.

"Now, if only I could as easily hide this." She held up her right hand, still covered in a bandage to protect the healing skin.

Glenna caught her eye in the reflective surface of the mirror, "It would be fruitless of me to point out that those who care for you will never be bothered a bit by the loss of a few toes and a finger because I know full well you already know that. Nonetheless, I do want to urge you to be kinder to yourself over the loss."

Edith nodded as she cast her eyes back down, "I was full of vanity my whole life. So taken with my appearance. It is not as marred as it could have been, I know. I still have a small voice inside that begs to know if anyone will be able to overlook not only my internal faults, but now my physical ones?"

"Are you thinking of someone particular or perhaps even yourself being unable to accept you as you are?"

"Both," Edith admitted. "I have a lot to learn about this new me, the physical and internal. I fear we have both been scared — and forever changed."

330

"Change can be beautiful, a caterpillar becoming a butterfly," Glenna said, giving Edith's shoulder a soft squeeze.

Edith turned on the stool so she was facing Glenna. "It is also painful. So I was admitting to myself how incredibly horrible I have been. It would have been easy to continue to be so. I was determined to be as difficult as I knew how, to everyone — keeping everyone at a distance." She paused and Glenna waited for her to continue, sensing that Edith needed to speak the words out loud without interruption.

"I was still filled with so much anger, so much pain, and lashed out at you, Doctor Tillman, Decker, and Patsy. It wasn't until Pastor Joseph quoted scripture to me during his visit from Romans five, *'And not only that, but we also rejoice in our afflictions, because we know that affliction produces endurance, endurance produces proven character, and proven character produces hope.'* that I realized what I needed. Hope. Hearing it unlocked something inside," she pressed her good hand to the center of her chest.

"I have a great deal of work to do on myself, on that voice in my head that screams of my lack of worth. Though, I have something that I did not have before. A much more humble outlook and *hope* for something better. That I can be someone better. Someone more like you."

"I have to leave for some business in town. Would you mind going to gather up the children from Theo and Hattie?" Holt asked Decker, shifting the now full milk bucket out of the heifers' reach and placing another one in its place, sending a steady stream of milk splashing into it.

"Sure can. When do you want me to head out?"

"I'm going to send Bowen and Gunner out to work the cattle," Holt said, working through the details in his mind. "Patsy and her beau will be out to fetch up Edith this afternoon. Around then would work fine. Take the wagon, invite Glenna to ride along if you like. Just be sure to give yourself enough daylight to head back."

Decker nodded, bending to take the full bucket. "I'll — um, take this in for you."

Holt smiled to himself. "Makin' the most of your time with Miss Carson under my roof, are ya?"

"Oh hell Holt, I'm gettin' raked over the coals between Gunner's constant ribbin' and Bowen's bad attitude. Don't you add to it!"

Laughing, Holt stopped milking and lifted both hands in defeat. "I'm the last man who'd give you a hard time for havin' your head turned. Lord knows."

"I'm glad for you Holt. Questionin' Glenna's sanity, but glad for you." Decker chuckled.

"Hey now, I'm a catch." Holt protested and finished up the milking. "Take this with you, Romeo. I need to check the hens." He handed Decker the other milk bucket and moved the milking stool.

"Holt," Decker said, stopping Holt mid-stride, "How'd you know fur certain?"

There was no need to elaborate. "I suppose it was the moment I tried to picture my life without Glenna and the sick feelin' it gave me. I was lucky, though. By the time I realized I was in love with her, we were already hitched." Holt laughed.

"Some help you are." Decker moaned.

"Give her time to mourn her father, console with her mother and sister. When a respectable time has passed, sweep her off her feet." Holt advised, pulling the barn door open.

"I — I have nothin' to offer a woman like Edith." He said dejectedly.

"I think you need to let her be the judge of that," Holt said, slapping him on the shoulder.

Decker finished the walk over the hard-packed snow to the house while Holt fetched the eggs and followed. Welcomed by the smell of fried ham and fresh coffee.

"We have a full day, boys." He announced, handing the egg basket over to Glenna.

"How so, boss?" Gunner asked, taking his seat at the table.

"I'm ridin' into town. I have some business I need to see to. Decker will be takin' Glenna over to Theo and Hattie's place to fetch the littles back home." He explained while peeling off his hat and coat, stomping his boots hard to remove the last vestiges of snow.

"I need the two of you to check the cattle."

Bowen nodded his understanding.

"You'll be leavin' Miss Edith here alone?" Gunner asked, raising an eyebrow.

"No, I will be leaving today to return home. I am expecting my sister and Mr. Helm this morning." Edith explained.

"All sounds fine to me, now can we eat?" Bowen asked, ready to spear a slice of ham.

———————

Pulling out the long winter coat she had found in the clothes gifted to her, Glenna inspected it a bit more closely now that it would be in use. It showed the wear of the previous owner, long, thick, and warm. She was thankful for it.

"I am positive your sister will come with whatever you require, however I would like to be prepared in case you need anything. This should work well. I also have a very warm scarf." She added them to the mittens laying across the foot of the bed and went in search of the scarf in question for Edith's trip home.

"I will be sure to return any borrowed items as soon as convenience allows."

"Now where did I put it?" Glenna muttered to herself and stopped her fussing long enough to spare herself a moment of reflection. It was in the quiet that she heard the sound of footfalls on the porch steps.

"Lands! I didn't expect anyone for at least another hour." Edith exclaimed as she moved slowly to the window that looked out over the front of the house. Her brow furrowed. "There's no wagon. Are you expecting someone on horseback?"

"Maybe one of the men forgot something. I'll check and be back in a few minutes with fresh bandages and that blasted scarf." Glenna assured her as the sound of footsteps headed their direction, paused at the top of the stairs, and moved past them.

Misgiving set heavy in the pit of her stomach. Holt shouldn't be back so soon from town. The footsteps hadn't sounded quite like Holt's either. These were heavier and determined in a way she didn't recognize. Worrying on her bottom lip, she turned to Edith, who was looking at her with wide eyes.

"Something must have gone wrong with his meeting this morning." She said quietly. Edith only nodded her understanding and took a seat on the chair that had often been occupied by Decker's girth.

334

In case Holt was very upset and didn't wish to speak to her about what had happened, Glenna made her approach as silently as possible. Reaching his half-open door without drawing attention to herself, she took a few steadying breaths as she listened to him pace inside his room, the bright midday light streaming in the windows casting shadows as he moved about the space.

"Where is it?" He muttered as the sound of something being dragged across the floor and papers rustling broke the stillness.

She knew that voice, "Bowen?" Confusion washed over her.

Glenna pushed the door so that it now stood wide open. It was clear she had startled him as he jumped a bit before a mask of calm replaced the look of shock he had given her.

"I thought for a moment — why are you in Holt's room?" She asked, suddenly unable to stop herself from stepping inside at the sight of both Holt's and Clint's boxes open, contents dumped, scattered across the bed, spilling onto the floor.

"I expected you to be gone by now."

"Plans changed." She said simply. There was no need to expound on the fact she had stayed to help prepare Edith for her travel and that Decker was perfectly capable of getting the children home on his own.

Bowen nodded, smiling sweetly at her, "I must apologize for startlin' ya." He drawled lazily. "Is Miss Edith still here?"

"No — she's already left," Glenna said, turning her head just a little, praying the conversation was carried to her room, and that Edith was listening.

Filled with a greater unease than she had felt when finding Gunner in a very similar position, Glenna eyed the mess of papers in disarray and Bowen. "What are you looking for? Perhaps I can help you locate it."

Bowen's face contorted into something altogether unfamiliar. The mask was removed, all pretense dissolved. "We can dispense with politeness. I'm here for Clint's second ledger and the deed to the ranch? Where are they?"

"Clint's what?" She feigned innocence, careful to keep her expression one of utter confusion as her mind worked to put the pieces together.

Bowen sneered as he took a menacing step in her direction. "You damn well know what I'm talkin' about. Where did Holt put it?"

"Bowen —" Glenna worked hard to keep her face impassively confused at his request. Realizing it was useless, she also dropped the pretense. "You? You're behind the missing cattle."

"If only it was that simple." He scrutinized her closely, sadly shaking his head. "It didn't have to go this way. Holt was ready to leave, relocate the children, and cut his losses. Plans had been carefully set into motion. The foundation work had taken years to set in place. Then you turned up with your looks of longin', honeyed voice, turnin' his head, and givin' him the one thing I had worked to remove from Holt's life — a future here at Crossroads."

He took a step nearer. "The Landry boys might collectively have only half a brain between them, but they can follow simple instructions fine enough." He was laughing now, the sound dull to her ears, as the world was set spinning. Nothing she knew seemed to make sense.

"Why steal and rebrand the cattle?" She asked, needing answers.

"Because sometimes a man has to take what should have been given," Bowen said menacingly, reaching behind his back and drawing forward a long hunting knife from its sheath hanging from his belt.

336

Glenna felt a shudder run the length of her spine, her mind racing. Where was the rifle? Would she be able to reach it before he could lunge at her?

"Clint found out, didn't he?" It hit her hard that Clint must have witnessed something Bowen had wanted to keep hidden, and this was the linchpin that lead to his writing the Brand Inspector, feeling he had enough evidence for an investigation.

"He saw things he shouldn't have. Stuck his nose in places it didn't belong." Bowen confirmed her suspicion.

"— You — you had Clint killed. Made it look like an accident."

"No," He shook his head, "I did that myself."

Sickness filled her throat, forcing it back down as she tried to regain her wits. She had to keep him talking, force him to keep his distance, and pray that it would give her the time to think of something, any way of escape for both herself and Edith.

"Why?"

"Why?" He barked back at her, "Why!" This time, Bowen shouted at her and advanced another step. "I was there. Did Holt tell you that? I was with the fool when he lost it all gambling. While he tucked his tail and ran for the hills, I came back to help rebuild the ranch. I stayed. Me!"

"I didn't know." She stammered honestly.

Bowen waved the knife between them, using it to emphasize his words with sharp movements of punctuation to his words, "*I* was here when their father ran the ranch. *I* was here for Clint all those years — and until Holt chose to grace his family with his presence. Before the Prodigal son showed his face, *I* was goin' to become a partner in the ranch.

"I had saved up enough to buy into it, absorbin' what Holt had lost. We could have not just rebuilt, but expanded. Holt wormed his way back into Clint's good graces and shut me out! After all those

years? All the work and dedication? No, I couldn't let it happen!"
The knife waved in the air, then stilled as Bowen narrowed his eyes.

"I knew those two imbeciles had been stealin' cattle and rebrandin' them. They hadn't been thinkin' big enough, small potatoes in taking a calf or yearlin' here and there. I knew I could use the Landry's, so instead of turnin' them over, I made them a deal. Help me get what's rightfully mine, and I'd help them build their herd up much faster."

Bowen took another step toward her. Glenna reflexively took a step back. This made him grin wildly. She had made the mistake of showing her fear. He was telling her this not because she had asked, but because they both knew he was not going to allow her to leave this house alive to tell what she knew.

Bowen's voice dripped with disdain. "Clint had caught on sooner than we had planned—too smart for his own good. Yet not smart enough. One clean shot from my rifle to frighten his horse." Bowen laughed darkly, "A fall — and one — two devastatin' blows to his head with a heavy rock. That stubborn bastard still refused to die, managed to get on his horse — by sheer luck, he was gone by the time his horse reached the homestead. I may not have watched his life drain away, but being the cause of it was just as satisfyin'. I was one step closer to gettin' everythin' that had been taken."

Glenna felt her thoughts blurring, trying to comprehend what she was hearing.

"You — you did all of that because Clint cut you out of partial ownership of Crossroads?"

"Clint didn't have to die. He made his bed by overlookin' those who had stood by him! I am just takin' what is due me, nothin' more."

"His life was due you? The life you took from his children, that life was due you? It's just land — it's just cattle —" She knew instantly she had said the wrong thing and Bowen's eyes narrowed at her menacingly.

"You would think that. You and Holt, the pair of you, all of it, just handed to you on a silver platter. Neither of you worked for the roof over your head, the food in your bellies, you didn't spend years buildin' up the herd, makin' the sacrifice, the clothes on your back aren't even earned — you stole them off the back of a dead woman." Bowen spat.

Glenna felt as if he had slapped her, the words stinging harshly.

"I did! I worked for it!" He shouted at her, the knife waving wildly. "I had all but talked Holt into sellin' and walkin' away — convinced him that it would be best for those little brats to get off this place — that he didn't want to be tied down to the ranch. Then... then you undid all my work — all my plannin' — gone in the blink of an eye. I deserve Crossroads — I paid for it — blood, sweat, and tears. Now, I aim to take what is rightfully mine."

"So you help the Landry boys with their cattle rustling. How does covering up their theft help you acquire Crossroads?" Glenna slid one foot a step closer to the door, pivoting to make her escape easier when the opportunity came.

"Who else am I goin' to pin it all on? They're both too dim-witted to know I'm usin' them as a decoy. They'll get caught, but not until the last of the obstacles to Crossroads are removed."

"By obstacles you mean Holt." It was not a question. "You shot at us spooking the horses. It was you that made the cattle stampede." Everything suddenly made sense.

"I was here... workin' the ranch with the other boys when those things happened. No one can pin either on me. It's my word... my long-trusted reputation pitted against the pair of feebleminded dolts. Who is goin' to believe either of them? No one. Not when upstandin' Theo, Hattie, or hard-workin' Gunner, and Decker are all my alibis for both events. It will be easy to point the finger at the Landry's. There is enough physical evidence at their place to hang them both." Bowen jeered. "So you can understand why I need that ledger."

"With Holt gone, there is nothing stopping you from purchasing Crossroads and running the cattle."

"I don't want to waste funds on purchasin' what should have been left to me. The deed, signed over to me free and clear, will do just fine and I wouldn't say nothin's in my way. How did you expect I'd get Holt to go along with my plan?"

"Ransom," Glenna exclaimed.

"Oh, no, I won't harm the littles. Not unless I have to. You, on the other hand… it would have been easier if you had gone with Decker. I suppose you can just as easily have an accident here." His tone sinister, the meaning clear.

"Accident?" Glenna knew she should be worried not only for her safety, but Decker was unarmed, some place on the road between here and Theo's. If Bowen had sent the Landry brothers to make sure both she and Holt met untimely ends, Decker was undoubtedly in danger.

"I didn't care how they do it." He waved a hand dismissively. "You and Decker were never meant to come back. Holt would be too distraught over the loss of his wife and friend to do anythin' except what I tell him to. The children are… my insurance policy. Now, this is the last time I'm going to ask, where are the ledger and the deed?"

There was no use in telling him a lie. "I don't know where Holt has the deed. As for the ledger, it was turned over to Sheriff Canton days ago. He and Holt are meeting with the Brand Inspector — right now, in fact. Your plan has already failed."

She had known that the instant those words spilled from her lips Bowen would rush her and Glenna had prepared herself for the action by inching closer to the door while he ranted, rattling off what he had been sure was a brilliant plan. When the charge did happen, she already had the door handle firmly in her hand and pulled it toward her with all her force, smashing it solidly into Bowen's right shoulder, jarring him, and forcing him to drop the knife.

Glenna instantly kicked the knife out of his reach and bolted for the stairs. She had to get downstairs, find a weapon of her own, preferably the rifle. There had to be a way to subdue Bowen, warn Decker, alert Holt and Sheriff Canton — if she could just hold off until Mr. Helm and Patsy arrived... perhaps...

The thought was abruptly knocked out of her as the full force of Bowen's weight crashed into her, propelling her forward with such violence her feet were swept out from under her, the air leaving her lungs as she crashed face-first to the hall floor, inches away from the stairs.

One hand clamped around her ankle like a vise, pulling her back toward him. Glenna kicked out with the other foot, making contact with his shoulder. Yanking her hard by the ankle he still held, she felt herself slide backward. Finding purchase, her fingers gripped the lip of the top stair and held on as she continued to kick back at him with her free leg. Hearing a grunt she knew she had hit him, his grip didn't loosen.

"No!" she screamed as her lungs filled with air.

Bowen pulled back with such force Glenna yelped in pain, her hip and knee now throbbing yet her grip held. Glenna thrashed out with her free leg, wild and desperate, her boot crashing down on any part of Bowen she could come into contact with.

He let go of her ankle, at the same moment one of his hands grabbed the back of her dress, holding her in place as he scrambled to his feet, hoisting himself above her, his other hand took hold of her hair, yanking her head upward painfully before slamming her face into the unforgiving floorboards.

Her teeth rattled from the impact, cutting into her lip as light burst behind her eyelids and muddied her vision as Glenna tasted blood.

A loud thud resounded, a cry, and a grunt of pain that wasn't hers. Glenna tried to register what was happening as Bowen's hands fell away from her completely. The sound of something heavy hitting bone made her stomach churn.

"Glenna!"

Edith was kneeling next to her, her face contorted into a mask of fury and fear. The fire poker held tightly between both her hands was shaking slightly. What had felt like a lifetime of torture had only taken seconds. Time that had offered Edith the presence of mind to arm herself and act.

Pushing herself up, Glenna sucked in a shattering breath through the pain. Bowen grunted, bringing both of their attention back to him. Crumbled next to the wall, he sat holding the side of his head, blood covering his fingers and staining his shoulder and front of his shirt.

Glenna pushed herself to stand, reaching for Edith as she rushed forward, "Run!"

Stumbling, both unsteady, they raced down to the first floor. Glenna pushed Edith toward the kitchen. Her mind racing. The rifle. Where had she last seen it? Should they run to the barn? It would take too long to get them both on a horse. Was Edith even able to ride bareback in her current condition? He was coming after them. She felt it in her bones as surely as she knew when he caught them, they would both die.

342

Twenty-two

"Holt, this is Dalton Wesley. Dalton, this is Holt Sterling."
Sheriff Canton made the introductions, and Holt shook the man's
hand. He was a few years older than Holt and weather-worn.

"We've been goin' over what you've found in your brother's
things." Dalton didn't waste time with pleasantries. "I need to do
some hands on research to verify, but I suspect you've got a strong
case against both Silas and Tripp Landry."

Holt felt a weight lift from his shoulders he hadn't known was
there.

"What do we do next?"

"Next, the Sheriff and I do some fieldwork while you go home.
As soon as I have been able to verify that any of the Landry cattle
have been rebranded, we will let you know."

"You — want me to just sit this out?" Holt asked in disbelief.

"You can't be involved in this part of the investigation," Canton
confirmed.

"Fine, but what about Clint? You know they had something to do
with his death." He pushed.

"Holt, unless we have a confession or find some kind of evidence
of involvement, there is no way we can prosecute either of them for
your brother's death." Canton said dejectedly, adding, "Even if I
suspect them of causing your brother's accident."

"I understand," Holt relented, feeling discouragement creeping up his spine. He might be able to prove cattle theft, yet Clint's death could go unanswered. The idea was maddening.

With an explosion of movement, the door to the sheriff's office burst open wide, and Gunner flew in, almost colliding with Dalton, righting himself panting and red-faced.

"What the devil?" Canton barked.

"Boss! I think there might be trouble at the homestead." Gunner spat out, ignoring Canton.

"Trouble?"

"You'd better take a breath and explain yourself, boy." Canton glared at him.

Gunner shook his head and beat his hat across his leg in a frustrated movement, "I should have told ya'... a few nights ago I went into town with Bowen after lights out. We just wanted to unwind," He gulped, seeing the look of disapproval on Holt's face at the admission.

"I was nursing my drink when I overheard Tripp talking to Bowen. He said somethin' about the deed to Crossroads — havin' you sign it over. Bowen said he was still lookin' for your copy."

"Bowen?" Holt repeated as confusion gave way to realization. "Is that what you were lookin' for when Glenna stumbled across ya?"

Gunner didn't bother trying to deny it. "It wasn't what it looked like, boss. I swear! Bowen wasn't supposed to be in the house, but I saw him leave from the back door. After hearin' what I had, I was suspicious. When I went in, I saw that he had gone through your desk. That's when Glenna came down and found me. I never would've taken anythin' that wasn't mine. You have to believe me, boss!" Gunner said with desperation.

344

"I believe you." And he did.

"I — I should have told ya about what I heard. I honestly don't know why I waited. I thought maybe I had heard wrong — or that there was some deal going on I didn't know about and sticking my nose into your business would cause problems — it wasn't until I saw Bowen in the house that I really started to suspect — something."

Holt understood. Gunner trusted Bowen, worked day in and day out, even lived with the man. Was it so impossible to believe in the best in someone, or rather, what they showed you of themselves? He had felt that way about Gunner when Glenna had told him about what she had seen. Now, hearing this about Bowen, Bowen had worked for his family longer than Holt could remember. His logic and his emotions were at war over the information.

"You have yet to explain why you believe there's trouble now?" Canton pressed.

Gunner looked at him, seeming to see him and Dalton for the very first time. "Holt sent Bowen and me out this morning. I thought things were normal, but when Bowen split off. He said he was going to check on the lower patch for stragglers.

"I didn't think much about it — after I got the ice over broken up on the stream, I went looking for Bowen. Boss, he wasn't in the lower patch, as far as I could tell he had never been there. I followed his trail to the Landry patch." He said with emphasis and waited for a reaction to his news. When no one pressed for more information, Gunner rushed on. "I saw him talking to both Silas and Tripp."

"Sorry Gunner, however witnessing a chat, no matter how despicable the participants, isn't cause for alarm," Canton concluded.

"But I thought — with the talk about deeds and Bowen actin' up the last few weeks… well, when I saw Bowen headin' back to the homestead and Silas and Tripp headed in Theo's direction that you'd want to know."

"Bowen was headed back toward Crossroads?" Holt demanded, something else Gunner said to him sparked in his mind. "The children."

Canton was on his feet, strapping on his holster.

"I'll ride out too." Dalton offered and checked the rounds in his pistol, placing it in his hip holster and reaching for the rifle Canton held out for him to take.

"They have a good head start on us," Canton growled, clasping Holt on the shoulder. "You can't be in two places at once."

His head was swimming. His family split, all of them possibly in peril. Resolution settled in the pit of his stomach and mixed heavily with the rage that was bubbling there.

Mind racing Glenna looked around the room for a way to defend themselves, there was no time to hesitate, running into the open yard of the house was foolishness, especially in Edith's condition and the barn would offer no help as the two of them riding bare back could be easily overtaken.

Taking into account her current surroundings, Glenna reached out and wrenched Edith by the shoulders, pressing her shoulders to the wall, out of sight. The poker had slipped from her fingers and went rolling toward the hearth. Edith's complexion had gone an ill sort of green color. Glenna knew she was going into a state of panicked shock.

"It's going to be alright." Glenna whispered, forcing Edith to meet her gaze, "It's going to be alright." She repeated.

346

There was only enough time to step away from her when Bowen charged into the room brandishing the knife he had retrieved.

Bruised and bloody, Bowen was like a wounded bear, growling and feral. Giving a guttural cry, he lunged toward her. Acting on instinct, Glenna reached behind her, fingers falling on the handle of the pot, and fighting the urge to pull back from the heat, she yanked it up and outward, flinging the scalding soup right into Bowen's face and chest.

Screaming from both surprise and pain, he stumbled while slashing downward with his knife hand, narrowly missing Glenna as she ducked to the side. Unable to stop herself from also stumbling, her feet catching her skirts, Glenna fell, hands out to brace herself, right in front of the fireplace.

"Glenna!" Edith's stretched.

Fingers finding and grasping the poker handle, she rolled quickly to her back, just as Bowen threw his full weight at her.

His momentum was suddenly arrested by a searing pop, followed by a deafening howl. Glenna hadn't realized her eyes had clamped shut until she opened them. Bowen was staggering away from her, the poker protruded from his right side.

One.

Two.

Three.

His steps halted there as if his mind caught up with what had happened. His free hand grasped at the poker, as if feeling it with his fingers would make it more real than it currently was. Eyes bouncing from Edith, who had stepped out of her hiding spot, to Glenna, who was scrambling to her feet, back down to the poker with an expression of disbelief.

Time seemed slowed to the speed of cool molasses being poured and for several breaths, no one moved. No sound was made. Then, with startling abruptness, the world seemed to explode into action. With a cry, Edith was yanked backward, away from Bowen's wild swinging arm by a man Glenna had never seen before, who had, it seemed, materialized from thin air out of the hall at the same time that Sheriff Canton had stormed through the kitchen door with such force it had nearly been knocked from its hinges.

"Put it down, Bowen!" Canton commanded.

Bowen had stopped mid-swing, eyeing the pistol raised in his direction.

"You know I can't do that." He said in a menacing, low voice, leveling his gaze at Glenna.

"It's over," Canton demanded.

"No!" Bellowed Bowen, rushing forward, knife raised.

The pistol blast sliced through the air, followed by a wet sounding thud. Red blossomed anew on his already stained shirt. Seeping through the fabric as it spilled down his torso. Bowen drew one hoarse, damp sounding breath, sinking to his knees, the knife clattering to the floor a split second before his body followed suit.

Still.

He was so still.

Canton kept his pistol leveled on Bowen, as the man Glenna hadn't recognized checked for signs of life, shaking his head.

"He — he —"

"Glenna, it's alright. I know."

"No, you don't understand. He killed Clint." She met Sheriff Canton's eyes, "He told me he was responsible, and he wanted Holt dead."

"I know." Canton said again.

348

"Decker!" Glenna yelped, coming to her senses. "Bowen sent the Landry brothers after him, thinking I would go with him to fetch the children."

A look passed between the men. Canton ducked out of the house and was gone.

"Are either of you badly harmed?" The stranger demanded.

Glenna shook her head.

"Alright, Mrs. Sterling, let's get both of you out of here and the body covered."

Glenna looked at the man who had pulled Edith to safety.

"I'm Dalton Wesley. I was meeting with your husband about possible cattle theft." He said by way of an introduction. Too emotionally numb and physically weak to speak, she carefully stepped around Bowen's body, and leaning on each other, she moved with Edith toward the front room.

Acting on instinct rather than any sort of self-awareness, in a daze that fogged her thinking, she sat Edith down on the sofa, the fact that the front door stood open, the biting winter air spilling inside hardly registering.

"I need to — change your bandages." She said mechanically, seeing red smeared across Edith's hands on the bandages of her foot.

"It isn't mine." Edith whimpered. "The blood isn't mine."

Glenna blinked, attempting to clear the fog from her brain.

"What?" Her eyes focused. Edith was shaking.

Something inside of her came unhinged and Glenna slumped into the open seat next to her, arms encircling Edith. Together they sobbed.

"I — I am so sorry." Edith managed.

"Whatever for?"

"I should have acted sooner. I knew I had to do something. That I had to help you. I froze, paralyzed with fear."

"No more of that. Edith, you saved my life!" Glenna cried.

Edith swallowed another sob.

"Are you sure you are both alright?" Dalton Wesley asked, announcing his presence and handing Glenna a wet washcloth that she pressed to her sore lip.

"Bruised and unsettled though otherwise I believe we are both mostly unharmed, thank you." Glenna answered.

"Hello?"

Three pairs of eyes turned toward the front door as a tentative hand pushed it fully open. "Glenna? Edith?"

"Patsy!" Edith threw herself at her sister, sobbing even harder.

A very worried and confused looking Patsy caught her sister up in a long embrace. John, looking equally baffled, stood nearby.

"Edith, what happened here?" Patsy finally asked, prying her sister away long enough to take a good look at her. "Are you hurt?"

"There is a lot to explain." Glenna gestured for each to take a seat.

Mr. Wesley listened as intently as the rest of their audience as Glenna and Edith recalled the morning's events in detail, sprinkling a few details from the past months to offer clarification when needed.

"And you have yet to hear from anyone at the Coleman's?" John asked when the explanation was finished.

"No," Edith said simply when Glenna was unable to find her voice to do so.

There was no way to differentiate the sound of Ranger's hooves pounding beneath him and the rapid beat of his heart. As if he could feel the urgency pouring off Holt in waves, Ranger pushed harder, giving a burst of speed that left Gunner lagging as his mount struggled to keep up.

The top of Theo's house crested above the hill, Holt leaned lower over Ranger's neck as the sound of a rifle blast reverberated in the distance. Terror tightened his chest, constricting his lungs, making it impossible to draw breath. Cresting the hill, a panicked sort of relief washed over him.

Decker was crouched behind the protective wall of the wagon, his pistol drawn, Blu crouched next to his feet. Across the open yard, Silas and Tripp had taken cover behind the open barn door. Their horses had been abandoned to the mercy of those they had meant to harm.

The brothers peered out, each aiming in a separate direction. Another rifle blast filled the air and Tripp folded in on himself, toppling face-first into the snow. Holt took one glance in the direction of the house and caught sight of Hattie, skirts flying, rifle held shoulder height, her silvery hair spilling out of its bindings.

Holt could see Theo inching his way nearer the barn door, just out of Silas' eye line. Giving Ranger his lead, Holt charged right into the center of the tumult. Blu's distinctive guttural growl sounded and sprinting from Decker's side, he rushed Silas, clamping down mercilessly on his arm with powerful jaws.

Silas cried out, swinging the arm out so that Blu's body made contact with the side of the barn. It was just enough distraction for Silas to pull his focus and for Holt to launch himself off Ranger's broad back, plowing into Silas, the gun flying from his hand as the two crashed to the ground just inches from Tripp's body.

Silas rolled, scrambling to regain his footing. Not before Holt had already sprung to his feet. He couldn't disguise his rage as anything other than what it was, and a white-hot fury sparked through him.

His fist landed, smashing the side of Silas' face with a satisfying crunch. Silas attempted a swing in Holt's direction, which was easily avoided as Holt landed another blow. Blood spurted from Silas's nose and split lip. Sputtering and spitting, his eyes cut back to Holt, who had drawn his pistol. Leveling it directly at his face.

"Give me more of a reason." Holt seethed.

"Holt — son —" Theo's voice was even, cutting into the fury pulsing through Holt's veins.

He made no move to lower his gun but tightened his hold on the grip as Decker stepped behind Silas, forcing both his arms behind him roughly while Theo tied his hands. Silas narrowed his eyes, and a sneer split his bloodied face.

"Coward."

"Shootin' an unarmed man is no act of bravery," Holt dropped his arm, gun sliding effortlessly back into the holster at his hip.

Leaning close to Silas, he allowed himself a smile. "Don't worry, you'll join your brother in hell soon enough. Before that happens, I'm going to have the satisfaction of watching your feet dangle from the gallows. Live the last of your days looking forward to this Silas. Not everyone's neck breaks, some suffocate. If you're lucky, you'll have blacked out before you soil yourself."

Decker yanked hard on Silas' trapped arms, forcing him toward the nearest fence post.

Theo placed a hand on Holt's shoulder. "You alright boy?"

Letting out a heavy breath, he nodded slowly, "Finn? Daisy?"

"They're safe."

Satisfied for the moment with the answer, Holt dropped to one knee, calling Blu to him with a click of his tongue. Blu limped, whimpered, and favored his side when Holt lifted him into his arms.

"Good dog."

Hattie met him on the porch where he leaned down, and over the top of Blu, placed a kiss on her cheek. "Nice shooten' Aunt Hattie."

"Well, I wasn't about to let anyone harm a member of my family." She retorted, "I love you — all of you." she added, pressing a hand to the side of his face, then pushing the door open for him to pass through.

Laying a cushion near the hearth for Blu, Hattie waited for Holt to relieve himself of the load before going to the closed bedroom door. "Finn," she called softly, pushing the door open.

Big eyes peered out, caught sight of Holt, and widened, "Uncle Holt!"

One arm scooped up Finn, holding the boy to him, blond head pressed to his shoulder. Daisy toddled out of the room after her brother, a wide grin on her cherubic face as she fell into Holt's free arm.

"Did you get them?" Finn asked, His face scrunched up, a deep line in the middle of his brows. "Did you get the bad men shooting at Aunt Hattie and Uncle Theo?"

"Yes, we got 'em."

"Good. Can we go home now?"

"We sure can." Holt gave a little snort of laughter and ruffled Finn's hair.

Rust-colored water sloshed over the rim of the bucket and spilled onto the already soaked floor. Glenna, on hands and knees over the crimson stain, took a shallow breath through her mouth. The thick, sticky puddle had started to smell rancid, filling her nostrils and coating her throat, making her cough and gag with the taste of it.

A second washcloth hit the floor, drawing Glenna's attention to the fact she was no longer alone in the kitchen.

"Patsy, you do not need to —" The protest died in her throat as Patsy ignored her and began scrubbing alongside her. The already ruddy water deepened in color as they sopped up rag full after rag full, ringing it out and repeating the process until a vast majority of the blood had been soaked up.

Edith had requested she and Patsy stay behind. She did not wish to travel with the body, and Glenna could not blame her. She also suspected Edith wanted to make sure Decker was alright and would be restless waiting for news in town. Wrapped comfortably in a quilt, she was instructed to stay in the rocking chair near the fire, Patsy brooking no opposition to the command that is where Edith had stayed.

By the third trip to the outhouse to dispose of tawny water, Glenna felt her energy fading. Bone-weary exhaustion born out of emotional and mental fatigue had settled in mixing with the sense of loss, betrayal, and worry. All emotions she was no stranger to. It was the addition of fear, fear born from love that was new to her emotional pallet, it felt too heavy for her to carry.

Returning to the kitchen Glenna was surprised to see that Mr. Wesley had removed his overcoat, rolled up his sleeves, and was adding his elbow grease to the cleaning efforts removing the last of the remnants of what would have been lunch that day from the floor and walls where it had splattered.

"We can manage here Glenna. Please go rest." Patsy implored.

"Thank you, though I need to see to the hall upstairs." She responded flatly, filling her bucket and gathering a washcloth for the job. Grateful for the chance to keep active, occupying her mind while waiting for word. Being idle as the minutes stretched out into painful oblivion was more torture than she could bear.

"I'll prepare a little lunch." Not waiting for Glenna to acknowledge her statement, Pasty set to work, stepping around Mr. Wesley and humming to herself.

Brushing past the table on her way out of the room, Glenna felt the tender mercy that was John Helm. He had been quick to suggest that he transport Bowen's body into town rather than laying him out on the dining table until Doctor Tillman could be summoned to the house.

There would have been no way of keeping her composure otherwise. Not the table where Bowen had shared meals with Clint for years, where he had broken bread with Holt, teased Gunner and Decker, or laughed with the children. Just the thought of it had made her stomach turn.

Alone, Glenna stood stock still in the upstairs hall, her gaze falling on the droplets of blood that scattered their way from the floor up the wall. Holt's door still stood open, leaving the papers dotting their way across the room in full sight.

Pressing her lips into a tight line, she dropped to her knees, set to scrubbing the blood from the walls and floor until all traces of it had disappeared into small wet pools of quickly drying water.

Once satisfied, she sat back on her heels, drawing a long breath to stave off the wave of nausea that flooded over her. The inner strength she had been clinging onto crumbled. Unable to keep herself upright, Glenna fell against the wall, her back pressing to the solid surface as her eyes flooded with tears, the numbness of shock fading to the dull ache of loss.

As if summoned out of her desperation for him, Holt's arms slid around her shaking shoulders, coaxing her to melt into the embrace as the reality of his presence washed over her. "It's alright love, it's alright." His voice was strangled with emotion.

"You're here —" she cried. "I thought — I thought maybe — I thought I lost you."

"I did too." He revealed, kissing her softly.

Incapable of fully trusting she hadn't been caught in an illusion of her own design, Glenna shifted to look at him, fingers making contact with any part of him she was able to grasp, arms, shoulders, neck, face. Something akin to a whimper. She folded herself back into his arms as if she could permanently adhere herself to his being.

"Canton arrived and told us what happened here with Bowen. I would have come sooner — I'm sorry, my love, I'm sorry I wasn't here." He lamented, lips pressed into her hair.

"No, you were exactly where you needed to be. I would have never forgiven you if you hadn't gone after the children." Glenna vowed.

The sound of Holt's reverberating laugh sounded through the wall of his chest next to her ear.

"That was my very thought."

"Where are they?" Glenna questioned, lifting her face to his, "Are they alright?"

Pressing hands to either side of her face, Holt pushed back the hair that had spilled from its casement. His brilliant blue eyes, as clear as a summer sky, held hers a breath before her attention was drawn in the direction they had turned.

356

"Gunner," Holt called out, and he appeared ascending the stairs, Daisy tucked into one arm, Finn holding his hand.

Daisy's expression was full of wonder, whereas Finn's held a trace of worry that should never mar a child's face. Glenna smiled at him and Finn broke free of Gunner and raced up the remaining steps, throwing his arms around her neck, almost knocking both she and Holt over with the force of his embrace.

Holt unhooked one arm and pulled Daisy down from Gunner's hold and right into the middle of the embrace. Gunner gave Glenna a look of sadness mixed with acceptance and she nodded her complete understanding. He turned and descended the stairs. Her heart going out to him, Bowen had been his friend as well, a trusted member of their makeshift family.

Their family.

Her family.

Laughing with both joy and giddy relief, Glenna kissed and hugged both the children individually, holding both of them to her fiercely. Perhaps a bit old for such displays of affection, Finn allowed it, wrapping one arm around her neck while the other slipped around Holt's. Daisy settled into Glenna's lap, her little hands pulling at the fabric of her dress as Holt's arms encircled all of them at once.

Burying her face into the crook of Holt's neck. Glenna breathed him in, relishing the feeling of his arms around her, of Finn and Daisy cradled between them. Listening with a sense of serenity to the sounds floating up from the first floor, the booming sound of Decker's voice. Gunner excitedly explained the scene at the Colman's to Mr. Wesley.

The sweet tones of Patsy and Edith joining in, Hattie barking orders from the kitchen and Theo's even toned replays. All of it adding perfectly to the chaos that was their home — her home.

She was unaware of how long the four of them stayed there, crushed together in the middle of the hall, each holding the other. Glenna felt as though an eternity could pass and it would still not be long enough.

The End

Epilogue

Standing at the Crossroads

Winter had gone, spring melting the snow into puddles that had soon dried up, the world turning green and alive with the promise of renewal. Changing the landscape of Crossroads as much as she felt changed inside, Edith thought to herself as the wagon wheels rolled to a stop.

"Hello!" Glenna waved from the porch with a wide smile.

"I hope you don't mind an unexpected visit." Rachel ventured, returning the greeting as she stepped down from the wagon seat.

"You are just in time for tea and biscuits." Glenna responded while pulling the apron from around her waist.

"We did plan our arrival perfectly." Patsy laughed, leaving the wagon seat and rounding the box to reach inside. "Of course we did not come empty-handed."

Edith slid from her place and retrieved the small brown paper-wrapped package from under the seat.

"And what is this?" Glenna laughed, holding the door open for the trio to enter the house.

"During that last rainstorm, the three of us hatched a plan that we just completed and although we could very well wait for the newest little Sterling to make his or her appearance, we thought the sooner we could celebrate with you, the better. It also gave us an excuse to ride out and see you, of course." Rachel offered with a glowing smile.

"We have some time yet before the baby comes," Glenna responded by placing a hand protectively over her abdomen. Edith had to admit that, as an expectant mother, she looked blissfully content with the prospect.

"It's a quilt for the baby." Pasty burst just as all four women converged on the other side of the front door.

"Oh, Patsy!" Edith cried.

"I'm sorry. I am no good at keeping secrets."

"She has been bursting to come out for days. I'm surprised she didn't send a card beforehand announcing we would be coming." Rachel laughed.

Edith handed the package to Glenna, who eagerly unwrapped the gift and held it for inspection.

"I — love it. It's perfect." She smiled, glowing.

"We each donated material and made up squares. Mrs. Tillman did that one. This was Clara. Hattie made those three. Even Mama added to it." Patsy indicated each patch in turn. Showing off the handiwork of each woman, indicating her own additions or those of Rachel or Edith last.

Blinking rapidly, Glenna hugged each of them in turn. "I can not thank you enough for this. Truly."

"There has been so much to celebrate and be thankful for." Rachel said, linking her arm with Patsy's. "A wedding, a new baby, everyone healthy and happy."

Edith's eyes darted from her sister, who no longer shared her last name, to Glenna and smiled her agreement with the sentiment.

"Come, I must have you write down all the names of those that contributed." Glenna motioned for the group to move to the kitchen. "I believe it's also time for some biscuits and tea."

Following behind Rachel and Patsy, Glenna fell into step by Edith's side, softly taking her hand, and leaning toward her with a conspiratorial whisper, "He's in the barn — if you perhaps feel that a short walk might do you some good."

Edith blinked, "I *do* feel as though I may need a bit of exercise after being sandwiched between those two from town."

Glenna smiled knowingly and, leaving her, walked into the kitchen where Daisy was twittering on to her captive audience. Before apprehension could arrest her steps, Edith spun in place and walked back out into the warm touch of sunlight.

The barn doors stood open and the sound of cattle lowing filtered out of them. Stepping inside cautiously, she walked past a few of the pens, some empty, others holding newborn calves with their mothers. Making her way back to the pen where a heifer stood, straining, large brown eyes looking miserable, rolling in her head.

The wide expanse of Decker's back faced her as he talked in a low, calming tone, hands feeling their way down and across her distended side. She watched his methodical movements as he checked for signs of birth progression, taking a rope down from a nail just outside the gate and working the loop over the head and neck. Giving enough lead so that the animal would have room to lie down if necessary before securing the other end to a post.

The skin of her hide rippled, then pulled tight as she strained again. A low painful sounding whine accompanied this. Decker walked to the back of the cow, frowned, his brows pinching together.

"Is she having more trouble than expected?" Edith asked, stepping closer to the gate.

Decker's eyes flickered over to her as his hands dipped into the bucket of water in the corner of the pen. Lathering up with the bar of soap to the elbows. Although Edith knew he hadn't noticed her until she had spoken, Decker showed no signs of surprise at her appearance, but offered a nod as the corners of his lips turned upward a fraction.

"She is. The calf is too big to go it alone. He's also tryin' to work his way into the world nose first."

"How do you know it's male?" She ventured.

"A female would never be this stubborn." Decker flashed her a full smile. It was impossible not to return.

"Is there something I can do to help?"

Decker eyed her from his side of the gate. "That's a mighty fine dress you have on today, miss Edith — this is goin' to be messy." He warned.

Edith pulled at the ribbons of her bonnet and tossed it onto the nail the rope had vacated. Then pushed her sleeves up her forearms, "It's just a dress." She grumbled, knowing he was teasing her in his way. Although, she had to admit she had hoped to meet with him on this particular trip to Crossroads and had worn her best dress. Now she felt silly and wished she had been more practical.

Not waiting for Decker to make any sort of reply, she pulled the pin holding the gate closed and stepped inside, fastening it and turning with a look of pure determination toward him.

"Go ahead. Wash up." He grinned at her while slipping the sliver of soap into her open hand.

She did as instructed, washing her hands and forearms with the tepid water and coarse soap. Decker had retrieved another length of rope, from where she had no idea. Working a loop into its length as he positioned himself at the rear of the heifer.

362

"I need to push the head back so I can reach around and grab the front legs." Gripping the tail, he lifted it high, "Here, hold this just so. It will be difficult enough without her slappin' me in the face with it."

"Alright,"

It was difficult to hold the poor animal's tail in the same position Decker had handed it off to her, as he was much taller than herself and the cow so wide it forced her onto her tiptoes to hold it in place. She tipped a little, falling on the cow's hip, unable to keep her balance for the duration.

"That'll do." He was smiling at her, as if enjoying how utterly ridiculous she must look.

The contact made it possible for Edith to feel the heifer straining and the sudden relaxing of the muscles. It was at just that moment that Decker pressed a hand inside, feeding the rope along with it. He grunted, straining against the resistance he must be feeling as both the calf and mother very much did not want to have the head pushed back down the birth canal.

"That's it, good girl, it will be over soon." He said, speaking to the cow, who was mooing in protest.

A few tense minutes passed before Decker cheered triumphantly, "Got 'em!" sliding his arm back out, gripping the rope at both ends.

"She is goin' to move a bit. Be ready."

The animal's muscles touching her torso went rigged. The heifer took a step forward, just as he had warned she would. Edith moved with her, Decker pulled up and away from her, alternating pulling on one end of the rope than the other. The cow took a few more steps forward, Edith practically hopping to keep up.

The small hooves and front legs of the calf appeared, followed by the nose, head, and shoulders. Decker switched to a downward arc, and the calf slid out, falling safely into the fresh hay at its mother's feet.

"Come here," Decker beckoned Edith to his side as he knelt next to the newborn. He handed her some of the straw, "Rub it in his nostrils. It will trigger a sneeze helpin' to clear things out."

Edith did as instructed. Decker dipped his hand into the mouth, sweeping out a good deal of mucus before the calf sneezed, and finding its voice called out loudly to his mother in protest.

"You're alright," Decker laughed and rubbed a handful of straw down his back.

Wide-eyed and wobbly, the calf tried to stand. It took a few attempts, unsteady he was able to gain his footing. Decker looked after the cord, scooping him up and moved to set him down in front of his mother, who promptly began to lick the newcomer.

"I've never witnessed anything larger than a puppy being born before," Edith said in awe, watching the pair. The heifer, who had only moments previous bellowed and strained, now seemed unconcerned with anything but her new calf.

"It's somethin'." Decker agreed, "I need to make sure to get the afterbirth, and then we can see if this little guy wants to eat."

Edith looked down at her hands, mucus and blood covered her fingers. She hadn't even noticed the transfer had happened. The water was even cooler now than it had been and the soap felt far coarser. She shook off the excess water and waited while Decker washed his hands as well.

Satisfied with her work, the mother allowed the baby to take a few steps away from her and toward where he instinctively knew he would be able to locate food. Decker leaned on the far wall of the pen, slid to the ground and gestured for Edith to join him. Wordlessly, they watched as the calf rooted, latched, and began tugging.

364

Edith smiled and glanced at Decker out of the corner of her eye. His head now resting on the rough boards of the barn wall, his eyes closed. A shadow of exhaustion had fallen over his strong features.

"I've been thinking about our last conversation." She ventured.

"Oh, I've been on your mind, have I? That's encouragin'." He teased, opening one eye to look at her with a smirk.

His lighthearted ribbing lessened the knot that had formed in her stomach a fraction.

"My answer is — yes."

She waited for her words to filter through his thoughts, watching carefully as Decker's countenance changed. All signs of fatigue dissolved, both eyes snapping open, head lifting as he twisted sharply toward her.

"Are you certain?"

Every trace of tension dissolved. "I've never been more certain of anything."

"I can't promise an easy life."

"I do not want promises. All I want — is you." She whispered, her throat tight with emotion. "I love you, Decker Hayes."

His mouth claimed hers in a kiss that shattered any semblance of self-composure Edith had thought she possessed. Soon she was fluttering like a leaf in the wind under the pressure of his hands, his lips, the way his arms encircled her so completely. The kiss was both imploring and demanding.

Edith felt herself press into the exchange, her hands skimming across the broad expanse of his shoulders to sink into the fullness of his shaggy mane. Whatever she had imagined, his kiss would feel like this wild thing with a life of its own had not been it. This, the reality of this new form of connection, was more satisfying than any amount of imagining could have been.

A revelation of touch and emotion. Edith wondered if she had ever taken a full breath prior to this moment and now that she could draw air, all she wished to do was take long, luxurious gulps, breathing in nothing but Decker.

"I love you." He breathed.

"I found them!" Edith jumped a little at the drawl of a new voice. Decker refused to allow her to pull away from him as he greeted their audience.

Gunner, Holt, and Finn all leaned on the fence, the men smiling like fools down at the pair of them. Finn with his nose scrunched as if he had smelled something particularly bad.

"They were bein' mushy." He accused.

With his one arm still solidly placed around her, Decker got to his feet, pulling her along with him.

"Edith accepted my proposal." He announced.

"We... gathered that." Holt laughed. "Congratulations to you both."

"I suppose this means I'll need to move my things out of the bunkhouse?" Asked Gunner.

"You won't need to move out of the bunkhouse, Gunner. We'll be settlin' on our own patch, but I appreciate the offer." Decker said with pride.

"We will?" Edith questioned.

"A place near Crossroads came up for sale not long ago. I won the bid." He announced.

"The Landry place." Gunner nodded his approval. "It will be good to have you nearby."

"Are you alright with that?" Decker asked, eyes on Edith. "It will be an adventure. The house needs a bit of work and it will take me some time to build up the herd —"

366

Pushing herself onto her tiptoes, she kissed his cheek. Onlookers be damned. "I'm ready for any amount of adventure as long as it's with you."

"Finn, would you run ahead to the house and tell Glenna that we will be cutting into that cake she's been hiding from us a bit sooner than she had planned." Holt chortled.

"Why?" Finn asked.

"Because it's time to celebrate!" Gunner hooted, tossing his hat in the air for emphasis.

Finn bolted for the house, Holt and Gunner on his tail.

Decker held the gate open for her to pass through, setting the soapy bucket of water on the outside, shutting the gate and dropping the pin.

"Life with you will never be dull, will it?" She laughed at the sight of Blu jumping up and catching Gunner's hat by the brim when he tossed it into the air a second time. The dog bolted, Gunner chased fruitlessly as the dog could easily outmaneuver him.

"Not with that lot around." He laughed, "You aren't changin' your mind now, are ya? Knowin' what kind of life we'll have?"

"Never." She promised as he took her hand, pressing a kiss to the palm before linking fingers. It was an odd sort of feeling. Being so undeniably happy. It was one she was looking forward to getting used to.

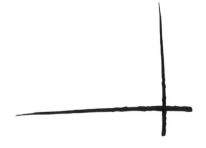

About the Author

B.E. Brown, one of nine children, had the privilege of growing up in a small Wyoming town. She was encouraged to use her imagination. Often that imagination would lead her to help build cardboard towers in the backyard with her brothers, slide down the stairs in their house while riding on a mattress, climb the local water tower, and of course, frequent visits to the ER after their shenanigans went awry.

Later B.E. Brown would learn that the power of imagination could take her around the world, to see and experience things she never dreamt of. Held between the pages of a book, she could climb mountains, sail the seas, go on safari, become a wizard, and this sparked a passion for storytelling. She began creating worlds on paper as young as six. Imagination and love of the written word continues to be a driving force throughout her life, inspiring her work.

B.E. Brown is a resident of scenic Wyoming, where she lives with her husband and three children.

"Writing is as much of an essential part of me as breathing. I wouldn't know who I was without the characters blooming to life in my mind and begging to live out their tales on paper. They refuse to be quiet until their stories are finished." ~B.E. Brown

You can also find B.E. Brown on FaceBook at
B.E. Brown Books and on Twitter @BEBROWN3

Other books by B.E. Brown found on Amazon
In the Absence of Light
The Love Letters
Lady of Leighton Manor

Made in the USA
Columbia, SC
15 November 2022

71261990R00204